DOCTOR BROOKLYN:

Love & Life at the End of a Knife

IRV DANESH, MD

Doctor Brooklyn: *Love & Life at the End of a Knife,* Published May, 2018

Editorial and Proofreading: Susan Strecker, Beth Raps, Karen Grennan
Interior Design and Layout: Howard Johnson
Cover Design: Howard Johnson
Photo Credits: Front cover: hospital photo, Max Danesh; Brooklyn to Manhattan: welcomia/Freepik.com; Brooklyn Bridge chapter opener: freevector.com; Statue of Liberty: pixabay.com; scalpel icon: Vecteezy.com; About the Author photo: Lou Goodman

 **SDP Publishing**

Published by SDP Publishing an imprint of SDP Publishing Solutions, LLC.

ISBN-13 (print): 978-1-7321115-1-6
ISBN-13 (ebook): 978-1-7321115-2-3
Library of Congress Control Number: 2018937036

Printed in the United States of America

ACKNOWLEDGMENTS

This is my sophomore book and it is time to re-thank the wonderful people who have helped influence my past as well as those who play a part in my future. Some are present, some are not, and some are in between; all are important.

First and foremost to my love, my life, I dedicate this book to you, Fanny. Since I am the romantic in our marriage, I cannot emphasize enough how my life has changed for the better since we met. Through the ups and downs the only thing I could ever count on was your love and support. Being the wife of an ER doctor, my *beshert*, the one who was destined to be with me, means you have had to endure my days of depression, days of doubt, days of mania and many days of poor choices. Fanny, through all those days and the good ones too, you have always had my adoration, my love, respect, and lust. You are my everything.

I would like to thank Yonia and Harold, Abe and Rita. Your examples of love in a marriage and as parents have always helped me differentiate the priorities in my life: being a physician is important, but I am a better physician because I have tried to be a better husband and father.

Thank you, Sam, Zach, Max, and Jake. I would have been incomplete without you. Seeing you grow up to become good men has been my greatest joy. Continue growing and achieving, especially after hard times, because (though it's cliché) nothing worth it ever comes easy.

Thank you, Mitch, Ari, Francine, and John as brothers, sister (and in-laws) you have had to support more *hazerei* than a human should endure.

Thank you, Aunt Lila and Uncle Bob Gofter. Many a day your home was refuge for a student who needed a safe place to sleep and a warm home-cooked meal. Your chairs probably still have the remains of my practice surgical knots.

I'd like to thank my mentors, because without mentors most of us wouldn't know how to pick up a spoon, let alone our noses. Thank you Ira Klonsky, Bernard Levowitz, Emmanuel Lambrakis, Lucio Flores, Sanjeev Rajpal, David Schwartzwald, Joseph Taff, Jack Jedwab, Joseph Dimayuga, and Mark Garber. You all made me the physician I am today. We learned from each other that the truly sick need our best efforts because being a physician means being the hero when no one else will.

Thanks to my artistic mentors. Andrew Lenchewski, Michael Rauch and Ruth DiPasquale, Mark Harrington, Deidre Horgan, Michael Espinosa, David Tuttman, Rich Frank, Paul Frank, Mark Feuerstein, Jill Flint, Reshma Shetty, Paulo Costanzo, and Campbell Scott, you opened a new universe for me. Thank you for complicating my life in the best possible way.

Finally, thank you to Lisa Akoury-Ross for her guidance and patience getting this book to press.

Irv Danesh, MD

PROLOGUE

"Free at last, I'm free at last."

Zach Maxwell, a freshly minted M.D., newly released from the hell of medical education tuition, was about to walk into the nirvana of a paid residency, specifically in surgical care.

After four years of matriculating at a private medical school associated with a private hospital, in a town he never really got to explore, Zach was free at last—free at last. He had made only two mistakes in his medical career. First, he hadn't studied hard enough for his boards so his scores were ... meh. His second mistake was his unrealistic view of the impression his resumé made.

Zach was in the process of becoming a good, if not great, clinician. He loved patient care and had spent more hours on the hospital wards of his rotations than any other medical student. The residents loved him because of his hard work, and so did the patients. As a student, Zach absorbed information by observation. He observed a lot and was able to apply his close, careful observations to patients under his care.

When it came time to pick a residency, he had decided on surgery. Because he had only rotated in a private hospital with patients who were rich, catered-to assholes, he'd never actually gotten to do any surgery. But he loved the sense of action he saw and all the best-looking nurses seemed to love surgeons. He knew he was an aggressive guy who liked action (including with the nurses) so he applied to only the absolute top programs in the country. For weeks he honed his match list, finally deciding on

UCLA, Stanford, and even though he hated the cold and snow, The Brigham in Boston.

The match list is part of a tradition in American medical schools and residencies. Zach and his classmates submitted a list of the hospitals where they wanted to do their residency in order of preference. At the same time, hospitals submitted their preference list. Both lists went into a computer and wham, bam, thank you ma'am, you were accepted into a residency.

Sometimes students listed a residency beyond their reach, and so it was common to pad your list with a few "safe" residencies you knew you'd get. Zach didn't—and so *boom*, no residency.

This was a very unpleasant situation few graduates ever found themselves in. In fact, usually the only medical students with this problem were students from obscure countries, whose names and schools had twenty-eight plus letters in them, or American medical students who graduated from schools in those countries.

Zach couldn't believe that no one on his match list wanted him and immediately knew there was a mistake. He ran to the dean's office.

The dean was a stiff, older doctor who practiced esoteric gastroenterology. "Esoteric" meaning he specialized in the gastrointestinal effects of Hermansky-Pudiak Syndrome. Since this disease affected between one in five hundred thousand patients to one in a hundred million patients, he was rarely needed to actually examine a patient. This left him all day to go to the various school meetings, conferences with national medical school associations, and hump his secretary at lunchtime.

"Sorry, Zach," the dean reported. "When we received the results of the match we couldn't believe it, so we contacted the match organization immediately."

"And so, it was a mistake, right? I'm on my way to sunny California, right?" Zach asked, not getting what the dean was telling him.

"Maybe on a vacation, but not for a residency."

Zach had sudden visions of being penniless, unemployed, and strapped with $250,000 in educational loans.

"But," the dean said, "never fear. This medical school will not let one of its graduates suffer the indignity of not achieving a residency. You said you wanted to be a surgeon … correct?"

"Yes, a surgeon," Zach responded hopefully.

And that was how, a few months later, Zach found himself in hot, humid, malodorous Brooklyn, standing in front of a sooty, old monument as big as two city blocks.

Chapter 1

There has to be some mistake, Zach thought, as he was both terrorized and shivering in front of the crumbling edifice in the Brownsville section of Brooklyn. The Pope Andreas Yiddish Hospital was rumored to have more violent crime reported within its walls than the rest of the Borough of Brooklyn. Its name came from two destitute hospitals that had served indigent Brooklynites. The City of New York recommended (in other words, demanded) they combine to create an interfaith hospital built out of the two old ones. Before shutting them down, Gracie Mansion allowed the Catholic Charities Foundation and the Jewish National Foundation to stop life-saving financial measures at both their hospitals. It must have been seen as a cosmic joke by the powers that be to name the new hospital after a pope rumored to be a Jew, and a dying language used only by eighty-year-old European Jews.

Thus PAY Hospital (or "No-Pay Hospital" for its lack of paying customers) was born. It was one of the world's largest charity institutions for the delivery of healthcare, and situated in the highest crime section of Brooklyn. Its subway station was known for having the leading murder rate in the five boroughs of New York.

Brooklyn, the tenth largest city in the United States, was thick with sidewalk boomboxes deafening inhabitants with the drumbeat of unintelligible sound and polluting the air alongside fetid smells recognizable to anyone who had spent time in a cattle barn.

It was 10 a.m. on June 23, 1978, Jimmy Carter was President, Andy Gibb's "Shadow Dancing" was hot on radio, and Zach Maxwell was going to interview with the Chief of General Surgery. It was speculated most of the residents interning in PAY's surgical program were never allowed to sleep. They appeared to their patients as zombies with a pulse--barely. Many a resident had started the surgical program only to mysteriously disappear from PAY. Those residents turned up years later as elected dogcatchers or Board of Health supervisors in towns with populations under 1,000. When those ex-residents were questioned about their time repairing victims of violent crime, they never admitted having heard of PAY let alone being students of surgery there.

The bus let Zach off across the street from the main entrance. Having already acquired a New Yorker's eye for survival, he scanned for potential muggers, murderers, or rapists, but didn't find anyone except hospital personnel and potential patients. He made it across the street and found a food truck near an alley between hospital buildings. He looked at his watch, but he was too nervous to stop for a cup of coffee before his meeting. Zach had barely participated in his surgical rotation at the small uber-wealthy suburban hospital and the surgeons were glad of it. The last thing any of them wanted was some med student putting his fingers in the wrong surgical holes or, God forbid, a medical student who was too familiar with a rich dowager. Zach had spent his surgical rotations reading *Sabiston's Textbook of Surgery* and trying to get one or two of the pretty nurses to play hide the salami in a utility closet. As with most things in medicine, paperwork completion was more important than the product itself. Zach finished his twelve-week rotation never having gone into the operating room, managing to examine two patients (one of whom was comatose) and score with one of the nurses (not comatose). The final exam in surgery was a joke. No real surgeon had the time to write up a test, so the director of education at the private hospital created a test consisting of three questions. The answers all came from the first page of *Sabiston.* Zach passed with a perfect score yet had never sutured or participated in as much as an abscess drainage. As a surgeon he was great on paper, but a patient with an exploding appendix would die in his hands.

He walked across the alley's access to the main entrance of the hospital.

How am I going to survive this? I've never even held a scalpel, he thought. Zach didn't want to be a surgeon for the sake of curing by cutting. He just loved the idea of being a surgeon. On TV at least, it was always the surgeon who got to *shtup* the blond nurse with the big tits.

His dean had known about off-the-match residencies for Zach because there were always hospitals that served very dangerous neighborhoods or had a history of lousy programs, or both. It was up in the air exactly which flaw PAY had but it was Zach's last chance for a residency that year. It was this or waste another year of his life—and his loans needed repayment.

On the last Friday of June in Brooklyn, Dr. Zachary Maxwell, hot, grimy, and already swimming in the sweat pooling between his polyester shirt and skin, was about to be thrown into the real world, without rose-tinted lenses to protect him.

Chapter 2

The Brownsville section of Brooklyn near Bedford-Stuyvesant housed mostly African-Americans, Hispanics, and a small contingent of Lubavitcher Hasidic Jews. Every night was party night, and the knives and bullets flew, fueled by a never-ending supply of cheap booze and drugs also flying into veins, up noses, and into mouths.

The hospital had close to a thousand beds with both old and new sections and an attached nursing home. The surgical residency trained eighty residents, doctors fresh out of medical school learning to cure patients with cold, surgical steel. PAY also boasted proportionally large residencies in Internal Medicine, OB-GYN, Psychiatry, Pediatrics, and Radiology. Day-to-day clinical services were run by senior residents, who in turn were supervised by the chiefs of service.

While Boston is considered the heart of medical research in the States, New York City is where hundreds of thousands of patients are seen and clinically treated for mundane illnesses such as pneumonia, and exotic illness such as leiomyosarcoma. Even foreigners know New York is home to the best clinicians in the world.

These patients were diagnosed, treated, and discharged on the bloodied, shat- and vomited-upon floors of the various wards of PAY. Patients were born, lived, and died all within its walls. Sometimes all three phases happened in a matter of minutes.

PAY was an unsung giant in the field of clinical education

and the Department of Surgery had trained countless hot-dog surgeons who could work on an abdomen blindfolded.

After four years of studying mostly theoretical medicine Zach had arrived at what amounted to a field hospital in a war zone. He plowed through the crowd into the cool marble lobby and took the elevator to the fifth floor, arriving at the door of Bernard S. Moskowitz, MD FACS. Dr. Moskowitz, chief of Surgery, Faculty of the American College of Surgery, a thoracic and vascular surgeon and author of numerous scientific articles, was Zach's target. Moskowitz had the power to advance his career or to keep him out of the society of medicine for at least another year.

Zach entered the outer office to find an older lady with red-dyed hair and horn-rimmed glasses. She was poring over patient charts with a smoldering cigarette in one hand and a yellow highlighter in the other. She looked up and was about to speak when the inner office door exploded and a tall man dressed in green scrubs and a long white butcher's coat emblazoned B.S. MOSKOWITZ, MD FACS appeared. His face was etched with deep lines and he had thinning gray hair combed back. His sapphire eyes glowed dangerously as he started screaming.

"Mudder, mudder, mudder—Phyllis, get that piece of shit of a chief resident in here … *now!*"

As fast as he appeared in the outer office, he disappeared into his office, slamming the door behind him.

The secretary didn't flinch. Zach had expected to see black smoke where the surgeon had been.

"Whadda you want, honey?" she asked as she picked up the phone and keyed in a number. Zach could hear tones of a beeper being accessed.

"Hi, I'm Zach Maxwell," he replied, still startled by the performance that had just occurred.

"And …?" the secretary stared at the ceiling as if counting water stains.

"Oh, sorry," Zach replied, mesmerized by Moskowitz's door. "I am here to see Dr. Moskowitz about a residency. I'm a graduate, Zach Maxwell from ... "

"Oh, are you one of those left-behind graduates? Who the fuck did you piss off that they told you to come here?"

"Uh, I'm not sure. I thought I might be a decent candidate...."

She breathed a motherly sigh. "You poor SOB. Manhattan is spiritually a million miles from here. Better start thinking Biafra or Haiti without the palm trees." She looked at Moskowitz's door. "Unfortunately, your timing sucks, honey." She took a beat. "Of course with him," she nodded at the door, "it will always suck."

At that moment the outer office door opened, filled with a giant of a man. He had black hair, bushy black eyebrows, coal-black eyes, wore a strange cut of vest, and suit pants under his long white butcher's coat. He was muscled, and his hands were large and looked very strong, like those of a bricklayer. He had a lopsided smile but otherwise looked exhausted.

"Phyllis, he bellowed for me?" the man asked in a thick Greek accent.

"Yeah, Hercules. Just to warn you, he is ready to do a complimentary tonsillectomy on you, through a hemorrhoidectomy incision."

"Sounds painful, but reportable to the *Archives of Surgery*. Maybe I can co-author?"

The inner office flew open again. "Where's that fucking ... Hercules! What the fuck are you doing to the goddam attending staff? They're ready to castrate you."

Hercules, noticing Zach for the first time, decided he had an audience. He smiled at Zach and stuck out a gigantic hand to shake.

"He only calls me by my proper name when his blood pressure is over 200 systolic. My name is Hercules Christospathos, but my friends call me Hercules."

Moskowitz then turned to Zach and bellowed, "Whadda you want?"

Zach was overwhelmed with the show and just stammered, "I'm … I'm … "

Moskowitz then yelled, "Look, if you're autistic, you're in the wrong office. Psychiatry is on the ninth floor."

Zach gulped. "No sir, I'm not autistic."

"So, what the fuck do you want?"

"Dr. Moskowitz, please," Hercules said, trying to calm down the surgeon. "Give the boy a chance to speak. He is obviously nervous, sensitive, and has never seen a middle-aged man act like a raving lunatic."

Moskowitz was apoplectic. His face had taken on a color not yet seen in nature. "Hercules, take care of him and see me later." Moskowitz again disappeared into his office and slammed the door.

"Way to dodge the bullet, Hercules," Phyllis said admiringly.

"Ahh, bet you say that to all the Greek gods. Now who is this, Phyllis?"

"This, chief resident, is Zach Maxwell, a new surgical intern from … " Phyllis looked at Zach. "Where did you say you were from, honey? Anyway, he is here to become a PAY trained surgeon. Know where he can find a mentor?" Phyllis responded with a flick of her cigarette causing ash to dirty the charts she had been working on.

"I don't know." Hercules frowned. "He looks too sensitive to me. Psychiatry?"

"Oh no, Dr. Christospathos, I'm the most insensitive person I know, I swear." Zach was mesmerized by Hercules, who exuded the confidence of a man in absolute charge of his role in life.

"I'm kidding, boy. Phyllis, get down his information and start him on my team. Also make sure Bullshit signs off on him so the head of education yammie knows." With that Christospathos swept out of the room, his butcher coat flapping behind him.

Zach looked as bewildered as he felt. Bullshit? Yammie?

"Hey! Honey! You still in there?" Phyllis laughed, slamming her hand on the desk.

"Uh … what's a yammie and what does it have to do with education and what Bullshit signs off on?" Zach stammered.

"You're one of the chosen people, right? You know: yammie, beanie, skullcap. You know, what those holy-moly Yids wear. A holier-than-thou Yid is boss of the education department. You don't know your own church? As far as Bullshit, well, our beloved Chief Moskowitz may be BS to his friends and admirers, but he is Bullshit only to his enemies."

Zach sighed. "Uh, yeah. I just don't understand most of what happened."

"Congrats, or maybe I should say condolences. My advice is you should sleep, eat, shit, and get laid enough to carry you through the next five years."

"Why? What just happened?"

"Honey, you were just drafted into Christospathos's team, starting now. You're with the new interns on the charity ward during the hottest part of the year. There is no air conditioning on that ward. The smells on the ward defy description. The patients are dangerous and there will be heavy casualties in the warzone of Brownsville. You are a soldier with the rank of scut puppy. Intelligence is predicting the ghetto will explode this summer."

"Scut puppy?"

"You sure are. Hercules will explain it all to you. Now try to survive the summer."

Chapter 3

The green of the trees contrasted with the blue of the sky, and white, fluffy clouds were its accents on beautiful July 1, 1978. The world was full of promise as Zach and his fellow riders got off the buses at the Linden Boulevard stop. There was a battle of wage-earners on the sidewalks, jousting to get to work or grab a cup of coffee in the many shops and food trucks in the area. Life was active on these streets and many patients milled around anxious about going to their appointments at the infamous hospital.

Zach hurried through the main entrance to the hospital. Even at five in the morning, the lobby was swarming with activity. People of every hue crossed the threshold of the hospital doors, bandaged, on crutches, and in wheelchairs, with the music of the newspaper kiosk vendors chanting the latest murder, rape, or building fire in the borough. "Read all about it!"

July first was a significant day in American medicine. In every teaching hospital, new interns are arriving to take on the medical needs of the sick in the hospital's wards and its E.R. The new interns with the ink still wet on their diplomas thought themselves ready to take on this monumental task. They would quickly discover how wrong they were.

Interns of both sexes walked onto the floors of patients admitted to Internal Medicine, Pediatrics, and OB-GYN. Only in Surgery were the interns solely male. Surgery was a man's specialty, and women were just not welcome. Zach and the other members of Christospathos's team gathered by the surgical ward's battered wood desk adorned with carvings etched into the wood and Formica: *GK is a stitch. Leave the RN alone. No, you fucking can't have more Demerol.* Some carvings were darker and more worn than others. The ward showed its age like a tree does by its rings. The nurses were busy gossiping and prepping medication carts. The interns and med students gathered on one side of the desk, warily eyeing the veterans of service: rookies in their gleaming brand new white coats versus the vets' coats stained with blood and other bodily fluids.

The team consisted of the chief resident in his fifth year of patient responsibilities and education in surgery, the fourth post-graduate year, or PGY-4, who was assistant to the chief resident, and so on down to the interns, the PGY-1s, just out of medical school. At the absolute bottom were a couple of boys representing the lowest form of hospital life, medical students.

"Jake," Zach happily recognized an old classmate, "how did you get on Christospathos's service?" Jake Ethan was a hybrid resident. He had had a hard time getting into an American medical school, so he started at a medical school in Europe, like many an American. He studied hard and took the first part of his board tests given to Americans in their second year of school. Fortunately, University of Pittsburgh accepted him into their third-year class, replacing a student who realized the true way to lots of money was to join his father in the male enhancement pharmaceutical business. Jake and Zach became good friends when they met at a rotation in Psychiatry. They both hated the rotation and so spent countless hours talking about the "when I graduate" hopes they had. They kept in touch when Jake left to go to the three-river city. Jake was one of the few who was proud of his start in a foreign medical school. He had told Zach countless times that living in Europe had made a man out of him and that without the foreign experience he would have never been able to face the rigors of the last two years on the wards of Pitt. As a testament to his exotic start in medicine, Jake had grown a large Frito-Bandito moustache that, he said, always reminded him life could be worse.

"Luck of being at the right place at the wrong time. I tried to match for a Urology residency at PAY, but they had just given the space to a kid from University of Ohio. So, figuring I had to do something for the year before I could try to apply again, I wandered down to Moskowitz's office. Unfortunately, some kid from the U. of Oklahoma was there and both the red-headed secretary and Moskowitz were drooling at the rare American student who ever showed up for a position."

Zach was dumbfounded. "They took you over a real four-year American med graduate … how?"

Jake chuckled. "Dumb shit thought he was too good for a rotation at a dump like PAY. He demanded a free residence at the hospital, no weekends, quit time at 5 p.m., protected study time … you should have heard the list."

"But, he is from U. of O. Doesn't that give places like PAY more panache from the American Association of Medical Colleges?"

"Maybe, but I don't think Moskowitz gives a rat's ass. I hope he survives the hypertensive stroke he is going to have eventually. I have never seen a reaction like that one to the crap that Okie was giving him. Moskowitz's face turned the deepest crimson I have ever seen. I swear smoke was coming out of his ears and the whites of his eyes turned fiery and bulged. Man, Moskowitz's brain valves were seconds from failing."

"You're kidding?"

"On my sainted father. That kid was lucky he survived to fly back to that Jesus state. I thought the chief was going to whip out a scalpel and colostomize him right there and then!"

"But, how did you … ?"

"Right place, right time. Red-headed secretary was holding Moskowitz back from making that guy into a *castrato* when this fucking Greek guy walks in, takes one look at the situation and tells Moskowitz to put 'the moustache' on his service. Moskowitz could barely get words out as the Greek guy kicked the Okie out of the office and told me ... 'Moustache, you're the new 'tern, don't fuck it up,' and disappeared like The Flash. They could have made a TV movie of the week."

"Shee-it!"

"Fuckin' A, partner. By the way, what surgical service is this? No one gave me any details besides I may die."

Zach started laughing. "I understand it's the hell service, but I think you'll enjoy the Greek guy. All your questions will be answered now. Hark! The Greek approaches and those residents look like they are coming to attention."

Having had one or more years treating patients, these residents were exhausted and dreading the arrival of their new colleagues. The residents were responsible for the actions and education of the new interns, but the new interns had a tendency, after the first month or two in their careers, to think they needed no such education or supervision. Each and every intern, armed with a gleaming white short coat with a red caduceus patch affixed to the left arm, had balls the size of grapefruits. Each thought himself the next DeBakey, Schweitzer, or Salk. The experienced residents knew this to be a very dangerous attitude. Each resident had learned in his or her internship year that medicine as clinically practiced is an art born of experience. The interns had no experience and would have to be watched closely to fend off preventable deaths on the surgical patient population.

Zach, Jake, and the other interns assigned to Christospathos's team were frozen in the knowledge the next patient disaster might be seconds away and they wouldn't know what to do. Zach knew he was in the big leagues. He knew he had never really taken care of a surgical patient. Hell, he had barely touched one. He had read all the books and passed all his clinical tests, but the patients didn't seem to come with multiple-choice answers to their problems. His self-doubt as to whether he had actually learned anything applicable to clinical practice was huge. An American hospital was a land of multiple rules, and punishment. The punishment hanging over his head was dismissal from the hospital, and probable oblivion. July first was the day he started running. He hoped he could avoid all the speeding cars there to knock him off.

Chapter 4

The institutional white-faced clock on the wall behind the nurses' station showed six o'clock.

"Good morning," boomed a loud, friendly voice. "I am Hercules Christospathos, your chief resident. This is General Surgery so if you were planning on checking a baby's ears or a lady's dripping coochie you are in the wrong residency. You can call me Hercules and I'd like to welcome you to ward 3G, your home for the next three to five years. We own the patients on this ward. They are our sole responsibility. We will diagnose and cure as many of these patients as we can. These patients come from the Surgical Clinic and the Emergency Room and they are ill and have only us to count on. Now, I'd like to introduce you to my assistant, the PGY-4 Dr. Rupak Pal and to the three PGY-3 doctors, Gervasio, Kane, and Abrams. The PGY-2s are John Lucas, Ike Aronsky, and Rob Chenoiel. Doctors, let me introduce you to the new 'terns, Chu, Gordon, Habib, Isaacs, Ethan, and Maxwell." Each of the doctors nodded at the group upon hearing their names. Hercules looked around, smiling. "We are quite a United Nations of medical care. This team of future surgeons is also charged with the education of our three medical students; Lustgartin, Goldberg, and Garber." Hercules took a breath and seemed deep in thought. He looked at the clock and made a decision. "We now have forty-five minutes to make rounds and get to the O.R. We will have three PG-1 teams with a med student assigned to each. Chu and Gordon, you watch Goldberg; Habib and Isaacs, you get Garber; and Ethan and Maxwell, Lustgartin is all yours. The PGY-2 will each be responsible for the PGY-1. Ike, you will have the pleasure of teaching Ethan and Maxwell; John, you get Habib and Isaacs; and last but not least, Rob, you have Chu and Gordon. Okay, someone get the chart rack and let's get a move on."

Like Moses leading the chosen ones, Hercules ushered his team down the humid and smelly hallway. Occasional moans or shouting could be heard from the doorways along with the flushing of toilets or clanging of metal objects like oxygen tanks. Ward 3G had old and cracked brown linoleum tiles on the floors and institutional, green-glazed cement block walls. The patient rooms had four beds with two TVs hanging from the ceilings on chains. Zach later learned that patients had gotten into fistfights or worse arguing over channels. At one end was the prep area where nurses were gathering the morning's meds to distribute.

The doctors and students stopped at the first bed occupied by a whimpering, young Hispanic male.

"Okay, who has the info?" Hercules asked.

Gervasio, the exhausted young Filipino doctor, looking like he was on drugs slurred, "He's mine. Mr. Lopez is a nineteen-year-old male who pissed off his rival compadres in some way. At approximately 11 p.m. he was found down in a pool of his and his adversary's blood by New York's finest. EMS was notified but couldn't do much of a scene assessment because the cops wouldn't guarantee the scene was secure. This was confirmed when bullet holes appeared in their ambulance, so the pre-hospital guys, being men of both intelligence and valor, grabbed Mr. Lopez and ran for it. He arrived in the E.R. sans I.V. or any other stabilizing therapy at 11:15 p.m. with a B.P. of seventy palp and a pulse of 140. He was correctly judged to be in shock by the surgical second-year resident who happened to be walking through the E.R. looking for some action. ... "

"Did you find Nurse Massey for your action, Gervasio?" Rupak laughed.

"No, Miss Massey wasn't available for any relief at that particular moment as she was dealing with a bowel disimpaction and was rather malodorous. By the time she might have had a moment … "

I understand that with you a moment is all it takes," Lucas snidely added.

"Dr. Lucas, Miss Massey has never complained, so fuck off," Gervasio retorted. " … I had to deal with Mr. Lopez."

"My apologies for the demands of your career. Can we get on with it?" Hercules urged, looking at his fingernails.

"I did a quick physical exam and confirmed the patient was in shock with multiple bullet holes gracing his abdomen and left chest. His abdomen was grossly distended and hard as a rock. He was cyanotic-appearing and there was subcutaneous emphysema noted over the left chest."

Hercules looked at the group. "Chenoiel, significance of the sub-q emphysema?"

Chenoiel looked scared. "Uh … pneumothorax?"

"Great, boy. Maxwell what does that mean?" Hercules turned his attention to his next victim.

Zach stammered. "Uh … he collapsed a lung."

"Good. Now Gervasio, were there any other interesting findings?

"Yeah, his trachea appeared to be deviated toward the right."

"Goldberg, are you worried about this finding?"

"I think so … ?"

Gervasio smirked. "In this business, you don't have much time to think, Goldberg—yes or no?"

Rupak broke in. "Give him a break, Gervasio, this is his first half-hour on the service, you can torture him for years to come."

"Tension pneumothorax … " Goldberg replied.

"Wonderful, Goldberg." Hercules smiled. "Now Gervasio, what did you do?"

"Well, first I yelled for the junior resident, who arrived a couple of minutes later adjusting his fly.... "

"Hey, no editorial comments," Abrams warned.

"I prepared to place a chest tube.... "

"Which looks like a winner. Pneumothorax successfully treated. Hercules, at this rate we'll never get to the O.R.," Rupak said urgently.

Hercules addressed the group. "Unfortunately, Dr. Pal is correct. Gervasio, what was found in the surgical exploration?"

"Oh, the usual, holes in the small and large bowel, which we repaired. The abdominal cavity was washed out with a copious amount of saline and Betadine solution and a diverting colostomy was created."

Hercules went to the supply closet. "Garber, Lustgartin, and Goldberg front and center."

The boys gathered around Hercules, who started stuffing all the pockets of their new white jackets with gauze, drains, tape, gloves, and other supplies, till they all looked like the Michelin Man. "Med students have dressing duty. Let's go check the incisions."

Pal had taken off the gauze covering Lopez's incisions, revealing a long cut to the abdomen that was stitched closed and a piece of bowel that was looped up through the abdominal wall and attached to the skin to form the colostomy. The students were taught how to re-bandage everything and the group went through the other patients on their service quickly. By Zach's count, Hercules's service had operated on three major trauma victims during the night. Hercules's only comment was that it had been a light night in the O.R.

Hercules nodded at Rupak. "You take the femoral by-pass with Bullshit and I'll get our charges squared away."

Rupak smiled. "Trying to stay out of Bullshit's sight for a while?"

Hercules laughed. "Yeah, but I was also the last one to do a fem-pop with Moskowitz … your turn. Chu, Gordon, Isaacs, and Habib to the O.R. Medical students to the yammie's office for orientation…."

"Or a circle jerk," Lucas spit out.

"Enough of that. Aren't you in enough trouble with the yammie bopper, Lucas?"

Hercules retorted, "Rest of new guys, breakfast with me."

"Boys, welcome to the team and PAY. I'm sure you're all scared and feel you need to defecate, but please do not shit. Your worries and fears are justified," Hercules announced.

Zach had had three minutes to meet with his fellow interns and the special second-year by courtesy. Jake had pointed out Chenoiel, and Zach sensed that Jake was not exactly a fan. Chenoiel was somewhat of an anomaly at PAY. Tall, thin, and prematurely graying, he was a fourth-year med student from Harvard who had wanted to be a surgeon. The surgical program at PAY was staffed almost exclusively by residents who had received their medical education outside the US. The hospital administration was exuberant that a Harvard grad would pick PAY. As an inducement, he was granted an automatic advance to PGY-2 based on his medical school rotations at Massachusetts General Hospital. Even with the probably illegal bump in grade, none of the senior residents knew why Chenoiel was here and not at a more prestigious hospital in Manhattan, or Mass General, or Brigham and Women's. Harvard grads as a rule went to whatever residency their hearts desired and their performance was always rated as A+ even if they acted like their IQ was south of the boiling point of water in centigrade.

"You are lucky, boys. You are on the unassigned surgical rotation at exactly the right moment in time. Unassigned means these patients have no docs of their own and the right time because Brooklyn is exploding with trauma and we get the majority of these cases with Downstate Medical Center getting the rest. If you don't see every type of trauma in twelve weeks, it isn't trauma," Hercules said.

"Dr. Christospathos, will we be able to assist in any open-heart surgeries? I want to try to get into a Cardio-thoracic program." Chenoiel asked.

"Hmm, you look more like the carpenter type …"

"Carpenter?" Chenoiel was puzzled.

"Bones—Ortho, boy. We don't do bypass if that's what you mean, but we do get a lot of knives and bullets in the heart region so I think even you will be happy. Now where was I? Okay, you will all be on rotating call every third night along with the rest of your team. You will be taught by all of us. For over one hundred years PAY has had a top-down approach to teaching. I teach the fourth-year resident, who teaches the third-year resident, etc. Work hard and your team leader, the PGY-3, or third-year resident, will love you. But, remember, along with love, shit also goes up and down the hill. Now finish breakfast and let's go to the O.R. for lesson one. You're in for a pleasure, boys."

"Pleasure?" Zach asked.

Chapter 5

Zach and Jake were led into the surgeons' locker room by Hercules. The room was like a gym's locker room. It smelled like B.O., stale cologne, and shit, but with the added stink of a hospital's medicinal antiseptic. Hercules pointed out bins of scrubs at one end of the room, toilet stalls around the corner near showers coated with black fungus, and the door that led to the operating rooms and the scrub sinks.

"Take any locker with a key in it and make sure the lock is engaged. Every year a couple of surgeons are ripped off in here and they never catch who is doing the ripping. Also make sure you put on the booties," Hercules said, pointing out another bin by the door, "before you enter the corridor or Braverman will make a eunuch out of you before you get three steps into an O.R."

Zach grabbed a pair of moss-green scrubs. They had the sheen of cloth that had been washed many times and were very soft. He was terrified as this was the first time he couldn't talk his way out of being in an O.R. His private fright was interrupted by Jake's joyful shouting, "Look Mom, I'm a sturgeon!"

In O.R. 7, Mrs. Collins was being rendered unconscious by the Egyptian anesthesiologist in preparation for her cholecystectomy, or gallbladder removal. Zach, Jake, and Chenoiel were ushered into a corner far from the actual operating table. Hercules walked in and smiled.

"Okay boys, first lesson, pay attention." Hercules went on to address the surgical nurses in the room, "Ladies, I present the virgins: Maxwell, Ethan, and Chenoiel, each smart and handsome, and at least some of them are single and available. Have at them, while I scrub." Hercules walked out of the O.R. to scrub for surgery.

"Okay, virgins, make a line," a nurse barked. "Ladies, fresh virgins, check them out."

The new doctors made a line and three scrub nurses walked behind them. In front was an older nurse who faced them.

"Gentlemen, I am Margaret Braverman, chief nurse manager and the head of operations for Surgical Services at PAY Hospital. This means that I am in charge and the absolute last word on anything that happens in the eighteen O.R.s that operate at this fine hospital. You will do absolutely nothing in these rooms unless I approve it."

Zach wondered what a beginning resident would do by himself in an O.R., but he guessed Braverman was reciting the rules, so any potential hotshot, almost-surgeon knew his limits.

"I believe that for most of you, this is your first time in this hospital. A word to the wise, gentlemen: a nurse, any nurse, knows more about medicine than any of you. If you are smart, and I haven't seen too many of you who are, you will seek the advice of the nurse assigned to your case and listen. Remember, she is the eyes and ears in back of your head. She also spends much more time with the patients than you do. Now pay attention as the nurses show you how to scrub, gown, and glove in a sterile fashion."

Chenoiel raised his hand. "Uh, Margaret: I'm a second-year and learned last year how to do all this stuff," he said as he moved toward the O.R. door. "I'll just get scrubbed. By the way, I use size eights in gloves." Chenoiel started to walk out of the O.R. There was silence as a freeze occurred in the middle of the O.R.

"Oh, excuse me, *Dr. DeBakey!*" Chenoiel stopped. "I didn't realize that we had an expert in our midst. You're probably too advanced for PAY. I'm sure you'd rather be in that fancy Boston hospital of yours," Braverman said, dripping sarcasm.

Chenoiel stiffened, then slowly turned around. "You don't have to be snippy. I merely said I've been through this training before and it would be a waste of time ... "

"Get out of my O.R., now," Braverman replied quietly.

"Look, Margaret." Chenoiel sneered. "Christospathos wanted us here to learn something I already know, and then observe this cholecystectomy." He checked his watch. "In any case, with this waste of time, I am behind with my personal patient rounds. I will discuss this episode with Christospathos." With that Chenoiel left the O.R.

Braverman's face formed a rictus of pure hate and her eyes had become laser-like orbs. She was obviously trying to calm herself; Zach and Jake saw her count ten under her breath. After a few moments of uncomfortable silence she said, "Any one of you want to join him, because you already know everything?"

Zach looked at Jake and answered for the both of them. "Neither one of us know a damn thing, Mrs. Braverman. We would be happy if you would teach us how to scrub."

Braverman motioned to her nurses, "Have fun, girls." She left the O.R.

Scrubbing is the first thing a baby surgeon must learn. Even small amounts of contaminant bacteria can cause an infection in the sterile peritoneal cavity, and thus eventual death. Sterility of hands, arms, and everything above the waist is learned on the first day of the surgical rotation and then practiced under the watch-ful eyes of the scrub nurses, probably until the surgeon retires or dies. The surgical sinks are engineered so that the surgeon can work the whole thing with his or her feet. Once the surgeon's upper extremities are sterile, they touch nothing except the part of the body operated on and the instruments that make that surgery happen. If one looks closely at an older surgeon's hands, one sees the effects of a lifetime of scrubs with the antibacterial soaps and brushes employed.

"Okay, boys, arms are always elevated above the waist, and when washing, elevated above the elbows. This allows the contaminated water to flow away from the hands. Start at those nails. Use the nail pick in the scrub brush to get under the nail and get rid of that auto mechanic schmutz."

One Rubenesque nurse looked at Jake's hands critically. "Hey, those nails are long. You ever hear of a nail clipper?"

Jake blushed. "What do you mean? I keep them trimmed and clean … "

"Not trim enough, Dr. Ethan. Have you ever seen a patient who had a post-op osteomyelitis of the sternum?"

"Uh, no," Jake stammered.

"It sucks. Now stop scrubbing. Get those nails cut and maybe tomorrow we will let you be more than an observer."

Jake looked like he was about to argue with the pretty nurse, but realized that she was probably right and just reached for a towel. He smiled and said, "Whatever you say … what's your name?"

She pulled out a scrap of paper and put it in his pants pocket, taking her time to do so. Jake just stood his ground, his cheeks looking like the red-hot elements on an electric stove.

"Name and number. Look at it later. My rates are reasonable for young almost-surgeons. For almost any of the surgical subspecialties, I charge a bit more."

She took off, leaving the impression of a great ass and a puff of roses.

Chapter 6

Blinking lights and soft audible beeps were coming from the far wall of the operating room. Mrs. Collins's body was now draped in dull green sheets, her head separated from the rest of the body by another sheet clipped to upright poles. Hercules was at the far side of the table with Gervasio, the third-year, on the other side. They were both looking down at her abdominal area like vultures ready to eat a carcass.

"Come on in, boys," Hercules boomed. "So, Dr. Gervasio, what kind of surgical malpractice are you going to practice today?"

Gervasio yawned through his surgical mask like he had been through this routine a million times. "Mrs. Collins is a forty-year-old biddy who always likes that extra slice of pizza, washed down with a chocolate milkshake and then a piece of coffee cake to push that down. She developed right upper quadrant pain...."

"Zach, what is Gervasio describing?"

Zach froze, his brain feeling like there was no electrical activity at all. The surgical gown felt like it was a ton of concrete because of his sweat. The surgical mask was definitely cutting off his oxygen, and as a last insult he had to take a fucking piss now!

"Zach...."? What are the five Fs?"

Zach thought. "Forty?"

"Good, and another?"

"Female, fertile, fat...."

"As a pig," said Gervasio under his breath.

"Don't like the well-upholstered, you skinny Filipino? What's the fifth F, Zach?"

Someone let out a loud raspberry in the O.R.

"Flatulence!" Zach said.

"Half credit because of the help, Zach." Hercules laughed. "Gervasio, do we have proof this lady has gall bag disease or are you just practicing on whatever piece of meat you can find?"

"Ultrasound noted stones and a thickened gallbladder wall."

"Sounds good to me." Hercules turned to the young scrub nurse. "Ramona, my sweet thing, knife to Dr. Gervasio, if you please."

"Certainly Hercules," she said as she slapped a scalpel into Gervasio's gloved hand. He took the knife and made a long incision underneath the woman's right rib cage. The skin separated and yellow, globular, fat swelled and protruded from the incision. It seemed a million dots of red blood appeared and grew into rivers of blood. Zach, behind the scrubbed doctors, gagged.

"Oh, God....! I don't feel well...." He started swaying.

Hercules instructed the pretty nurse who had previously conducted Zach's inspection to catch him before he incurred a head injury.

She ran over to Zach, catching him just as he went down, vomiting.

"Shit, you fucking bastard." Zach's vomit had ended up on her chest causing a very smelly, wet T-shirt effect.

Zach, now sitting on the ground, looked up weakly. Her face was beautiful. Even with her surgical cap he could make out honey-blond hair. Her face had just a touch of pale-blue eye makeup to complement the grey-gold eyes, and there were cute pale freckles across her nose. She looked like a concerned angel come to save him. "God, they are beautiful," he said, groggily smiling at her breasts now outlined in half-digested breakfast.

Her face went scarlet with embarrassment and she yelled, "You'll never know just how beautiful they are." With that she took off out of the O.R. to clean up.

"What happened, Zach?" Jake was with Chenoiel in the call room looking at a very embarrassed doctor.

"I have a problem, okay? I've never been in the O.R. That blood and the yellow stuff, is that fat? Christ, she was full of that stuff."

Chenoiel started laughing. "Shit, look at you, a fucking he-man. A little blood makes you sick? How do you expect to become a surgeon—with your eyes closed?"

"Hey, give him a break, Chenoiel," Jake responded. "He'll get used to it. He just needs time to acclimate."

"You guys are amazing. Didn't you do anything besides read textbooks, drink, and fuck whores in that shithole they called a medical school? I've logged hundreds of hours in the O.R. and I'm not that much ahead of you."

"Fuck off, Chenoiel. Not everyone has a daddy who had pull with Harvard Med, making sure their small-dicked son had a place to go," Jake retorted. He hated Chenoiel's sense of privilege because his father was the head of a medical society. Jake knew there was always a back door for those who had either the connections or the money. Chenoiel had both.

"Jealousy makes you weak, Jake. Besides, I earned all I have, so go fuck yourself."

"Hey, even sick, I can take your head off and the blood won't bother me a bit," Zach said, getting off the bed.

Chenoiel looked at him, then Jake, and bolted out the door. "Screw you!"

"God, I thought we were done with those assholes," Jake lamented.

"You are never through with assholes in this life. Forget him. He is technically in charge of us as the PGY-2, but I think his word doesn't count for much here."

"Why do you say that? You heard the rumors about his father."

Zach smiled at Jake. "You think a guy like Hercules Christospathos gives a fuck what a twerp like Chenoiel says?"

Jake nodded. "I see what you mean."

Chapter 7

It was time for the second set of rounds as dinner trays were distributed to the patients allowed to eat. Zach and the other interns spent the day being supervised in patient care by the senior residents. This time the interns had had their lab coat pockets filled with four by four gauze squares, tape, Betadine bottles, gloves, and sterile drain packages. In short, Zach felt like a walking cupboard. There was no evening meal for the patients who were fasting because they were on the surgical schedule in the morning. Most of these patients were grumpy about being examined.

"Zach, get the chart rack please," Hercules said. "Meet us in 302."

Zach went to the nurses' station while the rest of the team went to see patients.

"I need some help here," came a shout from a room down the corridor. Zach looked around for a nurse or his team and neither was around.

"Oh fuck." He hated the feeling that he had to urinate now, bad. He wanted to run toward the departing surgical team, but the bright, red caduceus patch on his new white jacket caught the corner of his eye. He remembered he was here to help patients to the best of his ability. Taking a quick look at the corridor leading to the restroom, he went running in the direction of the shout, dreading what he would see when he got to the emergency. He almost slipped on the floor and thought that the janitor should have put up a sign about wet floors when he looked down and saw the wet was blood spreading across the threshold of the room. His legs and shoes were splattered in blood. Zach looked down the corridor for the team, praying that someone was in the hall. No such luck.

"Fuck, I've been here twelve hours. Oh my God." Zach gasped as he entered the room. Nausea struck him as he started sweating.

"Who are you? You're not a real doctor." The pretty, dark-haired nurse was on her knees next to a large black man who was lying in what seemed a lake of blood, barely conscious and sweating profusely. Zach immediately got down next to the patient, trying to keep from fainting and vomiting at the same time, and felt for a carotid pulse in the patient's neck. "I'm one of the 'terns. Can you get a pulse?"

Chenoiel sauntered in. "Hey Maxwell, what do you think you're doing?"

"You're still basically a student … " the nurse yelled at Zach.

"Stop what you're doing, Maxwell. We need a senior resident to be present before any procedure. Stop or I'll report you," Chenoiel yelled.

Zach blocked out Chenoiel's and the nurse's words, quickly accessing the patient following the ABC rules he had read about: airway, breathing, circulation. He found the patient's carotid artery in the neck. The pulse was fast, weak, and not normal. At the same time, he listened for air going in and out of the patient's mouth and looked at the skin color for cyanosis or blue-tinged skin. He touched the patient's skin, feeling only a cold and clammy surface. This patient was going to die unless something was done now.

"Get an I.V. setup with saline or Ringer's, also a large bore angiocath, stat! He's in hemorrhagic shock and needs volume, now."

The nurse paused for a second and then ran off to get the I.V.

"Damn you Maxwell, I swear stop or I will fucking have you kicked out of here," Chenoiel yelled.

What to do, what to do, Zach thought. Training and instinct took over as he grabbed pillows from the surrounding beds and got them under the patient's legs. He slipped in blood and landed on his knees just barely stabilizing himself with his hands now covered in blood. This was the Trendelenburg position, a way to elevate the blood pressure and thereby perfuse the brain with blood. It was then he noticed that the blood appeared to be coming from the patient's rectum. The nurse ran in with the equipment and Zach grabbed the I.V. start tray and put a tourniquet around the patient's arm, searching for a vein. He tried to forget his aversion to blood. It was the warm, sticky feeling combined with a rusty smell that Zach had trouble ignoring. There was a sound of running in the hall and Hercules filled the doorframe. "Shit, what happened, boy?"

Chenoiel tried to take command. "I told Maxwell we needed to wait for you. The patient is in shock and needs I.V. access. He is bleeding from somewhere."

"I think he's bleeding rectally. He must have gotten out of bed and collapsed," Zach said while still trying to get in a line.

"Does he have a pulse?" Rupak asked, getting on the other side of the patient's body and grabbing his other arm. "By the way Zach, good job not panicking."

Zach looked up. "Thanks," he replied.

"Veins are collapsed on this side, you find anything, Zach?"

"No dammit, this guy needs access. I think he's still bleeding."

Hercules motioned to Jake who had arrived with the rest of the team. "Grab his legs and let's get him off the floor into the bed."

Hercules and Jake swung the patient off the floor and into the bed.

"What's his story?" Hercules asked.

Lucas responded, "Fuck, he's the post-op hemorrhoidectomy I operated on with Not-a-surgeon Milsap. Not-a-surgeon insisted on clipping the vein himself. That guy can't see three inches in front of him. How does the chief continue to let him in an O.R.?"

Rupak motioned to one of the third years. "Get a CVP kit … no get two.

"Chenoiel, what does CVP stand for, and what does it mean?" Rupak asked.

"Central venous pressure, it is a measure of pressure in the vena cava and blood returning to the heart."

"Great answer, now Chenoiel, tell the nurse to call the blood bank and get two units of O negative up here, stat," Rupak ordered.

The CVP kits in blue plastic trays were brought into the room.

"Zach, get on a pair of sterile gloves. You'll put in the line."

"Wait a second, Hercules. I'm senior to Zach. I should be the one to put in the line," Chenoiel protested.

The room went silent. Residencies ran like a military organization. It was rare that a junior, especially a lowly PGY-2, question the chief resident who acted as a General in the hospital. In fact, only attending physicians questioned the chief residents. Chief residents had put in five hard years of training and were considered senior in knowledge and skills to much of the rest of the staff.

Hercules took a breath. "By that logic, I should be the one who puts in this line, but since I've put in close to 400 lines in my career, I doubt I would learn much and we are all here to learn, aren't we, Chenoiel?"

"Just my point, Hercules. I've never put one in and I'm a year ahead of Maxwell and, no offense to Zach, I'm being groomed by Bullshit to be chief. I'm sure he'd want me to receive priority in experience."

"Chief?" Rupak laughed. "Getting a little ahead of yourself aren't you, Chenoiel? Moskowitz usually makes the decision about advancement on the recommendation of the senior residents, not on who the sperm donor was."

"That's enough Dr. Pal," Hercules admonished. "Chenoiel, Zach is rewarded for intervening in a critical situation. His assessment of the emergency was right on and he didn't wait to see who was watching him as I seem to remember you doing."

"That's not fair," Chenoiel cried. "I waited to intervene because an experienced doctor is supposed to be present when the junior acts."

"That is true, but in this case the assessment of a critical patient, who needs an immediate intervention, trumps." Hercules gave Chenoiel a dismissive look. "Would you have made this decision if you were the first on scene? Maybe one day, before I end my tenure, you will. For now, this was Zach's good call and his reward. Zach, do you have your gloves on?"

"Look Hercules, Chenoiel is right, he is senior...."

"Subject closed, prep the right neck and clavicular area with the Betadine."

Zach robotically followed Hercules's instructions, cleaning the area and then injecting the local anesthetic under the clavicle. He was handed a small syringe with a very long needle on it.

"Christ," Zach breathed, "this is a weapon."

Lucas laughed. "Yeah, a weapon for good, so try not to spear anything important like the aorta, heart, or lung. Better get a move on—Hercules, this guy is getting more tachycardic by the minute and I can hardly feel his pulse."

"Okay, Zach and those of you unfamiliar with this procedure, insert the needle under the skin and then under the clavicle. Our target is to cannulate the … Jake, what are we cannulating?"

"The subclavian vein," Jake answered.

"Correct, my boy. Now, Zach, advance the needle parallel to the clavicle."

Zach was following the instruction step-by-step like a robot. He tried to get under the clavicle but kept hitting something that wouldn't let him move. "Hercules, I can't advance the needle."

"Don't panic, boy, you're hitting the clavicle." Hercules said reassuringly. "Come back out with the needle and then point more cephalad, toward the head and under the clavicle. Just don't go too deep and hit … What shouldn't he hit Jake?"

"The subclavian artery," Jake responded.

Hercules chuckled, "Good, and a hell of a lot more dangerous if you hit it, but what other structure is more common to hit? Chenoiel?"

"The lung, Jake. Jeez, you are a moron."

"Dr. Chenoiel, that kind of response is not allowed on my team … *ever.* Now, as you are so smart, why are we attempting to cannulate the subclavian vein?"

Chenoiel stuttered, "Uh, because it is … large?"

Hercules seemed satisfied when he looked at Chenoiel: "Incorrect. Because it doesn't collapse at a low blood pressure, and thus can be cannulated even in hypovolemic shock."

"Come on Zach, that fat subclavian vein is waiting for you," Jake said, cheering Zach on.

Sweating, Zach did as Hercules advised him. Procedures and needle placement were always a matter of 3-D geometry so Zach pictured the relationship between the clavicle and the subclavian vein that snaked under the bone to connect to the superior vena cava. He also pictured where he thought the dome of the lung was. Puncturing the lung and deflating it was a known complication, but this patient didn't need added complications, especially at this time. Sweat ran into his eyes as he plunged the needle under the collarbone into the patient's chest wall.

"Pull back on the plunger of the syringe," Hercules advised. "Don't worry, you're doing great."

Zach drew the plunger back, which came slowly as the end of the needle was against tissue. Suddenly it released as the end of the needle entered the subclavian vein filling the syringe with blood.

"Great job, now carefully remove the syringe from the needle. Don't move the needle though," Hercules encouraged.

Zach did as he was told, the barrel of the syringe turning by microns. "Come on, this guy will die of old age before the syringe comes off." Rupak cried out.

Zach got the syringe off and blood gushed out of the needle left embedded in the chest, hitting him in the chest and covering the rest of his brand new white coat and pants in crimson.

"Not to worry, boy. Here is the wire you are going to put through the needle. Take it," Hercules ordered.

Zach found the wire hard to grab and difficult to control, as it was made out of a springy core, and the end of the wire didn't want to thread through the needle. It didn't help that Zach's hands were shaking.

"Calm down Zach, or we're going to have to treat you for a seizure disorder," Jake reassured. "Breathe man, you're doing great."

Zach smiled and took a deep breath, and his shaking decreased.

"Hercules, come on and take over," Rupak begged. "We have to get to the O.R."

"Hold on a moment, he'll get it. Besides, I seem to recollect the great Rupak having twice as much trouble putting in his first central line and, if I remember right, learning how to put in a chest tube the next minute."

Rupak quieted down, blushing in embarrassment. "I guess so...."

Hercules turned back to Zach and said, "Take your time, it will go in, just take another deep breath...."

"I got it, it's in."

"Great, now just put enough of the wire through the needle so you can still hold onto it. We don't want that wire to disappear into the vein. You know why, Zach?"

"Uh, no, why?"

"Because, then we have to call the cardiothoracic guys to

crack open this guy's chest to pull that wire out of his heart. Know what happens after that?"

"No," said Zach horrified.

"We all call our malpractice lawyers." He laughed. "Just hang onto the wire. Now carefully get the needle out of the guy's chest.... Good. Rupak, give him the scalpel."

Zach took the knife.

"Now Zach, widen the puncture the wire is going through...."

Zach cut into the skin.

"Excellent. Now take this.... "

Zach was given a large tube that was over a plastic dilator.

"Put the end of the wire into the end of the dilator and, making sure you never lose the wire, advance it through the dilator." Slowly, Zach fed the wire through until it came out the other end of the dilator.

"Okay Zach, almost done. Now grab the wire at the end where it sticks out of the catheter, and using the other hand, shove the catheter/dilator into this guy. Push hard but steady."

Zach started. It was harder shoving it in than he thought, but he was pleased to see he had finally gotten the culvert pipe into the guy's chest.

"Now remove the wire and dilator, leaving the catheter, and you are done. Someone find the nurse and find out where the blood is. We are ready for it."

Zach straightened up. Leaning over the patient with all the stress of doing the procedure had tied his back in knots. He looked toward Christospathos. "My God, I feel like I was sitting there for hours."

Hercules laughed. "I'll admit, not a speed record, but okay for a virgin. Next time you'll do it faster."

The nurse ran in with the blood transfusion set up.

"Come on everyone. We have an asshole to repair. To the O.R., boys!"

Chapter 8

Zach was happy when he read his schedule for night call. Not only was he teamed with Jake, but he found his immediate supervisor was Ike Aronsky. Ike was a tall, blond graduate of Guadalajara who was a neighborhood boy—that is, if you counted the area next to Brownsville where the Jews and Italians lived as part of the neighborhood. He was married to a perpetually happy lady who was also blond and had two small blond children. Ike had gone from neighborhood to Mexico and back to childhood neighborhood, where his support system of parents, in-laws, cousins, aunts and uncles, made him one of the most stable residents on the surgical service.

Ike gathered Zach and Jake in the surgical call room. The room, as usual, was filthy with gray, mussed-up sheets and old food wrappers and containers. He handed them the surgical schedule.

"OK, team," Ike smiled. "This surgical schedule reflects tomorrow's scheduled cases. It doesn't have emergencies and disasters on it, which are the rule, not the exception at PAY.

Zach looked at the schedule with dread. "There are twenty cases scheduled for tomorrow that we have to check in. How do we do this?"

"With efficiency and gusto, boychik. We will split up the list. Quick histories and physicals—the H&Ps—draw the blood tests and make sure they get to the lab, and then general orders, like no food or drink after midnight. Then we gather the results of the labs and put them in the charts with the H&Ps. That's it."

Jake smiled, "That's ten per man, piece of cake."

Ike laughed, "Oh, I remember the last time I was naively happy. You are on the trauma service. We have gunshots, stabbings, and motor vehicle accidents or MVAs, all night. Almost all cut into your time and almost all go to the O.R. Don't plan on sleeping. The E.R extension on your pager will become the most hated number you will ever see. The two of you will take alternate cases to scrub in all night and as I have to be in the O.R. for all the cases, you'll end up doing some of my Pre-ops also."

"Holy shit," Jake blurted, "how do we survive this?"

"Don't worry, boychiks, you were paired with the most efficient PGY-2 there is, and I will teach you the way," Ike boasted.

Doctors had been training in this fashion for decades. The team split up before the trauma cases started rolling in.

Before Zach left, Ike told him, "Zach, on tonight's plate, besides the twenty patients to pre-op, we have three consults for central lines for which, thank the Lord, we will only have to do one of those central lines tonight and all the consults in the E.R. I take it you know how to do a surgical history and physical?"

Zach replied confidently, "Yes, I get the CC, chief complaint, then the HPI, history of present illness, then ... "

"Fuck that. This is surgery. Surgeons are considered barely literate enough to put two coherent words on a piece of paper, let alone write a sentence. At Harvard, all the guys who don't know grammatical English become doctors, those who are fluent in the Queen's English run for President. The key to this process is 'short'."

"Christ, it will take us all night and tomorrow."

Ike smiled. "This is Brooklyn, baby. If we only had to do those H&Ps, we would be in bed snoozing or fucking at 9 p.m., but starting in about two hours we will go to the O.R. for the first of the stabbed or gunshot citizens. That's why we need to get as many of these elective H&Ps done ASAP."

Ike was wrong by about forty-five minutes.

"Dr. Zach Maxwell, report to the O.R., Dr. Maxwell, O.R.," the hospital overhead speaker screamed. Fuck, the O.R., he thought. The bile was already starting to travel up his esophagus. This has to stop or I'm in for a very long year. He got an idea and ran to the pharmacy for pharmacological fortitude.

Chapter 9

The patient was a typical denizen of the area. Sixteen years old, black, and bleeding from his crotch. Pal, Ike, and Zach all met in the O.R. to assess the damage.

"He shot his balls off?" Ike exclaimed. "Jesus, that must have hurt."

Pal just nodded. "No doubt. Well, I think we will open him and check for any intra-abdominal damage, then the pee-pee docs need to take over. I think he still has some testicular tissue, but I can't tell in that mess. Hell, if there is anything worth saving, he is going to need a sac for what remains of the ball."

"We still might be here for hours," said Ike. He called to one of the nurses. "Can you page the other surgical team. Maybe they can cross-cover the ward and help Jake?"

Pal looked at Zach. "Ike, why don't you scrub out. I only need someone to hold sticks and we have scut boy here. Go get the ward ready for tomorrow."

"Thanks, Rupak, see you later. Zach, page me when you finish here." He backed away from the table and out the door.

Zach was hearing this interchange and trying to keep from vomiting. His bright idea to combat the nausea didn't seem to be working. He sensed that his bright idea wasn't going to cure a brain that just didn't like the sight of blood. How could anyone shoot another person in the balls?

Pal nodded to the Egyptian anesthesiologist. "Hey, chief, you got him down?"

"Just about. Now can you all go scrub? That educational talk is disturbing my sleep."

Pal smiled. "Let's go scrub." He signaled to one of the nurses. "Sweetheart, could you tell the office that I need one of the dick-docs here in about an hour? This guy has a ball problem." With that, Pal motioned to Zach it was time to go scrub.

After an hour of debridement and electrocautery to seal the small bleeding vessels, the place smelled like hamburger on a grill. Zach mostly observed, but occasionally Pal would hand him an instrument that was already placed in the wound and tell him not to move. His hand and arm would stiffen and eventually the stiffness would turn to pain and tremors, but he had no nausea and doubted at this point that he would vomit. He didn't dare move through it all, deathly afraid that his movement would cause Pal to slip and cut something important.

The O.R. door swung open and an overweight, spectacled man in scrubs and mask strode through. Jack Taff, MD, Chief Resident of Urological Services was an expert in dicks, balls, nut sacks, and a fine comedian to boot. He peered thoughtfully at the surgical field.

"What the absolute fuck did this asshole do to himself?" he asked as he looked over Zach's shoulder at the surgical field. "Pal, my brother from a lost tribe, lift that piece of *hazarei* there." Pal, having now worked at a half-Jewish hospital for four years, had picked up enough of the lingo to understand that "hazarei" was Yid for pork or unclean meat. What this had to do with genital tissue he wasn't sure.

Pal took the surgical pickups and pulled a piece of meat that looked like the other pieces of meat in the field. "This piece, Jack?"

"No, the piece that looks like New Jersey."

"New Jersey? This piece?"

"Nurse," commanded the fat doctor, "give me a Kelly."

The nurse balked. "Dr. Taff, you know better than that. You need to scrub."

"Cram it, sweetie, I'm not going to touch anything with my hand. I'm just using a sterile pointer so that I can teach my Hindu prince here what Jersey looks like."

The nurse sighed, knowing she would not win the argument and flipped him a Kelly clamp.

"Pal, this piece … this part is Camden. Have you ever been to Camden, Pal?" Taff asked as he flipped around mostly macerated tissue. "Camden, the home of where Campbell's soup is made, and where God is sticking the enema tube when the earth needs a bowel movement."

"Thanks for the geography and anatomy lesson all in one, Jack—now can we get on with this, as I have other work to do?" Pal hissed.

"Yeah, sure, you guys can go. I'll finish up in here." Zach was curious as to what the urologist made of the mess that represented this guy's genitals.

"Dr. Taff, wha do oo dink oo ca' do for duh patient?" Zach asked. He was surprised as the words came out slurred, and he was having problems moving his mouth the way he wanted to.

"Who are you, voice at the end of the table? Don't answer that and what's with the weird dialect?"

Zach was startled. "Ahh don no. Ahh tink awm havin ahh stroke."

"Fuck, Pal, you're killing the interns already? He hasn't been here even a week. A stroke at the age of, what, twenty-six or seven? Give me the sticks, new stroked-out intern. Pal, go help him."

Pal, obviously concerned, turned the table and the patient over to Taff. Zach was now having major spasms in his neck and face, and his right arm wasn't working too well. "Zach, are you having any pain? A headache? Nausea?"

Taff looked up from his dissection of the patient's scrotum. "Hold on a second." He studied Zach and commanded a nurse to pull Zach away from the O.R. table and pull off his mask. "Pal, stand by for brilliance that all have come to expect from the name Taff."

"What the fuck Jack, he is stroking. I have to get him down to the E.R. now."

"Oh, my Hindu prince, so engrossed in his surgical studies he has forgotten his basic medicine. Allow me to take over this lowly intern's case at the same time as I am saving this gangbanger's ability to create future gangbangers."

"Fuck you, Jack," he yelled. "Okay, what's wrong with Zach?"

"Zach, you have a problem with vomiting at the sight of blood?"

"Yeth, ahh puke," Zach managed to get out. The spasms were getting worse, tightening his face and neck into pretzels.

"Have you embarrassed yourself by vomiting in the O.R. in front of your masters, i.e. the Greek and Hindu gods?"

"Mufferfucker, ha did you know?"

Taff pointed a scalpel skyward. "Ah ha!"

"Dr. Taff," a scrub nurse admonished. "Put that knife down now!"

"Sorry," Taff said meekly. Even he was scared to death of Braverman's wrath. "Get an I.V. into him and give him twenty-five of Benadryl and two of Cogentin push. He'll be right as rain in a half-hour. Just remember to continue the Cogentin for three days—unless you enjoy looking like a stroke victim?"

Pal turned to Zach and yelled, "You mudderfucker, did you take Compazine?"

Compazine was used to combat nausea and vomiting. While safe, it occasionally caused something called a dystonic reaction. Patients started having spasms that made them look like stroke victims.

"Ahh din't wanna puke agan."

"Come on Zach, let's get you fixed up and let the dick doc … "

"Smile when you say that, Pal," Taff admonished.

"Excuse me, Professor Taff. Zach, let the esteemed surgeon of dicks and balls, and now neurology, work. We have some other lives to save."

With that Pal moved away from the table and made for the exit, stripping off his gloves and throwing them into a trash bucket. Zach shuffled after Pal's lead, also trying to dramatically strip the bloodied gloves from his hands but found he couldn't. So, with as much dignity as he could, he stumbled out with his gloves half off his hands.

Chapter 10

Zach's new day became a night that was just as busy if not busier than the day. Ike told him to stop at Mrs. Braverman's office and pick up a copy of the elective surgery schedule. Unlike the other private surgical services, the schedule on the residents' service was just a suggestion of the next day's fun and games. The private surgeons usually had few actual emergencies so the residents on those services usually had a fixed number of patients and O.R. cases. The usual fare consisted of hernia repairs, gallbladder removals, maybe a vascular case or two, and tumor removals.

The "schedule on service," as the resident's cases were called, was just a vague idea of the next day's events. Service was always mass chaos. Just because there were twenty cases on the schedule didn't mean that the schedule couldn't balloon to thirty cases in a matter of hours. Brooklyn had more trauma cases per hour than a major war. The nature of the neighborhood had blacks against whites against Hispanics, and the Asian gangs were particularly violent. Those cases were the daily diet. The frosting on the cake was kids who ran into the streets after rolling balls and the cars that found them. The falls, building collapses, fires, and other mayhem made the PAY operating rooms a twenty-four/seven business. All the non-scheduled cases were add-ons. All these cases needed to be evaluated, prepped, cut-on, and followed post-op. It was said that the surgical intern who survived his year in the operating rooms of Brooklyn was invincible to any other calamity that might occur in life.

Ike looked at the schedule and assigned Zach some of the pre-op cases to do a history, physical and prep on. There was little help. The nurses did not start I.V.s or give any meds unless a written order was given. These assigned cases were Zach's responsibility, though if Zach didn't get them done it was ultimately Ike's ass.

After leaving the O.R. Ike led Zach back down to ward 3G. The heat, humidity, and smells immediately made Zach woozy.

"Jesus, Ike, isn't the air conditioning working?"

"Stinks like the sewers with a fine over-smell of *je ne sais pas,*" Ike replied, laughing.

"Yeah, what is that smell? It's sweet with a smoky … Fuck, it's weed!"

"Dr. Maxwell, this is America and *cannabis sativa* is illegal. There can't be weed on this ward," Ike said sternly, then broke out into a smile. "Unofficially, the nurses allow the more asshole-inclined patients to smoke quietly at the far end of the hall. It keeps them calm and sometimes if they really like you, rumor has it, they share. They usually have really good pot compared to the crap I can afford."

"Damn, who'd have thought," Zach mused. "They smoke out in the open. Doesn't hospital administration worry about the cops?"

"Boychik, this is the neutral zone of the neighborhood. The gangs end up here as do the cops, politicians, business people, Mafiosi, and even Hassidic rabbis. When I was a student here they even had an Indian shaman who ended up in this neighborhood and got himself shot. There were all sorts of weird people hanging around him. He had brought his daughter, a real beauty, and the last chief of medicine, a boozer, ran away with her. PAY is a true melting pot of shitomas from all over the world. The authorities certainly don't want to rock the boat as they are afraid the whole structure will come down. Now you and I have had enough of a break. If we plan to make kosher smorgasbord we better get a move on. Tell you what, you take the right-side rooms, I'll take the left."

"Kosher smorgasbord, yum." With that Zach started moving down the darkened hallway toward room 301. His first patient, Shanaya Brown, was a forty-five-year-old and scheduled for a routine cholecystectomy in the morning. This shouldn't be too hard, he thought.

Armed with his trusty pad of pre-printed forms to write the history and physical of the patient, Zach entered the room and encountered a massive woman eating directly from a half-gallon container of Breyer's ice cream.

"Mrs. Brown, what are you doing?"

"Now with that white coat and all, you look like an educated person. What the fuck does it look like I'm doing?"

"Eating ice cream," Zach replied nonplussed. "Who gave that to you? Didn't the nurses tell you that you aren't allowed to eat or drink before your surgery tomorrow? Now we're going to have to cancel it."

"That's fine with me, sugar," Mrs. Brown said defiantly. "Get me the fuck outta here so I can go home and have real food to wash this down with, you mudderfucker. Who do you think you are telling me what to do? I'll fucking kill you.... "

"Mrs. Brown, please, not eating is for your safety during the surgery. The anesthesiologist doesn't like full stomachs for patients who are going to sleep during surgery. If you vomit, you will vomit into your lungs. Maybe we can ... "

"Maybe I can take this ice cream and shove it up your ass. See if you can vomit that you piece of ... "

"Hey, what's going on here, Dr. Maxwell?" Hercules had heard the commotion as he was making a pre-check before the morning's surgery.

"I'm sorry, Dr. Christospathos, Mrs. Brown is scheduled for … "

"Shanaya," Hercules cooed, "why are you giving Dr. Maxwell lip? He is just trying to make sure you have smooth sailing through the surgery so you can get back to those thirteen kids you have waiting at home."

"Dr. Hercules, he was disrespectful, accusing me of breaking the rules. I won't put up with that fucking shit, I won't."

"Shanaya, it's not your fault. The nurses and I must have forgotten about telling you not to eat the night before surgery. I apologize for that, but please don't take it out on poor Dr. Maxwell. He was just genuinely concerned about your safety. He is a hero, he saved your life."

Hercules turned to Zach. "Good job, Dr. Maxwell. With Mrs. Brown's body habitus, she would have surely aspirated that delicious-looking ice cream, setting her up for a pneumonia and possibly death. You truly are a hero and I'm sure Mrs. Brown will be grateful to you when she realizes how close she came to death."

"Well, I … "

"Mrs. Brown would really like to thank you, she just was misinformed of your concern. Right, Mrs. Brown?"

Mrs. Brown looked like a lightning bolt had hit her. She took the ice cream container and pitched it into the trash. "Dr. Hercules, what am I going to do? I can't get my sister to come up from Georgia again to watch my babies." Tears started running down Mrs. Brown's chubby cheeks.

"Dr. Maxwell, after you examine Mrs. Brown, I want you to call the O.R. scheduling office and switch her to last case of the day … about five in the afternoon. Mrs. Brown, remember no food from now on."

"Okay, Dr. Hercules," she looked sadly at the trash. "What a waste of good ice cream."

Hercules laughed loudly. "Boy, I think after Mrs. Brown gets through the surgery and is feeling better, you owe her a half-gallon of Breyer's best. What do you say?"

Zach smiled, as did Mrs. Brown. "I think that's a great idea, Dr. Christospathos."

"That's the way she goes," Hercules said, happily exiting the room.

Chapter 11

"**Ike, how many** fucking fat, forty, flatulent, fertile females are here in Brooklyn? You think we'd have run out weeks ago."

Ike looked up from the I.V. that Zach had tried to insert and failed … five times … on a particularly obese woman. "Well, I, for one, am thankful. Eventually, the third-year residents will have their fill and little ol' me and the rest of the second-years will get their chance to slice and dice into these bodies."

Zach looked at the patient nervously. "Ike, the patient.… "

"Don't worry Zach, she doesn't speak English." He turned toward the patient. *"No hablas inglés?"*

"Sí," was the single word that came out of her mouth with a smile.

"Ike, sometimes I wonder how you got out of La Mexican Escuela de Medicina with your hide intact. You are so fucking disrespectful.… "

"As if you aren't, Zach," Ike retorted. "You speak pidgin Spanish at best and when the patient talks to you, you just bob your head and say, go yentz yourself, with that sweet smile. Anyway, I went through the Mexican system and have no loyalty or respect toward this American system of yours. The players are as shitty to each other as they were in Mexico and if you think the system itself is more honest, you don't know about the pay-offs to get accepted to a US school."

Zach was thoughtful. "I guess you're right. With money and contacts anything can be accomplished here. Look at Chenoiel. I can't believe he was a top choice for admission to any med school."

"I'm pretty sure you're right. Chenoiel's father is a medical society president. He is a bigwig at Downstate Med and I'm sure that counted for a lot. Hey, look," Ike said excitedly, "I hit oil in a sausage."

"Thank God. I thought we'd be here a whole night trying to get the I.V into this whale. I'm hungry and I smell smorgasbord coming our way."

"You're always hungry. How many more pre-ops do we have?"

Zach checked the list, "Done this one, this one, that one.... Damn, only one left." Zach squinted at the paper. "Shit."

"What, shit?" Ike looked up alarmed.

"Leiber, Jonah. Rabbi. Room 201. One of Bullshit's cases."

Ike looked like he was about to kill himself. "How the spiritual Moses fuck did that holy roller end up on our service? Please Zach, I know I'm supposed to do him, but please, the last time that rabbi was in I lost feeling in my left arm for three days from the S&M device he made me put on."

Zach chuckled. "First of all, S&M is in your perverted head, they are *tefillin* and it's an honor when someone as high up in the Lubavitch Jew movement asks to pray with you. Second, if it is a joke and Leiber is trying to get you into S&M, just think how much fun it might be when you get Goldie between the sheets and bring up a little something spicy."

Ike's face fell. "First, keep my sainted wife … "

"She can't be a saint, she's Jewish."

"Well, keep my angelic wife out of this. Besides, she is seven and a half months gone and with my schedule I don't have the strength to get over the hump. My dick's atrophying." Ike looked deep in thought. "Hmm, maybe Leiber's S&M device is what I need."

Zach went to the phone as if to make a call. "Yeah, I need Friedman … no, not vag Doc Friedman, Head Doc Friedman for a stat consult."

Ike laughed. "Okay, quit clowning around. Please get the H&P. I'll go to the lab and grab the lab results and then we'll meet for smorgasbord."

"Okay, what is Bullshit doing to him tomorrow?" asked Zach.

"Bullshit bypassed a blockage in his femoral artery about two years ago. He now has a lump of some sort just below the femoral takeoff. Bullshit thinks it could be just scar tissue, but he wants to make sure. If it turns out to be a pseudoaneurysm, there is going to be a very long case tomorrow for anyone unlucky enough to have to scrub in on it."

"I'll go and do the H&P, but I swear if he tries to convert me … "

"He can't. You're already Jewish.… "

"I mean convert me to a holy-roller.… I'll make sure you'll burn at the stake."

"Fair enough. Remember, do a good job. He's still Bullshit's case and for some reason the chief seems to tolerate you. Don't ruin it."

"He likes me? I didn't think Bullshit liked anyone. Look how he treats Hercules."

"I didn't say he likes you, but toleration from Bullshit is just as good. Besides, he respects Hercules, so he gives him a hard time. I think Bullshit thinks this will hone Hercules into an even better surgeon than he already is."

"Well, I wish he wouldn't tolerate me so much. He made me scrub with Flora on an AV fistula. Five hours of pure torture."

"It could have been worse. He could have loaned you to Mitchell in Groinocology. You don't want to know the horrors that pussy surgeon can invoke."

Chapter 12

"Hello, Rabbi Leiber. I'm Dr. Maxwell and I work on Dr. Moskowitz's team," Zach said. "You're here for surgery on your right leg? Dr. Moskowitz noted previously that you had a blockage in the femoral artery, causing pain with walking. He did a fem-pop bypass two years ago and now you have developed a lump."

Zach reviewed Leiber's medical record, noting he was a man in his fifties with high triglycerides.

"Rabbi, your chart notes that you have had high cholesterol since you were a younger man," Zach asked.

"I thought Dr. Ike was going to admit me. We go back a long time you know."

"Yes, Dr. Aronsky sends his apologies. He's tied up with an emergency in the E.R.," Zach lied smoothly, wondering if God was going to hit him with a lightning bolt.

"Yes, high cholesterol is the burden Ha Shem has given me. You know Ha Shem, Dr. Maxwell?" asked the Rabbi.

"The Name of God, right. I graduated top of my class in Hebrew school, Rabbi. Now I see that you had a heart attack when you were about thirty. Any chest pain recently?"

"Nah, maybe a little indigestion when I eat corned beef."

"Your doctor told you this wasn't healthy for you, Rabbi. I see you had another heart attack and then started developing pain in the legs."

"Ach, I know, but I only eat a small sandwich with French fries. A pleasure Ha Shem has given me."

"What brought you to see Dr. Moskowitz originally?"

"Leg pain when I prayed to Ha Shem. He gave me a sign that my legs needed care and I went to see Dr. Moskowitz. He fixed me and he will fix this lump too."

Zach started palpating the leg while still talking to Leiber. "So up to now you haven't had problems with the Gore-tex graft?"

"No, the graft carries my blood around the obstruction, just like the doctor told me."

Leiber was physically overwhelmed by his hospital room. A cardiac monitor connected by wires to his chest, a respirator that was stuck in a corner not being used, mayo stands and multiple overhead lights all seemed to close into this man with a bluish tinge to his skin. Zach saw a man who had the signs of tissue under-perfused of oxygen, a sign of cardiac insufficiency. Like most of these men with absolute faith in God, he was always smiling in total acceptance of a future in God's hands.

"You are Jewish, Dr. Maxwell?" Leiber asked with a smile.

"Yes, but I'm not religious. I'm afraid I haven't been inside a temple since my bar mitzvah." Zach, forewarned by Ike, tried to keep the interview out of the Jew world realm. He just wanted to pre-op this guy and get to smorgasbord.

"It doesn't matter that you don't come to *schul*, you know … the synagogue. It does matter that you try to come back to God. Please do me a favor and just say one prayer with me while you put on *tefillin*. It will take two minutes, maybe less. Hurry, thank God it is summer and still light out. We have a few minutes left for you to complete the mitzvah. You know what a mitzvah is, right?"

Ugh, Zach thought, smorgasbord was quickly depleting to the benefit of his hungry teammates.

"Rabbi, I really don't believe in religion and I don't have time because of my workload. Dr. Moskowitz wants me to get your blood tests started, insert an I.V., and make sure to tell you not to eat or drink after midnight."

Zach quickly took his stethoscope and listened to Leiber's lungs and bowel sounds. He prodded the rabbi's abdomen, noting no abnormalities. He then checked the previous operative site in the groin. The pale skin appeared swollen adjacent to the old scar from the bypass. Zach palpated a four-centimeter mass, causing the Rabbi to quietly groan. "Sorry, Rabbi, I didn't realize you had pain in this area."

"It's not that painful, more like a shock when it is touched. Just unexpected, I suppose."

Zach noted no buzzing—or a "thrill" in medicalese—on palpation, and then took his stethoscope and gently placed the diaphragm of the instrument on the mass. No rushing fluid sound, that meant no bruit. That was strange, as when he moved the diaphragm directly over the Gore-Tex graft site he could definitely hear the whoosh of blood flow. Could it be a solid tissue mass, and not a weakness in the graft, causing an aneurysm?

"Dr. Maxwell, please, one little act from you to God. I promise it won't hurt and then I'll do whatever you want me to. I promise. Are you a righty or lefty?"

"Rabbi, please...."

"We could have been finished by now." Leiber reached into the bedstand and pulled out a blue velvet bag stitched with gold lettering. "I have them here, it will be quick."

Zach felt his head throb and his cheeks get red hot. This was implicit blackmail. If he didn't do as Leiber requested, he couldn't get his work done. On the other hand, if he gave into this BS, he would have to continue with this religious mumbo-jumbo whenever Leiber was admitted or until he dropped dead of his vasculopathic condition.

The clock was ticking and he was sure the lean parts of the pastrami were already gone. "Okay, please be quick, I'm starving."

Leiber grabbed Zach's left arm and quickly placed the straps after putting a yarmulke on Zach's head. "Repeat after me … Shema Yisrael.… "

Zach, a reluctant graduate of the San Diego Conservative Jewish Hebrew School, just went with it and recited the prayer which was a declaration of God's oneness or some such. "Okay, I'm done, right?"

Leiber smiled. "So you do have some background, I'm surprised."

Zach started undoing the straps and smirked at the Rabbi. "A mitzvah is a good deed. Just because I don't practice doesn't mean I haven't been exposed. Let's get this medical stuff done and then I can eat and you can sleep."

Chapter 13

Death by stabbing, death by gunshot, death by motor vehicle.

Death by overdose, domestic violence, fire, pestilence, boils and plague. PAY had seen it all and tried to minimize the numbers the reaper claimed through its house staff.

Zach's night was a blur of noise, bright lights, flashing lights, and bad smells. This was American inner city medicine on a war footing. He lost count of how many patients he saw and helped treat. The starched white coat he had proudly received barely three weeks ago was a reeking, biological disaster area of every bodily fluid created.

His skin was sticky and his hair was greasy. He vaguely remembered seeing Lucas during the early morning hours. They waved to each other in one of the hospital's darkened corridors. Zach was running from the blood bank to deliver blood to an O.R. Zach remembered thinking that Lucas looked terrible.

Dawn finally broke and the last of the emergency O.R. cases were parked in the recovery room. Those who had survived the night still had a long way to go before seeing the exit door of the hospital. Zach made his way to the ward for morning rounds. He couldn't get his mind around the concept that he still had a full day's worth of surgery to go before he could sleep.

"Zach, do you have your numbers for Hercules?" Ike inquired.

"Yeah, thanks for telling me how to organize this. Who could memorize all this info after a night like last night?"

"Last night wasn't even considered out of the ordinary."

"Good morning, boys," Hercules boomed. "Light night I see. That's great, as we all have cases this fine day, so let's get a move on. Who has the first case?"

"I do," Ike replied. "Mr. Baranowski decided to defend his pharmacy from the urban blight that is Brownsville. The socialist who decided that drugs should be free for all tried to impart justice by taking a steak knife and attempting to do an open-heart procedure. Fortunately for Mr. B and to the greater glory of the Lord, the point of the knife hit the St. Christopher's medal that he has worn since his grandmother gave it to him. The knife point slipped on the metal, burying itself in the lung, and allowing Mr. B to get his .22 revolver free and shoot his assailant quite dead. Mr. B received a chest tube and is doing well.

"Great.... Ike, why don't you go check on him and the rest of us will go see ... OK, which of you has him or her as a patient," Hercules said while checking his watch.

"I do." Zach semi-yawned. "She is Señora Perez pre-op for this afternoon. Perez is a fifty-six-year old diabetic with right upper quadrant abdominal pain. She is afebrile and hydrated. She seems to be stable for now. Medicine was consulted about her insulin requirements as she is NPO.... "

"Zach, what does NPO stand for?" Lucas asked. He had almost graduated from a prestigious classics college when he was caught shtupping the Latin professor. The college was forced to allow him to finish his degree because his GPA was in the stratosphere. To med school he went, but the snooty Greek and Latin major never washed out of him.

"Uh," Zach brilliantly replied.

"They are not teaching the classics anymore, are they? I tell you it is a sign of the downfall of civilization. NPO stands for *Nil per os,* or nothing by mouth.... "

"That must have been a big disappointment to you, when that Latin teacher finally refused what you were offering, Lucas." Rupak laughed.

"Fuck off, Rupak. I'm just trying to class up the joint," Lucas replied.

"Okay, let's go see her." Hercules moved the group into the room to see Mrs. Perez, who turned out to be a short, fat, smiling lady. "Mrs. Perez, how are you this morning?

"I just want this surgery over with, Dr. Christospathos. My stomach hurts and I'm hungry at the same time."

Hercules looked at Zach. "What are her numbers, boy?"

Zach pulled out a stack of index cards and found Ms. Perez's. With the volume of surgery being done all the doctors carried a card for each of the patients. "White count is 11.4 with a 'crit of thirty. Her sodium is 132, potassium is 3.8 and her glucose is running 120."

"What are we running in the I.V., Zach?"

"D5Normal Saline at 120 mls an hour.... "

"Potassium in that?" Rupak questioned.

"Yes, twenty milliequivalents per liter."

"Sounds good. Where is she on the line-up?" Hercules inquired.

"She's first up so we can get early help managing her diabetes in case the surgery destabilizes her sugars," Gervasio responded.

"Brilliant. Mrs. Perez, we will see you in the O.R.," Hercules said. "Okay, onward boys."

Rounds continued, seeing all last night's emergencies and today's pre-ops. As usual, rounds were quick, focused, and everyone prayed they revealed no surprises.

Chapter 14

Eleven hours later, Zach was hallucinating. The last case of the day ran two hours and was, in a word, disgusting. PAY, being in a poor section of Brooklyn, had a higher proportion of patients than the general population of the US who were obese and diabetic.

Zach mentally reviewed what he knew about diabetes. It was a bad chronic disease that attacked the small blood vessels, giving rise to poor circulation. In the lower leg, this manifested as pain on walking and/or numbness in the feet. The numbness was especially bad for the patients as they couldn't feel a lot of pain. The patients cut themselves from walking around in ill-fitting shoes and either didn't feel it, or had their usual neuropathic pain that competed with the pain of the laceration. Wounds weren't noticed, so didn't get cleaned and got infected. Poor circulation allowed infections to really take hold, killing tissue and forming abscesses. Patients still didn't notice till they noticed drainage or pus that smelled like shit or the foot turned black from dry gangrene. This is where the surgeon came in. The treatment was debridement of the dead tissue and drainage of the pus. The surgeons would initially attempt to cut away the infected tissue. This was a gruesome, everyday chore that Zach hated on Christospathos's service. One of the scut puppies would go from floor to floor with a jacket bulging with scalpels, gauze, and tape. He would take the knife and start hacking away black, green, and always malodorous tissue until it bled freely. The bleeding indicated healthy tissue. Sometimes debridement was not enough, so when the infection and necrosis was bad enough, an amputation was done. PAY did amputations wholesale—toes, half-feet, below the knee, or above the knee. There was even an unofficial competition how fast an above-the-knee amputation could be done from first cut in the skin to stitching the stump.

The attendants brought in Mr. James, a forty-eight-year-old black male with hypertension, coronary heart disease, and chronic renal failure. In the words of Dr. Samuel Shem, he was a classic example of PPP or piss poor protoplasm. There wasn't a hell of a lot working on this relatively young guy, and now the surgical team was going to take a leg, putting him in a wheelchair or crutches for not a very long life.

"Kazi," Pal taunted the anesthesiologist, "is the patient asleep this time or are we going to hear him scream when we cut off his rotting leg?"

"Fuck you, you Indian piece of yak shit. Maybe if you learned how to cut off an appendage quickly the patient would stay asleep."

Zach marveled that in this United Nations of hospitals, ancient enemies like Pal and the Afghani gas passer, Jews and Arabs, Christians and everyone else, actually got along, aside from the humorous banter. He realized they were all in this together, hopefully for the good of the patients.

Mr. James was being medicated into anesthetic sleep and soon Pal was instructing Zach to grab the toes and lift the leg off the gurney. "Congratulations, Zach, you have just become a living piece of surgical equipment."

"What?" Zach asked. His nose was near an area of the leg, dripping pus, and smelling like an animal-waste processing plant.

"If this fucking hospital would lay out some cash, we would have the attachment to the O.R. table that would suspend the leg, but *c'est la vie*, the hospital doesn't buy basic equipment because they have cheap labor, i.e., you."

"You mean I have to keep this leg suspended in the air?"

"Yup, till the leg can leave the room without the patient. ... Don't let it drop, or else!"

Zach didn't have to contemplate the "or else." Pal made a paintbrush from a ring forceps and a wad of gauze, and proceeded to paint the entire leg from foot to groin with the brown soap called Betadine. He finished the process and started all over again while Zach tried to forget his arm muscles were cramping.

"Okay, here we go.... Kazi, vitals stable?"

"Go ahead, butcher," Kazi mumbled.

Pal quickly made a circum-thigh incision, blood welling from the cut edges, and exposing first the fascia, then the muscle underneath. Zach thought it so strange that he was here in the middle of the operating room, watching the deliberate maiming of a man and no one seemed at all indignant, sad, or had any emotion except boredom. Was he feeling too much and would he ever feel so little?

Chapter 15

"**Okay boys, that was** the last patient. I'll see you tomorrow on morning rounds. Go get drunk, laid, and make sure to get some sleep," Hercules slurred.

Zach couldn't believe he hadn't been to sleep in thirty-six hours. He had never felt so gritty in his life. His white coat was stained with bodily fluids, his blue shirt felt like paste on his chest, and his crotch itched something terrible. Drunk and laid, more like shower and sleep? Surprisingly, he was jacked up and didn't feel much like going right to bed. The last thirty-six hours had been a panorama of the evils that could befall a man, but also showed that evil was fought by professionals trained to correct these situations. He saw babies, blue with their last breath, turn pink; alcoholics seizing, now calm; and gunshot victims with no blood pressure have their holes closed, to be shot again another day. Energized, his physical condition no longer bothered him, as he knew it was well earned.

Hmm, drunk and laid, he thought.

"Hey Zach, how did the night go?" Jake asked. "God, you smell like a sewer. What happened?"

"You don't look so great yourself. What happened, bladder couldn't hold it?" Jake was showing a large, wet, yellowish area on the front of his once-white pants.

"Funny," Jake answered. "One of my lovely alcoholic patients with end-stage liver disease decided to give me a sample of his gastric contents. Fortunately, most of the liquid appeared to be at least eighty proof with just a hint of chicken piccata juice for freshness, I'm sure. Now I'm going to have to boil my manliness or never have it used again."

"Well, we men in surgery are bathed in the fluids of life. To tell you the truth I should be in a coma, but I just feel like partying. I know I should get some sleep, but damn, I saw life and death last night.... I just can't sleep."

Jake shook his head. "I know what you mean. Suddenly, all the shit that we went through in school seems worth it. We are actually saving lives."

"I know what you mean. So, what should do this evening?"

"I bet Sandy would like a night out. Mind if she tags along?" Sandy was Jake's significant other. They had been together forever, but never married. Jake had told Zach that marriage would probably ruin the relationship. Zach liked her. She was sarcastic, witty, and very loyal to Jake. Sometimes Zach wished he could be in such a situation. "Sure, tell her to pretty up and come-a-drinkin'."

"I think I know a place, sort of a hospital dive, not too far from here." Jake replied. "Go home, get cleaned up, and we'll pick you up in an hour-ish."

Chapter 16

Snooky's was a neighborhood saloon in Park Slope, a better part of Brooklyn. The brick façade with a welcoming, weathered, carved wood sign was a tradition among the young doctors in training at PAY. Snooky's took its place among the other fabled hospital bars, The Recovery Room in Manhattan, Intravenous in LA, and Microbes in Atlanta. The bar's patrons came in casual dress or scrubs, dirty or clean. The décor was dark wood and leather with the smell of steaks, fried foods, and beer from the tap. It was a place to unwind, interact, and not have to worry about a sick patient flying through the door.

Jake and Sandy picked up Zach. "Hey, Sandy, how are you doing? Proud of your stud muffin surgeon?"

Sandy was a brown-haired cutie on the thin side. She always smiled except when she was discussing Jake's current work place.

"Yes, of course I'm proud," Sandy replied. "I just wish he would be home more often, and awake. Two nights ago he came home, and I had made him his favorite, spaghetti and meatballs. He took two bites, told me he was full, and went to sit on the couch in front of the TV while I cleaned up."

"Sounds boring, unless you're cleaning up the final X-rated scene for my innocent self," Zach said with a playful leer.

Sandy's voice became tremulous, "No, I'm beginning to think all that X-rated stuff happens in the hospital. With me, he just falls asleep. Maybe I should buy one of those nursing outfits to rev him up."

Zach uncomfortably said, "I can attest to Jake's fidelity to you and his right hand, and even when he is on a date with said hand, I hear him murmuring, 'Sandy, Oh Sandy!'"

Sandy gave Zach a smile, and Jake said, "See babe, it's always about you."

Because the PAY neighborhood was so dangerous, Jake had found a small apartment in Queens. It could take Jake an hour to get home, depending on traffic. He was already spending less time with Sandy than he ever had, due to the demands of the residency. Even though she realized it was immature of her, and a temporary situation, Sandy was afraid of what it was doing to the relationship. She loved Jake with her heart and soul, and knew Jake felt the same about her, but men were men and when they weren't getting their needs satisfied at home.... Well, her father had left her mother years ago, taking up with a newer, less busy, model. Her mother never recovered and Sandy did not want to make the same mistake.

They navigated the streets of Brooklyn, finally finding the bar on a commercial street serving Park Slope. Even from across the street, the bar had a lively sound coming from it. The patrons entering its doors had smiles on their faces and looked like they were ready to party.

"What will it be?" the bartender asked. "Want to look at the menu, as I don't seem to recall ever seeing you here?"

"We're the new interns from PAY, and Snooky's was recommended," Zach responded.

"Well, you are in the right place. PAY owns tables ten through twenty. Methodist Hospital, tables one through five, and Lutheran, six through nine. Try to stay within your assigned area."

Jake shook his head. "Assigned? I don't understand?"

"Fewer bar fights. Management is tired of having to buy new

tables and glassware when you young doctors tie one on. You are assigned space as to size of your hospital. ... PAY is the biggest, you have the most tables."

"Well, good to know we're number one," Zach said. "How about a round of beers for my friends and me?"

"Money first, por favor. That's another policy of this establishment ... no credit."

Zach ponied up the cash for the first round and they looked at this extension to hospital social life. The patrons were almost 100 percent residents, as was reflected in their garb. Dirty white coats and green scrubs were the uniforms, even here in a public bar. Zach wondered what non-medical patrons of Snooky's thought about the drinking that went on. The young doctors and nurses all looked exhausted, except for their eyes. Their eyes were wandering from nurse to doctor and doctor to nurse, like wolves checking out a herd of deer. The more exhausted-looking the residents were, the hungrier they appeared. The nurses, mostly in uniform, but some in slinky dresses, were made up, faces carefully painted and hair done perfectly. Their hunger for the residents was obvious. Many of them, Zach knew, considered places like this a hunting ground to catch a future husband. Well, when in Rome, thought Zach.

Jake and Sandy told Zach they were going to wander. "Zach, why don't you find a nice girl to ... "

"Take home," Sandy said with a smile. "You both need some exercise and unless Jake drinks too much, he will get some tonight. That leaves you."

Zach blushed and mumbled, "Well, maybe."

He spied Lucas among a group of women. "Maybe there are more women than Lucas can handle," he said and walked to the group.

Lucas was looking bleary-eyed and greasy. Zach knew he had been on last night and had gotten pulled into a ruptured aorta case. The pressure in the aorta was high, so when it ruptured, death was quick from exsanguination. Five hours of surgery, and twelve units of blood, and the man had still died. It was a valiant attempt, but even the best doctors can't undo a cataclysm. Lucas looked like he had found the medicine to cure his defeat, and that medicine was vodka and women.

"Lucas, this is quite a place; it's like a clubhouse."

"More like a bordello, 'scuse me, ladies. *In vino veritas*." He smiled with a half bow. It was obvious the vodka had destroyed his inhibitions. There were three women with Lucas, two were instantly pissed off, but the third just looked concerned. She was a dark-haired, olive-skinned girl, slender, with full, wet-looking lips. "Lucas, don't ... "

"You heard about the aorta? The mudderfucker died," Lucas growled.

"I'm sure you did your best."

"Fuck that! Now I have to explain the case at Morbidity and Mortality conference. Bullshit is going to have a field day with me." Lucas looked like the air had just blown out of him. "I'll see you later, *deus vobiscum*," he grumbled as he walked toward the exit.

"Maybe I should go after him," Zach said. "God, he really looked depressed."

"No, he'll be all right. He just takes the bad outcomes hard. When you see him on rounds tomorrow, he will be fine. By the way, he also has no manners. My name is Dharma Motola."

"Zach, I'm an ... "

"Intern at PAY. Good move with Mr. Malone, by the way."

Zach was confused. He didn't remember a Mr. Malone or a good move that he made. "Uh ... thank you, I guess. Who is Mr. Malone?"

"Zach, you really ought to try to remember the patients whose lives you've saved. I mean in medicine it seems that moments like that can carry you through the next defeat. Malone, the guy bleeding out of his ass. It really was the talk of the nursing grapevine."

"Oh, that guy. Well, I don't think I did anything that spectacular. I mean all I did was order some fluids for the guy. You seem to know a lot about me."

"I also work at PAY. I was on the floor when you revived poor Mr. Malone. That was quite a save for your first week in a real medical institution. You may just be a contender for the Most Likely award."

"What is the Most Likely award, and what floor are you a nurse on?"

"Now, why do you think I'm a nurse? You know women have many different kinds of jobs in a hospital nowadays. I'm a social worker—or the one person you will come begging to help you with a patient."

"Beg?" Zach questioned. "I don't understand."

"When someone who is older than God comes on your service, and you can't get rid of him or her, then you will beg me to help you out. I know all the social service agencies and their phone numbers. I am a whiz at placement. Placement is absolutely necessary at PAY, as there are too many patients with nowhere to go."

"Is that so?" Zach asked. He was falling in love or lust with her beautiful, full lips.

"Well, Dr. Zach Maxwell, I'll let you in on a time-honored PAY tradition."

"Tell me, please," Zach replied eagerly.

"All the arriving interns are discussed. Background checks are ordered and then you are all rated."

Zach laughed. "Background checks? I doubt if any of us have robbed a bank or proposed treason against the United States. What could anyone want with a background check on us?"

"It helps to decide your desirability."

"I still don't get it? What desirability?"

"As a husband, dummy." She laughed. "Didn't your mother tell her prince how the girls would throw themselves at you because you were a doctor?"

Zach thought she was beautiful. Her warm, open face, raven hair, and olive skin gave her an exotic, enticing look. But she also had a serious side, and a serious job. The one thing he had already learned at PAY was that if you didn't get the patients out of the hospital beds, they stuck around like rotting fish.

"So, do I rate? I mean if you are not a nurse, I must be on a couple of rating systems. Nurses are sort of clique-ish. I don't think they allow non-nurses into the club."

"You are correct, except that I'm a major supplier of the information they need. The hospital wants to make sure the residents don't go off the deep end from all the work and horror you are involved in, so I get the keys to the personnel files. I do a little psych social work on the side. Just enough so the hospital doesn't have to involve the shrinks with you, but enough, in case one of you looks like he is going to dive off the roof to get to his car. Some of you guys are fascinating reads."

"Why don't we discuss it over a drink?" Zach said.

"I've got a better idea. Why don't we go to my place and have whatever?"

"Whatever?"

"Yes, whatever."

Zach took her arm and they made a quiet exit from the bar.

His head was pounding as he found himself naked under the thin sheet of a messy bed. Where was he? The room was a typical New York apartment, a studio with the bed taking up most of the room, exposed pipes, peeling paint, and a dingy window that let in some light. He smelled coffee and toast, and then Dharma came into sight wearing nothing but a smile. Her hair was disheveled, and she had not a hint of makeup. The rest of her body was almost boyish, cuppable breasts, and small muscular butt. The sight brought a smile to his face.

"Hey sleepyhead, I was about to wake you."

"What happened?" Zach asked.

"Well, I think it's obvious. Hope I don't get pregnant. I think I forgot my birth control, and I know you didn't have a rubber."

Zach went cold. He couldn't remember anything of last night. Pregnant? Oh boy, he was in trouble now. How much did he have to drink? Oh, shit, I don't even remember the highlights, he thought.

"I'm sorry, I don't know what got into me. I ... " he stammered.

She laughed. "I'm only kidding you, Zach. Actually, you were a perfect gentleman until you vomited all over yourself. I got you cleaned up and by then you had gone into a coma. I took the couch. You better get a move on, it's 5 a.m. and don't you have rounds at six?"

Zach jumped right out of bed, forgetting he was naked. Unfortunately, his embarrassment was compounded by her nakedness and the physiological response of morning wood. He found Dharma examining his growing predicament and turned beet red.

"What a shame the evening ended the way it did. It looks like something wanted to have some fun," she commented, pointing at his groin. "Maybe next time, sport. Your clothes are clean, and on the couch. Now get a move on, or you'll certainly go down in the ratings."

Zach took the hint and hurriedly moved on.

Chapter 17

"But Doctor, the patient has a temp and he can barely talk. Maybe you should take another look at him."

Rhonda was a senior nurse working PAY's emergency room. At the moment she was having a mega-problem with a resident. In her twenty-plus years in practice, she had seen it all. Her experience with the doctors-in-training taught her not to trust them until you knew you could. With the education that she and her level of nurses gave, most of the doctors became fine clinicians. They would learn to listen to the nurses they worked with in a partnership for good medical care. She thanked God there were more of those doctors than the group of docs Chenoiel represented.

"Fuck him, Rhonda. He is a fucking, pathetic addict looking for his next fix and we have Demerol, the legal heroin right here at PAY. I'm not playing his goddam game." Chenoiel got himself off the chair he was slumped in. He had barely touched the patient, spending most of the minute he was with him at the exam room's entrance. "Call me when the internists have a legit consult, otherwise I'm catching some shut-eye. Bullshit has an aorto-bifemoral bypass tomorrow, and I plan to be bright-eyed and bushy-tailed when I scrub in on it."

"I don't think you should discharge Mr. Zinman, Dr. Chenoiel. I think there is really something wrong.... "

Chenoiel grabbed the chart from Rhonda and took his pen like a weapon, scrawling a note. "There, it is official—drug-seeker Zinman is well and discharged." Chenoiel threw the chart at Rhonda, which bounced off her hand and landed on the floor. "You catch like a girl." He sneered and stormed out of the E.R.

What an asshole, thought Rhonda. I should call Hercules, but he's in the O.R. Rhonda looked around the E.R., and saw Zach palpating a woman's abdomen. She had never worked with Zach directly, but the grapevine had him up there. Maybe she could persuade him.... "Dr. Maxwell, do you have a second?"

Zach looked around, feeling like sand was lubricating his eyes. He was on his nineteenth hour straight, and could expect to be in the O.R. with the woman he just examined. She had right-sided guarding, an elevated white count, and was anorexic. He was just waiting for the pregnancy test to come back from the lab to make the decision whether to call Rupak to confirm his diagnosis of acute appendicitis, or to find out she was pregnant, and get one of the groinocologists to rule out an ectopic pregnancy. His muscles were cramping and he had problems focusing on the nurse who had just called to him. He squinted at her—a pleasant-looking, older blond-haired lady—and her name badge.

"I'm Zach, what can I do for you, Rhonda?"

"Look Zach, I know you are busy, but there is this patient who was seen and discharged, but I think is too sick to leave. I'm not sure what's going on, but he is a drug addict and has a fever. Would you mind taking a look at him?"

"Sure." Zach sighed. "Who discharged him? Drug addicts have problems with infection I know. Where is his chart, maybe I can … ?"

"Here it is, Zach. Chenoiel discharged him even though I told him it's not a good idea."

Crap, thought Zach, Chenoiel of all people. Zach had developed a quick loathing for the guy who walked around PAY like he was already Chief Resident in Surgery. Moskowitz was grudgingly promoting him as the ad for American grads to come and apply to the program. He knew the College of Surgeons always came down on PAY's surgical program because the only American applicant who wasn't a reject like Zach was Chenoiel, and it took offering him an automatic second-year slot. Even with good recommendations, probably from his father's cronies, and decent board scores, Chenoiel was a walking malpractice suit. He was never around for the scut work and as a result could barely perform any of the procedures necessary in his future as a general surgeon. He didn't do rounds with the group, and only saw patients with the private docs or Moskowitz. When, in a candid moment, Zach asked Hercules why he tolerated Chenoiel not attending rounds, he just shrugged and said karma, karma would deal with him. Besides, Hercules had decided Chenoiel didn't want to be taught, so why care if he was on the team? When Chenoiel completed rounds on the patients he had scrubbed on, he ran to the O.R. and found out which case Moskowitz was scheduled for so he could make himself available. Braverman had put out word not to tell Chenoiel any information about which doctor was doing what case, but Chenoiel was able to find out anyway. Rumor had it he had a mole he was fucking, working in the surgical office. Zach was sure that Chenoiel's wife would not be too pleased about this.

Zach looked at the E.R. chart and read the triage note. The patient complained of a sore throat and a fever. He was put in one of the cubicles where the primary nurse had taken his vital signs, noting he had a temperature of 102.3, a heart rate of 120 and blood pressure of ninety over forty. Zach was immediately concerned. Sepsis was a condition where bacteria from an infection anywhere in the body ended up in the bloodstream. The signs of sepsis included fever, tachycardia, and hypotension. Zach also knew that drug addicts were not known for the best of immune systems, complicating the danger level. It seemed like Chenoiel had totally discounted these vital signs and the patient's social condition.

"Rhonda, where is this guy? I'll go and take a look at him. Why did the internist get a surgical consult anyway?"

"The internist thought his throat looked funny, but didn't expand upon that observation to me," Rhonda said, miffed.

Rhonda led Zach to a cubicle in the Internal Medicine part of the E.R. It was in an overflow area that patients were stacked in till someone could get to them. The lighting was terrible, and the walls were the usual green-glazed block with the added esthetic of chipped exposed concrete, and old bodily fluid stains that had colored the blocks in a bizarre zebra pattern.

Zach opened the curtain and saw a barely living corpse. Charles Zinman III lay on the gurney looking like most of the other alcoholics who populated the E.R., but his color was a dusky blue-gray, and there was a sheen of sweat on his face. He smelled of urine with a load of dog shit added in. In the tradition of an inner-city E.R., his hospital johnnie was crumpled, damp, and had the opening in front. His stained jeans and socks and shoes had been left on. Unofficial hospital law disallowed anyone from removing socks and shoes because of the horrendous smells that came with that act. Zach could see that he was excessively drooling.

"Mr. Zinman, I'm Dr. Maxwell. I know my colleague has examined you, but if you don't mind, I'd like to take a look at you."

Zinman, whose eyes had been closed, barely opened one of them and growled, his voice raspy, "Who the fuck are you?"

"I'm Dr. Maxwell, this won't take more than a couple of minutes. Please, I'm just going to sit you up."

Zinman now had his eyes open. "Fuck, I'm in pain, I need something for my pain," he said, having problems getting the words out with all the saliva in his mouth.

"We will take care of your pain. Can you open your mouth really wide? I need to look at the back of your throat," Zach said as he prepared a tongue depressor, "then we will see what we can do about your pain."

Zinman tried to open his mouth, but it wasn't open enough to give Zach a good look. "Please, Mr. Zinman, try to open up. I really need to see.... "

Zinman grabbed Zach's hand holding the tongue depressor and feebly knocked it away. "I can't open any wider than this, asshole. Now get me some fucking pain meds or I'll leave. Where are my fucking clothes?" he croaked. With the outburst, Zinman was spent, and collapsed back onto the gurney. "Okay, you win," he whispered, "just help me."

Zach again tried to get Zinman to open his mouth, but it was obvious his jaw was not cooperating. Zach finally wedged the tongue depressor in and with his penlight got a look at the back of the throat. There was a big bulge in the tissue on the right side and it seemed like Zinman's uvula, the hanging tissue at the back of the throat, was shoved over to the left. Zach leaned back, and Rhonda saw his worried expression.

Rhonda asked, "Zach, what's the matter with him? Was I right or do you think he can be discharged?"

"No, you were right. Let's get an I.V. in him and give him some Demerol. That should help decrease his pain, and maybe we can get his mouth open more. He needs antibiotics and an ENT guy. I'll page the rez on call."

"You won't get him. They are all in the O.R. on a gunshot to the face.... "

"Fuck, I think this guy has a peritonsillar abscess and it needs to be drained. I need a real ENT doctor, now."

A heavily accented voice spoke from the next cubicle. "May I help you, my friend?" The curtain parted, and a small Arabic-looking gentleman in an intern jacket appeared. "We met on rounds the first day with Dr. Christospathos, my name is Habib."

"Dr. Habib, I don't know, I think I really need an ENT guy,"

Zach stammered. "I'm not even sure if my diagnosis is correct. Ike is stuck in an intestinal obstruction, Lucas is nowhere to be found, and Pal is with Ike. The ENT guys are getting a hard-on in the O.R. putting someone's face back together. Goddam it, if I'm right he'll either tank of sepsis or airway obstruction."

"Calm yourself, my friend," Habib said seriously. "Do you mind if I take a look?"

"Sure, be my guest for all the fucking good it will do him." Zach and Habib turned to Zinman who, if it was possible, was looking worse. Habib grabbed another tongue depressor from the drawer in the room and then pulled a head mirror out of his pocket, and put it on his forehead. "Please pull that surgical light down, and try to focus it on the mirror," he said while concentrating on Zinman's face. The light hit the mirror, and was reflected into Zinman's eyes.

"Hey, what are you trying to do, blind me?" Zinman asked weakly, trying to get out of the light.

"Sorry my friend. Zach, adjust the light down a little." The beam was now over Zinman's mouth. "Better, much better. Please open your mouth as wide as it can go." Habib saw what Zach had previously seen, a mouth that couldn't open all the way and the swelling on the right side of the patient's pharynx.

"Zach, your diagnosis of peritonsillar abscess is absolutely correct. The patient has trismus, which is his inability to open his jaw wide. The bulge is a collection of pus in a pocket. This pocket must be drained. You say the ENT residents are unavailable?"

"His nurse says she was left word that they are all in the O.R. What am I supposed to do now, watch his blood pressure bottom out or his face turn blue? We are interns, and I for one have never seen a peritonsillar abscess, let alone drained one. I mean, even if I knew how, Braverman would never let me in the O.R. without a senior. Fuck, this guy is going to croak on me. What am I going to do?"

"Why, you'll drain the abscess my boy, and save the day," Habib ordered.

"I told you, Habib, all the ENT guys are unavailable, and I don't know how to cut into someone's throat."

"Don't worry, in Egypt, third-year medical students can do this. I will teach you."

"You'll teach me, but you're an intern and not even ENT."

"My boy, here in America I am an intern, but when I trained in Egypt I became board-certified in ENT, then I went to Britain and certified there. Guess what I am going to be doing here in Brooklyn?"

"Train and certify in ENT?" Zach volunteered.

"And they say Americans are dumb shits." Habib smiled. "First, go find a number eleven scalpel and some surgical tape. I will go get some other things we will need. I will meet you back here in five minutes."

Zach ran, hunting down the equipment he needed, and collecting Rhonda along the way. "Come on, we are going to drain Zinman's abscess. We may need you as a just in case."

"A just in case ... what?" Rhonda replied, bewildered.

"A just in case I really fuck this up, and we need an extra pair of hands to resuscitate him. Grab the code cart, will you?" A worried Rhonda peeled off to get the red metal, resuscitation cart with the defibrillator on top of it.

Zach arrived to find Habib calmly setting up a suction set with a Yankauer suction tip. It was a long, hard, plastic nozzle connected to plastic tubing, which in turn connected to a vacuum bottle plugged into the wall. "We will need this so the patient doesn't drown in his own pus." Spying Zach's tape and scalpel, he rubbed his hands together like Uncle Ned contemplating the Thanksgiving turkey. "Exactly what we need." He took the scalpel and removed it from the packaging. "I need that tape you brought."

Zach handed it over to Habib, who proceeded to wind the

tape around the blade till just a bit of the scalpel's sharp tip was exposed. Zach asked, "Didn't you just contaminate that sterile scalpel with that tape?"

Habib just chuckled. "Zach, we are sticking the knife tip into pus, not the cleanest substance known to man. This scalpel won't infect the patient, the patient will infect the scalpel."

Zach smiled. "Yeah, that was a pretty dumb statement. I guess Americans are dumb shits. Okay, how do you do this?"

"I will tell you how to do this, with Rhonda's help. Mr. Zinman, please open your mouth as wide as you can. I know it is difficult, but if we are successful you should be able to open it a lot wider than you can now. Rhonda, please stand to the right side of Mr. Zinman. Now take the suction and place it in Mr. Zinman's mouth. Very good."

"Rhonda is going to suction the pus out of the abscess, right?" Zach asked Habib.

"More like Rhonda is going to try to vacuum the pus away before the patient swallows, or worse, aspirates or breathes the pus down his trachea and into his lungs.

"Why the taped scalpel blade, Habib?"

"Do you remember your anatomy? What is just behind the tonsil anatomically?" Habib questioned.

Zach thought, but his brain was gummed up by lack of sleep. He slowly peeled back layers of tissue in his brain: tonsil, then.... Fuck, the carotid artery is just behind that abscess. "What if I cut too deep? I'll end up cutting his carotid artery, and ... "

"It wouldn't do to cut too deep. The tape prevents that. Don't worry my friend, this Egyptian will help the Jew build a pyramid," he smiled.

Zach was now profusely sweating from nerves, and his hands were trembling. "It isn't even Passover."

"Okay Zach, take the Cetacaine numbing spray, and spray it into his mouth, aiming at that bulge."

Zinman immediately started gagging. "What the fuck was that, rotten bananas?"

"It is a topical anesthetic, Mr. Zinman. Sort of tropical, don't you think?" Habib asked reassuringly.

"Go fuck yourself!" Zinman, by this time, was having problems getting most of his words out, except the word fuck, which seemed easy for him to ejaculate.

"Hmm," Habib replied primly, "we had better get on with this. Rhonda, suction in mouth. Try to be aware of where Zach is going to incise and keep the tip of the suction there. Zach, slowly jab into the middle of that bulge."

Zach did as he was told, and suddenly a flood of thick, green-yellow pus came out of the abscess. Rhonda quickly vacuumed the vile fluid. "Lord, does that stink." Zach gagged.

"Well, that takes care of the acute problem. Put him on an antibiotic like penicillin or Clindamycin, and leave a consult for ENT. They should take him to the O.R. for a tonsillectomy in a couple of days. Good job, Zach."

"Yeah, fucking great job. Now, where is my pain medication, you fuck?" Zinman looked better.

Zach was about to get Zinman off to the ward when Chenoiel came crashing into the cubicle.

"What the fuck, I discharged this asshole. Who asked you to look at this guy, Maxwell? They and you are in a tub full of shit."

"Mr. Zinman couldn't even get himself off the stretcher. You were gone so I volunteered to take another look. He had a colossal peritonsillar abscess, Chenoiel. He could have died without treatment."

"Bullshit, he was just faking. At worst, he had a viral upper respiratory infection. Big deal!" Chenoiel looked around the room noting the blood on Zinman's johnnie and the vacuum canister with the putrid liquid in it. "What did you do, you shit?

"I did what you should have. I drained him. If I hadn't he would have gone septic and in his state probably died."

"Fuck you, you don't know what you're talking about. I want to know who told you to re-examine this worthless asshole and who helped you commit malpractice cutting into his fucking throat?" Chenoiel's voice was loud and high-pitched by this point. He was inflamed with his hands balling into fists. A lot of patients and medical personnel were witnessing his explosion. Zach didn't know how to get the fight out of the eyesight of all the people staring at them. Every time he made a move, Chenoiel blocked him.

"Dr. Chenoiel, maybe you can take this argument away from the patients and into one of the conference rooms," Rhonda commanded. "I can't have you making a spectacle of yourself here in the middle of the E.R. Please go now."

"Who are you to tell me what to do? You're a nurse and don't know shit. Now just walk away." Chenoiel's face became a rictus of anger with the vein at his temple throbbing. His hands kept clenching and unclenching. It was obvious to Zach that something bad was about to happen.

"Chenoiel, I asked you to recheck the patient and you just yelled at me and walked. Now, leave the E.R. until you get control of yourself." Rhonda got right in front of Chenoiel and wouldn't move.

Chenoiel looked like someone had just punched him. "You are the one who asked Maxwell to see my patient. You countermanded my order to discharge him, you fuck, I'll.… " He raised his hand as if to strike her, but before he could a large hand grabbed his arm.

"Now, now, Dr. Chenoiel, I am sure you were just stretching that arm to relieve a cramp. Is the cramp gone?" Christospathos spun Chenoiel around to face him. "You need to calm yourself, and then apologize to Rhonda. She is a superb nurse who has worked here for years, and has taught countless young doctors medicine, even the irresponsible ones. She has a very difficult job, and commands respect."

"Apologize? I will not. She is only a nurse, and she disobeyed an order. I am a doctor. She will obey me."

Hercules turned to Rhonda and Zach and shrugged his shoulders. He then turned to Zinman. "Are you feeling better, Mr. Zinman?"

"I am, Hercules. That young fuck, Maxwell, I think he may have saved my life. So did that babe, the nurse. I couldn't open my mouth."

"Well, I'm not sure young Dr. Maxwell did the world any favors with your mouth, but I guess he gets points anyway."

Zinman let out a cackle. "Eat scata, Hercules."

"Same to you, Zinman." He turned to the nurse. "Now Rhonda, will you make arrangements for a bed upstairs, and ENT to consult when they get out of the O.R.?" Hercules chuckled, and addressed Zinman, Zach, and Rhonda. "Did you know, Zinman and I go way back? I saved his life when he was shot the first time. Zinman, you don't know it, but I left a clamp in you on purpose. I put it in low in your pelvis. If you mouth off to Rhonda, or are anything but polite, Rhonda has orders to turn a magnet on you. It should come out of your body, ripping your dick off with it. Understand that, Mr. Zinman?"

Hercules then turned to Zach and Chenoiel. "You two come with me." He started walking out of the E.R.

Chapter 18

Hercules led Zach and Chenoiel into the nearest on-call room.

"Chenoiel," Hercules bellowed, "if I ever see you make an aggressive move toward a nurse, doctor, patient, or a rat scurrying on the floor, I swear I will have your ass out of here so fast you won't know what time zone you're in."

"Try it, Christospathos. My father will … "

"Your father will do nothing. He won't want his son mixed up in an investigation questioning mental stability. You think I can't get an investigation started? Try me. Bullshit won't put up with your crap. He doesn't want a complaint to go from the nurses' union to administration about your abusive behavior. You are banned from the O.R. for ten days, now get the fuck out of here."

Once again, Chenoiel's face turned purple, and his eyes fiery. He was about to go ballistic, and then thought better of it. He shrugged and said, "Okay Hercules, you win this one. Just remember I'm the one who's going to assure PAY's surgical program stays accredited. How far do you think you'll get if you give me a hard time? In the end, neither Bullshit nor the rest of the administration is going to take a chance that the residency commission judges there are too many foreigners like you, and too many subpar Americans like Maxwell in this program. Look at my face, this is the future of American medicine, not a bunch of second-raters."

Zach looked at Christospathos and saw a man who was

about a nanosecond away from committing an execution. Hercules took a deep breath and calmed. "A real doctor, you're a real doctor, Chenoiel," Hercules replied, shaking his head. "God help the world, if real doctors are like you. Now get out of my sight."

Chenoiel walked out of the room, but not before he said, "Remember Christospathos, if I even feel I got one less case, I think I should have my father hear about it—and you can kiss your career bye-bye." The door to the room banged open, letting in fresh air from the foulness that Chenoiel had created.

"I'm sorry, Hercules. I probably shouldn't have interfered with Chenoiel's case. I just thought that Zinman looked like he was going to die. Maybe I was wrong," Zach said forlornly.

Hercules smiled at Zach. "Never apologize for having good judgment. You probably saved Zinman days in the ICU and maybe worse. I've known Zinman for years. He was one of my first traumas. No doubt he can be a total dick, but he has had a very tough life. He was in Vietnam when his pregnant wife was killed by a drunk driver. He got word almost a week after her death because he was on a hush-hush mission. By the time he got back, she was in the ground. Because of a paperwork glitch, it took almost a month to track down his child, who was sent into foster care. I never did find out what happened to the child, but Zinman had to be institutionalized. He started drugs right after that. I doubt he ever had a chance to be anything but the drug-addicted guy who shows up here whenever he can't score a fix. On a happier note, Habib did show you how to emergently drain a peritonsillar abscess."

"Yes, he told me he had some experience in these types of cases."

Hercules grunted, "He had some experiences, huh? Just goes to prove to you how full of itself the American system is. Habib was the equivalent of a full professor at the All-Egyptian Hospital in Cairo. He was considered one of the best head and neck surgeons in the Middle East. Even the Israelis wanted him over the border to work at the Hadassah Hospital. He told them his country needed him. Two years later they accused Habib of being anti-government, mostly because he saved a protester who suffered major trauma at the hands of their Secret Police. Poor Habib, a nebbish who just wanted to serve his people, had to run for it. He escaped to England where they made him start all over again, and then kept him from an academic appointment because he was an Egyptian. Now American medicine has a chance to abuse him. You can put on your resume that you trained with the world-renowned Dr. Habib."

"There is going to be fallout from this, isn't there?"

Hercules looked out into space. "Maybe, but no one ever said this was a safe profession to take up. Why don't you get back to work? It's going to be a long night, so don't make it longer than it has to be." Hercules walked out of the room only to be replaced by Dharma and Jake.

"We just saw Hercules leave. Are you canned?" Jake asked, frowning.

"Not so far. How did you hear about this so fast?"

Dharma looked smug. "I told you I'm the source of information for many of the hospital groups. Please don't worry. Bullshit takes a very dim view of irresponsibility in patient care. I doubt if Chenoiel's father worries Bullshit politically. Chances are, if push comes to shove, the board will back Bullshit in the running of his own department."

Jake had a haunted look come over his face. "You don't understand, Dharma. Most of us weren't top picks. If we bounce out of PAY, there isn't another hospital to go to."

"Well, I still think Chenoiel and his father are a minimal threat to a place like PAY. The whole place is run by the United Nations of doctors, all considered at the bottom of the food chain. The secret is hospitals like this survive and save patient's lives. The city knows and counts on doctors like you, Hercules, and

Habib. If they had to count on doctors from America's top schools, the poor in boroughs like Brooklyn would riot."

Zach sighed. "Jake, we both knew this would not be easy. We'll just hope that there just isn't any more trouble. I'm going to try to keep a low profile and all that shit."

"God, why should we have to, but you're right. I'm off to administer my fifteenth disimpaction since arriving in these hallowed halls. See you at smorgasbord," Jake said, as he started walking down the halls.

Chapter 19

Two a.m. and the corridors in the hospital were dark except for the red lights of the EXIT signs, and the dim lights from the nurses' stations. An occasional muffled cough or groan could be heard from a patient room, but otherwise this was the first quiet night Zach had experienced since he had arrived at PAY. Maybe a half hour of work left and, if he was lucky, a two-hour nap before he had to get up and start the numbers collection he was responsible for on all the service patients. There was some quiet laughter and clinking of a coffee carafe being jostled, but in the distance Zach thought he heard someone crying. He followed the sound to an almost pitch-black corner of the supply closet.

"Are you okay?" he asked, barely seeing a small person huddled in a corner. He came close and saw it was Dharma bathed in the shadow, only a sliver of light catching her eyes. Eyes that were bloodshot and puffy. "Dharma, what's the matter?"

"Go away, Zach. I really need a little time alone."

"I'm not going to leave you in the corridor." He reached out and took her hand. It felt icy. "Come on, we'll go to the on-call room. I have some food stashed, we can talk or not. Let's just get out of the corridor."

Dharma followed Zach. The call room was empty with trash from old take-out on the lone desk. The bunk beds were disheveled with sheets that looked like they hadn't been changed for weeks.

Dharma looked around. "Lovely place you have here. Is it the maid's century off?"

"Probably. Unfortunately, none of us can afford to keep a maid, let alone the prices at the laundromat. The unspoken rule is don't lay down if you have anything communicable, like leprosy."

"Leprosy, huh. Who do you think has it?"

"I don't know, but if I find a dead dick in the bed I'm going to strongly protest to the powers that be. Now, if you want to talk about it, what's going on, Dharma?"

Dharma gave Zach a half-smile. She was young, vulnerable with a bitter sweetness about her. She was a woman who, in her role as social worker to a ghetto population, had been a warrior fighting for the disavowed of Brooklyn for a long time. Her caseload of child abuse, elder abuse, domestic abuse, and the abuse of the month was legendary. She always had a smile and a can-do attitude.

"I screwed up. I gave into one of the biggest clichés in a teaching hospital and I am so fucking pissed off at myself." She went silent as the tears slowly traced down the lines of her cheeks.

"Please tell me what's going on. Maybe I can help."

Dharma turned to face Zach. "I became the other woman."

"What does that mean?" Zach asked.

"I fucked someone's husband. The worst part is that I fucked the biggest shit in this hospital and I don't even know why."

Zach couldn't get words out. He hadn't known she was seeing anyone, let alone that there was someone she was sleeping with. In fact, he thought she was alone after the drunken night in her apartment. He swallowed twice before answering her.

"I didn't know.... Who? Wait, I'm sorry, that is none of my business, but I mean ... hell, I don't know what I mean."

"It was a one-night frolic, and it was my carelessness. There wasn't any love, just booze and need and I satisfied that need carelessly. That shit Chenoiel is married, with two little kids. He doesn't care he dishonored his family but maybe I do."

Zach instinctively reached over and held her hand in the semi-darkness. He knew he had nothing to say that would help. How could she be with Chenoiel? Life in the hospital was filled with problems that had no pat answers or simple solutions. As crazy as it sounded, sitting with Dharma, feeling the warmth of her body and the strength of her hand locked in his, there was jealousy. She had picked a lowlife over him. As much as he was jealous of the sex, he was almost more jealous because here was someone he could be close to, because she knew exactly what he had to face every day. After the ridiculous night they had almost spent together, he had hoped she might want to give him a chance at creating a relationship. He needed a special person in his life and thought she might like the same.

He gathered her into his arms and she came willingly. His hand lifted her chin and he looked deeply into her eyes. He kissed the tears from her cheeks, and then she found his lips. Hungrily he kissed her neck and unbuttoned her blouse while she undressed him. They lay on the gross, stained sheets, naked and devouring each other. Her orgasm was loud, driving him to explode.

They lay there catching their breath. He felt happy, but at the same time, realized he had just complicated her life and his. Zach reached out to her, touching her shoulder. She stiffened and pulled away from him.

"Dharma, are you okay? That was wonderful," he said.

"Yeah, it was great, but it shouldn't have happened." She got out of bed, quickly putting on her clothes. "I'm sure we both needed it. Forgive me, I'm at fault. I just don't know what has gotten into me, but I really need a time-out."

"But, I don't understand. I thought we both ... " He felt he had forced himself on her, but she had seemed so willing. He got up to go to her.

"No, just let me go. I don't want anybody to see the both of us leave this room together. Zach, it was very nice, but it can't happen again, promise me."

"But, maybe we can help each other?" Even as the words left his mouth they felt like dust.

"You can't help me, and I can't be your girlfriend. Just promise that you'll stay away from me." She left the room quietly, leaving Zach, who didn't know whether to be relieved or hurt. He did know he had just added to the loneliness he had in him.

Chapter 20

September came and the surgical service never slowed. To Zach the pace just seemed a little saner. As the medical students and residents became incrementally more proficient at what they were doing and as the senior staff trusted them more, an easier rhythm pervaded the hospital. Rounds started at 6 a.m., and at 8 some of the team went to the O.R. and some went to breakfast. After breakfast, if there wasn't a case to scrub into, Zach started work rounds, the drudgery of seeing each patient in more detail and writing notes. E.R. and floor consults usually came at the most inconvenient times, and the day wound up at about 6 p.m. for evening rounds. That left the next twelve hours to admit the new pre-ops, get lab work done, I.V.s started, write orders, eat, have a bowel movement, catnap, read the headlines of the *New York Times*, and take the three seconds left to realize what a shitty life this was. More consults, go to the O.R. with emergency cases and the calls from the floor for med orders that hadn't been written during the day that were usually caught at 3 a.m. by a nurse. Phone orders weren't accepted, so he'd get out of bed and walk to the nurses' station to write the order for a medication. Zach sometimes argued that he would come and write the order later, but the nurses just insisted and kept calling. It was the way most of the RNs got back at the interns' accumulated slights against them during the day.

"Hey Zach, wait up." Ike trotted to where Zach was putting

the final touches on a post-surgical note. "Whatcha doing this weekend?"

Zach looked at Ike. "My usual, after working 140 hours this week. I'm going into coma at my aunt's. You know, I'm surprised my aunt even lets me in the apartment. I get there, she has this beautiful meal ready for me. I start eating, trying to make conversation. As the seconds go by, my speech slurs and I find everyone looking at me, wondering if they need to call an ambulance for my stroke-in-evolution. Thankfully, I usually make it through the meal without face-planting into the brisket and crawl to the couch in the living room. Next thing I know, it's 11 a.m. the next day, and I am still on the couch in scrubs. Why do you think my aunt puts up with me?"

Ike laughed. "She gets free medical care for life, which she may need if they get rid of Medicare. Besides I can do you one better. I actually did face-plant into dinner, except it was the chicken soup. I was picking a combination of matzo ball and carrots out of my nose for a week and treating first degree burns. Not a pretty sight. Thank God the soup was not boiling, or this pretty face would have been permanently scarred."

"I guess you win," Zach laughed. "So, what's up this weekend?"

"High Holidays, fool. Weren't you circumcised seven days after birth?"

"Shit, I forgot. My parents would be batshit if I didn't make an attempt to check in with the big guy. How can I get off? I mean the patients aren't taking the time off."

"Don't worry, Hercules and Bullshit work out the schedules so the non-Yids cover and the Yids return the favor on Christmas. Works out for all. So, what I was thinking, you come home with me and meet my wife, kids, parents, neighbors, the garbage man, etc. You can come to services, see what the congregation has to offer in nubile, young, Jewish potential wives and we can do Slivovitz with my father-in-law."

"It sounds like fun. I'd be honored—and by the way what's Slivovitz?"

"It's plum firewater. About 120 proof. Great, I'll tell Goldie Abigail you're coming. In the meantime, it's back to work."

Zach looked at the almost completed pre-op list. "Have you seen Drushkin yet?" Zach asked.

"Crap, he's back?" Ike cried. "Bullshit is just whittling that guy down piece by piece. He's a middle-aged, obese, diabetic who has an aversion for doing anything his doctors advise him. He eats every dessert he can find, drinks like a fish, only intermittently injects his insulin, and only when he feels he needs it. Because of his very unhealthy habits, he has developed major vascular problems. The diabetes has affected the arteries in both his legs and eyes. He was classified as legally blind last year, and every six months, Moskowitz takes him to the operating room and tries to bypass another blockage in his arteries. The surgery usually fails by the next month.

"Christ, he sounds like a disaster," Zach said sadly.

"Yeah, when the bypass clots he returns to the O.R. to amputate more and more of his legs. What started as a couple of toes removed from each foot progressed to the removal of half his right foot, and then an emergency amputation of his left lower leg for gangrene."

"What happened this time? More gangrene because he decided a cold leg was normal?

Ike sighed. "Something like that. Your friend Jake admitted him from the E.R. two days ago because he decided to follow his usual behavior, drinking himself into a stupor and not taking his insulin. He didn't check his glucose level.... "

"And his sugar soared," Zach guessed, "so he became acidotic.... "

"Which means?" Ike questioned.

"Drushkin was in diabetic ketoacidosis, the asshole, mudderfucker."

"Excellent diagnosis, young scholar," Ike praised. "What do you think Jake treated him with?"

"Well, I would have started hydrating him, gotten an arterial blood gas...."

"Which is what?" Ike quizzed.

"Blood collected from the patient's artery, in this case to check the pH of the blood. If the blood is acidotic, the patient is in danger of going down the toilet."

"Good, Zach, now, treatment? And by the way, Jake did a good job."

"Fluids, fluids, fluids, and I.V. insulin. ICU admission and very careful monitoring."

"Close enough for folk music or a dumb surgeon, but as Paul Harvey says, 'and now for the rest of the story.' While being pretty much immobile in an ICU bed, he developed a clot in the right popliteal artery that went unnoticed for at least twenty-four hours."

"Shit ... malpractice city?"

"Never mention that particular town in this hospital. You don't get paid enough."

"I don't get paid what the janitor is making ... not that I'm complaining."

"As may be," Ike replied grimly. "To be fair, Jake and his team were trying really hard to save his life. He crashed at least four times with pressures in the sixties. My guess the low-flow state of low blood pressure caused the clot. Anyway, he is better, with a cold right half a foot, and Bullshit is dying to try another bypass on him. He thinks that he can restore circulation to the foot."

"Should I schedule the bypass for tomorrow and the amputation for next week?" Zach said innocently.

"Shit," Ike exclaimed looking around to see who was near them. "Don't let Bullshit hear you talking like that. He has a very poor sense of humor when it comes to his vascular work. Besides, maybe the fourth time is the charm."

"From your mouth to God's ear. I'll connect with Jake and see Drushkin."

"Okay, make sure you get the consent, and try to get Jake to write the insulin orders. Remind him that Drushkin can't eat or drink after midnight so he needs the insulin adjusted, capeesh?"

Zach took off to the SICU or Surgical Intensive Care, a launching pad to heaven for the majority of its inmates.

Chapter 21

The first thing Zach noticed, walking into the SICU, was the eerie silence coming from the anonymous bodies in the ten beds. The only sound came from the beeping of the monitors, murmuring from the nurses, and an occasional clang from an instrument hitting a metal object. It was as quiet as a cemetery, which Zach thought was very appropriate.

The second thing he noticed was the musty, rancid smell with an overlay of industrial cleanser. The stink made Zach's eyes water and hurt his sinuses.

The nurses in the MICU (Medical Intensive Care Unit), SICU, and the Emergency Room were considered the elite nurses. This specially trained group had seen it all and were certified to do it all. Many a resident had had their orders countermanded unceremoniously by these nurses in the presence of a high-ranking attending physician. Sometimes even the high-ranking physicians had their orders revoked by these same nurses. They were the priestesses of critical care, and the final word on day-to-day care of their patients.

"Excuse me, who is in charge of Mr. Drushkin's care?" Zach asked the unit secretary.

"Honey, that's Sara, and she is not in a very good mood today, so tread carefully," the secretary replied with a sigh. "She is over there with Drushkin, bed seven."

Zach looked over to the area the secretary had pointed out, and saw a short, black-haired woman dressed in a dark blue set of scrubs, masked and gloved. She was removing dressing from Drushkin's left leg. Even from this distance he could see the once-white bandages were stained and wet with a thick green pus, and as Zach moved closer the smell was overpowering.

"Hi Sara, I'm Zach from Surgery. I'm here to get Mr. Drushkin ready for his bypass."

Sara stopped her dressing changes, and violently ripped off her gloves tossing them into a red can. "Mr. Drushkin, I'll be back to give you some more pain medicine and finish your bandage changes. I need to talk to this doctor." Drushkin appeared barely awake and just grunted. "Why don't you come with me?" She started walking to an exit toward the rear of the SICU, leaving Zach to catch up.

Zach found himself in a small lounge area. "Hi, I'm Zach Maxwell. I was sent to see Mr. Drushkin and get him pre-opped. I also need to speak to Jake and get his insulin requirements set up for the next forty-eight hours, through the pre-op and post-op period. Do you know where Jake is?"

"No." Sara stood like Lot's wife, stiff and salty, her face, back, legs, and arms rigid, in a pose that left no doubt she was immovable.

"Look, Sara, between you and me, I have better things to be doing myself, but Bullshit wants to operate, and Drushkin wants him to operate. You and I have no say on the matter, and I for one want to keep my job."

"You are a fucking coward. How many bypasses do you think Drushkin can tolerate? Besides you can't get a legal consent from him. He is barely able to stay awake, let alone understand your explanation on the risks of the surgery."

Zach let out a big sigh, ending in a grimace. Though he personally agreed with Sara that this new surgery would probably do nothing for Drushkin, and might kill him, what choice did he have? "Look Sara, what can I do? Bullshit has more experience than the both of us. I'm sure that if Drushkin himself didn't sign for this, there must be some legally designated family member who did. Let's face it, without trying to restore some circulation, that leg is coming off. He needs surgery, no matter what."

"He is suffering and can't take another general anesthesia. His heart, lungs—fuck, every system this man has, is shutting down. Can't you tell Bullshit that he is too unstable?"

Zach thought about Drushkin's clinical situation. She was right, surgery would be a method of execution. Might as well take the syringe of potassium and inject it to stop his heart. He needed to find a way to convince Bullshit to stop these procedures. Suddenly, an idea popped into his head, but he needed help setting the plan up. Hell, he needed to make sure that the idea itself wouldn't kill Drushkin. "Sara, do you know where Kavi is? I need his medical expertise and clearance."

"Didn't anything I told you make any difference? I forbid this surgery."

Zach drew himself up. He liked this feisty woman who cared, plus she wasn't bad looking, but orders were orders. Maybe he could solve two problems with a third answer. "I'm going to try to make this easier on Drushkin. Your main objection is his cardiovascular status isn't strong enough. Do you think Kavi will agree with you?"

"What are you planning, Zach?" she asked suspiciously.

"I'll let you know. In the meantime, I need his family here ASAP—and Kavi before I see them."

Kavi was the Hindu anesthesiologist who had a reputation for being hot-tempered in social situations, but the coolest performer around when the hard cases came through or the true emergency was thrust upon the hospital.

"Of course, his heart status sucks. Why are you putting Drushkin through this major surgery? The anesthesia will kill him. He is barely maintaining himself in his present state. I agree, ultimately his leg has to come off, but at least that won't take hours on the table," Kavi said.

"What if Bullshit could do his bypass under regional block or spinal, with some sedation? That should take care of your concerns about his heart status."

"You fuckin' surgeons. You think you know anything about anesthesia? Let me tell you, you know shit," Kavi exploded. "That man is a medical and surgical disaster, and Bullshit thinks he can pull a miracle out of some fuckin' hat? Fuck you and fuck Bullshit!"

"Please Kavi, I'm trying to get this guy through his next surgical disaster. Maybe Bullshit is right, and we can keep him ultimately to do a BK amputation after the bypass. Can you do it?" Zach begged.

"Of course I can do it, you fuckin' white boy. Who the fuck do you think you're talking to? Make sure that SICU resident talks to me about Drushkin's insulin and I.V. fluids, and you make sure he is NPO. You know what that means, white boy?"

"Nothing by mouth, I'm not stupid."

"No, moron, it means *Nil per os,* so keep everything out of his mouth after midnight." Kavi stormed out of the lounge, leaving Zach smiling. Now the crucial part.

"Hercules, the gas-passers won't clear him for general anesthesia. Something about his heart not being strong enough. I went to talk to Kavi to try to overrule them, but he told me to fuck off."

"Fuck, Bullshit is going to go apeshit. He wants to save as much of the leg as possible. Well, let's go see Bullshit."

"Wait a second. Kavi says he can do this under spinal if Bullshit insists on—and I'm quoting him—this useless surgery."

"Kavi said that, huh?"

"Well, I might be paraphrasing or maybe he said something in Hindi I didn't understand. The point is we can do the surgery, just not under general." Zach thought Hercules was coming around to this idea. If only he could convince Bullshit.

"You know Bullshit won't care. He'll get to do the bypass, and you know maybe Bullshit is right. I mean if we can keep it to a BK, maybe we can still fit him for a prosthesis? I'll go talk to Bullshit, you go get Drushkin ready."

"Okay, Hercules," Zach said with relief. He turned to go write orders for the next day's surgery when he felt a hand on his shoulder.

"Good job, Zach. You have a future in surgery and politics," Hercules told him.

"What do you mean?"

"Zach, I have been working with Bullshit for five years now. I also have been a doctor for five years longer than you. You don't think I know how you manipulated this?"

"Hercules," Zach replied, feeling the icicles of fear. "Drushkin is a poor risk. He won't survive general anesthesia according to Kavi and Sara. Even I could see that. I just figured there was a way to give him a better chance and yet satisfy Bullshit. For the record, I respect Bullshit and he obviously has more experience than all of us put together, but I'm sorry I didn't tell you."

Hercules smiled. "Don't worry. As a doctor you need to advocate for your patient. As an intern, you are here to follow orders. It took a lot of skill to accomplish both. I am only disappointed that you didn't think to come to me for help, but you did it on your own, so, kudos. Next time remember I am your teacher and friend, and you are allowed and required to come to me for help."

Zach felt elated. He didn't like manipulating people. It went against his nature, but damn it, Sara, and Kavi, and even he had been right. Drushkin needed a way to survive what might be a necessary procedure, so said the expert Dr. Moskowitz. "Thanks, Hercules."

"I'll see you later, on rounds." Hercules slowly walked off down the hall to talk to Bullshit.

Chapter 22

"**It's the patron saint** of legless men. We are so honored here in the lowly SICU."

Zach had come to the SICU to check on Mr. Drushkin after his bypass. It had been five days since the surgery and so far, he seemed to be holding his own. The leg was almost pink with the new blood supply and it looked like the antibiotics were helping to clean his skin infection. He was even coherent at the times he was awake. Maybe, Zach thought, Bullshit had finally pulled it off.

"And a big hi to you too, Sara. How's tricks?" Zach was happy to see the brassy nurse was working. Aside from being a little on the combative side, she was obviously smart, committed to her patients, and had a killer body. Maybe she would be interested in coffee or dinner sometime.

"Well, as far as tricks, that trick you pulled for Drushkin was admirable. He seems to be making improvement, and even his leg looks better. So, on behalf of Mr. Drushkin, his family, and the SICU team, I thank you."

"It was a little thing in the life of a saint." Zach chuckled. "Maybe you would like to grab a dinner?"

"I don't think so."

"A drink?"

"No thanks."

"A cup of coffee?" Zach asked hopefully.

"Look Zach, I really don't date guys from the hospital. In fact, I hardly have time to date at all, and I am not looking for a husband. You seem nice enough, and I am impressed that someone who is studying to be a surgeon has any humanity."

"Would it help to tell you that I wanted to be a psychiatrist, but was shanghaied into surgery?"

Sara paused and then shook her head. "As much as I am sure your story is interesting.... "

"Tragic, actually."

"As I was saying, interesting. I just do not date here at PAY. Thank you for thinking of me, but I have patient rounds now and I'm sure you can find a more willing RN to go out with."

"A can of soda from the vending machine? I can steal a bottle of ginger ale from the patient's supply."

She laughed, and walked off, leaving Zach more determined to get her number.

Chapter 23

"Zach, this is Goldie, my wife, and my kids, Lewis and Abby. Welcome," boomed Ike. Zach had run back to his apartment after three hours in the O.R. holding sticks for Lucas and his colon re-section. Now, shaved and dressed in a nice button-down shirt, dress pants, and a sports jacket, and armed with a bottle of red wine, he called a car service to take him the two miles from inner-city drug ghetto to Jewish-Italian suburbia—the jungle of Canarsie. The houses were mostly cubicles with a small patch of lawn, driveway, and an occasional tree. Zach could instantly make out the Jewish homes from the Italian by the statue of the Virgin in the front yards. Canarsie and Brownsville were like the Angel and the Devil. It all depended on what side of Linden Boulevard he was standing on that predicted his chances of being shot, stabbed, and in either case robbed. Canarsie and Brownsville were two sides of one coin named Brooklyn. Ike had told him that the Jews were grateful to their Italian neighbors for keeping the streets of Canarsie safe … and by "Italian neighbors," Ike meant the made-men of La Cosa Nostra. These guys insisted their neighborhood streets be safe and quiet. They always said there was enough dodging bullets at work.

The house smelled like his mother's house during the holidays. Chicken soup vapors combined with brisket, potatoes, kugel, and green beans. The silver candlesticks and challah peeking from beneath the embroidered cover made him feel somewhat homesick. It was funny to Zach that though Goldie and Ike were only a year or two older than he, they already seemed like his parents, especially Goldie. He was sure that Goldie was college-educated, and probably at one time wanted a career, but Ike had told him Goldie was a housewife, and taking care of the kids and taking care of him was a harder job than he had. He also said most of the time he was grateful for the anchor in his world that gave him stability. Goldie was blond, short, and pleasingly curvy. She always seemed to be smiling, especially when either Ike or her babies were near her. Her house was spotless and festive, and her babies were clean.

"So, Zach, Ike has told me a lot about you. Does San Diego have a large Jewish community? Do you have a girl back there? Here?" Goldie went to work on her prime responsibility to Zach. God forbid any Jewish male was to live a lonely life without the support of a Jewish wife and Jewish children. She also didn't want Zach's bachelorhood to become a bad example for Ike. Ike was a young surgeon and she was sure there was a lot of temptation at the hospital.

Zach knew Goldie had notified the Jewish mothers in the neighborhood. "Get your daughters ready for a potential husband." Zach wondered if Goldie would make a commission if he got engaged.

"Not as large as Brooklyn, no, and I'm too busy." He laughed. "My schedule is the same as Ike's, Goldie. There aren't too many women who would put up with it."

"Oh, I think you wouldn't be too surprised that being a doctor is a commodity in this market, and that many a fine girl would be willing to work with you on that problem. Now, what are your preferences in a girlfriend, and are you free any weekend?" she asked, as she grabbed at her phone book.

"Goldie, please leave Zach alone. He has no time for relationships, and his needs can be taken care of in one of PAY's many well-appointed call rooms. They even have locks on the doors," Ike admonished her.

"Meaningless sex? He doesn't want that. And how do you know about locks on call-room doors, Dr. Ike Aronsky?" Goldie accused.

"Sweetie," Ike replied innocently, "I know nothing, I see nothing, I hear nothing except what stud muffins like Zach tell me. Honestly, I mean when you have steak at home, why look for hamburger elsewhere?"

"That better be true, Sergeant Schultz, or no more kugel for you, and you know I'm not talking sweet noodle dishes."

"I'd never do anything to get cut off from the kugel supply, and I know what you mean by kugel. Maybe we should all sit down and eat. Temple awaits."

Dinner was a pleasant diversion from the rushed meals of smorgasbord or the quick cafeteria sandwich. It certainly was more interesting than fixing himself some canned soup while half-asleep after call. Zach found himself sitting next to an older woman who introduced herself as Clara Rosenberg, Ike and Goldie's neighbor across the street.

"So, Dr. Maxwell, I understand you're unattached, from San Diego, and a surgical resident. How do you like Brooklyn?" Clara asked.

"I'd ask you how you obtained all that information, but my guess is there is a Canarsie branch of the CIA in operation."

"Well, if I told you I'd have to kill you. Besides, then I'd have no one to be a matchmaker to. How is your training going? I have known Ike since he was a little pisher. I have never seen him look so worn out. Frankly, you look like you could use a year off on the beach yourself."

"The training is intense, but I guess this is what makes a surgeon. I'm so tired that the only time I really notice it is when I step back into the real world, like now."

"That is why you need someone with you."

"Clara, I doubt a relationship is a good idea while I'm in training. I'm sure that any normal woman would feel neglected if we attempted a long-term relationship. I know this is not very Jewish, on this high holy day, but I think a monastic, celibate, life is about all I can handle. It is nice that you thought of me, and thanks for the offer, but no thanks. Besides, I believe matchmakers usually get paid, and I once figured out I was making seventy-nine cents an hour. I can't afford you." He chuckled.

"I wouldn't worry about your lack of time. A smart girl understands Project Maxwell is an investment toward a brighter future, and as far as payment you can be my *pro bono* case."

"I just wouldn't want you wasting your time. I take it you are a native of Canarsie?"

"Born and bred. Most of us Canarsie folk are born, live, and die all within a few blocks of our childhood homes. Both the Italians and Jews feel comfortable here. We all pretty much know each other and know members of different generations of the neighborhood families. Ike's father and my father used to bowl together on Wednesday nights. Down the table there is Mr. Russo. His father used to supply both our fathers with his homemade red wine. We have all attended christenings, brisses, bar mitzvahs, weddings, and funerals from all the families. It really is a shame."

"What's a shame, Clara?"

"Oh, just that people like Ike and Goldie will soon be moving out of the neighborhood, and that in ten years or so, Canarsie will just be another Brownsville. White flight has started here, and the families will be dispersed to the safety of Long Island. I guess for now we should all enjoy the life with our generations of neighbors."

"I guess we should drink a 'L'Chaim' to that, Clara."

"What a sweet boy you are. I will keep an eye out for a special lady. Until then I hope you make time to have fun with the practice nurses in the hospital. Remember all work and no fun will make Zach a boring boy between the sheets." She laughed.

Zach blushed, not being used to such talk from an older woman. This evening was turning out to be adult-rated fun.

Chapter **24**

"My boy, a true doctor is expected to know how to treat the basics," the short, jaunty surgeon with a veddy British accent intoned.

"What do you mean, Dr. Ginsberg?"

Dr. Nathan Ginsberg was the epitome of anyone from over there. He dressed British and thought Yiddish. Born Natan Goiningstein in Poland just before the war, baby Natan's parents prophesied death in the future, being Jewish and living in Poland. So, believing in the Prophets, they ran for it, ending up in Dublin, Ireland. Natan was a studious boy who became an extroverted young man. He was admitted to the Royal College of Surgeons, where he completed medical school. He had grown tired of his little hometown of Dublin. Natan, now Nathan, decided to expand his horizons. He yearned for wealth so he could afford the biggest Cadillac manufactured, and decided that America was truly a land where the streets were paved in gold. He applied to and was accepted into PAY's surgical program. Five years later, he opened a private practice at PAY, where he buried his Polish origins along with his real last name and never corrected his patients or the residents when they commented on his British style. Ginsberg personally thought it was classier to be a Brit than a son of the auld sod, even though the Irish in him was forever leaking out.

"Lad, a doctor, any doctor, be he internist, surgeon, or a fookin' radiologist should know how to treat a myocardial infarction, cardiac arrest, hypertension. He should be able to deliver a baby, stop bleeding, and oxygenate a body that is cyanotic. No excuses."

Zach thought this little leprechaun had the wisdom of the ages, plus he was going to let him scrub in on his cholecystectomy case. For Zach, this worked out perfectly. Stitch some skin, and then out of there for rounds and home for dinner. Zach had room service coming over. In the weeks at PAY, his resolve to only be a studious kind of guy had modified because of plain biological need. He wasn't going for the priesthood and the nursing staff were as horny as he was. What the hell, she was a fine young thing from the lab who was into blood, obtaining it and analyzing it. Rumor had it she wasn't into finding a husband, which made her a rare bird, but that she did enjoy something different. Zach wasn't sure what something different was, but who cared. He hadn't even met her but had called her at the hospital and arranged a meet. This was so typical at PAY, where every aspect of life was hurry up. Who had time for pre-meets? Call, and go for the main event. This was an evening's entertainment, and since this was his third night of rotation, at least he had slept last night. There would be no difficulties where dessert was concerned.

All went as planned. The cholecystectomy was routine, the post-op orders were written up, and rounds were made. Zach signed out to the intern on call and took off across the street to his apartment. He started the dinner, the only thing he knew how to make: salad, pre-frozen potato something, and marinated two skirt steaks he had taken out of the freezer last night before going into coma. He put some muzak on the stereo ... so suave, he thought.

He came out of the shower, dressed, and right on the button, there was a knock at the door.

"One moment." Final check in the mirror, and off he went to answer the door.

"Hi Zach," she said as he let her in. "I'm Lysistrata, but

you can call me Lizzie." Zach gave her a sort of discreet look. Dark, almost raven, hair, black clothes, tight, showing all the requisite curves. Her makeup created shadowy eyes, and deoxygenated blood lips. She was a knockout, straight out of the comic books that featured tall, ebony-haired, well-endowed women of the superhero kind.

"Welcome, can I take your … cape?" Boy, he thought, a cape?

"Sure, do you have something to drink here?"

"White, red, or beer?"

"Red. So you are the wonder boy that saved the guy losing all that marvelous blood?"

"Boy, that story isn't getting old. Yeah, I guess I am, but it really wasn't a big deal."

"Well, you sure showed up the heir apparent to the throne."

Zach was now really confused. "Heir to the throne? Who is that?"

"Why, Chenoiel of course. He came to PAY to become its black king. He wants to be Chief Resident, and then take Bullshit's place."

Zach was amazed. She really was something different, walking around the room touching the furniture, and taking in his cheap posters on the walls hanging by scotch tape. The swishing of her velvet-silk dress occurred with every move. Zach noticed the black nail polish she wore.

"Wow, I mean, I think that is sort of ambitious, even for Chenoiel. I mean, he really is an intern, just like me. That is long-term planning for anyone."

"I have tasted Chenoiel, and he tasted like moldy socks. What I say is true."

Zach had no idea of a response except, "Tasted him?"

She laughed, changing the subject, "I'm hungry, what's for dinner?"

"Steak, how do you take yours?"

"Rare, darling. Very bloody."

"Sick doctor coming through, make way for the sick doctor," Ike yelled, wheeling Zach in a wheelchair like this was the Indy 500. He made a hard ninety-degree right turn, almost dumping Zach onto the floor, and eliciting a horrifying shriek.

"What the fuck are you doing, Ike? Trying to kill me?" Tears were flowing down Zach's cheeks from the pain.

Ike stopped at a radiology exam room. "What did she do to make that shoulder dislocate? I mean Goldie and I can get pretty adventurous, I mean, she did me on a Wednesday night.... Shit, a Wednesday. There is a God."

"She had me tied up, and then started biting me.... "

"You mean, teeth cutting skin?" Ike's eyes were wide and he was looking flustered.

"You're a fucking surgeon, what do you think these are?" Zach declared. He unbuckled his pants and pulled down his underwear.

"Holy mudder of hell!" Ike looked like he was going to puke. "There?"

"Fuck yes!" Zach screamed. "I'm already circumcised. If she decreased it by even one millimeter ... "

"It's okay, Big Guy, and since you are Jewish you know I'm lying about the big part. The marks will fade, just like this nightmare. Let's get a shot of that shoulder, and then I'll call Putzman."

Zach turned paler than he was before. "Putzman, not Putzman, please not Putzman," he begged. Dr. Ari Putterman was an American born to an Israeli weightlifter and an American shot-putter. No one ever had the guts to ask which athlete was the mother. Putzman was six feet, six inches, and muscled like the Amazing Hulk. Putzman was an orthopedist. He was a man of few words who could reduce any joint or fracture without the use of pain medication or muscle relaxants. To send a patient to Putzman was to get back a patient who had fear of God, and Putzman, in his soul. Not necessarily in that order.

Painfully, Zach was positioned for the x-rays by the tech. He had never, ever had an experience like this. Now he knew what Lizzie meant when she said she had tasted Chenoiel.

Three hours before …

The steaks were bloody, the wine was red, and the dessert was a chocolate cake with raspberry filling. Their conversation was mostly about hospital antics and gossip. She was funny, and pretty, and seemed pretty much into anything at all. The conversation moved to Zach's couch, and his soundtrack went to mellow love songs. Soon they were kissing and fondling each other. Zach was happy. This was an easy way to let off some biological pressure.

"Zach, turn off the lights.… "

Zach turned to do as she requested. He turned back to her, finding her blouse was open, and she wasn't wearing a bra. Even her silver dollar areola and nipples were blood red. She unbuckled him, and opened his shirt, sucking on his nipples. Zach was in heaven. He started reciprocating, latching on for life, while trying to get to third base.

Lizzie shuddered, "Oh my, you are hard, my heroic boy." She nuzzled even closer, squeezing the life out of his tent pole. "Zachie, let's play a game."

A game, he barely thought, he couldn't even think, as the blood had rushed out of his brain to parts south of the border. "Absolutely Lizzie. What game do you want to play?"

Giving him a last squeeze making him gasp, she got off the

couch, and went to her bag. Out came colored things and metal things and rubbery things. Zach couldn't believe the number of objects coming out of her bag.

She shrugged off the rest of her clothes, standing before him like a Botticelli painting, except with larger breasts. "Maybe a bed would be more appropriate?"

Zach jumped up, and got out of his clothes, and led her into the bedroom with the two twin beds that came with the place. "I will shove them together."

"Don't Zachie, we can be closer together, and the game will be more fun. Now, let me put this on you." She put a silk blindfold over his eyes.

"I can't see you. I want to see you," Zach protested.

"Hush now, and lay on the bed, close your eyes, and give me your hands." She gave him a sly smile, which he couldn't see.

"What are you going to do?"

"Don't you trust me, love?" she asked, as she swooped down and kissed his penis wetly.

He gasped. "I trust you, I really trust you." He closed his eyes and put out his hands. He heard a double click. He found that his hands were bound with—handcuffs? "Hey, I can't touch you." A suddenly lightning-bolt sensation hit him in the groin, spasming his body. "Jesus, that was ... " Again, the lightning bolt hit his groin, and his penis was being sucked. "I can't breathe. ... Oh my God."

"Now, my love, do you like this?" He felt wet kisses and licking down his chest. "Or this?" She nibbled his earlobe. "How about this?" He was treated to a white-hot pain the like his groin had never felt.

"What did you do, stop!" he screamed.

"Oh baby, the line between pain and pleasure is so close. We should use both to become closer," she purred, and bit in his groin again.

"Please stop, it hurts too much!" he yelled, now trying to get out of the cuffs.

"Isn't this the best, sweetie?" she questioned, putting something on him that pinched his right nipple hard.

"No, it isn't...."

Lizzie then grabbed his penis, putting a rubber band around the base. This restricted the blood flow, making him hard as a rock and bigger than he had ever been, but it also started starving the tissue for blood. The pain was intense. She placed herself on him and started screaming herself.

Zach shook violently, trying to free himself from the cuffs, and get her off him. She orgasmed, and was flung off the bed, twisting him so his left shoulder dislocated. Somewhere in this he fainted. Lizzie slapped him multiple times to the cheek and pulled off the blindfold.

Zach came to in pain from every part of his body, but especially his left shoulder. "What did you do to me? Are you crazy?"

Lizzie looked truly confused. "Wasn't that the best sex you have ever had, baby? I came so hard I think I passed out."

"No, it wasn't, and my penis and shoulder are killing me." He looked down to his groin first, noting multiple bite marks, and then noticed the rubber band was still on his penis that was almost black, and huge. "Oh my God, get that rubber band off, now."

Lizzie, now looking more confused than ever, tried to pull the rubber band off, accidently snapping it in one of her attempts. The searing pain went directly from Zach's groin to the penis center of his brain. He fainted.

"Well, I think Lizzie isn't that bad," said Ike. "I mean she did call me to come and get you. She even gave you a little kiss to your schvantz. Not every date does that, especially in front of another guy." He chuckled. "I especially liked the part where she started licking your abrasions."

"Yeah, thanks for pulling her off me. Hopefully the wounds won't get all infected with her mouth bacteria."

The tech brought in the films, and as expected the shoulder was out of its socket. Ike went to call Putzman to reduce it, leaving Zach in the cold x-ray room wearing a thin johnnie. He decided he was finished with women. His recent history of two left him with one woman who ignored him, or actively tried to avoid him, and another who almost had killed him or attempted to literally emasculate him. It just wasn't worth it. He needed to concentrate on the residency and becoming a surgeon, even if he still became woozy at the sight of blood. No more romantic ideas for the future.

Zach was so deep in his thoughts that he didn't even hear Ike and Putzman sneak up behind him. He was grabbed by Ike to his back while Putzman grabbed the arm with the dislocated shoulder and twisted, pulling at the same time. For the second time in less than eight hours, Zach fainted.

Chapter 25

"**Hello there, can you tell me** where Dr. Chenoiel might be?" A beautiful, elegant-looking woman in her late twenties stood before Zach. He had just finished morning rounds after a whole night of admissions, and three trauma cases that went to the O.R. An alcoholic who decided to come into the E.R. for his perforated stomach ended up baptizing Zach in a combination of bile, blood, and Thunderbird. Zach was malodorous. Pungent just didn't cover it. The woman had just moved into position, and her eyes started welling up and her nose got all crinkly, like she was going to sneeze.

"I apologize for the smell, it was an action-filled night and I haven't had a moment."

"Funny," she replied in obvious disdain. "Dr. Chenoiel has never come home smelling like an open sewer and looking like he wasn't a knowledgeable, successful surgeon."

Yeah, that's because that piece of mold never gets close to a patient unless he is practicing malpractice on him, Zach thought.

"You must be Mrs. Chenoiel. I'm one of Chenoiel's colleagues, Zach Maxwell."

"Dr. Chenoiel."

"Yes, Chenoiel's colleagues."

"No, Dr. Maxwell, his name is *Dr.* Chenoiel. You must have respect for him and the others on his team."

"His team," Zach blurted, nonplussed.

"Yes, you all must realize that Dr. Chenoiel will be Chief sooner than later, and that the niceties must be observed."

Zach was ready to vomit into his own mouth. "If you come with me, Mrs. Chenoiel, I'll see if he can be paged."

He led her to the nurses' station. She was a study in ice. White porcelain skin, blond hair, and a tight figure. She hadn't cracked a smile, just tightened her lips covered in blood-red lipstick. Even so, she was quite a looker. Not that Zach knew anything about the price of women's clothes, but her clothes probably cost more than he made in two months.

Zach picked up the phone and told the page operator to have Chenoiel call back and waited. Mrs. Chenoiel did nothing to initiate conversation, and after waiting three minutes, the silence was uncomfortable.

"Maybe he is in the O.R.," he said. "I'll call and see what he is up to and how long he'll be."

"I'm sure it is very important. Don't bother, I'll see him tomorrow; he is on tonight," she said frostily.

Zach's radar instantly went up. Zach was on call and he usually kept track of who he would be working with. Chenoiel usually worked opposite days, so to his good fortune, he didn't have to deal with him after 6 p.m. Maybe he had switched with someone. That would suck.

"Hang on, I'm sure he would be disappointed if he didn't get to see you before tomorrow night." Zach called the O.R. office and was told that Chenoiel was not scheduled for a case, and no one had seen him this morning. Zach then tried the surgical specialty clinic, and was told Chenoiel wasn't there, thank God!

Zach was now uncomfortable, wondering where the hell Chenoiel was hanging out. He looked at Mrs. Chenoiel and since meeting her, for the first time, saw a hint of sadness on her sculptured face.

"You know, there is one place in the hospital the beeper system doesn't work too well," he lied. "Maybe he is there."

"I don't want to take you away from your duties, Dr. Maxwell. You have been kind enough to try to find him. I'll just go now. Thank you."

"It's no trouble, it's just downstairs. It won't take but a few minutes to get there."

Zach started down the hall, with Chenoiel's wife in tow, toward the stairwell. He headed for the on-call room, hoping the asshole was napping and shirking his duties as usual.

He reached the on-call room with her. The door was characteristically closed, and Zach didn't want to disturb anyone in there who was legitimately asleep. People who were coming off night call, or going into night call, sometimes took catnaps to help them get through till 6 p.m. sign-out.

He gently tapped on the door and got no response. He could hear some muffled movement inside. "Dr. Maxwell, I'm sure he's not here. I'm going home." She looked agitated as she started toward the stairwell.

"No wait, let me check." He slowly opened the door. The room was pitch black, but there were human groans, and then a sudden explosive commotion. "Close that fucking door, moron, didn't you see the glove on the door knob?"

"Glove?"

All of a sudden, Chenoiel in his tighty-whities appeared at the door. "The glove means the room is occupado, capeesh, you fucking douchebag!"

"Excuse me, Dr. Chenoiel, your wife was looking for you, and I was trying to help. You weren't answering your page."

Chenoiel suddenly froze. He hadn't noticed his wife standing behind Zach.

"Hi, Robert, I'm sorry we disturbed you. You must be very tired from working so hard." Her voice quivered with sadness and hurt. It didn't seem to affect Chenoiel any; he just looked more agitated.

"What are you doing here? You know how busy my call days are. Are the kids all right?"

She reached into her bag and pulled out a small gift-wrapped box. "I wanted to give this to you. It's our anniversary. I know you're busy with your patients, but today is a special day."

"That is very nice of you, but it could have waited till tomorrow when I came home." Zach could not believe what an asshole Chenoiel was. What the fuck was she doing with him? "Hey, Maxwell, can you walk my wife out? I got to get dressed and make some rounds."

"I can find my own way out, Robert. I just need to use the facility before I go." She made to go in the room.

"Wait, you can't use the bathroom here, it's filthy. Maxwell, take her up to the nurses' lounge."

Zach said, "Sure, but that is two floors above, maybe … "

"Robert, please, it doesn't matter. I just … " She pushed the door fully open, and stopped cold. The light from the corridor had illuminated the room, revealing a very topless woman who, as the door swung open more, was bottomless as well.

Mrs. Chenoiel let out a short cry, and then turned away quickly running down the hall.

"Fran, this is not what it seems." He grabbed his scrubs off the floor and quickly put them on. "You fucking piece of shit. I swear, Maxwell, I'll destroy you." He ran down the hall after his wife, but she had already disappeared.

Zach looked at the naked woman now retrieving her bra and panties. She frowned. "Now do you understand why we can't be together? I'm a morally corrupt woman with no self-esteem."

"Dharma?"

Chapter 26

They sat in the corner of the coffee shop, out of sight of the dozens of patients and staff running to clinics, the O.R., or appointments.

"Why Chenoiel, Dharma? He's such a fucking ass. I know you told me it was an episode of need, but I can't even believe he cares about you."

"He doesn't care but he's safe. I would never want a permanent relationship with him. Even if I wanted a commitment, I could never get him to separate from his wife. She has a fortune, which he has become used to. Besides, sex with him was mediocre at best. A little problem with not being attentive to the two-player rule, and premature endings. He was into solo ... his solo."

"But, why? You are such a kind, beautiful woman. He is an uncaring ... "

She looked directly into Zach's eyes. "Zach, there is so much pain in these walls. It is oppressive. You know why people screw around here?"

Zach remained silent, watching the tears once again trickle down her cheeks.

"They need a happy fix so that they can try to help these patients who come to us with almost unsolvable problems. We can fix the hearts, take out the bad gallbladders, and remove the bullets. What we can't solve are the real problems in their lives, the lack of education, the superstitions, the hardness of life situations that can and will eventually crush them. The absent fathers, the kids on drugs, the poverty, hunger, homelessness, and the abuse they use against each other, all unsolvable because it's in poverty's DNA."

"But Dharma, we try and that has to be enough. You must have happiness and security in your own life, and how about love?"

"You can't love when you feel powerless to change your situation. Let me be honest, and say I've tried to love and it never works. You'll see as you work here, Chenoiel's situation isn't so uncommon. In fact, even your friends with solid relationships have been known to slip … usually temporarily, but sometimes this place destroys the loving relationships they came in here with."

"But, I can't believe that Chenoiel cares about anything besides his career."

She gave him a thin smile. "Even a sub-human like Chenoiel has times when the blackness invades him." She paused. "But, in this case it was me who needed a body, and he just happened to be there. Great choice, huh?"

"What happened?"

"I had a patient who was being seen for depression, and then developed a GI problem. It was determined the two were related, and I was assigned. I worked with him for months, and it was going well. His symptoms decreased, mind and bowel. His grades in school started going up, and, the best part, his home situation improved. His absentee father had finally landed a stable job, and unlike most sperm-donors, actually owned up to paternity, and started being a positive influence in this kid's life."

"Sounds great, you should be proud."

"I was happy. He was joyful, and then one day on his way to an after-school program for college-bound kids, a bullet found his head, and that was that. They never found the gunman. The father, who had had another child with the mother of this kid, disappeared, and the mother turned to drugs to comfort herself. I turned to Chenoiel."

"But Dharma, you tried. As sad as this is, there are other patients that need you and ... "

"No, I can't do this anymore. My shrink has upped the doses of my meds just to keep me going. Frankly, I don't want to live the life of a pill popper to get me through the day. Lilly Pharmaceuticals has offered me a position as a detail lady." She winked conspiratorially. "Fuck, you know rumor has it they only pick handsome men and beautiful women, so I was very honored. The sales region is far away from Brooklyn and I will never have to see a body with half its head gone. Oh, did I tell you I was in the E.R. with a patient when they brought his body in after he was shot? He was such a beautiful baby, with fantastic corn-row hair."

She let out great sobs of pain, and when Zach tried to hold her to comfort her, she pushed him away.

"Enough," she sniffled. "I want you to leave so I can get a new face on. If we should pass in the hall before I leave, just know I'm not there."

Zach slowly pulled himself out of the chair and walked away.

Chapter 27

"We are off for the weekend. Want to go out to a movie or for dinner at the Italian place?" Jake pleaded. "I haven't had any real life for the last two weeks, and Sandy is scratching the walls. Did I tell you she took up knitting, and to date has made me fourteen too-big or too-small sweaters? I swear, not a one of them fits right."

Zach looked up from his copy of *Sabiston's Textbook of Surgery*. He was about to scrub on a hemicolectomy with Bullshit and didn't want to look like an idiot when Bullshit's question-pimping started. Bullshit's philosophy was a good mentor always tested the student, and thereby increased the student's knowledge in surgery. In other words, he made them all look like dummies. Even Hercules got tripped up by Bullshit occasionally. Bullshit's knowledge was encyclopedic, there was no doubt. "No, you and Sandy should spend some alone time. She has called me very occasionally looking for you. She didn't say as much, but I think she thinks you are doing the horizontal monkey dance with one of PAY's preferred nurses. I assured her she was wrong."

"She's been calling you?" Jake angrily asked. "Does she realize I'm here trying to gain a profession so she can have all the palaces she demands?"

Zach looked at his friend quizzically. He had never heard Jake so defensive and aggressively angry at the same time. "Hey, buddy, chill a bit. You know that woman of yours is 'til death do you part. Even without that broken glass and $5,000 bar bill. You need to tell me something," Zach said.

Jake gave Zach a stony look, then smiled ever so slightly. "No, I guess I'm just tired. Sandy is just not getting what I'm going through, though to be fair what spouse or friend could who isn't working in this fucking place. The smells, sights, sounds ... the brutality.... "

"Yeah, but the roast beef on Wednesday and fried fish on Friday ain't bad, and it's cheap," Zach replied, trying to keep the conversation above the plane. "Besides, what else did you want to do with your life ... tooth fairy, scum-sucking lawyer, used car salesman? This profession gives you a respected position, and then you can settle down with that woman of yours and make me a God-uncle."

Jake smiled wanly. "I'll have to think about it ... with Sandy." He took a sudden deep breath. "Sandy? I don't know—for fun, but kids and permanent?" He shook his head and got up suddenly. "I have to check on some patients. I'll catch up with you later." He ran out the door.

Zach sighed. "PAY destroys another relationship."

Chapter 28

"You know, I occasionally bleed when I take a crap. I mean I know it's hemorrhoids, but lately it's happening more often, and I'm getting constipated at the drop of a hat. I'm a young guy, but with my job I know I eat lousy food and can't always drain the snake or pinch a loaf when I want to."

Zach was in the E.R. doing internal moonlighting. Internal moonlighting was a hush-hush subject that the hospital and Bullshit didn't want the RRC, the Residency Review Committee, to know about. The RRC felt residents should not be off making extra money when they were in residency. They should be reading in their off-time. The hospital and Bullshit felt the E.R. needed the extra personnel to handle the human onslaught that occurred on a Saturday night. Bullshit's one caveat was that when the resident was on trauma service, they couldn't moonlight as it was too fucking busy. Anyone on any of the private services or the subspecialty service could go down to the E.R. after they pre-opped their patients and lend a hand. Bullshit was a great believer the more patients his residents saw, the better doctors they would make. If the hospital double-paid them when they were on-call, fuck it. It didn't come out of his budget.

"Any abdominal pain? Vomiting, diarrhea?" Zach ran quickly through the standard abdominal problem questions. Mr. Fred Siegel was a forty-five-year-old male, well-muscled from years of running his own trucking and transport company. He still loved getting into the truck and delivering to the local stores, where he would schmooze with the merchants. He had married a nice-looking girl who had given him three sons. It was obvious his family was everything to him. He didn't smoke, moderately had a shot of vodka after a long day and was obviously exercised from lifting boxes. Zach palpated Siegel's abdomen and felt no masses.

"I'm going to do a rectal exam. I put a finger in your rectum to feel for abnormalities, like hemorrhoids. Turn on your side and face the wall, please."

"Hey Doc," he replied nervously, "we aren't even engaged. I mean I like rectal play as much as the next guy, but I prefer a size five glove with skinny, soft, fingers not, what do you got there, eights?"

"Seven and a halfs, but who's counting. I'll be gentle."

Siegel flipped on his side and Zach lubed up a gloved finger. "A little pressure now."

"That's what you guys all say ... oof!"

What the fuck, Zach thought. I can't advance my finger all the way in. Wait, I found a way in. Zach felt a hard something in the rectum. Could it be his prostate? A hard prostate—no, the mass was in the wrong ... oh fuck, I found a tumor. Zach withdrew his finger.

"Hey Doc," Siegel cracked, "if you found gold it's mine."

Zach wasn't really listening. Of course, he had read and heard about rectal cancers, but had never felt one, and this was such a young guy. He couldn't have a rectal cancer ... could he?

"Hey Doc ... I'm still here."

Zach came back into focus. "Sorry, Mr. Siegel. I want one of my colleagues to redo my exam."

Siegel looked panicked. "Is anything wrong? Why do you need someone else to do the exam again?"

"I just want to make sure that I'm correct in my findings."

Fuck me for what I have to do next, Zach thought. He needed to talk to his senior about this case.

"Hey, Chenoiel, I need you to check my findings on a case. They don't make sense to me."

"Well, I think that probably makes sense to me. You never get the diagnosis right," Chenoiel answered with a smirk. He was standing in front of a beautiful nurse with auburn hair and a figure from Playboy. Chenoiel turned to her and, acting like Zach wasn't even there, said, "You know these inexperienced, young residents have no knowledge of medicine. I'm required to check every little thing they do and usually find that they could have killed the patient. Why don't we meet for dinner later?"

The nurse giggled and nodded. Zach just shook his head. What a douchebag, he thought. "Chenoiel, come on. I have a zillion things to do, and I can't let this guy go without you checking out his rectal mass. Please just examine him, and then you can go get laid or whatever."

"Jealous, intern? I bet you wish you could get prime meat like that nurse."

Zach just clenched his fists. "Look Chenoiel, forget it. I'll get Shusterman in Medicine to check me. He isn't a surgeon, but he is available and experienced. I'm sure Bullshit won't mind when he sees the note Shusterman leaves on the chart. Let's see.... Asked by Dr. Maxwell to see forty-five-year-old white guy with perceived rectal mass.... Nah, Bullshit won't mind. I mean we consult for them often enough."

Chenoiel's face froze in pure hate. "Are you threatening me, you zero? I swear I'll mention you to my father.... "

"And I'll get fired. Fine do it, call your father, but if you don't come see the patient I'll call Hercules and get the fucking consult. He'll want to know why you weren't here. Want me to tell him your father approved of your extracurricular activities?"

Chenoiel looked around quickly to see if anyone was listening. "Fuck you. Where is this guy?"

Zach took him to see the patient. "Mr. Siegel, this is Dr. Chenoiel, my senior resident. He would like to examine you. Then we will go discuss the findings and give you a plan of action. Okay?"

"Chenoiel, I remember you. I came in here about three months ago for rectal pain. You told me it was hemorrhoids. I was amazed because all you did was feel my stomach. I was really happy because I had thought you'd have to either stick a big instrument up my ass, or at least a finger. Think you can just feel my belly again?"

Chenoiel scowled. "Normally, that is what I would do, Mr. Siegel. I don't think a young, healthy guy like you is apt to have anything more than a couple of 'roids. In fact, if you refuse the exam, I'll write you for some topical anesthetic and stool softener like last time."

"Damn, yes, I refuse," Siegel said with a wide grin. "You're right, I'm a healthy guy. Why would I have anything wrong?"

Zach was pissed. Chenoiel was practically begging Siegel to refuse a medical exam. "Dr. Chenoiel, can we speak privately for a moment?"

Chenoiel looked over at Zach with a saccharine-sweet smile. "Oh, it's all right, Zach. Everything with Mr. Siegel is all right. It's a hemorrhoid, write his prescriptions as I told him, and discharge him. I'm sure Mr. Siegel has places to go and people to meet. Sign him out."

Zach was desperate. "Dr. Chenoiel, please take another moment, and do a digital exam."

Chenoiel looked at Siegel. "I'll get the discharge papers prepared, and the nurse will come and discharge you. Dr. Maxwell, come with me."

Zach followed Chenoiel into the physicians' locker room. He walked into the room, and he felt lightning hit his face. He went down, stunned. "You are insubordinate and shouldn't be able to call yourself a physician. Don't you ever question me again in front of a patient. In fact, never question me, period." Chenoiel then strode out of the locker room.

By the time Zach gathered his wits about him and got back to the E.R. Siegel was gone.

When Hercules asked him how he got the shiner, he just said he walked into a door and left it at that. His concern now was how to get Siegel to come back in to be checked.

Chapter 29

Tony had just stabbed Bernardo. Maria was crying in the corner, being held by her friends, who were angry and packing heat. Zach was trying to pour the blood that was gushing out of Tony's abdomen back into his belly, but the blood wanted its freedom from the confines of a shit-laden peritoneal cavity. As Tony was turning whiter and whiter, Zach was getting woozier and woozier. That's when Maria stood and came up behind Zach. She reached down, and between his legs grabbed his twig and berries and squeezed.

"What the fu … !" He woke with a start.

"I thought you were going to fall asleep doing CPR on the stabbing," the cute nurse chided. "I had to act fast."

"Okay," Zach mumbled. "Let's call it. Time of death 11:05 p.m., September 29, 1980, year of our Lord … "

"Year of *your* lord," Jake added as he ran past the resuscitation with a central line kit for another case.

"As Zach was saying, year of our Lord, county of kings, city of Brooklyn… *Requiem aeternam dona ei, Domine,*" Lucas intoned.

Zach, still woozy, yelled, "But what about Tony and Maria?"

"Man, you need some sleep. Gangbanger who died ain't no George Chakiris and that needle-tracked, syphilis-brained prostitute ain't no Natalie Wood," Chenoiel observed.

"Hey, a little respect for the dead. Zach, go home. Hercules and I will make quick rounds by ourselves."

Zach tried to shake out the mental cobwebs. At this point he had been up twenty-nine hours without food or catnap. "No, I'll come. Let's just get this day over with."

Rounds were perfunctory, and he was out of the hospital in a half hour. He opened the back door to the hospital, crossed Hegeman Avenue, noting the evenings were chillier and there was a fine mist making halos around the streetlights. He breathed in the fresh air, or as fresh as the air came in Brooklyn. If he had known what pain his eyes would see, would he still have pursued this career? He was three months short of his birthday. All his high school and college friends had sunk into history. Most of his college buddies were married, working on their second homes, second kids, and in some cases, second wives. Their retirement accounts were slowly accruing money, and most of them seemed only slightly miserable. He guessed he shouldn't complain. He was housed in a very cheap, large apartment with a view of the Verrazano Bridge running up to mid-town Manhattan. At this time of night, the lights of the city were like a zillion fireflies buzzing around in the black of the sky. The shame was, if he stepped a hundred feet away from his building he'd be mugged, or worse. He received free food from the hospital cafeteria, refrigerators, and anything the nurses didn't hide away. He was never more than fifteen feet away from a coffeemaker with age-unknown coffee in its hotpot. He was even clothed for free, though the style reminded him that his situation was the same as Communist China's. Everyone wore the same cut of clothes. At least they were the best, softest, and strongest scrubs money could buy ... and he never had to wash them. He had friends around him who understood exactly what he was going through, and he understood what they went through. Why was he so discontented?

A stiff breeze shook him awake, and he ran into his apartment building and up the elevator to his beautiful view. The mattress was on the floor, giving him more room to stretch and less chance of falling out of the single bed. He collapsed on the mattress, dirty scrubs and all, and was snoring almost before his head hit the pillow.

Chapter 30

Sirens, no the beeper, where is it, where … damn!

Zach opened an eye to see the dark room only lit by the lights of lower Manhattan. "What the fuck, who was calling … the hospital?" He quickly grabbed the beeper off his shirt and saw it hadn't gone off. "Not the hospital … " The phone stopped ringing. Must have been a wrong number, he thought as he closed his eyes.

Ring … ring.

"What the fuck!" He picked up the receiver. "Uh-yuh?"

"Dr. Maxwell? Zach?"

"Who is this? What time is it? What day, month, year is it?" Zach tried to wipe the drool off his cheek.

"It's Clara, Clara Rosenberg, and it's midnight."

"What year, and who is this?" Zach gurgled.

"Oh, you are silly, Zach, you know what year it is, and Ike told me you guys worked all night. I hope it's all right I called, I'm so excited. I just had to call."

"Claire?!"

"No, Clara, Ike and Goldie's next door neighbor … from Canarsie?"

"Oh yeah, the neighbor. I hate to be rude, but did Ike happen to mention we were up all last night, worked all day and I just got home at eleven?"

"No, he didn't, Zach. I can call you Zach, Dr. Maxwell, can't I? I mean I have such news."

"They close the Canarsie ghetto, Grabstein's run out of Romanian pastrami … ?"

"Wha … ?"

"Never mind, Clara. How can I help you in the middle of the night on a situation that doesn't end in a dead body?"

"My next-door neighbor … "

"Ike?"

"No silly, why would I call you about Ike? I'm sure you know more about what goes on with him, being in that hospital.… "

"Clara, focus!"

"You don't have to yell."

"Sorry, I'm just sleepy."

"My neighbor Isaac."

"Isaac?"

"You know Isaac the tailor. He lives next door."

"No, I am not personally acquainted with a tailor named Isaac. Please go on … quickly!"

"There is that yelling again," she said crossly.

"Clara, I swear I'm going to hang up. My eyes feel like hot lead leaking from my face."

"Okay, Isaac has a beautiful niece visiting from Boston. She has to be your age and she is educated and … "

"Thank you, Clara, for thinking of me over I'm sure the rest of the hundreds of single Jewish males in your matchmaker's rolodex, but like I told you, I'm not interested."

"But, I … "

"Let me save you the time and trouble. One, I'm too busy working twenty hours a day. Two, I have sworn off women. Who needs them? You can't trust them, they emotionally suck you dry. Three, see number one. Finally, four, I need some sleep. Good night, Clara."

"She doesn't wear a bra."

"What?"

"She doesn't wear a bra, and is a dancer. Her boobs are very perky."

"Clara, I'm surprised. I have never heard of a Jewish female pimp. How much is this Isaac paying you to sell his niece the dancer into white slavery?"

Clara chuckled. "Oh, Zach, I don't make any money putting people together. I do it for love."

Zach knew when he had been trounced. "Perky, huh? Fine. Does this dancer have a name? Or is her name Candy or Cinnamon or some such?"

"It's Shoshie, and Isaac, her uncle, is expecting you should call her at his house this week … like tomorrow."

"Shoshie, what kind of name is that?" Zach asked.

"How should I know, but I know she is unencumbered." A loud cackle hurt Zach's ears. "Get it—unencumbered, you know, swinging freely."

"Send your bill to Isaac, Clara. I'll call when I get a second and don't sound like I'm on smack. Night, night." With those words he hung up the phone with Clara still laughing. He was in a deep coma within seconds.

Chapter **31**

"Okay, boys," Dr. Taff boomed, "forty-seven minutes and thirty-six seconds till free slops in the cafeteria. We have ten pre-ops to do, history and physicals on the elevator after we grab the patients from admitting. Only one thing is slowing us down. What is that, young Californian Maxwell?"

"Uh, you actually have to talk to the patients, master?"

"Not even close, young grasshopper. You must go back to Master Po, the Kung Fu blind guy for more training. The answer is simplicity itself. I can't do a rectal in a public elevator. The administrators tell me it has something to do about lack of sterility, loss of privacy, the customers think it's unbecoming.... I forget which. We will split up. Official urologists take two each, I get three as king of service, and our guest urologist, Zach Maxwell, MD, direct from the butcher service, will get one."

"Jack, I don't think that is fair. He should get to work up three patients to repay our hospitality. I mean shouldn't he stay here helping us hard-working plumbers? We are teaching him the mysteries of the dick," Freddie Greenbauch, MD, second in command for urological services, complained. Freddie was an American grad who picked PAY's urological program because it was exactly ten minutes from his mother's house. Freddie, while officially interested in women, only seemed to show interest in the only woman he had ever been seen with, his mother.

"Freddie, remember, manners," Jack admonished. "Zach is a guest, and I feel that he may be your junior resident one of these days, as he will find the mysteries of the dick and balls too mysterious to leave. So, as we all count on each other to get home at a decent time either to take care of the kids or your mother, let's cut him a break and let him take it slow for a while."

"But Jack ... "

"No buts. Freddie, you did get the fucking 10 p.m. call from Clara, didn't you?"

Zach had listened to this experimental drama piece played in front of him with disinterest, until the name Clara came up. No, he thought, it couldn't be the same Clara. He was tired, having spent most of the night holding sticks, or retractors, as they were known in the surgical trade. A neighborhood socialist tried to share the wealth of a capitalist and didn't realize the capitalist was carrying a Glock. Instead of receiving a wallet, the capitalist had given him lead. The socialist survived and was transported to PAY for a trip to the O.R. to run his bowel. Twenty-seven holes had to be closed, and non-viable pieces of bowel needed to be removed and re-anastomosed. It wasn't pretty work, and the amount of fecal contamination to the peritoneal cavity was impressive. The socialist was sixteen, and his chances of living were less than fifty percent. His chance of taking a dump out of his asshole was less than twenty percent. Because some of the bullets had ricocheted within the abdomen, tissue in his pelvis was torn up, so actually getting a boner and fathering children was probably less than ten percent. Zach thought about his life when he was sixteen. Brooklyn was a different world. After the O.R., the surgical team made morning rounds, and Zach went off to another building where the urological patients were kept. He joined rounds in progress and then scrubbed on a nephrectomy. By 5 p.m. he was smelly, sticky, and achy. Hearing something like Clara called should have concerned him, but he was just too brain dead to care.

Chapter 32

Taff was as good as his word. At 7 p.m. the urological team signed out to the resident on call and went to their respective homes. Freddie to his mother, Taff to his wife and four kids, and Zach to an empty apartment.

Zach was looking forward to a shower, a beer, and a steak he had defrosted the night before and then, if he made it that far without face-planting into the steak from exhaustion, sleep in his own bed. His move toward the shower was immediately halted by the ringing of the phone. He briefly considered not answering it, but he was responsible for the patients he had admitted or scrubbed on. So, with a heavy sigh, he picked up the receiver.

"Hello?" he tentatively answered.

"Dr. Maxwell, Zach, it's Clara, you remember, Ike's neighbor?"

Zach's hand gripped the handset of the phone like it was a walnut and he was trying to crush it open. "Clara, I thought we went through this. You can't call me at night. I'm too exhausted to talk about anything. I'm going to hang up now. Have a good night."

"Zach, please call Shoshie, she is a sweet girl and knows no one in town. She is lonely, and so are you. It is worth the effort."

"I will, I will, but not now, I'm too fucking busy with patients and learning and keeping myself alive." He had run out of steam emotionally. Why was he so stressed? He was doing important things in a situation where even the minor problems could turn into life-saving situations. He glanced at a mirror and didn't recognize what he saw. His hair was still thick, but the Irish Setter red had lost its shine. His face was pale and greasy. When had he grown dark bags under his eyes? He was growing a paunch where he had had a flat abdomen. That, he knew, came from eating a lot of carbs and the greasy food that only a kosher kitchen could produce. It was what the mirror didn't show that bothered him the most. The lack of a smile where there had always been one was telling of his new life. He had friends galore within the walls of PAY, but his attempts at starting a romantic relationship had been a total disaster. He guessed the old saying, don't shit where you eat, was true. The fact of having to participate on a minute–to–minute basis in societal calamities was like steel wool rubbing on his soul. He was one of a team of people trying to help, and was damn proud of that, but he could see the damage it was doing to the people who, like himself, were trying to help. Could someone in his situation even have a normal relationship? He was in a world where a quickie in a closet with a nurse was considered the height of having a great love life.

He thought about Chenoiel and his wife. Did aggressively pursuing a chief residency in Surgery require a shield from any responsibility to any romantic partner? Well, Chenoiel was an asshole. His marriage was probably a failure before he met his wife. But look at Jake and Sandy. They had been so sweet together, and head over heels in love with each other. Now, they were barely speaking to each other. Jake had taken to telling anyone at PAY that Sandy was a cold bitch who was just slowing him down. He would say that the only reason they occupied the same apartment was to split costs. Privately, he had told Zach that Sandy had banished him to the couch, and he hadn't touched her in months. He told Zach a man couldn't live this way and that he had a plan to get that little redhead lab tech in the closet to do a semen analysis.

An hour later he walked into a call room only to find Jake, his eyes inflamed, rubbing his face.

"What's the matter?" Zach remembered asking.

"Nothing, I'm just allergic to something in here, probably that half-eaten tuna sandwich from two weeks ago."

"Come on, I've known you for years. What's going on?"

"Sandy wants me out of the apartment. Fuck her, I should. Let her take care of the monthly rent. I can bunk in one of the call rooms, like you, Zach."

"Move out, away from Sandy? You love each other. She's just pissed at you. Don't be a schmuck."

"No, Zach, she delivered her order in a very clear rational voice. In fact, she told me she doesn't blame me for the break-up, said it was Bullshit's fault."

"What did you say?"

"I just laughed at her. What a dumbo. Well, fuck her. She can screw with someone else's life."

Zach wondered, was it the residency's fault? Maybe the problem was only being physically and mentally present for a couple of hours every third day?

"Zach! Are you still there? Zach, did you collapse, should I call 911?"

Zach came back to reality with a sick feeling in his stomach, the phone in danger of being crushed in his hand. "Clara, I can't call her. I'm way too busy building my future. Take my word for it, unless she's looking for quick, non-satisfying sex and then getting tossed like a used piece of toilet paper, she should consider herself lucky."

There was sudden silence on the other end of the line. Zach could feel the vacuum closing in on him. "I'm sorry I bothered you, Dr. Maxwell. Good luck with your career."

Zach heard a click on the other end of the phone. He slowly put the receiver down and went to lie down. Sleep didn't come easily though.

Chapter 33

"Suction here please. Hey, scut boy, pay attention. I can't see for shit here."

Zach, Ike, and Rupak were in the third hour of repairing an aortic aneurysm. It was very touch-and-go for the patient in terms of life expectancy. Neither of the three residents was fresh as they had just closed on multiple GSW to abdomen, resulting in a colon looking more like Swiss cheese than anything else. There was a commotion in the hallway and Jake appeared with a couple of nurses and attendants from the E.R., driving a gurney on which was a sixty-five-year-old male with a barely registerable blood pressure.

"Ruptured Triple-A. Needs a butcher stat! Know where we can find three?" Jake yelled.

The three started running for the O.R. next door. "Where the fuck is Kazi?" Rupak yelled at Mrs. Braverman, who had just come out of her office to see what the commotion was about. "We have a ruptured Triple-A, I need him tubed and put to sleep, now!"

Braverman turned back into her office and suddenly over the PA came "Dr. Kazi to O.R. six, stat. Kazi to O.R. six. Kazi zip up and get your ass into O.R. six!"

"Well, that should go over big with the administration," Ike said as they helped get the patient positioned on the table.

"Zach, Ike, strip him, and then Ike scrub and Zach paint

him. Put on a pair of sterile gloves before you handle the sticks to paint."

"No, he needs to scrub first."

"Margaret," Rupak ordered, calling Braverman by her first name. "If we do this by the book, he's dead. Now let us work. Did you find Kazi?"

"Yeah, he is just washing his hands and will get this guy down. We are short on scrub nurses so I'll be assisting."

"An honor, Mrs. Braverman," Rupak said. Braverman started to walk out of the room to scrub. "Wait, you sure you remember what to do?" Rupak asked.

"Smart ass, I was assisting when your mother was cleaning your tiny thingy," she laughed.

Zach grabbed the gloves and grabbed the sticks, which were ring forceps. He also grabbed a bunch of the special four by fours, gauze squares that had a radio opaque thread in them in case a gauze sponge went missing. Someone then could x-ray the operative site and see if the gauze had been left in the abdomen. These he folded into a triangle and clamped the bundle with a ring forceps. "Nice paintbrush, now for my Sistine Chapel miracle."

He started painting with Betadine. From the bellybutton to the periphery of the abdomen, in ever-enlarging circles. When he got to the periphery, he'd drop the used gauze into the waste basket, hand the used stick to a nurse, grab a fresh stick and start the process over again. The purpose was to kill as many of the skin bacteria as he could.

"Okay, enough painting. Go scrub, Zach, and then get your ass in here. Braverman, number ten scalpel to Dr. Aronsky. Zach, get a move on," Rupak barked.

He was in the middle of scrubbing when Lucas stuck his head in the scrub room. "Zach, get into room two, Hercules needs you."

"Room two, I'm with Rupak and Ike. They are expecting me."

"Fuck that, Hercules takes precedent. I'll tell Rupak Hercules needs you, now move, and whatever you do, do not break scrub, Hercules has a hot one."

Zach ran into room two with his hands raised above his waist, cap and mask on and booties in place. Life had already changed from three months ago. His mind clicked on the patient on the bed, already asleep and tubed. He put on the sterile gloves and surgical robe that two nurses were holding for him. If Zach was even thinking at that point, he would have chuckled, thinking that maybe this was how fast Batman got into uniform while going down the pole to the bat cave.

"What do we have here?"

"Air-conditioned abdomen. Air-conditioned by stab wound. I need a surgeon and I picked you."

"Hercules, where is everyone? I'm not ready for this, really."

"First, Brooklyn just exploded. The whole team is either in the O.R. trying to stop bleeding, or the E.R. trying to stop bleeding. Second, I tell you when you are ready, boy."

Zach broke out into a cold sweat. "I'll fuck up.... "

"No, you won't because you have a great surgeon and teacher on the other side of the table. Now get over here," he said. "Nurse, number ten scalpel to Dr. Maxwell."

The nurse slapped the knife handle into Zach's outstretched hand. "Midline incision, Dr. Maxwell. Let's go."

Zach performed like a robot. Hercules gave him instruction and Zach precisely performed the command. Sweat collected under his arms and at his crotch. The itching skin was like a fireball with each touch of the scrub cotton. His wish to just drop the instruments and scratch his balls was unbearable. He forced himself to concentrate on the abdomen in front of him and Hercules's commands.

He opened the abdomen, cauterizing bleeders as he went. Red blossoms appeared in the yellow fat. The intestines floated in a bath of blood. No pieces of shit in the blood, a good sign. Where was the blood coming from? Quickly he thought, do a gross inspection of the four quadrants in the abdomen. Bleeder, bleeder, come out, bleeder, wherever you are.

Zach adjusted the self-retainers, clamps that held the abdominal incision open. Shit, the fucking liver was ripped open. The patient was going to bleed out.

"I found the bleeding, Hercules. The bastard is going to bleed out."

"No, he won't, we'll pack it. What do we pack a bleeding liver with, and don't say egg and onions. That is an old joke beneath you."

"Uh, wait, you want to take down the omentum and stuff it into the liver?"

"'Stuff' is not exactly language approved by the American College of Surgeons, but you are correct in thought. Start taking the omentum down off the stomach, boy, and hurry it up. This guy is bleeding like stink."

The omentum is a big drape of fat connected to the stomach and intestines in the abdominal cavity. It has a blood supply and can be partially disconnected from the stomach and put into a liver laceration like packing. Large sutures then secured everything and, with a little luck, no more bleeding.

Cut, tie, cut, tie. Hercules and Zach pulled the sheet of fat away from the stomach and stuffed it into the liver laceration. With Hercules's help, Zach learned how much pressure to close the liver-omental sandwich with.

"Looks dry, boy. What's next?" Hercules queried.

Zach, mentally and physically exhausted by this time, was having trouble getting words out. "Uh … irrigate and run the bowel?"

"Is that a question? Of course not. Do it."

Zach irrigated the wound with warm saline and then suctioned it out. He then ran the small intestines through his gloved fingers looking for perforations and found nothing abnormal. A check into the pelvis was normal.

"I think we are ready to close, Hercules."

Hercules looked at the circulation nurse. "Sponge count good?"

"Yes, Dr. Christospathos, all the sponges that went into the wound were taken out. You can close."

"Thank you, dear. Zach close, I'll scrub out and start the note."

"Three-0 Proline, if you please nurse, let's close and get outta here."

Zach felt like he had grown an additional ten feet, had a hard six-pack, and a nine-inch cock, one less than monumental because he was Jewish.

Chapter 34

Zach left the O.R. suite just as most of the surgical team got through with their cases. They were a sorry-looking lot, though on the other hand, they were all feeling good about themselves. The team so far had not lost a single patient. Some, like Rupak's ruptured aneurysm, still were fifty-fifty, but that was the surgical game.

Outside the suite's door, Zach saw a woman trying to question the residents as they left to complete floor work or make rounds. She was beautiful, blond, and had muscular calves. She looked and walked like a dancer. As he got closer, he heard her question.

"Does anyone know where I can find a Dr. Maxwell? I need to speak with Dr. Maxwell."

He went to her. God, she even smelled good, but then he had been stuck in the sweatbox O.R. for hours, so anyone smelled good at this point. "I'm Dr. Maxwell, can I help you?"

Zach didn't see it coming, but did he feel it. He thought his jaw was dislocated and he was seeing stars.

"Listen, you pompous surgical piece of crap. Don't you ever insult my friend. Who do you think you are?"

Zach was still reeling, but at least his vision had cleared and his jaw could move. He looked around embarrassed as his fellow residents had frozen where they were to observe the spectacle. "Hey, Maxwell, lovers' tiff? Did you leave her unsatisfied? Remember, she is supposed to cum first."

The crowd laughed at Zach's obvious discomfort. He grabbed the blond woman and went into an empty exam room, kicking the door closed.

"What the fuck? Do we know each other? And who is this friend of yours I supposedly insulted? I've been stuck in this hospital for thirty-six hours and I've had no contact with the outside world. Jesus, my jaw is killing me."

"You don't even remember who you insult. Damn, you are a self-centered piece of shit. Does the name Clara ring a bell in that overeducated, underused brain? How dare you, she was trying to do you a favor. You could have politely just told her you weren't interested."

Dawn suddenly hit Zach. Well, she was as pretty as Clara had said and, he stole a glance, yep, she was unencumbered and cute there, too. "Damn, I didn't know besides being a matchmaker, Clara had a hit squad. For your information, Shoshie, and I take it you are Shoshie, I never insulted her. I just told her to cease and desist, especially cease the midnight phone calls. I hardly get time to sleep as it is."

Doubt entered Shoshie's face. "She called you at midnight? Really?"

"Yes, and on nights after being here thirty-six plus hours without sleep. I was nice and politely told her not to call, and at that time told her I wasn't interested in a date. I was too busy."

"Listen bub, if you think I'd go out with you, you are as brainless as I thought. I do apologize for the midnight phone calls, though. I didn't realize she was doing that."

"Do you always go and beat up the person you think is screwing with your friends? Very chivalrous of you. You must have very loyal friends. In fact, if that is the way you defend friends, I don't see why you need to troll for dates."

"Troll for dates, you are an insulting worm. I don't need a date, but I bet you do. I can't imagine any woman would go out with you, even as a mercy date. Plus, what is that stink. Do you shower?"

"Oh, I wouldn't worry."

"I don't, Dr. Maxwell. I am sorry I hit you, and will speak to Clara about the phone calls. Good evening."

With that, she turned on her heel, opened the door and strode down the corridor. The view from the back was as good if not better than the front. God, she was feisty. He briefly contemplated chasing after her, but he was just dead on his feet. Zach shuffled toward the ward, contemplating the hours of work he still had before he could get out of there. She was beautiful, though.

35

He couldn't get her out of his mind, but work took precedence and he was putting in close to 130 hours a week. This didn't leave much time for romantic interests. He did have ample opportunity for linen-closet relationships as did most of the residents, nurses, and support personnel. Zach had survived one of these liaisons, barely, with the vampire. He saw how they worked for Chenoiel, destroying his marriage. He mourned Jake and Sandy's breakup. Jake was running around the hospital sticking his dick into anything, and it certainly wasn't making him happy. He decided to try to avoid the horizontal calisthenics as long as biologically possible.

"Dr. Maxwell to the E.R., Maxwell to the E.R."

Fuck, what now, he was only a quarter through seeing the patients on the service. He went down to the E.R., and found Chenoiel standing next to a gurney in the trauma room. Chenoiel, never known for his smile, had a big, shit-eating grin, as Zach went over to find out what the hell he wanted.

"Hey, Maxwell, got a great admission for you here."

"Yeah, what do you have?"

"Twenty-six-year-old white male with mental status change and alcohol on his breath."

"Okay, I'll bite, what is surgical in this patient?"

"Oh, a little present to improve your surgical skills, from me to you."

Chenoiel lifted the sheets, and Zach found that the patient had slashed the skin of his abdomen multiple times just deep enough to get down to the fat. Christ, it would take hours to put it all back together again.

"Isn't this, as the surgical E.R. resident, your job to put him back together, and get the medical residents to handle his alcohol intoxication?"

"No, I am admitting his surgical problem, and you can take care of the rest of his problems also. Besides, isn't that what Bullshit always says? Surgeons can handle any problems for twenty-four hours, then transfer to another service."

"I really think he'd agree that surgery would stitch this guy up and then let the medical boys handle it."

"Dr. Maxwell, your senior resident, having more experience, commands you to sew him up and admit him, deal with his alcohol withdrawal and then who knows. Toodles, I have lunch with a stunning blond now that you have screwed up my marriage."

He left with Zach holding the bag on this guy. He went to the nursing station and got what little information was available including Chenoiel's note:

C.C. Mental status change

HPI: Mid 40s Caucasian male, mental status change Arrives EMS intoxicated. Visible cutting of skin abdominal wall

Abdomen soft BS normal

GU normal

Zach flipped down to the conclusion.

Benign abdomen with heavily intoxicated male, unresponsive to commands except with deep stimulation

Probable self-inflicted slash wounds
Surgical repair and observation
Surgical resident called for admit

There really wasn't much here. He glanced at the physical, which only listed that he had a head, was breathing, had a beating heart, and the slashes.

The chart didn't even list the patient's name, making him a John Doe, or in this case, a José Doe. "Hey, *señor, como estas?*" He got nothing.

Next, he lifted José's hand, holding it about a foot above his face, and then let go. Zach thought the coma was real. No one faking a coma hits his own face. Reflexes kick in to divert the hand away from the face. Zach opened José's eyelids. No, the pupils were not pinpoint, so no opiate overdose, and they were reactive to light, all normal signs.

Zach looked for a work-up but found next to nothing. He also saw the vital signs were not addressed, which were worrisome. Blood pressure low, and he was very tachycardic with a rate of 130 beats a minute. Sure, alcoholics could have faster heart rates, especially if they were withdrawing from alcohol, but usually their blood pressure was on the hypertensive side. This guy was acting dehydrated.

Zach looked closely at the patient's head, and the smell of alcohol on his breath was evident. In fact, the smell was so evident it made Zach's eyes water. It was deep, sickeningly sweet, musky … Wait a second, sweet? Zach thought. Oh, fuck.

Zach called over the nurse who had been taking care of the patient. "I don't see any notation on the chart, but did anyone get lab results on this patient?"

"I don't think Dr. Chenoiel ordered any. I think I asked, but he said the guy was just a drunk that needed his cuts closed and to sleep it off. I thought maybe some basic labs since he was insistent on admitting this guy, but who am I? Just a lowly nurse here to serve The Chenoiel."

"I need saline at 250 an hour, and I need a finger stick glucose, and a cathed urine dip, and I need it now."

The nurse looked questioningly at Zach. "Why, what is going on?"

"I think the guy is going to crash. Let's move, do you have urine?"

The nurse looked at the patient's pants that hadn't been removed and then at the sheet. "You can wring it out."

"Never mind, I'll cath him, get me the glucose, and then draw CBC, Chem-7, LFTs, and get urine drug screen, EKG. ... Oh yeah, most important, get an acetone."

The nurse's eyes widened at the mention of the serum acetone. "Oh shit, you think he is DKA? Chenoiel has had him here for hours with this mental status and didn't do shit."

"We will see."

Zach fetched a Foley kit, and after stripping the patient of his pants, placed the catheter into the patient's bladder via his penis. The patient didn't move. "God, this guy must be deep." Clear urine drained into the collection bag and Zach retrieved ten cc in a small cup. The nurse had started giving the patient fluids and was doing a finger stick glucose.

"Sugar is reading too high to read. You are right, the guy is DKA."

"Not yet, we need to do a dip on the urine, and shit, I also need a green top tube for respiratory therapy to do a venous blood gas."

"I have an extra green top. I'll go page the respiratory thera-pist. The urine dipsticks are in the nurses' station." She went off to call respiratory.

Zach found the dip sticks and the ketones were three plus

positive. Basically, Chenoiel had assumed that the guy's smell was from binging alcohol and not what it really was, ketones in the blood. The body didn't have enough insulin to process the glucose so the cells could use it for energy, so the body burned fat, producing the ketones. The ketones got to too high a level, and essentially poisoned the body, causing coma. The high glucose also caused the body to get rid of a lot of water, and the body dehydrated. This decreased the blood pressure, which the body tried to compensate for by increasing the heart rate. If left without treatment, all the compensatory mechanisms would collapse, and the patient would go into metabolic failure and die.

The nurse returned with a lab slip. "ABG is 6.9, he is a sick mofo."

Zach sighed, not only a sick motherfucker, but almost a dead motherfucker. "Start an insulin drip, he looks like he is a hundred kilos, so ten units regular insulin I.V. push, and then ten units per hour in a drip. Glucoses q one hour, and he needs an ICU bed. In the meantime, also give him cefazolin one gram I.V. push and then q six. I'll clean up these cuts and close them, see if you can find the medical resident. I need to speak to him."

"What about Dr. Chenoiel? Shouldn't we let him know?"

"I've had enough of Chenoiel. I'm sure he will eventually find out what happened to this patient."

Chapter 36

"**Ike, wait up,**" Zach yelled as he saw Ike leaving the O.R.

"What's going on? I haven't seen you in a while and Goldie just mentioned she misses you."

"Oh, you know, saving the dregs of society, achieving my place on the shortlist for Surgeon General, shit like that. Plus, I didn't know if you or Goldie were pissed at me."

"Why would we be pissed?" Ike asked. Then it dawned on him, and he gave Zach a crooked smile. "Oh yeah, I heard you got your ass whipped by a girl. Pretty embarrassing if you ask me."

"First of all, she sucker-punched me. Second, she had no reason to be pissed at me. It was that friend of yours, Clara."

Ike laughed. "Clara, let me guess. She is trying to set up a shiddoch."

"A what?" Zach asked.

"A *shiddoch*, a Jewish shotgun wedding. This is really funny. Why didn't you just firmly tell her, not interested? I mean she is harmless and usually takes direction."

"Ike, she was calling me at midnight, bugging me to call this girl. I did tell her no, but she called again. I don't get enough sleep as it is. I'm sure she is a nice lady, but the second time she called, I was fried and I blasted her. She wouldn't … anyway, I told her that if she was offering the girl for quick, nasty sex, I'd call her, but otherwise forget it."

Ike winced. "Oof, now I see why Clara gave me the stink eye. I thought it was because I bumped into her garbage cans with the car. Yeah, I guess you went a little overboard."

"Actually, I went a lot overboard. Clara's fix-up is the girl who came here to kill me."

"The fuck you say. Well, I guess your instincts were right. What guy wants to date a girl who has a mean right cross and takes no hostages. She probably was a dog anyway. Clara really has no taste, you should see her husband."

"No, no, Ike, she is beautiful. I mean green-grey eyes with flecks of gold in them. Kissable mouth, great legs and above … and fire. I think I want to go out with her, but she hates me already. It usually takes a girl two or three dates to hate me."

"Hate you, because of what you said to Clara? I can take care of that if you play ball."

"How am I playing ball? Oh fuck, take care of it, whatever playing ball is I guess I'll just have to do it."

"You sure will. Hey, I just realized, this is the second girl that beat you up. You really are an embarrassment to all males everywhere."

"I told you I got sucker-punched, and the vampire wasn't even in the realm of reality."

"Sure, sure … you got beat up by two girls."

Chapter 37

Fecal Impaction: shit that has so compressed it is like drying cement. Unmovable. *See severe constipation, also disgusting (visual and smell).*

Zach was wrist deep in the Nana's rectum, pulling last week's creamed corn that now wasn't creamed, and shredded wheat, out of her ass. He wore a plastic surgical gown and two sets of masks and gloves. Inside the mask, he had painted benzoin, a medical glue with a very sweet smell. He had seen this trick on the TV show *Quincy, Medical Examiner.* Those fucking TV screenwriters really didn't know what they were writing about. The stench of decayed, fecalized, ancient-nursing-home, old-lady manure was more than he could take. His eyes were tearing profusely.

The door to the patient's room opened and there she stood. Clara's braless dancer, Shoshie. Right behind her was Ike acting like a tour guide. "Shoshie, this is a typical patient room.... "

"Oh my God, Ike, what are you doing. I'm doing a disimpaction here. Get Shoshie out of here before she vomits." Zach yelled at Ike again, "Quick, she looks green."

Ike pulled her back out of the room. Zach could hear retching and crying on the other side of the closing door. He gathered up the products of his labor in the drop sheet he had laid down and dumped them, his gloves, gown, and mask into a plastic bag. Quickly washing his hands, he ran out of the room to see Shoshie looking green and woozy, half bent over trying to get in fresh air. All the while Ike was trying to hold her up. "Jeez, Shoshie, sorry about that. I thought that room was empty and I had no idea Dr. Maxwell was in there working. Since you saw him last, he has had remorse about insulting our mutual friend Clara. I am his senior and I felt he hadn't made amends enough so I adjusted his surgical assignments to fit his crime. Please forgive this unfortunate incident."

Shoshie tried to speak, but instead just gagged while trying to keep herself upright.

"What the holy fuck is wrong with you, Aronsky? She needs to lie down, not listen to your crap. Come on, Shoshie, this room is empty."

He led her into the empty patient room, followed by Ike still yakking about the advantages of working at PAY. "Ike," Zach said, "please just leave. Better yet, run down to the pharmacy and get an anti-emetic for her. I'll stay with her until she gets back on her feet."

"But she wants to apply for a job here."

"Not now, she doesn't. Now go to the pharmacy and then find an appendix to do or a brain for that self-transplant you need."

Ike snorted and theatrically left the room, but not before he gave Zach a wink when he thought Shoshie wouldn't see. Zach's mouth flopped open. He prayed this wasn't Ike's plan to get him a date with her. No, he couldn't believe he would torture her just because he thought Zach needed a date.

He went into the closet, and pulled out a washcloth, and then ran cold water over it in the sink. Carefully wringing it out, he folded it into a long rectangle and put it on her forehead. "God, I'm sorry you had to see that, Shoshie. That procedure is not for viewing by civilians."

She opened her eyes and Zach marveled how beautiful they were. Her skin was flawless, and she smelled so good. "What were you doing to that poor woman? She was so old."

"She is a nursing home patient, Shoshie. She has advanced dementia. She can't walk, can't talk, and barely knows how to eat anymore. To try to feed her invites something called aspiration, which means the food, instead of going into the stomach, goes into the lung. This can cause pneumonia and she could die. But she still can chew if the aide puts something in her mouth, so she gets fed. It all ends up in her colon and Presto Change-o, shit-cement. Someone has to manually get rid of it."

Shoshie quietly said, "What will happen when she stops eating? Does she just starve to death?"

"We surgically create a hole in her stomach and connect the hole to another hole we make in her abdominal wall. We then place a tube and drip liquid nutrients directly into her stomach."

"What a horrible way to live." She sat up and removed the washcloth. "I feel like I can breathe again. Thanks for saving me. I think I'll go home, take a long hot shower and scrub hard, and then look for bartending jobs." She got off the bed, and after a little dizziness, started to walk away.

"Uh, Shoshie ... "

"Yes, I'd love to go out with you Zach, at least for a drink. I know your time is not your own and after talking to Clara, I understand why you flipped out, especially after today."

"Uh, that's great," he said. After Ike's meddling, he thought he'd seen the last of those beautiful eyes.

"I'm going to make this low pressure. Call me when you have time to go out. I'll wait. If you need to just talk to someone outside of the inmates of PAY, you can call me. If possible, call me even if you are busy, and tell me when to call you. I stay up late. This way we won't disturb my uncle with a ringing phone. Okay?"

Zach smiled. Could he have a real life along with a medical

life? He really didn't know. "That's great, thank you, I can't wait. By the way, where did your name come from?"

She gave him a little smile. "You'll find out when you buy me a drink."

38

"**Welcome to the SICU.** First rule, you do nothing unless the nurse approves."

Zach blinked. "Uh, you mean the nurses set up treatment? So what am I supposed to do?"

Sara was the new head of the SICU nurses. The last nurse manager had disappeared under mysterious circumstances. Rumor had it that during a patient catastrophe she had attempted to make one of the interns into a eunuch. The patient was a train wreck, fifty-five years old, with diabetes and coronary heart disease. After a routine scoping of his right knee, he had developed a fever. The orthopods, being brilliant carpenters, but a little weak in general medicine, failed to recognize the knee had become a mutant bacteria laboratory. Within twenty-four hours, the knee had blown up to three times the size of the other and had become red and very hot.

The surgery was done on Friday and because it was a holiday, weekend rounds had slacked off a bit to accommodate attending staff who took a break from driving to PAY, and house staff, who took advantage of the situation. In any case, by the time anyone realized the fever had escalated to 105, culminating in the patient having his first seizure, the damage to the knee and leg was done. There was no choice but to rush the patient back to the O.R. and amputate the leg. The patient's blood pressure crashed during surgery, causing a stroke and a minor myocardial infarction. Blood cultures revealed bacteria only found in Inner Mongolia with a resistance to most antibiotics.

The Infectious Disease fellow put the patient on triple antibiotics, a "Hail Mary" in the ID trade. The antibiotics at first seemed to be working, and then the patient developed Stevens-Johnson syndrome. This disaster causes the skin to necrose, leaving large, black patches of dry gangrene all over the patient's body. He suffered a second heart attack, and then a second major stroke, and was pronounced brain-dead by the almost English-speaking neurologist. The hospital's lawyers, smelling a multi-million-dollar lawsuit, called an unofficial SICU meeting and warned everyone to not get a DNR from the family, with the hope that even if he went into cardiac arrest, something could be salvaged, and the dollars to be paid out to the patient's family might be less.

The SICU nurses had very strong positions against this but realizing most of them would be dragged into this doctor-induced disaster, formulated their own plan to minimally attempt to resuscitate the patient, or slow-code him—more when, than if, the patient's heart stopped.

The resident assigned to the SICU during this episode was a devout, right-to-life Catholic. Orvis, the resident, believed he was instructed by God to save life, no matter the circumstances. The nurses, all veterans of the horrors of disease gone terminal, believed in the right to die. The patient was brain-dead and to prolong the animation of this decomposing body was a sin both for the torture of a living corpse that was once a person, and the abuse of his family.

Slow code would not be found in any hospital policy book or in any medical textbook. The unofficial procedure was, if the patient's heart stopped, a very slow stroll to the patient's bed, a couple of quick superficial chest compressions, maybe an I.V. squirt of some drug, and then call it, and mark the time of death. The nurses didn't count on Orvis doing anything except unofficial policy, but God told Orvis to save this life and gall darn it, he would.

The nurses legally had no choice, but in the thirty-seventh minute of resuscitation, with the body smoking from multiple attempts at defibrillation, multiple cracked ribs from CPR, and the makings of a tension pneumothorax from Orvis's unsuccessful attempt to place another central line, the nurses balked, led by the nurse manager. When Orvis called for another shock, the nurse manager took the paddles, turned around to where Orvis was standing and shocked him with 300 joules. Orvis screamed and then went down, convulsing.

A hospital review mandated the quiet firing of the nurse manager with recommendation for psych evaluation. Orvis was placed in the lab where God allowed him to kill rats to his heart's content.

Thus, the unofficial policy of residents following the recommendations of the nurses was born.

"I thought the idea was for me to write the orders and a treatment plan. Isn't that the reason for a residency?"

"Yes," Sara said, "except in the SICU the patients are really sick, and the technology is cutting-edge and complicated. No resident is anywhere near qualified to touch a patient here. If you are a good boy and do as you are told, we might allow you to write the notes on your own."

"Damn, four years of med school, and I'm qualified to be a glorified secretary. Does Bullshit or Hercules know about this arrangement? Hard to believe they do, considering if an Attending Surgeon takes away a case from the resident, there is all hell to pay."

"In fact, yes, they do. Bullshit wrote rule twenty-three himself."

"What is rule twenty-three? I don't remember anyone mentioning it."

"Rule twenty-three is super-secret. We only notify him and you, if you break it."

"You mean I might fuck up some secret rule I don't know anything about and be held accountable?"

"Well, not exactly fuck up, but the spirit of what you say is spot on."

"Great. Look, if it's easier I don't show at all, please tell me. This is a perfect time of year to say, be out on a golf course, learning golf."

"You don't know how to play golf? What kind of AMA card-carrying doctor are you?"

"Obviously not the right type."

Over time Zach came to like the SICU. To be admitted here, the patient had to have had a surgical catastrophe. Most of these being the shocks, either hemorrhagic or septic, and occasionally a cardiogenic shock induced by surgery.

Zach loved the quiet of the place that was almost like a tomb, especially at night. The nurses would turn down the light dimmers, so the only bright lights were from monitors or desk lamps. The environment at night reminded him of his days studying in the college library where students quietly roamed the stacks like human shadows floating in the dimness. Only here, the shadows were the nurses, and the stacks were the very sick patients on their hospital beds connected to IVs and monitors. The patients were either, very rarely, in condition to talk, or had an endotracheal tube down their larynxes, preventing even sound.

Zach would check the vital signs on a large monitor in the nurses' station. By protocol, labs were automatically drawn in the morning, and run stat for morning rounds. At 4:30 in the morning, the radiology tech came and took chest x-rays of all the patients on a ventilator. All Zach had to do was coordinate the computer screens to the patient's electronic chart. After being on the wards and running to deal with up to fifty patients a day, dealing with eight patients was child's play, even if these patients were the sickest of sick.

After preparing for morning rounds and examining the patients, Zach handled problems as they arose, or did bedside procedures. He loved bedside procedures. They weren't like putting miles of intestine together, but there was nothing as simple and satisfying as putting a big central line in someone's chest or neck, or doing a bedside tracheostomy. In the first week of his SICU duty he had done three of these.

There were cardiac arrests every day or so. Fluid and electrolyte problems done on the computer, and even an occasional intracranial pressure monitor to play with. Every procedure done, even if painful, was accomplished in near-silence. Unlike the E.R., no patients had to be tackled and mostly no one needed to be tied down. Zach just did the procedure.

While Zach thought this was wonderful, it did have a negative effect on his soul. Wordless, unresponsive patients became lumps of flesh under a thin white sheet. When he stopped treating Mr. Smyth and instead dealt with the ulcerative colitis in bed six, a certain humanity was lost. Some older doctors even said this might be a good thing. How many dead and dying patients could any one man deal with at a single time? This was a necessary defense mechanism, the senior physicians would say.

The attending surgeon in charge was an Egyptian named Kamuzu El Sayed. He was an interesting character, being an early graduate of the PAY surgeon-making machine. Bullshit found him a competent surgeon without the emotional stamina to handle any surgery longer than an hour. Bullshit theorized that Kamuzu's metabolism ran at such a high rate that after an hour, his cells had eaten all the glucose his bloodstream could supply. This caused his brain to starve, setting off a cascade of Kamuzuist problems. Behind closed doors, Bullshit admitted to his assistant director that El Sayed, at the hour mark, started making minor surgical errors, usually nothing too bad, but at an hour and fifteen, the crude language would emerge, usually directed at the nurses, and finally, at an hour and thirty, Kamuzu was screaming like a banshee and throwing objects, including scalpels.

It would have been easy for Bullshit to throw out Kamuzu, but he liked the guy. When not in the O.R., he was funny, kind to patients and their families, and most importantly, brilliant in diagnosis and treatment.

A miracle then occurred, rewarding Bullshit's intuition. The head of the SICU at that time was a retired surgeon who wasn't up on modern critical-care medicine. He was overweight, smoked two packs of cigarettes a day, and ate two pastrami sandwiches for lunch almost every day. At rounds one day, after consuming four fried eggs, crispy bacon, and home fries, he started having a belching episode followed by a horrible pressure in his chest. He retired to an unused bed in a darkened corner and flipped the monitor switch so the readings would not appear on the central monitor. He then put the leads on himself, huffing and puffing, as now breathing was difficult. His blood pressure, now monitored, sky-rocketed as he saw he was in ventricular tachycardia. He tried to beat on his own chest quietly, so no one would know he was having problems. Unfortunately, he never achieved the two to five joules of energy a chest thump was supposed to supply in CPR, went into ventricular fibrillation, and died. His body was only noticed when the smell from his bowels evacuating post-mortem occurred. Bullshit, speaking at his funeral, noted that this was a surgeon who did it on his own and never asked for help even at the end.

Bullshit appointed Kamuzu immediately and never was sorry.

"Zach, Mr. Cavelli's temp this morning is up to 99.5 rectal. Do we need to do anything about this?" Kamuzu asked.

"I ordered blood cultures times two, a urine culture, and already checked the chest x-ray, which showed nothing. I think it's probably in the urine, but we need to check out those incisions," Zach replied.

Zach put on gloves and started taking down the dressings. The incisions were seeping a small amount of yellowish material that had the musky, sour smell of diarrhea.

"I think we may have found Mr. Cavelli's problem. What do we need to do now, Dr. Maxwell?"

"Shit, we are going to need to open up this wound and see how deep this infection goes. I'll get a suture removal kit."

"Considering this guy had perforation of his bowel, we might consider getting a CT of his abdomen to see if the pus extends into the intraabdominal area," Kamuzu replied.

Zach shook his head. "If that is the case, Hercules and Ike are going to have a long night in the O.R. cleaning this guy's abdomen out."

Kamuzu chuckled. "If I know Hercules, his dick is going to get hard just thinking about re-opening this guy and hunting for a possible bowel leak and pus pockets."

"Okay," Zach replied, "let me rephrase that. Ike is not going to be able to get his dick serviced tonight. Instead of going home, he'll be in the O.R. fixing his patient."

Kamuzu took another look at the incision and said, "Okay, Zach, open up the incision, culture the shit, and pack the wound edges open."

"Dr. Maxwell, you have a phone call on line two," the unit secretary chimed.

"Take a message, I'm not exactly in the position to pick up a phone." He gestured, holding up bloody, pus-covered, gloved hands. He went to work on poor Mr. Cavelli removing stitches, irrigating out the yellow fat layer, and then covering the raw wound with clean gauze.

After re-bandaging, arranging for the culture to be sent, and ordering a CT, he was about to call Hercules.

"Hey, lover boy … your phone message … "

"Oh, fuck, thanks." He took the scrap of paper from the secretary.

He read the cryptic message. "I said whenever, but not never … 718-555-1017." Zach hit himself on the forehead. Fuck, Shoshie, he thought. It had been three weeks since Ike had tried to make her vomit. She expected a call and a drink, at least, but he had just gone from one crisis to another and rarely got to the apartment before midnight. At which time, his speech was so slurred from exhaustion he didn't understand himself. He had become familiar with his days like an inmate's, stuck in a jail without phone contact, and never seeing anyone except guards and other inmates. He quickly called both Ike and Hercules and notified them that Mr. Cavelli would be needing their services tonight. As predicted, Hercules sounded up for the game and Ike just moaned.

He hung up and checked the time. It was 5 p.m., she should be home. The phone rang and then, "Eh, hello?"

"Hi, is Shoshie available?"

"Who vantz ta know?" The woman who answered had an accent so deep and thick, Zach barely understood the words.

"I'm Zach Maxwell, I met Shoshie a couple of weeks … "

"Ohch za sturgeon. *Vos machts stu?*"

"Well, I'm not a surgeon. Is Shoshie there?"

"Du isht nischt a sturgeon. Du liest? Isaac, es da boychik o Shoshie. Isht nischt a sturgeon."

In the background he heard a deep, rumbly, male voice. "Vus? Nischt a sturgeon?" Then in the background he heard Shoshie's voice, "Okay, show over. Stop torturing the boy, Aunt Luva, and mind your own business, Uncle Isaac. Now, if you don't mind, give me the phone and some privacy."

Uncle Isaac yelled. "Is nischt a sturgeon, I don like it."

Shoshie sighed. "Please out, both of you."

Zach heard steps and then Shoshie came on the line. "You have any European, post-World War II relatives in San Diego? If not, I have extras I will pay you to take."

Zach chuckled. "Only my mother, but I'm used to her accent. I guess I called at a bad time, sorry."

"Oh, don't worry about it. You would have gotten the third, fourth, and fifth degree eventually. This experience will either turn you off, and you'll never call again, or it will temper you like fine steel."

"Steel is my middle name. Look, I have to apologize; it has been hectic and the only time I get is two nights usually around midnight, and I'm so tired I don't make much sense. I swear I want to at least have that drink with you. How about Sunday about seven p.m.? I'm off, so I can actually have an adult beverage."

"Well, Zach, I'm sorry I'm busy … have a date."

Zach felt shot down. What did he expect? He was sure she had a bunch of guys lined up. She wasn't going to put up with his schedule and lack of life now. "Oh, I'm sorry. Maybe some other time."

"I don't know, Zach. I mean you had three weeks to sneak a thirty-second call in. You know, 'Hi, it's Zach, not the surgeon. I'm thinking of you, but I had to go save a life or open a smelly disgusting abscess.' You know, that kind of call. In the meantime, Clara set me up with this investment banker, $400 suits. Tall, handsome. No bags under the bags under his eyes and doesn't smell of old blood and vomit."

"Oh, I mean, yeah, I understand. I guess my last line to you is always sorry. Look, I gotta go if I want to get out of here by 10 p.m. Have fun on your date, he sounds … dreamy." Zach hung up feeling strangely numb. What a shmuck he was. He didn't even know this girl, but he knew he wanted her.

"Dr. Maxwell, 2917, 2917 Dr. Maxwell." He picked up the phone and dialed the extension.

"Hey, Zach." Jake's voice came over the handset.

"What's up, Jake?"

"I'm off tonight and saw that you are, too. Thought we'd go over to Snooky's and scout the talent. Whadda ya say?"

Zach thought for a second before replying. Jake was spiraling ever closer to the sun and would soon burn. It was rumored that Sandy had permanently kicked him out of their apartment. She told him that she would always love him, but the relationship had to move forward and instead was moving backward. Instead of listening Jake had stormed out of the apartment, telling her to go fuck herself. Sandy had called him, and demanded to know what had happened to the sweet boy she had followed to New York? Most mornings on rounds, Zach could smell the booze on Jake's breath. He also knew the third floor exam room, and the volunteers and lab techs he brought there. Zach supposed the worst part was that he was neglecting his residency. Notes weren't getting written, surgeries he was supposed to scrub into usually had a substitute for his presence. His hands had started to manifest a fine tremor. Zach knew he needed saving, but Zach wondered how he'd go about it when he couldn't save himself.

"Come on, Zach, let's find us some pussy. I need my wingman."

"Not tonight, Jake. I'm too fucking tired and frankly you don't want to go either. Why don't you meet me up at the apartment? I got some cold ones in the fridge, and I'll order some Chinese. You can even crash and we can be at rounds bright and bushy-tailed."

"There is no pussy in your apartment. I need pussy, actually my dick needs the pussy. I could give a shit about the sweet young things … good for fucking only."

Zach was shocked. He had never heard a misogynistic word from his friend. Christ, he was in a bad way. "Jake, you don't want to do that. You have Sandy, she just needs you to clean up your act and meet her halfway. She doesn't want to lose you and you really don't want to lose her."

"Cunt ... "

"Jake! Stop it." Zach was genuinely shocked. What was this residency doing to everyone? "Please, just come over and we'll talk."

"Fuck you. Go home and jerk off, you Boy Scout." The line clicked off. Zach could only think the future was going to be grim for Jake. He got busy finishing the day's labors. God, he needed something besides this.

Chapter **39**

Zach finished evening rounds and set up lab and radiology orders for the morning. He put in the TPN orders so the pharmacy could make up the total parenteral nutrition fluid for the morning. This was a custom-made, expensive, intravenous fluid that was the food for patients who couldn't eat. TPN was a liquid five-course meal, i.e. calories that were infused directly into the bloodstream. Figuring out the individual patient's calorie requirements, how much fat, how many carbohydrates and vitamins, was time-consuming and exacting. Zach was proud that he had learned how to do this. He had even been complimented by Habib on his cuisine ideas. The formulations were so complicated that the orders had to be in the pharmacist's hands by a certain time, or the patient didn't get the TPN and starved for twenty-four hours.

He opened the door of his apartment at 11 p.m. Another eighteen-hour day had come to an end, when his beeper went off. He almost tossed it out the window. "2619 Dr. Maxwell, 2619, 2619. Dr. Maxwell, call the E.R." He was off, fuck, let the E.R. go find another schmuck to deal with the problem. The beeper quieted and then started up again. "2619 Dr. Maxwell, 2619, 2619."

"God fucking damn it," he cried and picked up the phone.

"E.R."

"This is Dr. Maxwell, I'm off for the evening. You paged the wrong guy."

There was a one second pause, "Hold the line, Dr. Maxwell."

"God damn it, I'm off … "

"Zach, it's Hercules. Sorry to disturb you, but I need some help. It shouldn't take more than a half-hour. Can you meet me in the E.R.?"

Zach took a deep breath. "Sure, Hercules. I'll be there in ten minutes."

"Thanks, boy. I need to get something straightened out and it can't wait. I swear I'll get you out of here as fast as possible."

"I'm on my way."

The E.R. was the usual mess. In one corner a well-known E.R. alcoholic was shivering in the classic sign of alcohol withdrawal. In one of the GYN beds, a woman was getting a vaginal exam, with total lack of privacy from a privacy curtain that never closed properly.

"Hey boy, over here," Hercules called.

Zach walked over to the gurney to find a rather pale Mr. Siegel. "Dr. Maxwell, I should have waited for you the last time I was here, but fuck, I mean I'm a healthy guy."

"I'm glad you're back, Mr. Siegel. I tried calling multiple times, but no one ever called me back. What happened?"

"I went to take a dump this morning and it hurt like a son of a bitch. Then I started bleeding like before, but it never stopped. Look at this," he cried out.

Siegel lifted the sheet to find him in very bloody boxers on a pad that was saturated with blood. No wonder he was sweaty and pale.

"Hercules, do we have a 'crit yet?"

"I need to discuss this case with you, Zach. Mr. Siegel, the nurse is going to put in another I.V. so we can give you more fluids and blood when you are type-matched. If you need to use a phone to contact anyone, ask the nurse. You won't be going home tonight."

"Okay, Dr. Christospathos. Whatever you say, I won't run again. Just stop this bleeding, please. I have a wife and kids at home." His eyes showed a fear of the future that only a condemned man would show. Zach felt sick to his stomach. He should have gotten Shusterman or Hercules to recheck this guy. He fucked up and now his patient was going to die.

"Dr. Maxwell, let's go." Hercules led him out of the E.R. and down to the coffee shop that this time of the night was open, but empty. They got cups of black, bitter coffee from the urn and went to a booth in back. "Zach, what happened?"

"I fucked up. I should have admitted him when I felt the tumor. I knew he had cancer, but I let him go and ... "

"I checked the old E.R. chart. You examined him and then it says you were going to call for a senior resident consult. The next entry in the chart says the patient eloped so no instructions could be generated. What happened with the consult?"

"Look, Hercules. This was my fault. The guy is going to die because of me. He is going to make his kids fatherless and wife a widow." Zach felt an ache in his chest and his eyes became moist. The room seemed to contract about him and he had problems breathing.

"Yes, it is your fault," Hercules said. "But not the way you probably think. Why didn't you call me when Chenoiel threw this guy out?"

Zach went rigid. He didn't want to bring Chenoiel into this mess. The chart had no note from Chenoiel about his consult. There was no proof of his being involved in the case, and Zach knew if he told Hercules of the crappy consult, it would just look like he was just trying to pass the blame onto a fellow resident who was hated by Zach. "I never got the consult. It was busy and I slipped up. I guess I figured it had to be hemorrhoids."

"Well, that is not how the patient remembered it. He remembers Dr. Chenoiel very well. He remembers the first time he came in with rectal bleeding, and remembers Chenoiel telling him that he didn't need a recheck of your findings. That he could refuse the rectal. So, I ask you again, why didn't you call me?"

Zach was silent. The damage was done and he should pay for it.

"Dr. Maxwell, you are guilty, not of improper diagnosis, not of being lazy. You are guilty of not having the strength of your convictions. You were correct, you knew you were correct, but you let outside influences silence you."

"I'll resign the residency. I am truly sorry." Zach felt suicidal. He deserved what he was about to get. Hercules was right. He had no guts. He didn't deserve this career.

"Sorry, too easy a way out and you will have no way to ever redeem yourself." Hercules looked at Zach. "Listen boy, we all go through a Siegel moment. Some of us may go through more than one. The good docs do, unfortunately. You will learn to rely on your own gut instinct. It is certainly good to get second opinions, run additional testing, consult a Ouija board. Sometimes, no, all the time, you need options for your patients. There is no patient whose picture is on page 422 of *Sabiston's Surgery*. Every patient is an individual, as his illness is. Your purpose during your residency is to see as many, and treat as many patients as you can. You need to become a diagnostician using what your eyes see, what your nose smells, and what your fingers feel. Your brain will then compare those sensations of the patient with other cases you have examined, and literature you have read. Then you work out the best treatment plan you can. Last, but not the least, never let someone who has not examined the patient dictate against your judgment. Chenoiel led you right into the sewer, and now Mr. Siegel is in there with you."

Hercules stood up. "For what it's worth, Chenoiel will have

some explaining to do. I hope he is smart enough to come clean. Now go home."

"I'll go and admit him."

"No Zach, go home, get some rest. I'm taking him up to the O.R., and stop the bleeding. Tomorrow we will sit, and try to save his life.

Chapter 40

He was tired. He couldn't lift his head. The last hour with Hercules had crushed him. To someone observing him, he looked like a question mark. The elevator doors opened, and he fumbled in his pocket for his keys. She was waiting by his door.

"Shoshie, what are you doing here?" Zach was genuinely confused. She was out with a date. What had happened? "Are you okay?"

"I'm fine, Zach. What happened to you? You look like the world has ended."

"I, uh ... " He couldn't tell this stranger of a girl he had probably killed someone. He didn't want her to see him this way, nauseated, with moist eyes. "I'm just really tired. It's been a bad day and I need to get some sleep, because tomorrow isn't going to be any better."

She stood by the door waiting. "Aren't you going to invite me in, Zach?"

"Uh, look, I don't want to be rude, but it just isn't a good night. In fact, it's probably not a good year. I'll take you downstairs. Is your date down there?"

"I don't have anyone with me."

"You told me you were going out on a date. Did he just dump you in this neighborhood? Doesn't he know this neighborhood boasts the highest murder and rape rate in the five boroughs?"

"Zach, I came alone. I am sorry, I fibbed about the date. Please open the door and invite me in."

"Great fake, Shoshie. I really thought you had moved on. Look, under normal circumstances I'd love it that you are here, and there wasn't another guy, but I don't think this will work out. Besides it is almost midnight and the cabs don't come into this neighborhood after one in the morning. You'll get stuck till at least five, and Uncle Isaac will be worried and angry, not necessarily in that order."

"Just open the door. Uncle Isaac is not your concern."

Zach bowed to the inevitable, opened the door and followed her in. The moment he closed the door, she enveloped him in her arms, holding him tightly. She kissed him gently on his lips. She led him to the couch, and lay him down with his head on her lap, stroking his chest. "Whatever it is Zach, it will be okay. Now rest, close your eyes, I'm here."

Zach did as he was told and mumbled, "So, how did you get your name, Shoshie?"

"I'm named after my aunt Shoshana. She was a dancer, too. I never met her, but I did have one picture of her in a tutu and on pointe."

"Why didn't you meet her?" Zach slurred, his eyes slowly closing.

"She didn't make it out of the camp."

Light streamed through the windows and Zach woke with a start. His first sight was of the most beautiful eyes he had ever seen. The light picked up their flecks of gold making them seem otherworldly. Then the panic set in. "Fuck, what time is it?"

"Don't worry, it's 5:15. You have at least twenty minutes to walk across the street," Shoshie responded, smiling. "I wouldn't have let you oversleep."

"Thanks, uh, did you sit on the couch a whole night with me on top of you … jeez that didn't come out right. You must be exhausted."

"Strangely, I feel fine. I think I closed my eyes for a while, but if you would be so kind as to get moving so I can get a cab and be back at Uncle Isaac's before he figures out I was gone."

Zach was embarrassed. "Oh, yeah, sorry." He got off the couch looking confused. "Why did you come over last night?"

Shoshie got off the couch, and picked up her coat and clutch, and headed for the door. "I don't know, Zach. I think you need someone, and I know I do, even as just friends. I'm glad I came. This was one of the much better non-dates I have ever been on. By the way, you snore." She walked out the door, leaving Zach wishing the night was not over.

He jumped into the shower and changed into fresh scrubs. Feeling better, he went out the door to face his future, if he still had one.

The beeper went off, "Dr. Maxwell 3644, Dr. Maxwell, call Dr. Moskowitz at 3644. Dr. Maxwell call … " Zach ran into the main hospital and picked up a page phone. He had shaking hands as he dialed the number.

"Dr. Moskowitz's office," the voice of Phyllis, Bullshit's smoke-shrouded secretary answered.

"Phyllis, this is Zach. Dr. Moskowitz paged me?"

"Yeah, Zach, the old man has been looking for you. He is in his sanctum with Hercules, and the room is shaking from the sonic booms of them yelling. Did you get caught stealing extra blintzes from the cafeteria? Get over here, stat. They're giving me a migraine."

Zach made it to the office in one minute, twelve seconds—a

new record if there were records. He was out of breath and sweating by the time he opened the outer office door. He figured Bullshit was about to give him his walking papers. Zach wondered if he could find a residency in Alaska.

"Oh, there you are. What took you so long?" She picked up the phone and buzzed Moskowitz's inner office. "Young Dr. Maxwell is here."

She hung up, the door to the inner office exploded open, and like the three-headed dog of Hades, "Zach, get your fuckin' ass in here," Moskowitz commanded.

Zach was so scared he froze.

"Move, now!"

He moved and went in, to find Hercules pacing the office, and Ike standing in a corner looking like he'd rather be at his own funeral. The door slammed shut, and Moskowitz sat heavily down behind the massive wood desk covered with stacks of papers. Behind him hung plaques attesting to one of the great surgeons and educators in the world.

"What the mudderfucking piece of unholy shit did you allow to happen in my hospital, boy?" Moskowitz yelled.

"Now, now, Dr. Moskowitz, remember your blood pressure," Hercules said, trying to diffuse the situation.

"My blood pressure is not the only thing exploding. Chenoiel's father is an asshole, but he is also a bigshot. He has influence on the board, and he will come after you, me, and Maxwell. He can't do much to me, he probably won't do much to you, though he might make it hard for you to get privileges here, but Maxwell ... I need to keep Chenoiel in the residency. Take my word for it, I would rather toss Chenoiel as far as I can, but ... well, there you have it." Bullshit put his head in his hands and rubbed his temples.

"Dr. Moskowitz, I should be punished. If I had asked for a review from Hercules or any of the other senior residents, maybe

Mr. Siegel would have a better chance of survival. I will resign, if that helps this situation."

"You will not resign, you will be fired if I so choose, and I don't so choose, so don't martyr yourself so quickly," Bullshit growled. "You're correct, you should have reviewed with another senior, but unfortunately the residency programs themselves discourage this. You are only really guilty of following rules and traditions assholes such as myself and the other fucking residency directors set up."

Hercules was deep in thought when he blurted out, "That might work. Maybe you and I should excuse young Maxwell here to get back to scut puppy duties, and we can discuss solutions."

With that Zach was excused by a wave of Bullshit's hand and an admonition to stay out of trouble. "And Zach, stay away from Siegel at least until we talk to him and his family."

Zach left Moskowitz's inner office, and immediately started hyperventilating.

"Zach, take it easy. Slow, even breaths," Phyllis instructed. "You're going to pass out, and then I'm going to have to call the Cardiac Arrest Team, because I don't know the difference between a twit who hyperventilated himself into a vasovagal syncopal episode and true cardiac standstill. I'm just a dumb secretary to you resident geniuses," she said with a smirk.

Zach couldn't help himself and started laughing.

"That's better, boy. I wish I could tell you 100 percent not to worry, but don't. Bullshit never throws a man he thinks could make a good doctor to the fucking administrative wolves. Besides, he hates Chenoiel and his father. He considers them both bottom-feeders and fake physicians. Between him and Hercules, they'll come up with a plan."

Zach's breathing had returned to normal and his light-headedness had disappeared. "You really think I'll survive this? I fucked up bad."

"Yeah, you did, but everyone has had a case that they really screwed up. You should hear about Hercules's case when he was an intern, or Ike's, and I'm sure if anyone was alive during the dinosaur era, Bullshit's case. Everyone experiences the darkness to become a good and careful physician. You're no exception, and no one aside from Bullshit and I understand this better."

"You, huh." Zach smiled. "How many years have you been at that desk?"

"Thirty-five years and counting. I've seen the greats and not so greats come and go. Now get out of here. I'm sure someone needs a disimpaction somewhere."

"Thanks, Phyllis," he said as he left to disimpact.

Chapter **41**

"**Dr. Maxwell, report to** three North, three North."

Well, at least it's not a stat call, he thought.

"Hey, boy," Hercules called out. Zach went over to him at the nursing desk. "Come on, I need to talk to you."

Zach's heart skipped a beat. What did he do now? He swore if he made it through the residency he was going to retire. Yeah, with $200,000 in school loans, I'll retire, he thought.

Hercules took him into an unused room. "We need to set some rules about Mr. Siegel. First thing is ... "

"Wait, Hercules, I thought Bullshit wanted me to stay away from him."

"Well, Mr. Siegel had other ideas. He told Bullshit he wanted you on the case. That you knew what you were doing when you saw him, that you offered him good advice on your findings and told him to follow up with his primary care doctor. Then he blamed Bullshit for hiring a guy like Chenoiel. He said he wouldn't sue, but as a token of Bullshit's and the hospital's gratitude, you were going to run the case."

"I can't run that case. I fucked up already. I'm going to be responsible for his death. Why would he want me?"

Hercules took a breath, then sighed. "Because you are a real doctor."

"I'm not.... "

"Oh, I agree with you."

Zach was crestfallen. "I, uh … "

"I should have said you're not a doctor if you're just measuring knowledge base or maybe judgment based on experience. Those things will come. But Siegel is right, you are a doctor. You care about the patients you treat, and work hard to learn what you don't know. I saw it with your first almost-solo case."

"My first solo case? What are you talking about?"

"That Puerto Rican-Jewish woman with the diabetic foot, Mrs. Hernandez? I'm pleased to report that I saw her last week in the clinic and her half-foot was great and her sugars were stable. She also told me she lost ten pounds. See what I mean? I doubt anyone looks at these cases like you do. Mrs. Hernandez probably thinks you saved her life, and she feels so much better because of you."

"Wasn't me. She did it all on her own."

Hercules looked skeptical. "Maybe, but you had a lot to do with her lifespan increasing at least ten years. She'll probably make it to see her grandkids enter college. She may even be able to walk down the aisle at their weddings because of you. She knows she has a good doctor, has faith in him and wants to please him. Same as Siegel. True, you failed him, but he is a man who understands being new, young, facing a hierarchy and trying his best to make the system work. Unfortunately, he also realizes the day he started bleeding, his fate was sealed. Zach, Mr. Siegel is going to die no matter what happens. Your little episode with him didn't kill him. His disease killed him way before he saw you the first time."

"If we can't save him, why is he here? And if I can't treat him, why does he want me?"

Hercules smiled, and got up off the desk he was leaning against. "I told you, he knows you are a good doctor and trusts that you will take the best care of him you can. Go examine him.

Figure out what needs to be done. I might recommend some library time on advanced anal carcinoma, especially papers from U.C. San Francisco." With that he left the room, and Zach feeling elated that he had potential—and scared because it was a losing game.

Chapter 42

Zach could hear a ringing in the distance. He opened his eyes but all he could register was a fog surrounding him. It couldn't be 5 a.m. yet, he had just gotten to sleep. It had been an emotionally trying day. He had gone to see Siegel right after Hercules had ordered him back on the case. He still didn't know how he had the strength to open the door to his room. The ringing was louder and he recognized it for what it was, his phone. God dammit, he thought. He told Clara never to call him at this hour.

He reached over and picked up the handset. "Clara, I told you not to call me at midnight. I'm hanging up right now."

"If it was Clara I would certainly hang up on her, but if you want any chance of a loving girlfriend, and I'm not saying that your chances are probable, I wouldn't be so fast slamming your phone down."

"Shit, Shoshie, it's you."

"And how the fuck are you? After our platonic night in sin, I expected communication. Are you, or are we, okay?"

"Oh, Shoshie, I seem to be forever apologizing. I'm sorry. I've been busy with a real emotional case that, along with the rest of the residency crap, is making it difficult to pick up a phone. I won't bore you."

"Why don't you tell me about it, slurred words and all, Zach?"

Zach felt so tired. He realized he must sound drunk to her

as his tongue seemed to want to go to sleep along with the rest of him. Shit, it was now after midnight. He had to get up in less than five hours. Yet he wanted to talk to her. She wasn't a jaded resident or a taskmaster attending. Still, he realized to the outside world the workings of patient care in the hospital could be disgusting, scary, and often cruel. He didn't want to scare her away or let her form an impression that he was a callous man.

"Shoshie, I would very much like to talk to you, but I'm exhausted and chances are you won't understand my mumbling," he uttered.

"I have an idea, Zach. Why don't I volunteer to be your sounding board? Even if I can't understand you, at least in your current state of mumbling, you'll have gotten some of the problems off your chest. I'll hang up when I hear you snoring." She chuckled.

"Some friend you're getting. I'll probably bore you to death."

"Let me worry about that. Besides, if it gets too tedious, I'll just do my nails and use you as background noise."

"Sounds like a deal. I'm off this Sunday. Can I ask you out on an official date?"

"Oh, a date. I'm not sure my official boyfriend would like that," she retorted. "So far we haven't even shaken hands."

"Well, you did slug me. I still think you took an unfair shot there, but that should count for something, and we did sleep together."

He heard her laughing, "First, there was nothing unfair about slugging you. You deserved it, and it woke you up as to what a diamond you were missing out on. Second, we didn't sleep together. You snored, and I was awake. The only bodily fluid we shared was you drooling on me. By the way, you should have offered to pay for dry cleaning my outfit."

"If I reimbursed you for the cleaning, I would have absolutely no money to take you out with. As it is, you'll be able to order anything on the menu that is a single digit before the period."

"Oh, a big spender, aren't you?"

"Well, they tell me I have potential."

She giggled. "Okay, Dr. Rockefeller, why don't you tell me what went on today. I have nails that look like they built a road."

Zach started telling her about Siegel, and before long he had slurred himself into a deep sleep.

43

The beeper went off. "Dr. Maxwell, 3505, Dr. Maxwell, 3505." Zach went to the nurses' station and dialed the number.

"This is Dr. Maxwell, I was paged."

"No one here paged you, Dr. Maxwell," the unit secretary responded. "Maybe the operator got the number confused. Ain't nobody here 'cept me. I wouldn't know how you got a page from the desk. Wait a second." Zach heard conversation in the background and then a lot of phone noise.

"Dr. Maxwell," the disembodied voice came from the receiver.

"This is he."

"Can you come down and see Mr. Siegel? He is looking pale and we lost his peripheral line."

"Fuck, he doesn't have any peripheral veins left. I guess we are going to have to schedule him for a port. I'll call Dr. Christospathos and try to arrange it as an add-on case."

"What do we do in the meantime?"

Zach thought. "Depends on what time his case runs. I'll call you in a bit."

Zach disconnected from the floor, and paged Hercules. "What's up, boy?

Zach admired how Hercules never seemed ruffled by anything. He wondered if he'd ever get to that state of Zen. "Hercules, Siegel needs a port. He blew his last I.V. and he had next to zero peripherals. Besides, the nurse reports he looks pale. Maybe he is bleeding again."

"Damn, boy, but I agree. Siegel is in for the long course, we better get better access into him. A port would work out fine, but I'm afraid it isn't going to happen today. Some *vlakas* on the BQE thought he could cut across three lanes to get to an exit. One problem with that."

"He was a fucking idiot."

"Good translation of vlakas, but no, he didn't apply the Pauli Exclusion Principle, no two objects can occupy the same space at the same time. He made a mess and we are going to be in the O.R. for hours cleaning it up. Put in a central line and start him on total parenteral nutrition until we can sort things out. Gotta go, boy. Later."

Zach went down to Siegel's room. He walked in and noticed a smell, sickly sweet. It was the smell of a dying man. Siegel had lost about twenty pounds. His eyes had sunken into their orbits and his skin had a yellow tone due to metastasis in his liver. Zach knew that the treatments weren't going to work. Why are we torturing him?

"Mr. Siegel, the nurse called me and said your I.V. wasn't working and you weren't eating. You need calories to keep up your strength and to fight the cancer."

"I try to eat, Dr. Maxwell, but everything tastes like shit and nauseates me. Even water has lost its taste, and water has no taste. What are we going to do about that?"

"I spoke to Dr. Christospathos and he recommended a port so you can get some of the calories and vitamins and minerals you need. A port is a small tube we put in a vein in your chest and connect to a small reservoir also buried in the chest. Then the nurse just punctures it to give you a special formulation of fats, carbohydrates, and the vitamins and minerals. The nurses won't have to hunt for a vein anymore."

"Another surgery, oh no, please, not another surgery." Siegel was sobbing. "I can't handle another surgery. I don't want the port. I don't want more pain. Please!"

Zach had never seen such a response to a simple procedure, and he frankly didn't know what to do except what felt natural to him. He took Siegel's hand in both of his, and when this didn't feel adequate, put his arms around Siegel and tried to comfort him as he would a child.

"Joe, I'm sorry you have to go through this, I really am. I know it isn't fair but you have to deal with it today. Hopefully, tomorrow will be better," Zach told Siegel. They were in this together, Zach by circumstance of not having the guts to fight for what he knew was right for his patient, and Siegel by bad luck or genetics.

Siegel calmed. "I'm sorry, you don't need to deal with water-works, and I'm sure you have better and more important things to do."

"Not really, and anyway, I've already cleaned enough bed-sores today. Hercules says when we hit our quota for the day, we get ten minutes to do anything we damn well please, but then back to the salt mines. Look Joe, putting a port in will decrease the pain of constantly trying to find a vein. It is done under a local anes-thetic with sedation. You won't even know it's happening. Please let Hercules put it in. It will help and maybe decrease the time you need to be in the hospital."

"Yeah, sure, do what you want." Siegel was staring out into space, his speech monotone, tears forming at the corners of his eyes. "You met my eldest, Harry?"

"We met, good kid."

"The best. You know, he was a thirty-week preemie. We thought we were going to lose him, lung problems, but he fought and fought. He survived, then battled reading disabilities, some more minor things, but he fought and won. He's studying for his bar mitzvah. He takes it so seriously. He told me he feels God pushing him to learn. Every day that kid sits, and it's like he tastes every letter in Hebrew that makes up his *haftarah*. You know what a haftarah is, Dr. Maxwell?"

"Yes, I know. I had some problems with mine in the day."

"God, he works so hard. He says he wants to make it perfect so his grandfather in heaven will know that he survived the Nazis for a purpose." Siegel suddenly gripped Zach's shoulder and intensely locked eyes with him. "I have to live to see his bar mitzvah, promise me Zach."

Zach couldn't breathe. His pulse felt like a jackhammer in his skull, and nausea was welling up from his abdomen. How could he make such a promise? Siegel was going to die, and die soon. His death wouldn't be the clean, quick end of a heart attack, a stroke, or even trauma. This would be a messy, disgusting death filled with surgeries, large needles, tubes in orifices, and indignities that God should never have one of his children suffer through. He couldn't promise. Siegel needed honesty and transparency, not lies and smoke.

Zach was about to tell him he couldn't make this kind of promise, but as he looked at Siegel, he realized this man's last request was all that was keeping him alive and sane. "I'll make sure you hear him sing for you and his grandfather, Joe."

Chapter 44

"**What do you mean** I'm not scrubbing today?" Chenoiel was on the warpath. Zach had heard that some of the attending staff refused to let Chenoiel operate on their patients. During his time as a medical student and a resident, Zach had never heard of such an action. PAY, being a teaching hospital, existed to teach young doctors. By not allowing Chenoiel to operate, the teachers were basically ending any surgical career he may have had. Chenoiel was angry, and it was obvious from his wild look he was going to blow a gasket any moment. He was also yelling at Lucas, who obviously didn't give a crap about Chenoiel and was the one who held the power over assigning junior residents to cases.

"I swear I'll go to Hercules and Bullshit about this. It will be you and not me who rots on the wards changing bandages."

Lucas, looking unperturbed by Chenoiel's wild man scene, quietly replied, "Chenoiel, I don't know that God has smiled on our patients and kept your inadequate knowledge and services away from them, but I for one am happy, and may even go to church on Sunday to thank God for this miracle. Now stop making a scene and get up to the floor. There is scut work to do, and I'm designating you scut puppy of the month. Now git!"

Chenoiel's mouth fell open. "I swear you'll pay for this, Lucas."

Lucas pulled out a toothpick, and proceeded to pop it in his mouth and chew on it. "Whatcha goin' to do, cry to your daddy, the wrinkle eraser? I mean, is that even being a doctor? Get the fuck out of here before I forbid you to touch any of our patients."

Chenoiel stomped off as Zach went over to Lucas. "Man, did you think maybe you were a little too honest with Chenoiel? I mean you might catch hell from Hercules or Bullshit over keeping Chenoiel out of the O.R."

Lucas almost whispered to Zach. "Who do you think told me to keep him out of the O.R.?"

Zach was shocked. "Aren't they worried about Chenoiel senior?"

"I don't know, chief. That's way above my pay grade. Now go scrub into the hernia with Rupak. I hear you're lucky; he's only in a shitty mood today. Probably didn't get his crown spit polished by his wife last night." Lucas winked at Zach and wandered down the hall. Zach took the hint and ran to the scrub room.

Chapter 45

Zach made another quick check in the mirror and didn't like what he saw. He was taking on aspects of his grandfather's face, and that scared him. The bags under his eyes, the yellow tinge of his skin, the lusterless hair, all symptoms of the mushroom existence he was living. He tried to remember when he had spent any length of time under the sun. Aside from dashing across the two-lane street to go from hospital to apartment and apartment to hospital, it was about zero. He scratched at his chest and neck. Fuck, this button-down shirt and burnt-orange corduroy sports coat were the pits. He was used to old cotton scrubs. Laundered a million times, the only components in the fabric were soft cotton and the fine steel threads that held the thing together. He took a sniff of his pits, thought the Mennen was holding, and left his apartment for his first date with Shoshie.

He maneuvered the ancient, faded green, Yugoslavian Toyota Corolla given to him by a graduating pathology resident through the streets of Brooklyn. He passed the bodega where both Dominican ampicillin and heroin were sold. Crossing the border of East New York, he was in Canarsie, home of Grabstein's Fine Deli and the thick-crust, train station pizza shop. Up to this point, most of the faces were black, and suspicious of a white boy cruising the streets. In Canarsie, they were mostly Italian men and young

Jewish families with their parents in tow, some still showing the blue numbers tattooed on their forearms. The houses here were still rundown, but the yards were mowed and all the buildings had intact windows. Finally, he made it to Mill Basin, home of Uncle Isaac, Aunt Luva, and Shoshie. Shoshie had told him her uncle had come to the States after the war with three other brothers. One of them was Shoshie's father, who, with her other uncle, lived in Boston. Isaac lived in Brooklyn and her other uncle, Max, lived in Queens. Of the brothers, Isaac was the most successful. He had apprenticed in the tailor trade and worked for a men's clothing store. In the garden apartment of his building, he had a full tailor's shop where he fitted and repaired clothes.

Zach walked up the steps and rang the doorbell. The door opened instantaneously, leading Zach to believe the family were either clairvoyant, or he had been under surveillance since he parked. An older woman with white-blond hair answered.

"Witamy. Du es dere doctor?"

"I'm sorry, I don't … " A gruff voice erupted from behind the woman. "What do you want? Fix that sports coat? It's a piece of shit. What an eyesore. For $500, I'll tailor you a suit." He was a medium-sized man with muscular arms and a semi-flat middle. His hair was steel gray, and his accent was middle European and thick. He spoke English and his wife spoke—Zach had no idea. He had picked up some Yiddish, some Russian, some German, and what he could guess was Polish, in the older woman.

"No, I'm Zach Maxwell. I came to take Shoshie for dinner."

"Shoshie for dinner," said the man, "We didn't know she was going out. She is too young to be going out." The man turned toward the stairs in the house and shouted, "Shoshie, were you planning on going out? I promised my brother we'd keep you from getting into trouble. If you made plans, tell this young man you can't go out till I find a chaperone."

Zach heard the word chaperone and thought he misheard.

"Sir, a chaperone? We were planning just to go to dinner in Brooklyn Heights. I'll have her back right after dinner."

"Uncle Isaac, you should be ashamed of yourself roughing up a potential suitor. Didn't Aunt Luva and you tell me to find a husband when I got here from Boston? Well, this is an attempt, and now you probably scared him off. Damn, he is going to be a surgeon soon, and would have had the potential to buy a mansion that the whole family could move into. Think of the fun. You would do the gardening, Luva and Ma would cook, Daddy would bartend and wash the cars. Besides, I'm pregnant and he is the father. No marriage, and you have a bastard nephew or niece. Wouldn't the busybody neighbors be interested?"

"Excuse me, young lady. While your family would be employed as domestic servants, what would you be doing?" Uncle Isaac asked.

"Oh, I would be the doctor's, no, the surgeon's wife. You know, up at 11 a.m., at the mall for the latest Chanel bag by 1 p.m. after lunch with my fellow surgeons' wives, and then back home by 6:30 to shower, perfume, and get into the sexiest outfit I have to entice my husband into making babies for Ma to take care of." She stopped suddenly and smiled. "Employ the family? No, you all get room and board in the servants' quarters." She laughed. "I mean, the surgeon and I need some privacy to fertilize those eggs. Daddy will explain that to you."

Uncle Isaac turned to Zach, who after hearing all this, had almost virtually turned to stone. He didn't think he'd leave the stoop alive ... fertilize the eggs?

Uncle Isaac started guffawing, and Aunt Luva just shook her head. "You were always a smart-mouth. Go have a good time and be back at a reasonable hour. You have want ads to answer tomorrow." He turned to Zach. "No funny business. I promised my brother, plus I own a shotgun."

Chapter 46

The smell of Lebanese spices and grilled lamb were melding with the soft Middle Eastern music coming from the old tape deck in the restaurant. The atmosphere had transformed to exotic Araby from smelly Brooklyn. Jake had once recommended this place as a romantic restaurant filled with exotic food and erotic smells. Having little knowledge of the neighborhoods that made up Brooklyn, aside from the one PAY was in, Zach decided that exploration to the unknown might also be a part of his new life. Maybe one that included Shoshie. They were seated at a small table covered with a white tablecloth, a small lit tea candle, and shiny flatware.

"So, my uncle told you about the shotgun? He has had to use it on only one of my boyfriends."

Zach laughed. "And what was this boyfriend's offense, if I might ask?"

"Oh, that boyfriend really committed no offense. Which is why he got shot. You see, when after the third date he didn't try anything, I was so offended that I told Isaac he tried to make a move on me. Poor boy, he never knew what hit him."

"So, I see dating you is dangerous. If you don't beat the boy up, you have him shot."

"Something like that," she replied, while absently twirling her hair. The candlelight reflected in her eyes. God, she was beautiful. Zach couldn't understand why she wasn't involved with a guy.

"So, how was your day, Zach?"

"I got a better idea. Let's talk about you. How was your day, and what want ads are you supposed to check?"

"Your life is more interesting. It would probably make better conversation."

"How about a glass of something alcoholic as an inducement to loosen your tongue?" He signaled the waitress and ordered two glasses of the cheapest wine on the menu. Residents didn't make much and Brooklyn wasn't cheap.

"Well," she started, "my day started with a cup of instant coffee. Luva and Isaac, being suave Europeans, drink only Lipton tea, but have an old jar of Folgers for guests. I opened the *New York Times* and looked at the job offerings. I wanted to be a kept woman when I arrived here from Boston, but Isaac had other ideas … and that shotgun. I found a bunch of secretarial jobs, but while I was an English major I am not that great at keyboards or computers. I kept looking for a dancer job, but alas, each ad advertised 'EROTIC' and 'LARGE CHESTED' and as you can see, Mommy didn't make me that way. Besides, when I studied dance, flat-chested and long-limbed were the requirements. I wonder what has changed."

"Well, being a surgeon, I know there is a cure for the former."

"So, Dr. Hotshot, you don't like what you see," Shoshie said indignantly.

"No, no. I don't think you should change a thing, but as a healer I can offer treatments."

"Two points off, mister, no matter the purdy words." She scowled. She saw he took her seriously and laughed. "Take it easy, Zach. They may be small, but they are cute and I am happy with them. Seriously, the day was a bore. It is tough to find a job in N-Y-C, yet I need one. I have a goal of moving out of Isaac's. He is a love, but there is no privacy, and I'm twenty-six years old and don't need or wish to have a chaperone for the rest of my single days."

"Maybe you can find a job at PAY. It is one of the bigger employers in the area. You could go to Human Resources and find out if there is something that might interest you."

"Maybe. Hmm, if I come, I don't want you to think I'm chasing after you."

"I promise I won't think that, but maybe I came up with the idea so I could chase after you."

"Great idea. Okay, let's eat. What's good here?"

Zach laughed. "I have no idea. Let's have an adventure."

Chapter 47

"Sandy, this is a pleasant surprise. What brings you out to our very dangerous world? More so, does Jake know you are here?"

He saw that Sandy was fidgeting and was concerned that Jake might show up at any minute. He loved them both, but he realized that he had neither the strength nor the power to make these two realize how much they needed and loved each other.

"Have you seen Jake lately, Zach?"

"Well, here and there. Sometimes on rounds," Zach replied. He didn't want to get into the fight they had had, nor Jake's increase in alcohol intake. "We both have been really busy. You know the residency has a way of eating up even personal time."

"Bullshit!"

"Excuse me, what's bullshit?"

"I know he got into a fight with you. I know he has been drinking heavily, and I know he has been fucking whatever warm, wet slit he can find. I hate it, but I have to accept it for now. You and I have bigger problems where he is concerned."

Zach felt uncomfortable. He knew as Jake's friend he should have tried harder with Jake, but shit, it was just so tough, between dying patients, Chenoiel, and the politics of the residency. "I didn't realize he had told you we had a falling out. Really Sandy, it isn't the end of the world. I'm sure we will patch things up when the pressure decreases."

"Christ, what is the fucking matter with you guys? You don't even care that you are falling apart. You are turning into a species unto yourselves. The Jake and the Zach I knew and loved are unrecognizable to me."

"Sandy, you're exaggerating. It's a little fight. Friends have them all the time. We will patch it up. I'm more worried about what happened to the relationship between you and Jake. He is hurting, I can tell."

"No shit. He is now so hurt that he is calling me at 2 a.m., and threatening to either jump, medicate, or perform surgery on himself."

"What?"

"You don't understand. This is how a surgical resident tells you that suicide is an option for him. You didn't even realize, and you essentially live in the same fucking house he does. Fucking PAY. I hate this place." Sandy walked off.

Zach shook himself as if he had just woken from a nightmare. He ran a few steps and grabbed Sandy by the arm.

"What the fuck are you doing? Let go of me this minute."

Zach let her go. "Sandy, you have to believe me. I care about Jake, but he won't take any help, evidently including mine or yours. If he is suicidal we need to notify … "

"Notify his chief? Are you kidding? You know what will happen if we notify anyone. They will boot him from the residency and then they'll take his license away. Even if he gets better, he will hate us both for the rest of his life and we will have destroyed his dream. He will never be a surgeon. Might as well let him take the pills, buy the gun, buy a rope, whatever."

"I don't think … "

"That's right, you don't think, but you do understand his dream to be a doctor, and to be something great. Isn't it the same dream you have?"

Zach was silent. That someone he considered his good friend

could be hurting that bad, and he didn't even seem to care was inexcusable. But he did care. Unfortunately, he was wavering on just the other side of a mental line that Jake had already crossed.

"Well?"

"I don't know what to say, Sandy. I don't … "

"Fuck you, Zach. With friends like you, why should Jake even care, and truthfully, with a girlfriend like me who loves him so much that I decided to have a child with him, well, fuck me too."

She started crying. Zach gently hugged her. He was in shock from the news that his friend was about to become a father. "Sandy, does he know?"

She just shook her head and walked down the hall.

Chapter **48**

Siegel had taken a turn for the worse. His abdominal midline incision, the result of his surgical anterior resection of the rectum to remove the tumor, had failed. The first sign was a redness to the sutured skin edges, and thin yellow fluid seeping through. In a hope that the infection would be beat, samples of the fluid were sent to the lab to plate in Petri dishes. If something grew out, it would be tested against multiple antibiotics to see which one would kill it. Within twenty-four hours, a collection of fluid had formed under Siegel's skin in the subcutaneous tissue and fat. Zach was forced to clip out all the skin sutures and wash out the sickly-looking fat below. He feared that the subsequent layers would also get infected, and eventually all the layers of the abdominal wall would open, completely exposing the viscera. This was called dehiscence, and a very bad sign for the future of Siegel's life.

Zach went to find Hercules and Ike. He had cultured the fluid, and an appropriate antibiotic was started. Siegel was still spiking temps and he was losing weight.

"He is dying, Zach. His body is burning through the limited amount of calories we can provide to him through TPN. He doesn't have the energy to make new tissue, so his wounds won't heal. In addition, did you notice how bloated his abdomen is?"

"Yes, but I don't know where the bloat is coming from, unless he is forming abscesses in the abdomen. I ordered a CAT scan to check, otherwise I come up with zero."

Hercules put on gloves and palpated the abdomen, and then said to Siegel, "I have to check something, but it may hurt."

Siegel, who half the time slept, and the other part of his day was too groggy or narcotized to really know what was going on, said, "Yeah, do whatever. Do your job. I don't care."

Hercules leaned down near Siegel's face and locked eyes with his patient. "You have to care, sir. Your life depends on it. If you are not hopeful, you will die quickly. If you can't be hopeful for yourself, be hopeful for your son, who will always tie his big event with your illness in his mind, no matter the outcome."

Siegel croaked. "I just don't know if I have the strength. I try, but the pain and the waiting for anything to change are mentally impossible."

Hercules gently squeezed Siegel's hand, and let it go. "Okay, I'll be fast." He took the index and middle fingers of his left hand, and laid them flat on Siegel's abdominal skin, and tapped, producing a drum-like sound. Siegel let out a yelp. He was very pale, and had a cold sweat. "Please, no more."

"No, Mr. Siegel, no more of this. I will send in a nurse to give you some morphine. I'll be back when your wife arrives to discuss our plan to treat your recent problem."

Hercules led them out of Siegel's room and into a small conference room. He grabbed the phone and paged Rupak to come and meet them. He arrived minutes later.

"Zach, what does my exam mean?"

"He has peritoneal signs. There is an infection in his abdomen, which unless we can treat it, will definitely kill him," Zach responded.

"Good, now, what are the signs of sepsis, Zach?"

Zach thought, and said, "Could be an elevated or low white count, a high lactic acid, low blood pressure, tachycardia … "

"And possibly hypothermia," Rupak said. "Hercules, if this guy has any chance at all we need to dump in a gallon of the strongest antibiotics we have, and then take him into the O.R. for the hunt, and see."

Hercules drummed his finger on the worn conference table in front of him. "We could kill him even attempting to put him under with anesthesia."

"But, we know he will die if we don't try to clean out his abdomen and secure that abdominal wall."

Zach was feeling more and more the witness to an execution. His guilt over his part of this death sentence would never leave him emotionally, but intellectually, rectal cancer was deadly, even with treatment.

"Well, boys, I think this may be one of the times we need to present the patient and his wife with options, and then let them decide. I just wish we had better options to give," Hercules said. "Zach, look at the results of the cultures and see if the antibiotics we started are adequate. Also, make sure his nurse pages you as soon as Siegel's wife comes."

They left the room to separately think about how they were going to tell Mrs. Siegel her husband was going to die, no matter what.

Chapter 49

"**Hey shithead, what were you** doing with my fiancé?"

Zach slowly turned from the chart he was reading at the nurses' station and confronted Jake. Jake's hair was disheveled, and he was sporting a three-day growth of beard. It didn't look as if he had changed his scrubs or white coat in days, and even from ten feet away, Zach thought he smelled of old alcohol mixed with even older sweat. He didn't want a public confrontation with Jake. Like a small town, hospitals were hotbeds of rumors, gossip, and innuendo. Once something was put out there, and heard by a doctor, nurse, or attendant, the news spread like a forest fire through dry trees and brush.

"Hey, Jake, let's go to the call room."

"Why, my best friend? I'm okay with talking here. What's going on between you and my ex-faithful future wife, Sandy?" Jake's feverish demeanor threatened Zach. "Hmm, have you been playing hide the salami, best friend?"

"No, of course not. Please, we can talk, Jake, just not here." Zach reached out to steer Jake toward the call room, but Jake slapped his hand away.

"Don't touch me. You don't order me around."

Fortunately, Jake started toward the call room, so Zach put the chart back in the racks, and followed. The door was open, and Zach entered the room to have his stomach connect with Jake's fist. Zach's breath was knocked out of him and he immediately doubled over in pain. "What the fuck," he croaked.

"You're fucking the love of my life. Why didn't you just stab me in the back?" Jake was crazed. His body was stiff, almost quivering. "How could you betray me like that?"

"Are you nuts? I saw Sandy for the first time in a month here. She came to me because she is worried about you. I haven't slept with her, let alone seen her, except yesterday for fifteen minutes."

"Bullshit, I can smell her on you."

"Please, Jake, nothing has been going on with Sandy, except that we are both worried about you. Please, I want to help. I know you are going through a hard time, but drinking and acting like a maniac isn't helping anything. Sandy loves you and wants you home, away from this place. Both of us are begging you, let us help. I'll talk to Hercules and Bullshit about moving your vacation up, so you can rest and think this out. Spend some quiet time with Sandy. Straighten out your relationship." Zach saw Jake's body deflate, like a balloon that had a slow leak. Jake opened his mouth as if to say something, but instead pushed his way past Zach through the door mumbling, "Just stay away from me and Sandy … or else."

Zach didn't know whether running after Jake or letting him chill out would be best. He finally just sat on the bed and put his head in his hands. He realized he didn't have the strength to solve Jake's problems when they were so close to the problems he had and couldn't seem to solve. He felt a chill and an ache in his chest. Finally, taking a breath, he got off the disheveled bed and reached for the phone.

"Operator, an outside line please." Zach dialed the number. "Shoshie? No, nothing is wrong. I just wanted to hear your voice. No, really, all is good, as good as it can be. Yeah, I'm not on tonight, but you know, we probably won't get to make rounds till seven and then I need to do some charting and such. Yeah, I'll be in the apartment by midnight. Sure, I can call you then, but it will be so late. ... Okay, but if I can't, we will talk tomorrow. Okay, later ... and thanks for picking up the phone, I prefer your voice to Uncle Isaac's."

He hung up.

Chapter 50

"**Dr. Maxwell, excuse me,** do you have a minute?"

Zach turned around to find himself face-to-face with Chenoiel's wife. She looked like she had lost weight since he last saw her. Her eyes were sad, floating in tears, and her mascara looked smudged, the blackness drawing lines down her cheeks.

"Of course, Mrs. Chenoiel, how can I help you?" He dreaded her answer. Since the confrontation with Chenoiel he had done his best to avoid being anywhere near him. The one thing he couldn't avoid in the hospital was gossip and rumor. He had heard enough about Chenoiel's current dealings to know that his missus had not come just to have lunch. Chenoiel had threatened to take Zach, Bullshit, and Hercules to court over prejudice against American graduates. His contention was he was being singled out because almost everyone in the surgical training program was a foreign graduate or a second-rate American graduate who couldn't get any other residency except PAY. He told anyone who would listen that, even though he had had offers from Columbia University, Harvard, and Stanford, he had come to PAY to make a difference. He continued by pointing out that the American College of Surgeons was going to shut surgical programs down staffed by residents who were foreign grads. Zach knew most of the nurses and doctors had been subjected to Chenoiel's line. They had either laughed in his face or ignored him. In the meantime, Chenoiel was getting no, to very little, O.R. time. The board-certified surgeons who brought in the private cases told Bullshit in no uncertain terms that Chenoiel had to go. They felt he was incompetent, lazy, and besides most of them were foreign also, so fuck Chenoiel and his father. Payback was a bitch. The situation was so bad that Chenoiel senior had shown up on Bullshit's doorstep and demanded that Bullshit not only force the boarded surgeons to let Chenoiel have the cases, but he also wanted an apology from the whole department written and placed in Chenoiel's file. To add the rotten cherry to the top of the cake, he demanded both Zach and Hercules be terminated. Zach assumed he meant fired, and not sent to a firing squad, though Chenoiel, senior and junior, had one and the same personality type, so he wasn't positive.

"Dr. Maxwell?"

Zach mentally shook himself. "I don't know exactly where he is, Mrs. Chenoiel, but I can have him paged to that nursing station over there. Unfortunately, I'll have to leave after the call is made. I'm very busy with patient care today."

"Please page him stat, I think you doctors call it, and please wait till he arrives. I would consider it a personal favor."

Zach saw her face had turned from wet and bloated because of her crying to one of cold granite. What was going on, and why did he have to stay? He didn't need another confrontation with that shithead. He looked at her face again, sighed, and walked over to the nurses' station with her in tow. "Dr. Chenoiel, report to 3S. Dr. Chenoiel 3S." Zach put down the phone and looked at Mrs. Chenoiel. "He should be here in a minute." So, they both waited, and waited, and Chenoiel didn't show or call. Zach was getting nervous. He had heard of Chenoiel's latest conquest, a separated nurse with four kids who had started seeing a lot of Chenoiel, and even defended his crappy care and attitude. Maybe he was in one of the call rooms showing the nurse his inchworm. Zach shook his head. "Mrs. Chenoiel, he isn't coming. He's probably in the O.R, saving a life."

"Saving a life, huh," she said quietly. "Okay, now I want you to page him like I told you before, stat."

"Mrs. Chenoiel, I can't do that. The stat page is used only in an emergency. I can get into trouble if I do this. Please, just go home. I'm sure I'll see him within the next few hours, and I'll make sure he calls. In the meantime, I'm having some problems and I don't need further complications from unnecessary stat calls."

"Zach," Mrs. Chenoiel interrupted, "my husband is the source of your problems, isn't he?"

Zach was shocked speechless, more for her calling him Zach and not Dr. Maxwell, but also from her admission she knew her husband was a source of trouble.

"Now, page him stat. Don't worry, at least some of your problems are about to go away. Now, please, I don't have all day and neither do you."

Zach picked up the phone, dialed and said, "Dr. Chenoiel stat 3S, stat 3S."

Nurses started coming out of the rooms into the hallways, each looking frantically around for the emergency. The stat page meant dire emergency, drop everything and come. Zach then heard rapid, heavy, running. He knew it was Chenoiel, but he certainly didn't expect Chenoiel's nurse, her blouse half-out, makeup smudged, and more interestingly, it seemed that her bra hadn't come along for the jog, as her large, heavy breasts were unencumbered and threatening to rip through the thin fabric of the blouse.

Chenoiel stopped in front of Zach. This close they could both see Chenoiel's face, neck, and chest had lipstick lips tattooed on his skin. "Maxwell, what the fuck are you calling me stat for? Didn't I tell you before, never call me stat?" Chenoiel suddenly noticed his wife standing behind Zach.

"What are you doing here, Fran? We didn't have a lunch

appointment, did we? The kids okay?" Fran Chenoiel remained silent. This was unlike the previous Fran Chenoiel, who had accepted her husband's abuse and her personal humiliation. She turned toward Zach and reached up to his face. Zach was so shocked by this level of intimacy that he almost ran when Fran Chenoiel drew his head toward her, and passionately kissed him on the mouth. She broke the kiss and said, "Thank you for your decency, Dr. Maxwell. I truly appreciate you trying to protect me from my husband's indiscretions." Zach looked around, and noticed the audience of nurses, fellow residents, and attendants. Most smiled, a few even applauded, probably because no one tolerated the asshole and felt Chenoiel had this coming.

"What the fuck, Fran? I don't know what to say to you. And you, Maxwell, when I get through with you no one will let you anywhere near a hospital. I told you don't fuck with me, and to be fucking my wife … "

Suddenly, Chenoiel was slapped hard across the cheek knocking him into the nurse who came with him. They both went down in a pile. The slap had drawn a collective gasp from the crowd. Chenoiel jumped to his feet, and it was unclear whether he was going to punch Zach or Fran. His fists were tight balls and his face was almost burgundy, with sweat running down it. Zach grabbed him and yelled, "Don't, you'll totally ruin your career."

Chenoiel froze, slowly realizing the situation he was in. "I'll ruin you, Maxwell, and as for you, my wife…. "

"You inadequate excuse for a man, you'll do nothing if you know what is good for you."

"What are you going to do, Fran? You can't live without me and you know it."

Zach wanted to run. He disliked family politics occurring in public, but he was curious as to why Fran had become so confident. In fact, Chenoiel was the one sweating. "Fran, maybe you and Chenoiel would like to go to the conference room and work this out. There are a lot of people here, and I'm sure some privacy would help."

Fran almost put her nose up in the air. "No, I don't think so. I'll be going home now. Zach, would you walk me to the exit?"

"Uh, sure," Zach replied.

She started down the hall, leaving Chenoiel and his nurse, who was still on the floor. She turned and addressed Chenoiel. "If I hear of one word of trouble for Zach, Hercules, or anyone else who you have threatened, you are through playing doctor." She continued down the hall, but suddenly smiled and turned a final time. "Oh, if your father initiates the trouble, just tell him this from Henry. 'Your society will be closed, and that fund will be forfeited.'"

Chenoiel turned pale. "You wouldn't, Fran. I'm still your husband and the father of our children."

Fran smiled coldly and flipped him the bird as she got into the elevator with Zach. Fran was obviously not the woman he originally imagined.

The exit from the lobby was crowded with patients trying to get upstairs for clinic appointments, and doctors trying to get to those clinics on time. Zach and Fran Chenoiel were in the middle of hundreds of people, but they were alone together.

"You know, he wasn't an evil young man. His personality failure is mostly his father's fault, but then again, the operative word is man. He is anything but a man. We were put together by my father, who was a successful MD-scientist. He worked with Chenoiel's father on botox for wrinkles. We were the same age and both our fathers thought they would create a dynasty. The problem was my husband was spoiled and was used to doing his daddy's bidding. He also looked to his father to get him out of trouble from the various social problems his weak personality caused. PAY was a calculated effort to create a chief of department. I was to be his entrance into higher society. What a crock, and I went along with it. He never really loved me, though I doubt he knows what love is. I found my role was wife, followed by mother. It was a stifling life when I realized the only one with freedom was my husband. This is not the first affair he has had. His father taught him that also. Oh well, the leash is on him. He won't give you any problems. He and his father are very dependent on daddy's goodwill. Would you mind telling Hercules that I send my regards and I'm so sorry?"

"You know Hercules personally?"

"Oh, yes. In fact, before he got married, or was a resident. He was still a brilliant medical student when I met him on a vacation to Greece. My father, in fact, talked him into leaving Greece to do his residency at PAY. I was so in love with him, but his heart was with the lovely Greek girl he eventually married. The three of us remained friends."

Zach didn't want to be having this conversation, but he was bound here with her, maybe to bear witness to the events that had just happened. "I'm sure your husband loves you, Mrs. Chenoiel." He blushed. "You are beautiful, smart, kind.... "

"He doesn't have that emotion. I should not have ignored his mother's life. She lives like a queen in that castle of theirs, but she has no say in her life. Her husband gives her the marching orders of the day, and off she goes, and follows them. God help her if she doesn't. You know the father drinks, and he isn't too nice on the fifth shot. The woman is so depressed, I wouldn't be surprised if one day I read she has had an accident or died of a strange disease. I can't imagine she would want to live the way she does, anyway. Well, it won't happen to me."

"What are you going to do now?" Zach asked. Fran just took her finger and touched his lips to quiet him. She was still a moment, then grabbed and kissed him deeply. "I think I will relocate, but I'll keep my husband on a leash till I decide what is good for my children and myself. Good luck, Zach, be a good surgeon and be a good doctor. Find a woman you love and loves you, and remember always that she is your priority, and the doctoring part will come naturally."

Zach followed her with his eyes as she walked out of the hospital.

Chapter 51

"I found a job!" Shoshie was overjoyed.

"That is great. Doing what?"

"Well, you ever hear of Jazzercise? I'm going to be a Jazzercise girl."

"Uh, really? What is Jazzercise again?"

"Don't worry, Zach, it's an exercise class set to music. Maybe you'll come."

Zach looked at his middle. He hated exercise, and he had a paunch that had grown since he left college. Hell, he grabbed meals here and there when there was time—usually pizza, bread, cheese, more pizza. He loved leftovers, like pizza for breakfast straight from the fridge, or the counter if he fell asleep before putting dinner away. Oh well, love me the way I am. "Sure, when I get a break I'll be there in my Spandex."

Shoshie giggled. "Now that I'd like to see. How was your day?"

Zach was in his apartment, and it was midnight. His eyelids felt like lead weights had been attached and were dragging them down. He knew he stank but had just been too tired to stand in the shower. He was also afraid if he lay down in the bath he'd fall asleep, and just slip under the water. The day, he thought, had been like most of the other days. Trauma calls from the E.R., consult calls from the floors, rounds, O.R., more rounds and notes and paperwork. Tons of notes and paperwork. "Same day as yesterday and tomorrow. People hurt, sick, or both, and we save them, or not. I'd rather hear about you. Your voice is such a beautiful thing to hear before I fall asleep." There was a silence at the other end. "Shoshie, are you still there?" He thought he heard some sniffling. "Shoshie, I'm sorry. I meant it as a compliment."

"No, Zach, I know. It was such a nice thing to say. No guy has ever … Anyway, thank you. You must be exhausted. Did you flip off your beeper? They can leave you alone for a while."

"You know I can't do that," he slurred. "Don't hang up. In fact, tell me a bedtime story."

"Dirty or clean?" She laughed.

But he was already asleep.

He was awakened by a very loud beeping, and an unpleasant vibration at his waist. He jumped up, and opened his eyes, seeing only the light of mid-town Manhattan and black sky. What the hell time was it, and what was that beeping? Shit! He pulled the beeper off his waistband and punched the received button. "Report to E.R. stat, E.R. stat." What the fuck, he was off for the night. Piece of shit operator must have read off the wrong call list, again.

He got up and went to the phone and squinted in the dark to dial the number for the E.R. "E.R.," someone answered. The background noise was deafening. It sounded like the apocalypse had just broken out.

"This is Dr. Maxwell. I think I was mistakenly paged. I'm off tonight. You need to re-page. By the way, what time is it?"

"Hold on, Dr. Maxwell."

"But, I'm off … " He realized there was no one on the other end of the phone. He then heard a click and a short ring.

"Hey, boy, this is Hercules. Look, I know you're off, but Bed-

Stuy just blew up … literally. I need help, so I'm calling everyone in."

"What time is it?" Zach asked.

"Three-fifteen in the glorious morning. Can you come?"

"Hercules, I just got off a thirty-six-hour marathon there, and have had less than three hours sleep, and haven't showered in over forty hours." Zach took a deep breath, fuck fuck fuck fuck fuck … "Give me ten."

"Try to get here in three. And as for your smell, you probably smell like roses compared to the average patient here. Hurry, I told the volunteer to make coffee with double the amount of beans."

It smelled like the trash fire from hell. There were no flames, just a heavy, sickening, oily, smoke smell. Zach found Hercules putting a chest tube in a partially burned victim.

"What the hell happened?" Zach asked Hercules.

"Radical anarchist felt that the local coffee emporium selling Colombian beans was exploiting the native peoples. He decided that no outlet, no exploiting, so he concocted a small explosive device to take out the coffee roaster, not realizing that the device was hooked up to a gas line. Result, crispy critters combined with blast victims. Look, our brother internists have graciously taken the pure burn victims and will apply the Parkland formula and start hydrating. Anesthesia is here accessing airways, so all we have to do is save the ones with holes or deformed whatevers. Start at one end of the E.R., and pick up charts triaged in red. Those patients are surgical. Good luck … man with the most saves gets a six-pack of domestic from Bullshit."

"Damn, I always knew he was a generous SOB. See you later." Zach went to the opposite side of the E.R. in a corner that was full of suffering patients but didn't have a doc already working it. As he looked around at the suffering, he saw almost every doctor, attending or resident, every nurse he could think of, and most of the attendant staff. Even more, he saw the volunteers that came from the community, circulating with coffee and sandwiches for the medical staff, or just holding the hands of their neighbors who had been innocent victims of a community horror. This, he thought, was what medicine was about. Not the Chenoiels, the patient complaints, the politics, or the insurance companies.

A nurse yelled over to him. "Zach, I need help here."

He ran over to find the nurse placing a mask on a young man who had burns to his face. It was apparent he was having problems breathing, and even with the mask on and the oxygen turned all the way up, his O_2 sat—the measurement of oxygen in his blood—was only in the 50 percent range. He was hypoxic and struggling. Zach took his stethoscope and listened to his chest and then his neck. He heard decent lung sounds but higher up in the chest and in the neck, he heard wheezing. Zach thought he was hearing sounds like he heard when the asthmatics were wheezing. This meant the airflow was going through a constricted space. "Crap, I think this guy burned his upper airway. He can't get oxygen down into the lungs. What's his BP and pulse?"

"220 over 110, and a pulse rate of 120, sat is now 51 percent on 100 percent oxygen."

"Double crap, we need an airway, his high blood pressure and pulse mean he is struggling, and he is struggling because he is hypoxic, and possibly fluid in his lungs. Where is a gas passer? This guy needs to be tubed."

"They are all tubing other patients, Zach. I don't think this guy has the time to wait. Do you?" the nurse replied.

"Fuck, no, I don't. In for a penny ... give him etomidate twenty mg I.V. push. We can't give him succinylcholine with all the burns, maybe we should just overdose him on fentanyl, and pray for the best that he maintains a blood pressure."

The nurse ran to the cart to get the meds, and Zach started bagging him. He managed to get him up to a barely 60 percent oxygen saturation. He thought that unless he could get some oxygen into the guy, the patient was a goner. Zach felt the sweat running down from his hairline into his eyes. He couldn't even wipe them as he needed both hands to keep a seal on the guy's face with the mask. Man, I have to take a piss bad, he thought. Maybe Mommy will take me to the bathroom, and when I get back this nightmare will be gone. "Lay out a seven MAC blade and a 7.5 tube," he ordered the nurse.

"Okay, Zach, you're ready. Want me to push the meds?"

Zach took a quick glance at the ceiling. "Dear God, Moses, Jesus, Buddha, and Zoroaster, don't let me screw the pooch and kill this guy." He looked at the nurse and nodded. "Push them now."

The patient visibly relaxed and started making deep snoring sounds. Another sign of upper airway obstruction. He continued to bag the patient and glanced at the O_2 sat monitor. 62 percent, probably the best he could achieve. He stopped bagging and grabbed the laryngoscope with the already fitted MAC blade and placed it in the patient's mouth. The inside of his mouth was like nothing he had ever seen. The usually pink mucosal tissue was an angry red, swollen, and at places ulcerated. There were pieces of black carbonaceous material all over his mouth. "Shit, it looks like this guy got a mouthful of flame or superheated air."

"There is nowhere to put a tube down into the trachea." The O_2 sat monitor alarm went off. The saturation of oxygen in his blood was now minimal. A couple more minutes of this, and this guy's brain was toast. What to do? he thought.

"Zach, what are you going to do? Do you need anything else?" The nurse looked at him with confidence. That was the baseline relationship between doctor and nurse in the E.R. If your rep was good, the E.R. nurses would give you a chance to earn their respect, but if you were a screw-up, you were shit and they would walk all over you. He needed help, but none was around. He kept thinking, man, it took balls the size of grapefruits to work here. No wonder E.R. docs and nurses felt they were so privileged.

"Zach, the O_2 sat is inching toward the thirties. He is going to die."

Zach internally woke up. Do nothing, he is dead. Do something, even something he shouldn't be doing without a senior doctor present. Well, even if he failed, he had tried, and it was always better to try than throw in the towel.

"Get me a number eleven blade and a 6.0 ET tube, now." Zach started bagging the patient again, but it wasn't helping the oxygen level.

"Wait, what are you going to do? You know you need a senior to cut."

"Like you said, do we have time to wait?"

She gave him a quick look and reached over to grab the items off the cart.

Zach quickly doused the patient's anterior neck with Betadine. Well, he thought, even if he dies, he won't get an infection.

"Here you go," she announced, holding out the items he had asked for.

He grabbed the knife, and carefully judging the midline of the patient's neck, made a vertical incision. If the incision was too far to the sides, he could inadvertently cut the carotid arteries or the internal jugulars. This would kill the patient from exsanguination. Blood welled up from the fat and the nurse, seeing the blood, grabbed some four by fours and dabbed the red viscous liquid away. Okay, great start, he thought.

"Sat down to 41 percent, heart rate is 138. If you're going to do something, do it now."

"Fuck!" He took his scalpel and made a vertical incision through what he hoped was the cricothyroid membrane, and was rewarded with the sudden whoosh of air exploding from his incision.

"Sat 32 percent, Zach. He's not going to make it."

"Yes, he is, get ready to hand me the 6.0 ET tube." He reversed the scalpel blade and shoved it through the slit he had made, then told the nurse to hand him the tube, which he placed into the resultant hole. The patient immediately started coughing through the tube, and his oxygen saturation came up. "Give me a syringe, and we'll blow up the balloon. He needs some oxygen by T-piece for now. Get a portable chest x-ray, and if there is fluid in the lungs, tell Respiratory he needs to go on a vent with positive pressure. Try to keep him over 90 percent O_2 sat."

"Good job, Zach. He needs sedation and a pulmonologist, but I guess the lung guy will have to wait. You want a milligram or two of Ativan?"

"Yes, and he needs some morphine for pain. Start him at four, and then give him all he needs. I'll sign for the grand total in a bit."

"Go on and write it up. I'll take care of the odds and ends, T-piece, x-ray, PEEP if fluids. I got it."

Zach went to the desk to chart when the shakes hit him. He had almost lost this guy, and God alone knew if he wouldn't lose him in the near future. Airway burns were a tricky thing to treat. Besides screwing up oxygen exchange with the blood, he was a big risk for pneumonia. He started writing orders for the ICU, including a pulmonology consult and antibiotics. It was time for victim number two.

Zach scrubbed on a crushed leg that, after two hours attempting an arterial bypass, was judged to have to be amputated. He also scrubbed on a perforated colon and helped clean up a woman who had burns to her left arm, leg, and torso. He did this under sedation, as the woman would scream if even light touch was applied.

By 7 p.m. Zach had been going for almost nineteen hours, and that was after only three hours of sleep. He had started seeing double about two hours ago but trudged on. His cricothyroidomy had been rounded on by Bullshit himself, who questioned Zach about the case, his reasons for doing such an invasive procedure and why he didn't get a senior resident to help him. Zach answered as best as he could. Shit, he thought, who was I going to get who already wasn't trying to save a life? In the end, Bullshit just grunted, and shaking his head, walked away. "Mudda, mudda, mudda," could be heard echoing from his lips as he disappeared down the hall.

They all looked terrible as they gathered for evening rounds at 10 p.m. on the third-floor ward. Every member of Hercules's team smelled of smoke and bodily functions. There wasn't a white coat among them, all being covered by soot, blood, and God knew what else.

"Boys, before we start, I would like to tell you how proud I am of you. Through your efforts, I think we conservatively got at least eight patients through a crisis and countless others able to be discharged after treatment. Dr. Moskowitz has asked me to express his gratitude and has told me to tell you that the Mayor of New York has called and congratulated your fine work. A special commendation will be placed in your individual files, and while I doubt showing it will buy you a Big Mac, it looks good, so what the hell." He smiled. "Dr. Moskowitz has also put a twenty-four hour hold on elective surgery, so we can tidy up those burn victims that need more debridement under anesthesia or other emergent procedures. He has also placed the specialty service on call tonight so you can all get some rest. Use this time to rest! While tomorrow should be a light day, you never know. Okay, let's round."

When they got to the last stop, the ICU, they found that Zach's pulmonary burn was holding his own. The pulmonologist had written a note that she had scoped him and found burns in the upper trachea not permitting a scope to advance, and scoping down the tube that Zach had placed showed minimal damage, just some low-grade edema.

Hercules dismissed all of them, but asked Zach to hold a minute. "Hey, boy, great job on the cric. Bullshit wanted me to tell you that it was gutsy, and you definitely saved the guy's life. He made mention of your big balls and that if you ever have to do something like that again, certainly save a life. But lie about the lack of supervision, at least to him."

Zach sighed. "Crap, I hope I never have to do that again."

"We all hope, never works out that way for the real doctors. People like Chenoiel will go through a career treating only safe patients and refusing to take risks even though that patient may have no other chance at surviving. Chenoiel will pass that patient onto another surgeon instead of taking responsibility himself. You took responsibility, you got him through his crisis, and now rightfully it is the problem of another doctor. All kosher. If you had decided to wait for one of us seniors, or heaven forbid just walk away from the guy.... Well, Hell has a special place for cowardly people who call themselves physicians. Go home and get some sleep. See you in the morning."

The elevator door opened at the residence and Zach, smelling like a three-alarm fire, and sweat, trudged down the hallway to his apartment, his eyes mostly on his feet, making sure they followed a straight line to the door.

"Zach, how many did you get?"

Zach looked up and saw Shoshie by his door. He was no longer surprised by her surprise visits when he needed her the most. "I lost count. They were brought in and then kept coming in. Saved a bunch, lost a few. All in all, I guess we won, at least according to Hizzoner da Mayor of New York."

"Well, my hero, you look like you were buried, and someone dug you up."

"You should see what my eyes think I look like. Man, I have never been through anything like that."

"Give me your keys. You need to get cleaned up before you sleep."

"Shoshie, what are you doing here? Not that you aren't the best sight I've had," he said, checking his watch, "in now thirty-one hours and twenty-two minutes. I got called in at around 3 a.m. yesterday and have been trying to keep up since then."

"I don't know why I'm here, but after hearing about the bombing, I figured you'd need someone to be here. I can leave, I won't be hurt."

Zach slumped against the door frame. "Please stay."

Shoshie took his arm and led him into the apartment. He headed for the couch, as it looked so inviting.

"No, no couch. You'll fall asleep on it, and I'll never get you up and cleaned up. Come on." She led him into the bathroom and started running the water for a bath.

"I shower, baths are for girls," he slurred.

"Well, right now, they are for very smelly, dirty, surgical residents who are sleep-deprived." She started stripping him of his scrubs, underwear, and socks.

He was awake enough to feel uncomfortable, though for the life of him he couldn't figure out why. "Shoshie, what are you doing? This is not the time."

Shoshie laughed, "Time for what?"

He blushed. "I can't, and I stink."

Shoshie's face registered shock. "You can't what?" she asked, as she continued stripping him of the toxic clothes. "Oh, you can't perform." She chuckled. "I think maybe you should think of me as a nurse and you as an accident victim."

He was naked and had feelings below his beltline that he

didn't want her to see. Shit, even as tired as he was, must be that primitive brain. He slipped into the tub and was instantly lulled into relaxation by the warm water. He closed his eyes and started dreaming that something was washing him. He knew it wasn't his arms because they felt like lead pipes. He opened his eyes and yelled, "Shoshie!"

She smiled at him. So beautiful, her eyes gray-gold with beautiful blond hair. Skin smooth, flawless, muscles covered with just enough fat to make sure she could never be recognized as anything but a woman. Her breasts small, but firm, with dark red, prominent nipples. A six-pack abdomen, and an ass and thighs that were all muscle. He was instantly erect, and squirmed around embarrassed. "What? I'm sure you've seen one or two naked women in your practice, doctor. Maybe better than this naked woman?"

"What are you doing? You're naked."

"No shit, Sherlock. How was I supposed to get you cleaned up? I don't have extra clothes here to change into and it didn't look like you were going to clean yourself."

Zach most definitely did not know what to say. He reached out and touched her cheek, and then the back of her head and drew her face close to his and kissed her. Her lips and mouth were sweet, and she relaxed into the kiss, her body on his, slippery yet warm. Her body excited him as they touched each other in the water. He flipped over her in the bathtub and bent down to kiss her breasts, her moans getting louder.

"Zach.... "

He responded by kissing her again while reaching down to her sex.

"Oh my God, that's good, Zach, but you have to stop."

He looked up at her smiling, glowing face. "Stop?" he asked dumbly.

"Zach, tonight can't be the night. You need some rest and I need to be sure."

Zach had never met a girl like this. Frankly, most of the non-relationships he had had included casual fucking. This was a new one to him. "Uh, okay, I guess. Is it anything I said or did?"

"No, it's just that I have been through the casual times with the casual relationships, and I've never seen anything wonderful about them. I know this sounds like a romance novel, but I think I really like you and I hope you like me. Maybe despite your schedule from hell, we can get to know each other better and see what happens."

He couldn't believe it: an old-fashioned girl. He knew then that he had feelings for her, but damn, where did he find time for a girlfriend, a deep relationship, and if it came to that something more permanent? He had had the one-night stand, the two-week relationship, and the friends with benefits. All great and exciting, but not one of those affairs turned into anything but a flirtation. Zach couldn't even remember the names of most of them, let alone want to call them just to shoot the shit. Maybe it was time to try something new. God knows, she had so far accepted all the limitations that his life now demanded. "Sure, Shoshie, I think I understand. We can be friends, at least for now."

She gave him a big smile. "Ten points."

"What's ten points? What does my ten points get me?"

"My undying respect and gratitude, and for a bonus, and since it is too late to get a car service, I'm going to stay, and keep you company until you're asleep. Which I predict will be thirty seconds after you hit the bed."

Zach smiled, happy that she would stay and maybe have a cup of coffee with him in the morning. "You take the bed; in my state, the couch is just as good."

"No, you need a good rest." She got out of the water and he was mesmerized watching the water drip off her body. He started getting excited again.

"Okay, enough of that." She laughed, grabbing a towel and wrapping it around her. "Where are your guest towels?"

"Guest towels." He smirked. "What do you think I run, a Holiday Inn here? I think there might be some clean hospital towels in the closet. I'll get them." He got out of the water, at half-staff.

"No, I think I've seen and felt enough. I'll get them. You stay right there."

"Well, that's your fault. Are you complaining?" he asked, smiling.

"No, everything is adequate." She laughed as she went to the closet. She came back and handed him a towel. "Actually, everything is perfect. Now dry off and go to bed. I'm taking the couch."

After arguing a minute or two, with Zach slurring more and more of his speech, he fell into his bed and was sleeping before she could turn out the light.

Sometime during the night, he felt another body in the bed with him. "Wha … "

"Shush, go back to sleep. It's cold on that couch."

Zach fell back to sleep with a warm feeling, centered at his back. He closed his eyes and snored with a smile.

Chapter 52

Hercules's face had a stony grimness to it before morning rounds. He wasn't his usual jokey, buoyant self. More worrisome, he, for the first time, did no teaching and rushed through rounds.

"Okay, Rupak, get all of them to the O.R. except Zach and Ike. You'll have to scrub with Bullshit on that aortobifemoral bypass. I'll make it up to you."

"Don't worry, just find him."

"Will do, boy," Hercules said cryptically. "Zach, Ike join me in the conference room.

They entered the conference room and Hercules shut the door. "Listen, Jake is missing. We have to find him quick before Bullshit has to officially find him."

Zach was confused. "What do you mean find him? He isn't in the hospital? He quit? I don't understand?"

"When did either of you see him last?" Hercules asked.

Ike thought and then replied, "I thought I saw him charting on the third floor at about 4 a.m. I thought it strange, as he wasn't on last night. Why would he be in early?"

"Bullshit came into the office at 5 a.m. and sat down to listen to his messages. Sandy called, hysterical that Jake had left their apartment at 3 a.m. after a fight, screaming that he had had enough of the crap he had to go through. He told her this would be the last time he'd feel pressured and left. She is afraid he is going to hurt himself and thought he might be heading for the hospital. Bullshit called me at home and told me to get my ass in and try to find him before anything happens." Hercules looked like he had aged a good ten years in twenty-four hours. "Can you think where he might go?"

"Why did Bullshit call you, Hercules? Why didn't he call security to find him?" Zach asked.

"If security finds him, his mental state becomes public. Under New York State law, Jake becomes a risk to the public and will have his license suspended. He then would have to go into a rehab. The fun starts after that. The Board of Medicine policy on doctors self-reporting mental problems or addictions is great on paper but, in reality, they essentially kill a physician's career. You know how many doctors make it out of that mess to practice again? Next to zero, that's how many. Bullshit wants to try to keep this quiet. Dr. Moskowitz supports his residents and doesn't want anyone to fall into the state's hands if it can be avoided. PAY has a very nice, private area on the psych ward that was unofficially but specially created to help treat these kinds of problems. Bullshit picked the best of the shrinks and obtained their word that only in the worst case would they officially report to the state."

Ike was shaking his head. "How many fucking times has this happened?"

"Too many. You know the training is stressful. Between sleep deprivation and the stress on social interaction, well, this is what happens. Now we must try to find him before he does something he can't come back from, or by noon. After that, Bullshit will have no choice but to make it official. So, where should we look?"

Neither Zach nor Ike had any idea, and PAY was gigantic, almost a city within itself. It also had many areas where one could hurt oneself. HVAC room, pharmacy, nurses' stations, hell, with a little thought, even the patient rooms could be a hazard.

"We need more info. I'm calling Sandy. Maybe he told her

something she didn't realize was a clue as to what was going on in his mind."

Zach went into a call room and dialed her apartment.

"Did you find him? Is he okay?"

"Sandy, we haven't yet and we are trying to keep it quiet so he doesn't lose his career. What did he say before he left the apartment?"

Sandy was crying on the phone, her voice trembling. "Zach, I love him, I always did and always will. If he hurts himself … The baby, he doesn't know about the baby." She was sobbing harder now.

"Sandy, we will do our best that doesn't happen. Could he have found out about the baby? Was that causing him more stress?"

"No, I don't think so. I had a test done at the clinic and didn't tell him. He was so stressed, yelling, and just pissed off. I didn't want to make things worse. He kept talking about our relationship, and how you were now my boyfriend. I kept telling him that I loved him, but he had to behave better, that I was under stress also, and couldn't live with this constant fighting and being ignored. He just kept focusing on you, and the last time he saw you in your apartment. He said it was a beautiful place, and that you didn't appreciate how calming your place is. That looking out the windows, one could almost fly to the magical city. That is what he called Manhattan. He loves you Zach, but he feels abandoned by everyone."

"Oh shit!" Zach yelled. "I know where he is. Look, I gotta go." He hung up the phone and then immediately paged Hercules and Ike. "Meet me at my apartment and hurry."

Zach ran out of the elevator and went to his apartment. The door was partially open. He was almost afraid of what he'd find there. Once Sandy told him that Jake was complaining about his abandonment by his friends, he knew that Jake would have headed to his apartment. One of the features of the apartment was a window that opened to a small balcony. During the summer, the balcony was a nice place to sit and enjoy the breeze and the New York skyline. It also was a place a person could easily and purposely climb over the rail and get to oblivion.

"Jake, are you here?" he called out. There was no response and then he noticed the open bottle of cheap vodka he had for special occasions. Jake knew where he stashed it, of course. "Jake, where are you?"

He walked slowly toward the balcony window and saw a large shadow moving around. "Jake, we need to talk."

"I don't think so, Zach. Do me a favor though. Take care of Sandy. She was the best thing in my life and I let her get away."

"Come on, Jake. Sandy and I are only friends. Please, she wants you home. She loves you, needs you. She told me that."

"Anyway, my career is down the tubes, though I guess if I had to blame anything on my current state, it's the fucking residency. How are you surviving this? The residency is literally eating away at our souls."

"Jake, please come inside. Sandy is crying her eyes out. She just wants you home. She especially needs you now, plus the dive off the balcony is not you. With your luck this won't end your problems, and you'll just end up in a trauma bay, strapped to a gurney, explaining what you did to your fellow residents. Please spare yourself that grief." Zach started for Jake, but he quickly got up on the railing.

"Not so fast, old ex-buddy. What about you and Sandy? You going to be together? Stealing the love of my life wasn't so nice you know, and I hope you think about that the rest of your life. I really do."

"Jake, there is nothing between us, besides being friends because of you. Please, I know I haven't been that great of a friend, but you understand what circumstances we are both in. They want us to be human, caring doctors, but we lose all that makes us compassionate just trying to take care of this mass of sick humanity."

There was a sudden commotion at the entrance to the balcony when Hercules and Ike burst in. Jake was startled and lost his grip and balance on the rail and started to tip over. Zach leapt to grab him, getting him by the ankle and getting dragged over the rail himself.

"Oh fuck!" Zach could see the headline: "Resident commits suicide, killing ex-friend." Shit, what a way to go. He then felt hands grabbing his ankles, jerking him so powerfully that he almost let go of Jake.

Jake yelled at Zach. "I changed my mind, don't let go, please!" He started thrashing in Zach's grip.

"Fuck, stop jerking, asshole. You'll kill yourself," Zach screamed. He looked back at Hercules and Ike trying to reel them back in and started laughing. "We all have to stop kosher smorgasbord." There was a moment of stunned silence, and suddenly Jake started laughing. "Motherfucker, I'm so sorry, Zach. Please get me up, and none of you drop us."

Hercules managed to drag both Zach and Jake up onto the balcony, all falling to the floor like a Keystone Cops routine. Jake started laughing and crying at the same time. "I'm so sorry, I wish I could say I don't know why I did this, but I do know. My whole life has been getting to the goal of being a surgeon. I wanted it, my parents wanted it, uncles, aunts, and cousins all wanted it. Most importantly, Sandy expected that one day I would become a great surgeon."

"Jake, I didn't care about you being a surgeon. I just cared that you'd be happy in whatever you wanted to be, and to be there with me. I love you and just want to be with you, and you with me." Sandy had come through the door. She immediately went to Jake and kissed him.

Zach, still trying to catch his breath along with Hercules and

Ike, said, "Buddy, there are other ways to make a living besides surgery. Maybe a slower, more personal specialty—Internal Medicine, Family Practice, Peds? The world needs those kind of docs, too."

Hercules got himself off the floor. "Hey, boy, we can help you. You have friends here, no matter what specialty you go into or don't go into."

Jake looked ashamed. "I don't know if I can ever practice. How am I going to even face all the people I was so shitty to? Zach, how can you even talk to me after I accused you of having an affair with Sandy? I knew you weren't. It was just an excuse for more bad behavior."

Zach replied, "Don't worry about it, though I'd ask Sandy to forgive you for accusing her of the bad taste of being with me."

Jake smiled. "I guess you're right."

Ike asked Hercules, as he was getting off the floor, "What do we do now? It's obvious he needs a rest, and I think he needs time to get his head straight." Ike glanced at his watch. "Shit, someone better get to Bullshit quick and tell him not to start the dogs."

Hercules said to Jake, "You need to be here for another couple of hours. Then you are officially on vacation, after being sick for a couple of days."

"How is that going to help? Bullshit was pretty firm on some sort of treatment. If Jake gets treatment, it's reportable to the Board of Medical Licensing. We'll never get him back after throwing him into that crappy labyrinth," Ike said.

"Bullshit knows what to do. Knowing him, he'll want to yell a little with Jake in his presence. Why don't you and Sandy go to a call room and lock the door? I'll go talk to Bullshit, and in a couple of hours, hopefully, some of this will be a bad memory."

Chapter 53

Zach was heading to the third floor to write notes on patients. This was a constant pain for all the residents. That the doctors saw the patients at least twice a day was not enough. They had to sit in front of a pile of loose-leaf folders and enter in notes about the patient visit. Surgeons, being very action-oriented, hated sitting down and recording the day's progress on a patient. Most of them would rather cut, stab, sew, place a tube, extract a tube, screw around with a tube that wasn't working, or just amputate something, than write. Surgeons were 180 degrees from the internist who would sit and write a novel based on a serum potassium reading. The last thing the internist wanted to do was actually touch a patient. The surgeons always thought condoms were invented for internists, though how did little internists get hatched?

"Zach, hold up."

Jake and Sandy were coming down the corridor with bright smiles. He looked like he had dropped ten rough years. "Why didn't you tell me, asshole? I mean I had a right to know and I wouldn't have ... " He hesitated, and the smile lost its wattage.

"Don't worry Jake, we both move on. Congratulations, I'm glad you are happy about the baby. What plans do the both of you have now?"

"Well, Sandy and I are going to eventually get married. We should have done this a long time ago, but ... " He again looked unsure and sad. "Zach, my priorities were all fucked up. I am going to straighten out this mess I'm in and try to be the best husband and father I can."

"Hey guys, and Sandy." Ike ran up to them. "Hercules asked that I tell you the news from Bullshit's office. He is sorry he isn't here himself, but he had to take care of an emergency in the O.R."

"I'm canned, or I have to see the shrink if I want to stay, right?" Jake said, sadly.

Ike responded in his best Bullshit imitation, "Well, not fucking really." Ike dropped the imitation and continued, "Bullshit thinks you could use some counseling, but thinks that you are a good doctor who picked the wrong field. He thinks this makes you a schizophrenic, and if we find the right place for you, your symptoms will go away, and we'll still get some work out of you. Besides, he said, if he had to send you to the shrinks in secret, he'd owe them. This way saves a ton of crap. End quote."

"But Ike, if I can't complete a year of surgery I'll have to explain it on my application for another program next year, and you know no program wants someone who fell apart. I'm screwed no matter what."

"Not necessarily, Jake. By the way, Bullshit says mazel tov on the pregnancy, and now please get married. He likes his residents to have family responsibilities even if they fuck themselves into a family. His term, not mine."

Zach laughed. "He's a bit old-fashioned, isn't he? I mean, they don't have to get married."

"I want to get married," Jake said as he got down on one knee, oblivious to the people walking around the four of them in the corridor. "Sandy Ethel Rosensweig, will you be my wife till the end of time? I promise to love you, be there for you, and listen to you. I also promise never to put you through what I just put you through."

There were tears in Sandy's eyes, and Zach's eyes, though he tried to hide it, and Ike was choked up. "I will, Jacob Ethan Marcus, come and kiss me, you lug." There was spontaneous applause in the corridor, and both Jake and Sandy blushed, murmuring their thanks. Jake then reached into his pocket, pulled out a piece of black surgical silk thread, and loosely tied it around her ring finger. "I don't have the money yet for a diamond. Will this do till then?"

Sandy's tears really started flowing as she kissed him and murmured, "I will always love you."

"Okay," Ike broke in smiling, "now as of," Ike checked his watch, "3:52 p.m. EST you, Dr. Jacob Marcus, are on vacation. Go call your parents and tell them the wedding is in two weeks in the PAY chapel, Rabbi Jonah Leiber presiding ... that is, unless Bullshit has to amputate something of Jonah's. The wedding is courtesy of Bullshit. Jonah owes him a couple of favors. Honeymoon, also courtesy of Bullshit, in Atlantic City, he has a comped hotel room there, and then after a week you, Jake, report to 5S at 8 a.m."

"Five S, that's the family practice floor," Jake responded. "Why there?"

Zach looked at Ike and realized that Bullshit, probably with the help of Hercules, had come up with a plan to both give Jake a little time to heal, and to continue a medical career at a slower pace. He obviously forgot to tell Jake. "So, the rumors are true, they didn't fill, did they?"

Ike smiled. "I guess not. Even a Sabbath program couldn't get them all the people they need to run a service as large as Family Practice." He turned to Jake. "They will take you into the family practice residency here. They will even give you credit for your months of surgery. It is a sweet set-up; night call is four blocks of three weeks. You work three night shifts in a row, and get the fourth off. Everything else is days. Most of it in their clinic. You'll have your own patients, and the best part, you'll refer worked-up cases to surgery. In other words, we win because we have a guy with surgical training on that service. No BS from you like the rest of residents give us."

"Oh my God, it sounds like a dream," Jake cried. "How can I ever thank you?"

"More like how can you ever thank Bullshit. He said don't. Just heal. Be a good husband, father, and doctor and have fun on your honeymoon, though, and I'm quoting him here, 'how much fun can you have with a knocked up broad on a honeymoon?'"

Sandy laughed. "Obviously, Dr. Moskowitz has no idea what pregnant female hormones can do."

Jake looked at Zach and said, "I don't know how you will ever forgive me for being such an A-hole to you, but I hope you do. I owe you my life, Zach."

"Just have a good time and come back healthy. Now why don't you two scoot, as Ike and I have work to do."

Chapter 54

At 11:30 p.m., the zombie-like residents were ready to go home. For those on call, the evening's high jinx were just starting. Their only luck was that the next day's surgical schedule was quiet. Zach felt like every muscle was a pulverized piece of meat ready to cook. Ike was on with him, and for once they decided to skip kosher smorgasbord and try to chill in the on-call room.

"So, what's going on with you and Shoshie, and when do I get to officially meet her, instead of making her gag?"

Zach remembered Shoshie's introduction to the surgical service courtesy of Ike. She occasionally mentioned how she didn't know how he tolerated the disimpaction, blood, smells, and other fluids. "Believe me, Ike, she remembers you. I guess it is going okay. She is nice, interested, and seems to understand that the residency comes first. I guess my problem is that I don't know where it goes or ends. This is a long haul, another four years, and, God knows, maybe two to three years after that for a fellowship. How do you keep your marriage with Goldie intact? I mean you guys were together from college on. Isn't the residency interfering with everything?"

Ike thought a moment before he answered. "Well, it doesn't help, that's for sure. Goldie sort of knew what she was in for when we came back to Canarsie. Medical school wasn't bad, for the first two years. At least aside from classes and labs, I was home, maybe studying, but home. The fun started in third year with the rotations. It seemed like I was never home. Things eased up when we got back to Canarsie. Her parents live five miles away, and my parents are a couple of blocks away. If she needs a break from the kids, usually at least one grandparent is available. The burden for family life is still on her, but I guess I'm lucky in a way. She takes the long view that one day I'll have my own practice, and our life can normalize."

"I wish I was in your shoes, so sure of the future. It's just that I'm not sure of my future. Shoshie is a great girl, and so far, she seems to be tolerating this life of mine, but we haven't really invested a lot."

"So, you haven't slept with her yet? I only ask because these Jewish girls, as liberated as they are, put a lot of stock in the act, hence, the investment. So, as much as I'm sure your putz needs the exercise, I recommend contemplating the consequences of your actions before, during and, if you're so lucky, after the act. And son, make sure to use a rubber, as my old man used to say."

"Uh, that's not any of your business."

"So, no." Ike laughed.

"Hmm, a gentleman never tells. I even have my doubts about a career in surgery. You know, I love the action in the E.R., the stabilization, the what is coming through the door next? I just can't get that excited about spending hours in the O.R. doing a bowel run or removing a gallbladder. If I am not excited about doing this work now, what will I be thinking in ten years?"

"Ten years, huh. I think you should worry about tomorrow. I know Bullshit is grooming you to be one of the chief residents. I'm sure he will be disappointed if you decide to jump ship. Besides, Emergency Medicine is hospital-based. You end up working for a hospital, seeing patients, but never following those patients. Slam, bang, thank you ma'am medicine. You really want that?"

"I guess not." But Zach wondered if that were true. Would sacrificing the follow-up be that bad?

Chapter 55

"**What is Chenoiel doing** out on the floor?" Ike asked Zach. Chenoiel had showed up on morning rounds and wasn't saying much. He just had a subtle hint of a smile, like the cat that had just eaten the canary.

"Damned if I know. Time off for good behavior? He was caught literally screwing the pooch. No one tells me anything here."

Hercules came on to the floor looking grim. He saw Chenoiel and looked grimmer. "I'd like to welcome Dr. Chenoiel back to the team. He will be assuming the duties of Jake and will be assigned tasks at Jake's level. He therefore answers to Ike."

It was obvious that Chenoiel didn't like what he was hearing, and was about to say something when he suddenly resumed just standing there. Zach looked at Ike and both could read dread in each other's faces. What had happened? Chenoiel was supposed to be in the lab for at least a year.

The team made rounds and then headed for the O.R. or the floor. Ike called to Zach to come over. "I'll get Hercules by himself, and we will hash this out. I can't believe he is happy about this."

"Yeah, I doubt it. Did you see the puss on him before he left for the O.R.?"

Chenoiel walked over to them with a big smile. "Happy to see me back on the team, boys?" When he didn't get a response, his smile became even bigger. "Yeah, tough luck for you two that your friend went crazy, and Bullshit realized that I was the only one who could save your asses. How is Jackie? In a rubber room?"

"You fucking bastard!" Zach was about to swing when Ike held him back.

Ike told Zach, "It's not worth it, Zach. Let him flap his mouth. He'll be back fucking rats in the lab before he knows it, or better yet the rats won't have anything to do with him, and he'll become a pharmaceutical salesman."

Zach calmed down. "Yeah, you're right, Ike. I guess his microdick is big enough for a rat. By the way, Chenoiel, how is your wife?"

"Good one, moron. Well, whether you two like it or not, I'm here and I'm staying. What case am I scrubbing on, Ike? I don't want to be late for my case."

"You're not in the O.R. today, you're the scut boy. Notes, and there are two disimpactions on the medical floors. Call Phyllis, she'll tell you where those consults are. Now get moving, or I understand those rats want their man to service them, your choice."

Again, Chenoiel's face turned tense, then instantly relaxed. "You can't keep me out of the O.R. forever." He walked off the floor.

Ike and Zach watched him go. "We are going to have problems with him again," Ike said. "Look, go scrub with Ginsberg. He has a cholecystectomy, and a cold, so he is pretty much going to let you handle the operation. I'm with Hercules and I'll ask him how we are going to handle this prick. Most important, stay away from Chenoiel. You blow up and whack him, and Bullshit will have no choice but to can you." He looked at Zach and added, "Please, I don't want to lose you, too."

"I'll stay away. I promise. Go see Hercules. We have to have a plan ASAP."

Chapter 56

"Thanks for the chicken soup, Shoshie," Zach said, sniffling.

"You guys are all doctors and you can't even keep yourselves from getting sick. Look at these on-call rooms. Are they ever cleaned? And what's with the overflowing wastebaskets full of snot-crusted Kleenex? Does everyone have a cold on this service?"

Zach chuckled. "I'm not sure all that Kleenex is snot-crusted. I'd stay away from them; one of those wads might be fresh and get you pregnant."

Shoshie looked stricken. "Ugh, why did you tell me that? They do 'that' in the on-call room?"

"Well, it's a hard life, and the lack of warm companionship dictates that a true surgeon has to take matters into his own hands. Of course, sometimes the nurses, lab techs, janitorial staff, in fact, any kind of female, is here to help."

"Dr. Maxwell, you are a gross individual, but I love you in spite of it."

Zach froze, as did Shoshie. The love word had reared its loaded head. Did she expect him to respond with "I love you, too"? The door to the on-call room banged open, wiping the deer-in-the-headlights expression he had, and the uncomfortable silence that had thickened the air.

Ike stuck his head in the room. "There is a big trauma in the E.R., everyone else is in the O.R. Let's go," he yelled. He noticed

Shoshie and said, "Oh, hi, Shoshie, wanna see something cool? Zach, give her your none-too-clean white jacket, and let's go."

"Uh ... Shoshie?"

Shoshie had noticed his reaction to her blurting out the word "love," and he didn't look happy. She straightened up, and said, "I'd like to go, Zach, if it's okay with you."

"Of course it's okay. Boy, are you are going to get an eyeful," Ike said, happily missing the tension in the room.

Zach gave her the jacket, too much in shock to voice any protest. They ran down to the E.R. where someone's mouth had a laryngoscope in it. "You *sha-mutta*, where are your motherfuckin' cords?" Kazi the gas-passer yelled.

Ike looked at the Egyptian anesthesiologist trying to get an airway in a woman who had obviously taken a baseball bat to the face and been stabbed multiple times in the chest. "Having problems, my Egyptian brother? She looks like someone tried to hit a homer with her head."

"Who the fuck is so angry that he not only tries to decapitate his victim, but also tries to cut out her heart? A fucking animal. I can't see a fucking thing in her pharynx. Blood, mucous, air bubbles, and her sat is going to hit snake eyes any second."

Suddenly, like an avenging angel coming through the curtains, Hercules appeared.

"What happened here, besides the obvious, boys? She looks like someone tried to kick a goal with her head."

Ike gave a low-key laugh. "See, Zach, in America, we see baseball, but in Greekland, it's all about soccer. Kazi, go take a sedative and let me in."

Hercules looked over the situation, noting a rapidly decreasing blood pressure and a rising heart rate. "Zach, look at her! Five seconds, what's happening with her? You win a prize if you get it right. Otherwise you're the goat, and you know what Greeks do with goats?"

Ike mumbled, "Fuck them?"

"Yes, Dr. Ike, but not the way Brooklyn Jews do. One, one thousand, two, one thousand ... Time almost out Dr. Maxwell, three ... "

Zach was sweating through his underwear. "What?" Then he saw it. "You have to crack her, Hercules, now."

Hercules called to the nurse, "Eight and a halfs for me, and seven and a half for young Dr. Maxwell ... also a condom. He is about to become a man. Plus, get the chest tray. Chop, chop." He turned to Zach, and for the first time saw Shoshie, white and trembling in a coat two sizes too big. "Which one of you morons brought the civilian?"

Zach froze. Bringing in non-medical personnel to a case, especially something like this, was strictly verboten.

Ike piped in. "Oh, that's Shoshie. She's a medical student who came in tonight for a tryout rotation."

Hercules shook his head. "A med student wearing Zach's toxic jacket and looking like she is going to puke and have diarrhea at the same time. Where is she a med student, Dr. Maxwell?"

"Ah ... "

Ike smiled. "Zach, don't be ashamed that your first cousin goes to a shitty foreign medical school in ... Haiti. Hercules, she is just observing ... really."

"Really, huh. Okay, but don't let Bullshit catch you."

Kazi screamed, "Hey, hotshot butchers, your patient just stopped breathing and BP is almost zero! Maybe it's time to attempt to save her or something?"

"You are correct, my Mediterranean brother from another mudder. Ike, give Kazi a break, and get him back to work and off his lazy ass. Cric her. Zach, you crack her."

Zach was sure he hadn't heard right. Opening a patient's chest who was in cardiac arrest was a senior-level procedure, not for a youngster like he was. "Hercules, I've never done one of these."

"I'm aware of that, young Dr. Kildare, but you won the quiz, and besides, I'm wearing my suit ... no-blood rule, you know. But let me help." Hercules unceremoniously stripped the sheet covering her upper body, revealing multiple stab wounds that had stopped bleeding, then took a bottle of Betadine and, extending his arm as far as it would go, emptied it over the left side of her chest. Not a drop of it, or blood, got on him. The patient had a pair of magnificent breasts that were at least double-Fs. Zach was mesmerized, not realizing that Shoshie was watching him. He felt a sudden slap to the back of the head. "Ouch," he said. "What did you do that for?"

Shoshie, now aware that both Hercules and Ike were staring at her, suddenly felt ridiculous. Zach had just proven he felt nothing for her an hour ago, what did she care? "I'm sorry, Dr. Hercules and Ike, I just felt that Dr. Maxwell's brain might have glitched and need a reset."

Hercules guffawed. "Reset, huh? You seem to be a smart medical student. If he doesn't do something soon, can you reset him again?"

Zach was so hot, it seemed steam was coming out of his ears. "Ten scalpel to me, nurse." He held out his gloved hand and a knife was slapped into it. He cut a continuous incision, going from the sternum, down under the breast, to the sheet. Suddenly, he was doused with cool, clear, liquid coming out of his incision. "What the fuck is this?" he shouted, as the liquid spilled, soaking his crotch.

"Shit, Zach, what the fuck? You could hold it till after the procedure." Ike laughed hysterically.

"Ike, leave the boy alone. You have your own task to accomplish. By the way, how is that hole coming?"

Ike had a small endotracheal tube in his hand, and with a flourish of his hands dropped the tube into a hole in the front of the patient's neck. "Done, oh Greek master o' mine. Kazi, get off your rug and bag her up." Kazi grabbed his bag-valve-mask and connected it to the tube and pressed oxygen into her lungs. The pulse oximeter started to rise to acceptable levels. "Hey, Greek, I'm oxygenating the pre-dead here. Maybe your fucking Jew of a boy could save her life now, and not piss himself?"

"I didn't fucking piss myself, you camel-humping drug pusher. The fluid came from her. What the fuck, did she piss on me? Oh, fuck! Her tit!" Her gigantic pillow of a left breast was now a flat, empty bag. "They were fake?"

Shoshie, who was shocked silent by the screaming, yelled, "You are such a shmuck, of course they were fake, now could you shut the fuck up and save her life?"

Hercules's mouth twitched, and then he started laughing. "Yes, shmuck boy, could you now impress us?"

Zach, who still had the knife in his hand, glowered at his audience. "Blow me!" He slashed through the intercostal muscle and was showered with blood. "Kazi, open all fluids, get me four units of O negative and fucking push it in. Rib spreader ... now." He didn't wait but took his hands and started pulling the two ribs apart that he had separated from their attachments to the intercostal muscles, and pulled them apart like a wishbone. Both ribs made cracking sounds, and all the muscles in Zach's arms grew more prominent with the strain.

"Look at his guns," Ike commented, "he's my ma-a-an."

"I saw him first, Ike," Shoshie commented. She had a rosy glow about her face and a fine sweat on her skin. Ike took a second look at her, and could have sworn she looked just like Goldie after he had his meal at the "Y." She hadn't just ...?

"I don't want him, Shoshie."

"Would you two shut the fuck up, and Ike, swing that lamp in here, I can't see a mudderfuckin' thing," he said, as he placed the metal rib spreader.

"Yes, stud boy," Ike responded. He grabbed the handles to the huge mega-wattage surgical light and aimed it into the patient's chest. Looking behind him, he yelled, "Goldie, I mean, Shoshie, get over here if you want to see her heart, literally, not metaphorically." Shoshie got behind Ike's crouching back. What was that scent? Oh fuck, just like Goldie. "You okay, Shoshie?"

She looked flushed and was obviously breathing hard. "Just a little warm," she croaked.

"Here, get in front of me, behind super-surgeon." He positioned her just behind Zach's bent body as he was staring at her heart. She bumped into his backside trying to see.

"Hey, watch it." Her body was really warm against his ass, her crotch involuntarily rubbing his ass every time he switched position. Her crotch was like flame against him, and that smell, shit, it was delicious. Oh God, he thought, as his crotch started responding to sudden quiet moans coming from her. He shook his head, fuck and dammit, where was the bleeding coming from? "Get me some goddam suction."

A tonsillar-tipped suction was placed into his right hand and he suctioned blood, both liquid and clot, away. "There you are, you fuckwad." He had found a slit in the heart muscle and surrounding pericardium that pumped out blood with every heartbeat.

"Hey stupid surgeon, she just rolled snake eyes BP. Do something or pronounce her," Kazi said. "And could someone find out what smells like a camel in heat? Jesus!"

Camel in heat, Zach thought. No time. The moaning behind him was louder and Zach was pretty uncomfortable himself. Shit, he couldn't stand up now.

"Zach, hurry!" Shoshie panted.

"Fuck! Foley catheter size twenty-two and ten ml saline in a syringe. Glove, Shoshie, I'm going to need hands."

Ike cautioned, "Zach, you sure? I mean, Shoshie?"

"You mudder, you set this up. She has to go to the O.R. We will need to transport. You and me pushing the gurney, you making sure we don't lose the cric. Me stabilizing the Foley and holding Shoshie while she straddles the patient and keeps that mudderfucking Foley under pressure against the hole in the heart. It's the only thing keeping our patient alive. By the way, watch that the patient doesn't fall off the gurney with your driving, and make sure the Greek keeps blood off that awful suit he is wearing, or we will have to hear about it, over and fucking over."

"Hey, boy," Hercules boomed, "this suit is from the finest Greek tailor in Athens."

"You should have found the finest Jewish tailor in Athens," Zach retorted. "Greeks are ignorant about line and fabric but they sure know about fucking sheep," Zach chortled.

"Zach, do something now," Kazi snarled. "She's dead and becoming a stiff corpse."

"Oh yeah." He grabbed the balloon-tipped Foley and pushed it against the blood-spewing hole and into the ventricular chamber. The nurse handed him the saline filled-syringe, and he injected into the Foley's port, inflating the balloon. He then gently started to pull the Foley out of the heart, but the inflated balloon was too big to go through the hole, and snugged up against the hole, sealing the blood in the heart.

"Pressure coming up," Kazi reported. "You, little Jewess, see if she is stiff yet."

"Ignore him, Shoshie. His people fuck four-legged mammals for entertainment."

Zach grabbed Shoshie's gloved hand and placed it on the Foley. "Pull gently, not too much. You want to keep the balloon snug against the wall of the heart. Too much and you can rip the heart further."

Shoshie's eyes were glassy, her skin was absolutely glowing, and there were small drops of sweat dripping down her cleavage. God, she is magnificent, thought Zach. "Got it, Shoshie?" Suddenly, he grabbed her face and kissed her on the lips. "Your lips are as sweet as nectar, my bride; milk and honey are under your tongue." Christ, Hebrew school was good for something, he thought.

"She is Zach's cousin?" Hercules asked Ike. "Boy, there are strange customs here."

"What, you don't have kissing cousins in Greece, Hercules?" Ike responded.

"Yes, stud, I mean, Zach, I've got it." She blushed even more than she had.

"Now up onto the stretcher and straddle her. I'll keep you steady."

She just nodded.

"Hercules, we are ready."

"Great job, though could have been a little faster. Oh well, next time for the land speed record. By the way, you owe that medical student flowers. I'm going ahead to the O.R. and meet Braverman. She'll be waiting and take over for Shoshie. By the way, Shoshie, if you need a recommendation ... "

Their eyes locked, and he winked at her. She gave a bashful smile. As Hercules went past Zach, he whispered, "Don't lose her, schmuck. Goats are not as much fun."

Off they went, tearing down the hall, with George Washington Shoshie upright on the boat of the half-dead patient to clear the way.

The O.R. team met them at the door of the O.R. suite. Braverman gingerly took the Foley into her gloved hand from Shoshie. She whispered to Zach, "Hercules says to grab the girl and disappear before Bullshit shows up. He says one hour, but if you are the man he thinks you are, take two. His final words, he approves." Braverman shook her head and looked up at Shoshie. "She is beautiful, better than you deserve. Now beat it."

Zach, with a big smile, mock-saluted. "I am relieved, ma'am." He grabbed Shoshie and they beat it.

They crashed through the first empty call room door and started ripping off each other's clothes. Lips met lips, hands touched hands, fingers molded and unmolded, tab A met slot B, and with gusto. Laughing, kissing, loving he was alive. Was it serious? Zach thought. Who cared for now? He felt wonderful, and she felt wonderful under him, and above him, and to the side of him. Those eyes, that scent was intoxicating, and he felt like a surgeon, and the world was spinning round and round and round …

Chapter 57

The patient lived, despite the possibility of bleeding to death before the surgery, and cerebral anoxia, traumatic brain injury, sepsis and/or pulmonary embolism after the surgery. Despite multiple surgeries to fix her face and fix a breast that a young intern had damaged during her resuscitation, she lived and finally was released, only to be found a month later, stone-cold, blue, with her eyes frozen open. A needle was buried in her arm, and the coroner ruled she had died of a massive drug overdose.

Zach got the call from Jake, who had quietly returned to become a Family Practitioner. He was in the E.R. when the paramedics brought her in. Her left post-thoracotomy scar was blue like the rest of her, but obviously a newer addition to a body that was a map of a hard and wasted life. Jake had heard about Zach's resuscitation when he was out on leave and knew Zach would want to know.

"Zach, over here," Jake called. "We just pronounced her a few minutes ago."

Zach walked over to the draped body still waiting for the morgue gurney and uncovered her face. Sightless eyes staring at what? He didn't know. He didn't even know if he truly cared about her death. They had worked so hard to resuscitate her, then to reconstruct as much of the damage as they could. The rehab was difficult, but she even triumphed there. What had happened? Hadn't she appreciated that whomever was in charge of such things had let her have another chance? He shouldn't let such losses concern him. Life was precious but if the patient chose unwisely … well, to hell with it. There were plenty of patients within feet of him who were praying for every last second. He covered her face and walked back to the elevator. He didn't feel any relief from the black cloud that had surrounded him, but duty called, and those patients wouldn't fucking check themselves. He entered the elevator wiping the tears from his eyes.

Bad times come in threes, so just in time for Zach to get ready for a quick tasteless sandwich for dinner, his beeper went off. With the mood he was in, the last thing in the world he wanted to do was answer it, but the minute the operator started talking he knew that if horrors came in threes, this emergency counted as one hundred. He doubted he would sleep tonight.

"Okay, I'll be right down. Has someone notified Dr. Chenoiel?"

"No Dr. Maxwell, the family doesn't want to see Chenoiel, and for good reason. They want you, now get your ass down here. He must be in a tremendous amount of pain."

Zach was steamed by then. "So get him four mg of morphine I.V. push. I'll be down."

"Now you know we can't do that. Hospital rules clearly state a doctor must come see the patient, and write, and sign, the orders before the nurse can administer them."

"But it'll take me ten minutes to get there. I'll write and sign the orders when I get there."

"No, Doctor, that is against policy. You best just hurry."

"Listen, you angel of perverted mercy.… "

"You're wasting time, Doctor." There was a click and the line was dead. Zach hated the 1099-ers, unionized nurses that used dumb rules so they could get away with working as little as possible.

He dialed the page operator. "Dr. Chenoiel to 3561, please." The phone rang back thirty seconds later.

"Chenoiel, meet me on the third-floor ward. Siegel is back, and it's bad." Siegel had survived his last near-death experience, but he never came back all the way. His mind never cleared completely, and he became wheelchair-bound because he was too weak to walk.

"I wondered how long it would take you to call me. The ward called me, and then immediately called me back, and said don't bother. I recommended they call his Jesus … you."

Zach again wondered how this subhuman got through a single interview for med school. He was about to blast him, and just as suddenly, ran out of steam. He hung up.

Zach could hear the screams at the elevator door. Pain, fear, and, if one listened closely enough, a loud and forceful command to God to end the pain and let him sleep, eternally. Siegel had been under this death sentence for months, living longer than anyone expected. He kept repeating that he had to see his son bar mitzvah. Siegel was now in hospice with a DNR order. The "Do Not Resuscitate" was for terminal cases who had no reasonable life-saving or even palliative treatments left. The only thing these people had was pain till the end. As such, for the hospice to send Siegel in, screaming the way he was, meant the "gallons" of morphine they were giving him were not working. Zach sighed and went into Siegel's room. The stench was thick, sweet, evil. It had overtones of feces and pus. Zach, who was now the expert of debridement of unviable tissue, knew this was gangrene, and gas gangrene at that. He lifted Siegel's hospital gown to expose his grossly distended abdomen. Siegel by this time had had three or four intraabdominal procedures, mostly to fix complications due to intestinal obstruction and problems with his colostomy. Zach knew Hercules was concerned about the healing of the incisions. Siegel would become weaker after each surgery, not interested in food and the calories that would help him heal his wounds. The second problem was Siegel's abdominal distention. The cancer was everywhere, including his liver, causing fluid in the abdomen to accumulate. The fluid's pressure on the wall caused the abdominal wall to stretch. Eventually, there was so much pressure that the veins collapsed and blood flow was obstructed in the abdominal wall. Over time, the cells would die, allowing gangrene. He saw a large, wet, brown stain on the gown over the abdomen, and knew his worst fears had been realized. Siegel's wound was going to open and eviscerate his abdominal contents. He ordered a large dose of morphine, told Siegel he was going to call Hercules, and went off to think while waiting for Hercules to come down, and tell him what to do.

Siegel was sleeping under enough morphine to kill the average person. It was a blessing being able to relieve such pain. Hercules came and had just finished his exam when Zach looked at him, and knew from the tensing of Hercules's face, it wasn't good.

"If we debride the gangrenous area, there is no tissue left to suture the incision in the abdominal wall. We will never get it closed. Unfortunately, this is going to happen soon, spontaneously. The abdominal wall will just split spontaneously from the rot."

Zach shook his head. "He'll die. He can't survive that kind of traumatic event. His heart is weak from the lack of calories, and his kidneys are barely holding on." He looked up at Hercules. He almost had no strength left to ask a question. Siegel and he had been through so much in the last months. They both needed time off. In Siegel's case, it would be permanent. "Hercules, he doesn't want a miracle. He doesn't even want to live a day more.

The only thing he wants is to see his son bar mitzvah. Then he can die. We need to do this for him. We are indirectly responsible for Chenoiel's actions, he was part of the team, is part of the team. His bad reflects on us."

"When is the bar mitzvah?"

"This Saturday, though there is another problem there. He needs to be in a synagogue. His kid needs a Torah. You know what that is?"

"Hey schmuck, you know how many years I have lived in Brooklyn? You don't think I don't know what that scroll bible is?"

Zach smiled. "I have an idea. Who is the head yammie-bopper doctor at PAY?"

Hercules laughed as he saw where this was going. "Well, Fogler is, but why do you need a doctor? I heard you're bosom buddies with the head bopper himself. In fact, I heard you removed a small piece of his foot, and he offered you herring and you, slut, ate it."

"I was hungry, and Leiber needed that piece of herring only if he needed me to debride his rotted *schmeckele.*"

Hercules smirked. "Hey, respect the *schmeckele,* it made fourteen kids. They say his wife's vagina is secretly called the Holland Tunnel because of that."

"The fuck you say."

"Greeks invented truth, I cannot lie. Go call Leiber, I'm sure if you give him the circumstances, he will help you. He is a good man deep down. Come back afterward. I have an idea."

Zach went off to call Leiber and was amazed how easily it all went. Leiber told Zach that it was a great mitzvah, or good deed, to help Siegel with his last wish, especially since the last wish involved the Torah. Leiber said that Siegel's rabbi was a friend, and he would make all the arrangements for him. The service would be held in the hospital synagogue. The morning of the ceremony, they would set up a corner of the room as a mini ICU, with monitors, vents, etc., and they would bring him down at the last minute so he could see his son become a man.

Zach was about to get off the phone when Leiber stopped him. "Dr. Zach, I want I should give you a blessing."

Zach needed to get back to Hercules and tried to put this off. "Listen, Rabbi, Hercules is waiting and he has an idea that may keep Siegel alive a little longer. Saturday, at the bar mitzvah you'll bless me, Hercules, the Arabs, the Israelis, Bullshit.... "

"No, you will take sixty seconds. This is important. This you will not make fun of," Leiber said sternly.

"Rabbi. ... " Zach knew it would be worse if he just hung up, and what the fuck. "Go ahead Rabbi, but I warn you, I'm not wearing a yarmulke."

"You're such a *schmendrick*. How God gave you a brilliant brain for medicine, eating, and *shtupping*, and not one for your soul? *Vay ist mir.*"

"Rabbi, please, let's get this going."

"Meyer ben Yitzhok," Leiber chanted, using Zach's Jewish name. "May God grant you the wisdom, strength, and cunning to keep his patient's life from the Angel of Death, if even for only a few days. May you grant Meyer happiness and satisfaction in his chosen career. May he save many lives. May you find him a worthy Jewish woman, one who is patient with his pig-headed ways but will know his golden heart. May they have much *nachas* from their children. *Oo-main.*"

Zach smiled. "Rabbi, with a blessing like that.... Well, how the fuck can Siegel and I lose?" He hung up the phone and ran back to the ward.

"It's called a Harvard sling."

Zach was looking at the simple but seemingly effective apparatus under Siegel's abdomen. It was a sheet, rolled and tied to the rails on his bed, creating a sling. Hercules had taken a lamb's wool incontinence pad that prevented bed sores, and wrapped it around the sling, making it very soft. With this, he elevated the protuberant abdominal wall in which gravity had caused a kinking of the blood vessels.

All of a sudden, the abdominal wall looked pinker, except for the gangrenous portion that had started, ever so slightly, to separate. "Certainly looks better."

"See the spot where it is separating? We will put a small drain there and hopefully if the fluid has a place to go, there will be less pressure on the wall. Maybe get an ultrasound in here, and look for abscesses that are subcuticular, and then we can aspirate them."

They walked away from the bedside. Even though Siegel was out of it because of the pain meds, they didn't want him more upset than he was. How does a condemned man even feel? "Hercules, how much time can we buy him?

"Wait, I will call 1-800 GodUThere. How would I know? Siegel was fucked from the moment Chenoiel missed his diagnosis by not examining him. The truth is, his tumor is so aggressive we probably wouldn't have saved him anyway. That he has lasted this long is a true miracle and more probably a statement of how his love for his son is giving him the strength to survive. Now we need to help him survive the next couple of days alive and awake enough to say goodbye.

"What else can we try?" Zach asked.

"I think drains, or better wicks. We get the ultrasound and find the bigger collections, and then wick them. It'll draw off the excess fluid and decrease the pressure."

"I'll get rays down here. Maybe we have a chance."

Chapter 58

"**Zach, the guy in room ten** sliced his forearm and is bleeding all over the place," Sheila, a nurse, told him. "Can you go look at him and try to stop the bleeding? We called Vascular, but they are tied up with that multi-vehicle crash. Lucas is swamped, so you were bachelor number three. The patient is messing up the floor, and the janitor is getting pissed. He is looking a little pale and sweaty, and I don't need a hypovolemic arrest on top of the shit I got going on here."

Zach had just left Siegel's room after the rays guys wicked all the abscesses they could find near the old suture line. They were doubtful it would help prevent full dehiscence, but they agreed it couldn't hurt. Zach was praying to every god he could think of, please, just a couple of more days. He was so tired, but Sheila was a great nurse, and had helped him and others out of big binds. Screw it, he should be able to stop the bleeding. Wasn't that what surgeons did?

He picked up the chart and walked into a blood-sprayed room containing what appeared to be a wild animal covered in blood. Shocked, he froze. A bomb exploded by his head, and all went black. The third bad thing had happened.

"Zach, can you hear me? Zach, oh, Zach? Earth to Zach!"

Zach painfully opened his eyes to see Ike applying a stiff cervical collar to his neck. Jake was holding an ice bag to his left jaw. "What happened?" He tried to get up but Ike put a hand to his chest.

"Not so fast. First a CT of your head and neck, and then you can go dancing."

"What do I need a CT for? Did anyone else get hurt when the bomb went off?" Zach saw Jake look at Ike worriedly.

Jake answered, "What bomb, Zach? There was no bomb."

Zach was more confused than ever. "What about that bleeding wild animal?"

Ike understood and laughed. "Oh, you mean Mr. Petralli."

"Petralli the street person? What does he have to do with this?" Zach said.

Jake, still looking worried, responded, "You know how Petralli collects empty bottles of Night Train in the neighborhood? Well, he put his arm in a bin that had broken glass, and sliced himself. He was pretty drunk at the time, and obviously wasn't taking any of his meds. The cops found him dripping blood, so they dumped him at his home away from home, PAY. He knows Sheila and he kept it together while she bandaged up his just-oozing arm. The alcohol and lack of antipsychotics finally got the best of him. Sheila didn't see that part of his behavior, so she left him in the room and I guess he started bleeding again, bad, and his blood pressure must have dropped and along with his natural hallucinations, the alcoholic thought you were here to take off his arm and eat it."

"No, he said, take off his arm and shove it up his ass," Ike claimed.

"Well, yeah. Sorry, I forgot. So, he did the American thing. He decked you," Jake responded.

Zach saw the gurney being wheeled into the room. "Here's

your ride. God, it seems we did something like this a couple of months ago. By the way, does it still get up and perform?"

Zach moaned. "You guys are hilarious. Where is Petralli now?"

"Why, you want to sue him or ask him out on a date? Rematch maybe?" Ike asked.

"He's in the O.R., Zach. I pushed Haldol into him with Ativan and Benadryl. He'll be okay," Jake answered.

Ike asked Jake, "Can you follow him from here? I got a shit-load to do, and now I got to write his notes?"

"Sure, Ike," he answered. "You're lucky, Zach. Ike was going to get one of the new nurses to give you a total bowel cleanout. He said it would clean, or was that clear, your mind."

Ike started down the hall. "Feel better, buddy; see you later."

Zach just saluted him with his middle finger.

He was battered and bruised, but his brain was intact, and besides some spasm in his neck, his cord was intact. He would be stiff and aching for days. Thank God he was in the profession he was. No time would be allowed for rest to think about the violence and its aftermath.

The phone rang, and he hesitated to answer it. He was tired and felt guilty he hadn't spoken to, or worse, seen Shoshie for days. After their, whatever that was, he was high on love and life, but he couldn't understand why the love, hope, intimacy, hadn't buoyed him for more than a half a day. He needed quiet and when the phone stopped ringing, that is what he had.

Chapter 59

The weekend had arrived and Zach, for the first time in weeks, was rested. He hadn't had the overnight on Friday, so instead of sleeping three-quarters of the day on Saturday, he was awake. So here he was in his boxers, having had the best night's sleep he had had in a long time, and a whole two days to forget his life as it was.

He called Shoshie and told her he was in the mood for his favorite Manhattan vacation.

"Manhattan vacation, now what's that, Zach? I thought you had the day off only."

"Yep, so I have to make it a vacation day. Breakfast out, stroll around town, see things, watch people, dogs, and birds, bask in the sun, and then dinner at a small steak house in Soho, and home. You with me?" he asked hopefully.

"It sounds nice. Tell you what. Where is the breakfast place? I'll meet you there, so you don't have to first come down to Isaac's and get stuck answering a hundred questions. We'll have more time, just the two of us."

"Can't wait to start our first vacation together." He put down the phone and went to shower, whistling his happiness.

The sun was shining and the birds were chirping. Shower time.

Even the drunks and addicts who had pissed themselves in the subway car couldn't dampen his mood. Next stop, the Village, and breakfast with a great girl. The car screeched to a stop and was plunged into darkness. "Passengers, there is an electrical problem on the line. Remain calm, we are sending out technicians to fix the problem." Fuck, thought Zach.

Zach ran to the street and headed for the coffee shop. He refused to have his mood diminished. He found out from the hostess, yes, a nice-looking girl had come, but since her friend didn't show she had left. He was now pissed at the city of New York and the subway system and was, in a foul mood, going to call Isaac's to see if she had come home. Then he heard a scream from behind the counter.

"Ahh, *Maman. Maman.*"

The woman sitting in a pool of yellowish fluid was young and black and very pregnant. It was obvious she had broken her water, and now was in the process of trying to give birth. Zach had seen many women give birth during his medical school training, and it wasn't all the beautiful crap the women's lit people put out. In fact, Zach thought it was the most nauseating medical experience he had ever participated in. He remembered his first delivery under supervision. He was standing in front of a very distended vagina, hearing an orgasmic screaming coming from the owner of the vagina. Suddenly, a shower of hot amniotic fluid and blood hit him full in the face, followed by a slippery mini-alien attached by a cable. The poor woman also picked that time to have a bowel movement right in front of him, getting his new sneakers soaked. Clamping his jaw and almost losing his lunch then and there, he managed not to drop the baby. He never wanted to do another delivery as long as he lived.

But medical education came first, so he managed not to vomit through another twenty or so deliveries without major incident. Now, in front of him was a woman who, by his quick exam, was at term and ready to go, but somehow looking not right. Her face was a rictus of pain, sweaty and …

"Fuck me … " Zach said, under his breath while feeling her abdomen. Her baby was breech, upside down in the uterus. This made for a potentially very difficult delivery if the baby didn't flip to come head first out of the vagina. Normally, if the baby didn't flip, a cesarean section was done.

"Call 911," Zach told the crowd that had gathered. "Mama, do you speak English?"

The mother started another contraction, which Zach figured to be about a minute after the last one, and screamed "No, *français!*"

"Can anyone here translate, anyone speak French?" Zach called out.

"I can," came a familiar voice.

"Shoshie, I thought you went home. The train got stuck and I had no way … "

"I thought something like that happened, but maybe we should talk about this later. So, you deliver babies too?"

"Uh, I have. Just a little problem with this one. It wants to come out ass first. I don't have a lot of experience in breech births."

Shoshie got close to him and whispered, "How much is not a lot?"

"None. Breechers are born mostly by C-section in the States. I can't section her here, and that baby wants out. The longer we wait, the more chance for a complication to baby or mother."

"Oh shit, " Shoshie cried.

"Yeah, oh shit. Listen, tell her the baby is upside-down and I need to turn the baby."

Shoshie went over to the woman, whose next contraction had just finished, and told her in French that Zach was a doctor and was going to help her. The woman, now sweating even more profusely, rattled off some French.

Shoshie grabbed her hand and tried to reassure her.

"Allons-y. Est-ce que ça va faire mal?" the soon-to-be-mother chirped, before the next contraction hit her.

"What did she say?" Zach asked.

Shoshie, looking worried, said, "She wanted to know why you looked so worried if you were a good doctor. I told her the baby was upside-down and you would have to turn him."

"She okay with this, Shoshie? I think if this baby doesn't come out, the risk increases."

"She said let's go, but wanted to know if it would hurt. Will it?"

Zach grimaced. "Yeah, like a bitch. Tell her to brace herself."

He yelled at the cook to bring him some olive oil and when it arrived, poured it over her protuberant abdomen. He needed to basically massage the baby around the right way in the uterus. "Okay, tell her to try and relax, it will help."

Shoshie grabbed her hands and murmured French at her like she was transferring strength to the woman.

Zach was just praying he didn't screw up. He felt for the baby's butt with both hands, and started slowly pushing and pushing. The woman let out a yelp, and then clamped down, only her eyes showing the pain. Shoshie was frantically rubbing her hands.

Slowly, the baby's body moved within the uterus under his hands. This maneuvering was done often in the Third World and very rarely in the States. External Cephalic Version or ECV was practiced only when C-sections were difficult to accomplish. The goal was to make the baby rotate 180 degrees. He just kept turning the baby slowly … when the mother had a seizure.

"Zach, what's happening? Is she dying?" Shoshie cried.

"No, she is eclamptic. We need to get the baby out. It's the only way to stop this, and probably the hypertension that goes along with it. Grab a rolled towel and try to get it between the woman's teeth so she won't bite her tongue off."

Zach held onto the baby's position for dear life. As the woman started relaxing with the seizure ending, he shoved the baby into position. The woman, now awake but unfocused, let out a scream and started pushing. Zach quickly positioned himself between her legs and tried to slow the baby from coming out too quickly. Suddenly, there was a slippery, stinky, blue baby in his hands. He grabbed the baby's feet and lifted the baby by them. A quick tap to the baby's soles resulted in a crying, pink, infant.

"Mon bébé. Mon bébé."

He once again yelled into the kitchen. "Clean towels, I need clean towels." He cleaned and swaddled the baby and put it in the mother's arms. "Tell her to hold her baby close. The baby needs the mother's warmth," he told Shoshie.

Shoshie was beaming. *"Le bébé es si beau."*

Zach was mentally exhausted, and in his exhaustion opened his mouth. "Boy, that is not for me."

Shoshie immediately stiffened, gave Zach a weird smile, and after reassuring the mother all was well, took off. Zach, now confused, wanted to run after her but the paramedics had arrived, and he knew he was going to have to write up some sort of chart. Miserably, he started into the paperwork.

"I just don't get it. Everything was great. She was helping with that woman who gave birth to a healthy baby girl and boom, she took off like a rocket."

Zach was in the call room talking to Jake. He had tried to

call Shoshie multiple times, but she wouldn't pick up, and when Isaac did and heard his voice, he just snarled and cursed him out.

"Maybe she was shocked by the whole process," Jake offered. "I mean while we see childbirth ... "

"No," Zach interrupted, "it was something else. I had just said I never wanted to do a delivery again, when boom she was out of there."

"You didn't," Jake said, amazed.

"I didn't what? You know I hate obstetrics. I vomit, though I didn't this time."

"Tell me, exactly what you did say?" Jake asked wisely. "What words did you use?"

"Uh, I don't really ... 'Boy, that is not for me?' Oh, shit, she thinks I don't want kids? But why would she be upset? We're not even engaged? I mean ... "

Jake just shook his head. "You are an amazing friend, doctor, and human being, Dr. Maxwell, but what you don't know about women, especially one who might be in love with you. Well, I'd start crawling back to her on hands and knees. You just told her that the man she was contemplating spending the rest of her life with doesn't want to get her knocked up. Dope!"

"Oh fuck!"

"Yeah, oh fuck, or in your case, no fuck."

Chapter 60

"Shoshie, please don't hang up," Zach said into the phone.

"What do you want, Zach?"

He had rehearsed what he would tell her if she picked up the phone, but just had trouble saying any words. The words now seemed so inadequate "I do want kids, Shoshie, but now, with the residency, and trying to make time for a normal life, and not taking you for granted, how do I juggle babies or even being a husband? Besides, I was talking about OB-GYN, not babies. I don't like deliveries."

"Look, Zach, I have to get a move on, so I'll make it short. I guess it just hit me with the beautiful place you and I were in, helping that lady and the beautiful baby, you should be happy. I know I was just so happy being in a situation where I could help another human being in such a difficult time. I was overwhelmed. Then you ruined it, and why? Because you can no longer see the beauty in having the skill to save lives. I also realize you don't see a family in your future. Maybe I'm just another girlfriend for a while. Sure, you need some human contact besides your fellow residents, and maybe that is all you want. I come over, you cry on my shoulder, we fuck, and then it's back to the hospital. I can't invest time in that life, but I guess I know and understand your needs. I just can't provide for them. Be well and have a great life." With that she hung up.

"Fuck." He slammed down the phone. What the fuck was wrong with him? He realized his life wasn't his own, but for crap's sake look at Ike, look at Hercules. They had wives and kids and someone to go home to. Hell, they even liked it. Ike had admitted their sex life wasn't what it was when they were dating, but he said he was just too tired most of the time. Zach remembered that he had a funny, lopsided, grin after he had admitted that. Zach had asked what he was smiling about. Wasn't boring, intermittent sex depressing? Ike told him after this place just having someone who cared about him, sleeping beside him, rubbing his shoulders, holding him, was better than all the porn sex he had always imagined but had never achieved. He told Zach one day he would understand having a friend who had your back, who supported you, who only cared about the safety and happiness of the family, the family you had created together with love, was better. Then he laughed, and told him a Saturday night blowjob was great, too.

It was the time of day when the nurses were rounding on their patients. He quickly went to the call room and took off his scrubs and got into his bloody clothes, hoping the blood and stink wouldn't be too objectionable. Fuck, half of Brooklyn was dressed the same way, and smelled worse. He left the room and snuck out of the hospital.

The cab pulled up to Isaac's house. It was then, reaching for his wallet that he realized it was missing, and he had no money. The Pakistani driver looked back. "That is $10.95, sir."

"Uh, I forgot my wallet. I'm sorry. Look, wait I'll get some money." Zach felt chest pain and shortness of breath. Here he was trying to win Shoshie back, and he now had to beg her for money. What a schmuck.

"You have no money? I am going to call the police. You don't go anywhere."

"Look, man, I just need to go to that house and they'll give me money for you. Just wait here."

"No, sir, you will wait in my cab."

Zach jerked open the cab door and ran up Isaac's walk. The cab driver got out of the car and started screaming at him. "You son of a whore, I will kill you!" The cab driver got back into the car, and Zach rang the bell frantically. When the door didn't open, Zach started banging on the door and ringing the bell.

"Shoshie, Shoshie, please open the door. Shoshie …!"

The door suddenly opened, almost causing Zach to fall through the doorway, but an older, portly man stopped him with one, strong, outstretched arm. He noticed the bicep's tendon disruption, making the arm look like Popeye's, and in the other hand, he saw the shotgun.

"Vat do you vant?" the man asked. He looked angry, and he wasn't Isaac.

"I need to speak to Shoshie. Can you tell her I'm here?"

"Who are ju? Vay you vant to speak to mein daughter?"

It dawned on him this was Shoshie's father, Abe, and he didn't look happy. Maybe it was the shotgun he had in his hand, or the index finger on that same hand that was twitching. "You must be Shoshie's father, Abe. Hi, I'm Zach." He stuck out his hand, but Abe just looked at it like it was a piece of rotting garbage.

"You're the *momzer* who disrespected my daughter. Get otta here. You hear me, get otta here before I give you a reason to go home by ambulance."

"Look, Abe, I need to talk to Shoshie, please, it is important."

Abe raised the shotgun and pointed it at Zach. "Tsu redn nischt English? Get otta here." Abe shoved the barrel of the rifle into Zach's gut.

"Not until I see Shoshie. If she wants me to go, I will."

Abe cocked the shotgun.

"Abe, don't do anything rash, please." Zach was feeling a

strong urge to urinate, but he'd be damned if he'd be run off by this ill-tempered Polish immigrant. "Look, five minutes, please. Just tell her I'm here."

"Too late, momzer, you're trespassing. Say your prayers."

"Abie! Stop that right now!" Shoshie's voice made Abe jerk, and fortunately the jerk pointed the shotgun up, letting off a blast that made both of them head for the floor. Unfortunately, Uncle Isaac now had pellets embedded in the plaster ceiling of the foyer. The broken plaster fell on Abe, covering him in white powder.

Zach shouted, "Jesus Christ," and grabbed the shotgun away from Abe while scrambling to his feet.

"What are you doing here, Zach? Do you need something? Maybe someone you can use as a part-time friend only when you have need of them?"

"Ya, git otta here, momzer," Abe added. "And gimme back mein gun."

"Abie, please go into the kitchen. I need to talk to Zach alone."

"Ach, you are always talking to these boys. Just kick them out, and if they don't go, I shoot them. When are you going to find yourself a real mon?"

"Abie, just go. You are making this worse. Zach and I were never serious. Please just go, now." Abe walked away muttering, and Shoshie stepped onto the porch and closed the door. "Why are you here, Zach?"

"I … I needed to talk to you. I couldn't leave it at our last conversation. Do you really believe I was never serious about you?"

"It wasn't a conversation, Zach. It was more my reporting on why you lost me as a girlfriend, lover, friend … whatever our relationship was. Your skill in saving those two lives made me so proud that I had a relationship with you. You made me think here was a man worth pursuing, but you then proved you are not someone I'd want to start a future with. Now, please just go. I am glad you are safe and healthy, and I hope you have a happy life."

"Shoshie, please. I'm sorry. I want to be with you."

"No, you don't, Zach. You want conflict and action. You want to be with the boys, drinking, screwing, getting yourselves into trouble, and I don't blame you. It sounds like fun, and if I were someone else, or younger, I wouldn't mind being part of it, but I want the mature relationship that might go somewhere."

Zach looked troubled. He wasn't like that. He hated the pressure and the frat-house mentality that had created a Chenoiel, or Jake's problems. He knew he wasn't the typical surgical personality. That ambience of uberman just wasn't something he wanted to subscribe to or acquire. He would always be Zach, that nice kid who cared about his patients, and cared about his friends and family. "I'm not like that, Shoshie."

She looked at him hard. "No, you aren't, but you go along, because that is what the surgical residency does to all of you. You know who the bravest of you is? Jake, who in the end, figured out that to save his own humanity, he needed to change his life. God knows it almost killed him to get there."

"Shoshie, I don't want that life. I want you to be my life and I want to be in yours. Whatever happens, I want it to start with you and end with you."

Shoshie's eyes glistened with tears, and Zach's heart leapt. Had he won her over? But, just as suddenly, he saw the glow leave her face, and a frown start to form.

Shoshie took a deep breath, as if to reset herself. "I believe you believe those words right now, but what about tomorrow? What about when the next tough stretch happens, and life gets complicated? Why would you even need another human in your life? You are building a future that is right out of those TV shows you used to tell me about."

She took another breath, and the steel in her straightened her frame. Zach wasn't sure that his dreams of a stable life with her were going to survive the next ten seconds, let alone his lifetime.

"Let me tell you what I want, Zach. I want a husband who will be there for me. A husband who wants a friend, a lover, a mother for his children. Of those three things, the friend is the most important and not just when you need someone as a pillow for your head, or someone to dry your tears, or someone to just expend the frustrations you have about your life in bed. I mean someone you want to just sit with, or walk with, or just wake up in the morning with. I know this is trite, but really, what else would you want from a life? I won't be a booty call, or your psychiatrist, or your mother. I want a real man who wants to be there for his family through good and bad and everything in between. In return, I want to promise my man the same."

"Shoshie, I … "

"Go back to your apartment, or better yet, go to Snooky's. There are nurses there who will understand your immediate needs and won't demand much. There is nothing wrong with any of them. In fact, the women nurses and the doctors are all in the same boat, needing a human for just a few hours at a time. I'm not saying I offer more than they do, in fact, looking at this from your point of view, I offer less for more work on your part, but I will always be there for you."

Zach was silent. He wanted to tell her yes, he would be all she wanted, but he was afraid that it was an impossibility. It seemed she was demanding he give up all he was working for. Medicine was a bitch that also demanded total loyalty to care for the sick, the helpless, but did that really make a good doctor? Where was the humanity?

The silence had gone on for too long, and they both knew it. Zach felt the sick pressure in his chest, where every breath came with difficulty. He was nauseous, his legs felt weak, and he knew he would have to turn around and walk back to that cab with the screaming driver. He looked at her for mercy, but saw none and, he thought, rightly so. Shoshie deserved the husband that would be present. He just didn't know if he could promise that.

"Goodbye, Zach." She reached up and kissed him on the cheek. "Go and make your dream happen." Her breath caught, and she turned and walked back into the house, closing the door behind her.

Chapter **61**

"**What the holy fuck** were you thinking?" Ike yelled as he re-established the I.V. fluids, and added a small bag with antibiotics in it to flow through the main line. "She was the best thing that ever happened to you, besides working with me."

"Leave it be, Ike. My heart will heal, and I'll be able to cover all your surgical goof-ups like I usually do." Zach lay back and looked out the window. Brooklyn was still alive. The lights of mid-town Manhattan still shined brightly, the world continued, and he heard the distant sirens of the ambulances going to retrieve the sick.

"Zach, call her. Tell her you want to be with her and won't let that dick brain of yours screw up again."

"Ike, she was right. She wants a guy like you. Goldie's husband is a guy who is always going to be there. Good or bad, rich or poor, your wife knows she is with a guy that counts. I don't know how you do it, but I doubt I can."

Ike was quiet for a moment. "I had an advantage you didn't. I married my best friend from grade school, and we have been dreaming the same dreams for decades now. Goldie and I went to school together, went through the rejection of the medical schools in the States, and the exile to a foreign country. We went through the surprise pregnancy, the surprise miscarriage, the rich days and the poor days, and we are now going through this. Frankly, if I didn't have her to face those years with me, I might have been the guy trying to fly off the balcony."

"You're a better man than I'll ever be. I can't imagine being a partner in anything and I certainly can't imagine being a father. Shoshie will find the right guy for her. Me, I'll get back to work."

Ike put a hand on Zach's shoulder. "You are making a mistake. Shoshie loves you and you not only love her, you need her to stabilize your life. You're going to be a surgeon, and believe me, as your responsibility for your patients increases, you are going to need the support more and more. Think hard after you get some rest."

Zach went back to the apartment. Manhattan's lights through his window beckoned, promising good times, good food, good drink, and beautiful women. At one time it was all Zach wanted. The MD, the surgical scrubs, the nurses in starched whites, and the antics that occurred between the sheets with them. He had tasted a tiny sampling of that life. It was fun and tasted sweet, but it was like empty calories. The only significant aspect of his life was represented by his patients. All else made very little difference. Could his professional life be enough? Manhattan's lights seemed to be signaling no.

Two days later he had gotten back to his regular routine. He wandered to the ward for rounds, only to find no one at the nurses' station. He walked down the hall looking in the rooms, but all he saw were patients, no doctors, nurses, or aides. What the fuck? Did the schedule change the two days he was gone?

"Surprise!" Zach jumped. Everyone had been hiding in the rooms, behind curtains and corners. Zach's heart was beating a mile a minute. Everyone was there, including Hercules, Ike, Jake, and even Bullshit. The guy standing behind him looked familiar.

Bullshit signaled for everyone to quiet down. "Your Honor, may I introduce Dr. Zach Maxwell?"

The Mayor of New York shook Zach's hand. Out of nowhere, a photographer snapped some pictures of them. "That was a great thing you did, son. The woman has been telephoning, as have the Haitian community leaders, as to what a wonderful thing you did. This city needs more doctors with your attitude of helping the residents of the great city of New York."

Zach mumbled his thanks to the Mayor, and then looked for an escape hole. Zach slowly moved away from the crowd and, as soon as he thought no one was paying attention, ran for it.

He ended up in the most cliché place he could, the chapel. At least here there was hardly ever any traffic. No one came to a hospital chapel to pray, and the only chronic users were residents fucking nurses who liked the illicit feel to the whole place.

Fuck, he thought. The door swung open and Hercules spotted him. "I thought the Orthodox didn't come into a Jewish-Catholic chapel. Besides don't you have miracle surgery to perform?"

"No miracles scheduled this morning. You never know, though. The day is young." Hercules chuckled.

I don't think the surgical life is for me, Hercules," he said.

"What do you mean, boy?"

"I need stabilization, a home to go to, a woman, kids, and God help me, maybe even suburbia."

"I agree with you, boy. This is a life for someone who already has a stable life, or for a sociopath who wants to be in a constant war state. Now, when you get out of residency, you can stabilize your life, but it works better if you already have a partner who has gone through this with you. If you wait till you are a full-fledged surgeon, women seem to think that you are ripe for the picking and have a tendency to spend all the money you make for themselves. Of course, that can happen with a wife that was part of this.... "

"Please stop, Hercules. I need something else besides this. I need to start working on an adult life, because being a kid was fun, but should be finite."

Hercules shook his head. "You need Shoshie and you need … " He paused, and as if a lightning bolt had entered his brain, a smile lit up his face, and he said, "I got just the right thing for you, but you will have to give up the O.R. You can and will still get to wear pajamas to work."

"What miracle is this?"

"Come on, we got to make rounds, and then you go down to the E.R. and ask for Garber."

"Garber? You mean that guy who directs that three-ring circus?"

"Boy," Hercules said with a smile, "he is the ringmaster of hell."

Chapter **62**

"**Dr. Garber, I'm Zach Maxwell.** Hercules said I should come and see you."

"I know who you are, Zach, and you can call me Mark. We are pretty informal here."

Mark Garber was a thin, salt-and-pepper-haired man with a large beard. He wore an earring, and his scrubs were as filthy as most of the surgeons'. "Well, to be honest, Mark, I don't know why I'm here. Hercules thought you could help me with a problem, but unless you are a life counselor … "

"Nah, nothing like that, but I can offer you an alternative life choice. I was impressed with your treatment of the alcoholic with the peritonsillar abscess. What was his name? Oh yeah, Zinman. You treated him like a patient and examined him. That was good work, especially considering he is a sub-human piece of shit who smells to high heaven, and has a mouth on him that would make a drunken sailor blush."

"Hey, he is a human being, and he was sick. I could tell that in my sleep."

"But he is a disrespectful waste of life."

Zach was getting mad. What was with Garber? "Listen, Dr. Garber, he was a patient, period. I had a job to do, and I tried to do it to the best of my ability. I'm sorry I wasted your time. Hercules was trying to help, but I don't think there is an answer here." Zach got up to go, but Garber's hand grabbed his shoulder.

"Hang on, young man. Hercules was right to send you to me. What do you know about the Emergency Department?"

"I know it's the last hope of the dying, and that everything ends up here. I know the office practices refuse to see last-minute emergencies, sometimes any kind of case, so they shove them into the Emergency Room. This is where the resuscitation happens, and there is an awful lot of chronic care and fishing for OxyContin going on. I know your doctors are the last people any of the ward doctors want to hear from, and that every specialty in this hospital thinks your people are fucking lunatics."

"Whoa, tell me what you really think." Garber laughed. "Well, I think that is a pretty fair assessment. So, let me tell you why you are a lunatic. Come and take a walk with me. I need a large cup of bad coffee. You look like you could use one, too."

Garber led him to a small room that had a large window with a view of the E.R.'s critical care beds. It also had a view of the entrance from the ambulance bay, where patients were continuously brought in by medics for evaluation.

"The key to being a good E.R. doc is observation," Garber instructed. "You need to be aware of almost all things going on in your department at all times. This room was set up to give the working docs and RNs a place to scream, cry, laugh, vomit, whatever he or she needs to do to break the tension, and still be in observational control of what's going on in the department."

Zach looked around, noting an RN stretching on a battered couch yet keeping an eye on the window. "Cushy arrangement you have here. How do you guys rate this clubhouse?"

"Cheaper than mental health counseling for employees on a twenty-four/seven basis. You're correct, everyone who works here is a lunatic. On the other hand, no one here can ever say they are bored. The Emergency Department is an outmoded term, it's the crisis center of the community. Give us your tired, your poor, your huddled masses, and we'll make chicken salad. The Emergency Department sets the tone for a hospital. In fact, we probably get away with more shit than the rest of the hospital combined, because no hospital can survive without us."

"You are a lunatic. No one gets away from stupid hospital rules, and how does anyone survive a twenty-four/seven battle zone?" Zach questioned.

"It takes a certain personality and skill set. Want to see if you have what it takes? There are pluses, including a stabilized life with set working hours. You walk in, and twelve hours later you are gone. You can actually plan a date and getting laid on a consistent basis."

Zach thought that life couldn't be this structured. "Look, Dr. Garber, it sounds interesting and insane, but Dr. Moskowitz would never let me out of my surgical residency, and I don't even know if this is for me. Going from one frying pan to another that is hotter ... well, I don't know."

"I'll give you a week to think on it. Maybe you want to talk to a significant other about this? Oh, and by the way, don't worry about Bullshit. He has already approved this if you want it."

"Approved it? How did he even know about this?"

"Well, I don't know for sure, but my guess is that your friend Hercules has been laying the groundwork with Bullshit, and finally got him to sign off on this. But Bullshit may have seen this himself. In the end, he wants happy, adjusted, doctors. He also wants excellent doctors who were trained at PAY and keep this dump in the worldview as a producer of healers. If he needs to give up making an ace surgeon, he'll claim helping create an ace E.R. doc. Look, go home, and think about it. PAY is about to start the first Emergency Medicine residency in Brooklyn, more specifically East New York. You will be the first resident in Emergency Medicine, Brooklyn style."

Chapter 63

Fourteen hours later Zach finished assisting on the third GSW to the gut. Two were still alive, one of those barely, and one died on the table. Too many holes and not enough time to plug them all. Zach was bone-tired and hallucinating. He went into the surgeons' lounge, and poured the hours-old, brown acid the hospital called coffee. No cream was available, as usual. He collapsed on the old, stained, mustard-colored couch, spilling some of the acid on his scrub top. He barely noticed, as the coffee maker could only heat the liquid up to tepid.

"Whatcha doing tonight, Zach?" Ike asked. "It is supposed to be beautiful."

Zach zoned his aching eyeballs toward his friend. "You're kidding, right? I think I'll take a ten-mile hike, in my dreams. Why, what are you doing besides going home and into coma? Hopefully, in that order."

"Yes, I guess you're right. I really wish I had the strength to at least go out for a drink. Goldie and I haven't had a date for months, and tonight is the only night I can foresee that happening for the next month."

Zach didn't know if Ike knew he was contemplating leaving surgery. He had wanted to make the actual decision as to his future in a private, meditative way, but he also didn't want to surprise one of his best friends after the fact. He thought Ike would be disappointed. He also knew Ike didn't think much of the E.R. His bottom line on Emergency Medicine was, they cause more patient problems than they are worth. "Ike, if you had it to do all over—if you could have gone into another specialty, would you have?"

Ike sighed. "Yes, in a New York minute. Truth is, I enjoy my home, and my wife and kids, and the residency is made for a man who is more like a priest than us mere mortals."

"I'm thinking of leaving surgery. I want what you have, but Shoshie didn't grow up with a boyfriend who wanted to be a surgeon. She met me under the worst of circumstances."

"What the fuck is the worst of circumstances? That you were in a training program so demanding that almost all your time is taken doing disgusting things to patients?" Ike asked.

"There is a mantra every little Jewish girl hears from the moment she hears sound. It goes like this, 'Marry a doctor, marry a lawyer, marry an engineer, marry someone who will give you a great life.' The problem is Shoshie actually wants a husband, not a roll of cash who will set her up in Boca every winter and give her a platinum Saks card."

"Crap, you mean I missed all that because I grew up with Goldie?" Ike looked skyward and addressed the heavens. "Thank you, Lord, for sending me Goldie at an early age, and keeping me away from evil, i.e. strange, Jewish girls and their mothers, for which I will give Goldie a foot rub, a back rub, and multiple orgasms."

Zach chuckled. "She'll be lucky if you stay awake through dinner. Well, I got some thinking to do. I do like the excitement of the Emergency Room, though I'm not sure dealing with the I-want-a-work-note patients, or the I'm-allergic-to-everything-except-P-P-P-Percocet patients, is what I want to deal with the rest of my career."

"You could spend the rest of your life doing gallbladders, which will probably be my fate."

"Yeah, I guess there is that."

This time Zach did it right. He carefully showered and shaved. He dressed in his best button-down shirt and slacks, and even put on a tie. He still only had the corduroy sports jacket Shoshie had made fun of, but it would have to do. This time, he made sure his wallet was in his pocket, and grabbed the dozen red roses he had picked up from the local supermarket in the morning. He left the apartment and went down the elevator and out the lobby just when the cab he called for showed up.

"Shoshie, would you go on a life adventure with me?" he murmured to himself.

The cab driver yelled, "What did you say? Be patient, we will be there in ten minutes."

"Nothing, just talking to myself," he said. "Shoshie, I've wanted to make more of a commitment for a long time." Jeez, so clinical, and as romantic as a soap-suds enema. This wasn't going to work. Suddenly, he was covered in flop sweat. "Fuck, I'm going to really screw this up."

The cab pulled up to her uncle's house, and Zach paid the driver and walked up the pathway. He was about to knock on the door when it opened, and Abe was pointing his shotgun in Zach's face. Zach had been in the middle of a knock on the door, causing him to lose his balance, falling into Abe. No longer having control of the gun, Abe fell backwards, with his finger on the trigger, causing the gun to go off. That was how Isaac's ceiling got a second hole in it.

"Abie, I am taking this gun away from you before you either kill someone or yourself. There are no Nazis at the front door. Second, it is time for you to go home, back to Rya."

"I will not go home with that momzer around. He might try to pull something, the *nischtgutnik*. I don't even think he is a surgeon."

"Abie, he is a surgeon. A surgeon in training, and he is a good one at that."

Zach, who was still shaken by his second near-death episode with the father of his future girlfriend, mumbled, "I'm not a surgeon anymore."

Abe, having abnormally great hearing when he wanted to, yelled, "See, I told you so. Not only is he a momzer, he's a liar. He isn't a surgeon. Ask him, Shoshie, if he is even a doctor, the momzer. Where is my gun? I'll kill him."

Shoshie was confused. She looked at Zach curiously, and then at Abe. "Abie, you misheard. Of course, Zach is a surgeon. Tell him he misheard, Zach."

Zach was silent for a moment. God, this wasn't the way he wanted this to work. "Uh, no, I'm no longer going to be a surgeon. Abe heard right. I need to talk to you, Shoshie. Please, just a couple of minutes."

"I swear I'm going to kill this momzer, liar, fake-doctor, nischtgutnik."

"Abie, go into the kitchen now," Shoshie commanded.

"Again, with the kitchen," he said as he slowly walked toward the rear of the house. He turned and gave Zach the evil eye. "I'm watching you, momzer."

"Come on Zach, let's take a walk."

It was a lovely evening. It had rained earlier, and the air was fresh and the leaves still had drops of rainwater, making everything glittery. They didn't talk, nor did they hold hands as they walked to a neighborhood park. "Let's sit down," Zach said.

"Why did you come, Zach? I understand you don't have time for anyone in your life. I can't just wait around. It is time for both of us to move on. You go and become … whatever it is you are going to do."

Zach saw she suddenly looked confused. She scowled and took a deep breath. Frozen by whatever thought she had, she remained quiet, waiting for him.

"I don't want to move on without you, Shoshie. I want to see where the relationship goes. I understand why you decided I couldn't make a commitment, but I'm going to change my life because I want to try to be a good boyfriend, and if that works, I will try to make you believe we belong together forever."

Shoshie looked at Zach and sighed. "Your life is going to be amazing. Treating patients, saving lives, but it has no room for me. I told you before Zach, I need to feel I am important in my partner's life. I can't be there just to put the bandage on the boo-boo, or when you need to release your stress into a convenient woman. I'd be happy to be there for those, as long as you are there for everything else. Zach, I want the love of my life. I want a home, babies, maybe even dogs or cats. I want to get up in the morning and see a man who loves me, adores me, and I will guarantee he will feel loved back. I'm here to listen to the good, the bad, the happy, the sad, as long as I can tell you all those things, too."

"Shoshie, I don't want to lose you. I'm leaving the surgical program and am going on a fixed schedule, but just not in Surgery. It will still be bad for a bit, but it'll get better. Please stay with me, I love you."

Shoshie looked shocked. "You're leaving surgery? No, I can't have that. You're good, and a natural. You'll just end up resenting me. No, no, no!"

"I love you, Shoshie. This isn't a sacrifice. It is rebuilding me—and more importantly, us."

"I know you love me. I knew it from the first time we met,

and I slugged you," she laughed. "Zach, you love being a part of the surgical team. You'll resent it, missing all the excitement, the blood, the drug addicts. What are you going to do if you don't practice surgery? I don't exactly see you as a pediatrician."

"God forbid, a pediatrician ... no. There is this new thing ... E.R. I'm going to be the guy who saves the patient who is bleeding, short of breath, or with no blood pressure. I'll save them without much of a medical history, without knowing the patient, and I'll do it as they come through the door. We can tell your father that I'm going to be one of the first Board-certified Emergency Physicians in Brooklyn, and I'll love his daughter for as long as I live."

Shoshie smiled, "Me? Tell him you're going to be an E.R. doctor, working in a hospital? This time I'm sure he'll actually shoot you and not the ceiling."

Chapter 64

"**Emergency Medicine can be** summed up with this check-off list: 'Sick/Not Sick. Admit/Don't Admit.' We are an easy specialty to learn. All the other strategies you may learn are pure, unadulterated, crap." Garber had welcomed Zach to his first day as an official Emergency Medicine resident with breakfast at the hospital coffee shop. He guessed all the specialties wanted to fatten the lambs before the slaughter of the residencies.

Zach looked up from his bagel and a schmear, trying to digest Garber's statement. Yeah, it was an easy specialty, except you needed to learn enough of every other specialty: Surgery, Medicine, Cardiology, GI, Pediatrics, even Radiation Oncology, to apply his simple statement accurately. Often, you had to do it with no previous information on the patient, and at breakneck speeds. The PAY E.R. was one of the busiest in the country. The average wait for the many non-emergency emergencies (colds, sore toe for three months, rash for years) was between eight and eighteen hours, depending on the time of day and the day of the week. The non-stop traumas and heart attacks were signals to stop everything else and try to save a life.

"As an Emergency resident you are second in command to the nurses. They are older, more mature, and have much more experience than you do. They will give you plenty of rope, though. Try not to hang yourself."

Zach's experiences with the E.R. nurses were generally good. Garber was correct about older and experienced. Like Braverman in the O.R., Mrs. Molchan was the nurse supervisor of the E.R. who ruled with a velvet-covered iron fist. Her two majordomos, Joni, and Mama Lisa, ran the place, when Molchan wasn't there, like a Swiss clock. Because the place was so busy and chronically understaffed, the unofficial word was, "If they walked in, they can walk out." The three of them taught, coddled, admonished, and begged the new residents to move the meat as fast as was safely possible.

The residency was to be a big experiment in the PAY E.R. and Garber was the man to do it. He had been a Vietnam-era surgeon, where triage, the art of prioritizing sickest from non-sick, was practiced both as a science and as an art. Pre-mortally wounded soldiers became saved soldiers because minutes hadn't been wasted dealing with lesser levels of sickness. After his stint in the Army, he went to Parkland Medical Center in Texas, and studied with the great trauma surgeons there. He learned those first minutes of resuscitation in the E.R. were the difference between life and death. He found other surgeons who felt the same, and a group was formed to create a specialty in Emergency Medicine. Zach was going to be part of that program.

"You're lucky, Zach. This is going to be easier for you than the rest of the newbies coming in."

"How so, Dr. Garber? I know I spent some time down here with the surgical program, but what I know about Internal Medicine or Pediatrics will fit on a very small pin."

"Ahh, those are subjects a monkey could learn. They are also specialties that don't teach you how to think on your feet. Ever been on rounds with medical or pediatric residents?"

"In med school. They were very long rounds."

"You know why they were so long, and boring, I might add?"

"Uh, no."

"Because when you're mentally masturbating, it takes a long time to cum. This is a good thing under certain circumstances. In Emergency Medicine, it means death."

Zach chuckled. "Yeah, I could never be an office internist, and Pediatrics gives me migraines."

"You have the wrong personality. I've watched you with patients. You are nice to them but comes a time when you decide action is needed, and boom you are sticking large needles into their necks or groins."

"That is the surgical way," Zach said. "That is the way Bullshit teaches it, that is the way Hercules teaches it, and I'm pretty sure that is the way most surgeons practice their specialty."

Garber sighed. "Bullshit is a great teacher of surgeons, and Christospathos is the last of his acolytes. The next generation of physicians will follow the rest of the sheep to the slaughter of medicine as we know it, practicing the fear of getting sued game."

"That can't be. Look at what happens at PAY, on a daily basis. We have a patient population that needs, demands, aggressive treatment."

"Zach, you haven't yet enjoyed the fruits of the private sector. Ever wonder why the community hospitals send so many really sick patients in here?"

"Uh, because they don't have doctors who are trained in critical care the way we are?" Zach answered, unsure if he was correct. There were damned sure a lot of patients from the peripheral hospitals showing up in their private ambulances on an hourly basis.

Garber laughed. "Where do you think those surgeons, internists, and especially the pediatricians, trained? Right here at PAY. Theoretically, their knowledge base should be greater than yours or even Christospathos'. More cases, more experience, more maturity, frankly. No, the reason the peripheral hospitals send all those patients in here is to die. They figure PAY, being a teaching institution, will give those patients their "Hail Mary" of care. If the Hail Mary doesn't work, well, they would have been dead anyway. The advantage for the community hospital of sending all these cases to us is their decreased mortality rates and decreased malpractice suits. If you don't believe me, take any of the major surgical procedures and compare mortality at the larger community hospitals versus any of the major teaching hospitals in any part of the country. More people die here than any community hospital. The why is because patients here are sicker, usually have worse healthcare, and less compliance with their physicians' advice. That is, if a lot of these patients even sought the care of a physician when their maladies might have been easier to fix. Places like PAY are truly a last line of defense, and the Emergency Department is where the war is fought. Welcome to a last line of true battle-ready physicians, Zach."

Zach felt a chill and suddenly cold sweat ran down his back. Could any human deal with the chaos of the sick and the dying, side-by-side with the social-problem patients or the minor-problem patients? All, by law, had to be medically evaluated, and cleared to either go home or be admitted for further work-up. "How do you deal with this circus?"

Garber smiled. "With class, looks, and a certain bonhomie."

Garber moved off with a wave. "See you on Monday. Go have some fun, because it will be work, work, work, in twelve-hour bites after that."

"Wait, I thought I was starting today."

Garber just waved as he disappeared through the entrance. Three days, what was he going to do with himself? Shit, he knew what he wanted to do. He grabbed a phone and dialed, please be home, please be … "Shoshie, what are you doing for the next three days?"

Chapter 65

Forty-eight hours later, his apartment had that musky, exciting, scent of sex, sweat, day-old pizza, and unwashed wine glasses.

Zach, naked, in bed, stretched his back. Next to him was the most beautiful back and butt he had ever seen. He felt a familiar heaviness below his waist and reached out to stroke the perfect skin.

"Oh, that feels good. So good." She turned around and gave him a smile. Her hair was disheveled, and her cheeks were a healthy pink. Her small, firm, breasts were pert with a hardening of her nipples. "What's up, big boy?" She looked down at what looked like a tent pole under the sheets. "Again?" She paused as if she were thinking about a great problem. "Oh, okay, but then we are getting out of this bed, and doing something vertical." She flowed into his arms, flipping him on his back. "I'll do the work. I need the exercise anyway."

They emerged from the shower, both physically and mentally happy and satiated. Zach thought about the rest of the day and tomorrow. So, this was love. He knew that whenever she was near and he looked at her, he felt like someone was there for him and he wanted to be there for her. Wasn't this what love was all about? All he really knew was he was happy and at peace for the first time in a long time.

"What's the matter, Zach? Second thoughts? You're frowning."

He smiled. "No regrets, second thoughts, and I'm very happy. I think I know what I want to do tonight."

"I'm sure I can figure out what you want, but sweetheart, as much as I want that too, I'm a little sore and need some rehab time. At least a couple of hours. How about vertical time?"

"Yeah, I want that too, but I actually had something else in mind, and your body doesn't have much to do with it."

She looked disappointed. "Tired of me already, you cad?"

"Never tired of you. I think I'd like to meet your father and try to make amends. Think he might allow me to visit tonight?"

Shoshie smiled, and let out a squeal, followed by a big hug and kisses. She then ran to the phone. "I'll call him and tell him that the shotgun better be stowed in the basement."

"Good idea. I might not survive a third encounter of that kind."

"Abie, this is Dr. Zach Maxwell. He is a doctor and is in a residency at PAY. He was studying to be a surgeon, but decided he wanted more time for a normal life."

Abie looked Zach over like he was a mule on a sales block. "Vat doctor has a normal life? He must be lying. He can't be a doctor."

Zach sighed. He figured switching from surgery would be strange, but he never realized that just trying to explain what an emergentologist actually was would be such a problem. "Abe, let me start by saying I'm in love with your daughter and ..."

"Shoshie, vai this boy? He's *nischt* a sturgeon, *nischt* a doctor. Vat kind of *nebbish* is this?"

"Abie, stop right now! He is a doctor and a good one at that."

"Shoshie, du hast a *gut hertzl*, but you are such a *schmendrick*. Look at him, he looks like a used car salesman."

"Abie, I assure you I'm ... "

Abe's face, quickly darkening in frustration, almost had smoke coming out of its ears. "You momzer, you're *nischt* a doctor. You're trying to get mein daughter and then leave her, you piece of shit. I'll kill ... " Suddenly Abe turned white, and the sweat started pouring out of him. "I'll kill ... " he murmured, as he collapsed.

"Abie!" Shoshie cried out.

Zach couldn't believe what happened. He had just killed his potential father-in-law. Shoshie would never be with him again. Fuck! Why couldn't his life be normal?

"Shoshie, call 911, now." Zach dropped to his knees and shook Abe. "Abe, can you hear me?" He felt for the carotid pulse and felt nothing.

"Zach," Shoshie cried, "what's happening?"

By this time, Uncle Isaac had run into the room, and seeing his brother collapsed on the floor, screamed that his brother was dead and Zach had killed him. He started to grab Zach, but Shoshie blocked him.

"*Gey avek*, Shoshie. He murdered *mein brudder.*"

Zach yelled, "Everyone, shut the fuck up and let me do my work." He made a fist, and came down on Abe's chest hard.

"You momzer, don't touch him. I vill fucking kill you." Isaac was livid.

"Zach, what are you doing? Please save him, please." She was openly crying.

Zach reached to find Abe's pulse again and came up with nothing. "Shit, maybe I did fucking kill the bastard." He raised his fist once again and punched Abe, while muttering a prayer to God to save Shoshie's father and he would make many Jewish children with his daughter. He then thought maybe this was too carnal an oath, and retracted it, smashing into his chest yet again.

Isaac couldn't be contained any longer and jumped on Zach, punching him. Zach was getting killed, and thought that now if

Abe had any chance, Isaac was keeping him from his patient. He yelled, "Sorry, Uncle Isaac," and socked him in the jaw. Isaac went flying backwards only to be caught by his wife. "*Vu ist duest*," she screamed.

Zach turned back to Abe to check a pulse, and as he was doing this, started to put his lips on Abe's mouth, when Abe opened his eyes, and gently pushed him away. "Give *mein* daughter a *kish* instead. She needs it more than I."

Zach smiled at Abe. "Do you still doubt I'm a doctor, Abe?"

Abe chuckled, then groaned. "Vay did you hit me so hard? Mein chest is killing me."

Suddenly Shoshie was down on the floor, kissing her father. "Abie, don't do that again."

"Hey Zach, you ever hear a daughter tell her father vat to do? Tsk-tsk, so disrespectful. Go to your *beshert*."

Shoshie flowed into Zach's arms, kissing him.

"Okay, okay, Shoshie." He kissed her, and knelt back down to Abe, checking his pulse. "Are you having any chest pain or shortness of breath? Do you have a heart history?"

"Yeah, you momzer, I have chest pain and shortness of breath. Where you socked me," he said with a smile, and a twinkle in his eye.

"Abie, vai don you tell him vat your doctor told you," Uncle Isaac yelled. "You almost died, because you are a *schmuck*."

"Zach," Shoshie said, "Abie has angina, and is supposed to keep his temper in check. He is not to get too excited. He is supposed to watch his salt and fat intake, so for lunch, instead of a pound of pastrami, he has three-quarters of a pound on rye with a large kosher pickle. To Abie, that is a vegetable, isn't it Abie? His cardiologist forbade him from going to wrestling at the Boston Garden because he got so excited he'd have angina attacks ... and where did you have your nitro pills? That's right, nowhere near."

"Ach," Abe croaked. "*Gay kaken afen yam.*"

"What did he say, Shoshie?" Zach laughed. "I think I remember my mother saying something like it, but I remember it wasn't very nice."

"I'm sure your mother would never say anything like that to a son she loved and who loved her with all his heart. Only a low-class, crotchety, know-it-all like Abie would say something like 'go take a shit in the ocean' to his beautiful, loving, daughter. Right, Abie, you bad boy?"

The sound of the ambulance siren could be heard outside. "Well, I think we can conclude this lovefest. I'll ride with Abie in the ambulance. Isaac, can you give Shoshie a ride up to the hospital? I'll make sure everything goes smoothly. I'm sure my friend Jake is on tonight. I'll get him on Jake's service, and then Jake can get a cardiologist for him."

Abe told Zach his cardiologist was in Boston. "Don't worry, Abie," Zach told him, "the medicine here is better than Boston, and we'll make sure we get you an excellent cardiologist."

"*A danke*, Doctor. I am in your hands." Abe grinned.

"Well, that's a change from trying to shoot him, Abie. Maybe an apology would be helpful," Shoshie scolded.

"Okay, let's forget about shooting, killing, and destroying ceilings. Besides, the ambulance crew won't allow shotguns. Shoshie and Isaac, get up to the hospital and I'll stay with Abe."

Jake looked at the cardiogram, and shook his head. They were in the cardiac care unit, with its monitors, beeps, and alarms.

"What?" asked Zach. "I really don't want Shoshie to think her father needs anything but anti-anxiety pills, or a chemically induced coma so he can't get to his gun."

Jake looked at Zach sternly. "You could have finished him off and had a stress-free girlfriend, but you had to save him."

Jake laughed. "The EKG looks fine, no acute changes. We will keep him here and rule out an infarction. Maybe adjust his anti-hypertensives a bit and keep him on a low-fat, low-salt, diet for twenty-four hours. That should cure him … not."

"But, he doesn't need a stent or bypass?"

"Not this time. I think he stressed himself into a vasovagal event and couldn't get himself out of asystole. He may need a pacemaker, but cards will decide that. Don't worry, a guy like Abie can handle a little cardiac arrest. You or I would be fitted for a pine box, and land in Beth Jacob's Cemetery. Just don't let Shoshie bring him the pastrami sandwich he wants to celebrate with."

Jake went off to see his sicker patients, and Zach went into Abe's room, where Shoshie was talking softly to him. "Good news, Abe."

"Ach, *ich vil nischt* surgery."

"Abie, you will do whatever the doctors recommend, or I swear I will tell Mom and you will be grounded. You know how unpleasant that will be, with Mom being the jailor," Shoshie told him sternly.

"Please don't tell your mother. She'll kill me. Better I should have been killed by the heart attack."

"Well, lucky you. They are planning to keep you overnight for observation and if all remains stable, send you out within the next couple of days."

"*Danke Gott.*"

"And you should thank Zach and Jake, now. And while you're at it apologize to Zach for doubting him," Shoshie admonished him.

Abe, with downcast eyes and a smile, said, "I'm sorry, Dr. Maxwell, can you forgive me?"

"Yeah, I forgive you. Just try to keep your blood pressure down and stay alive."

Abe looked tired, so Zach recommended that they go and he get some sleep. Abe murmured, "Take care of Shoshie, Dr. Zach."

"What happened to Isaac, Shoshie?"

"He hates this place. He has had his prostate treated here, along with various cuts, bruises, and an occasional broken bone. He's not wild about doctors to begin with and hates this hospital."

"I'll get you a car to take you back to Isaac's house."

"You mean you're not inviting me up for a drink?"

Zach smiled. "Don't you think Isaac will be angry if you spend the night and then tell Abe?"

"You saved his brother's life. I don't think there will be a problem."

"In that case, come home."

Chapter 66

"**Zach, there is a** new patient in ten. Short of breath."

Zach had just arrived and received sign-out from the night shift doctor. He had grabbed a cup of coffee, and a couple of Motrin. His back was cricked from last night's kama sutra practice. He smiled, thinking it was a small problem in exchange for a wonderful night. He had arrived early, and snuck up to Abe's room, and found him still asleep. The nurse had told Zach that the blood tests had come back positive, but they thought that was from the chest compressions. They were planning to stress him later in the morning. Zach made a mental note to get ahold of Jake, and ask him about a stress test versus a catheterization. Zach looked at the computer and signed up to see the patient in room ten, with a foreboding. The patient was Mr. Siegel.

Siegel had been pumped up with a triple cocktail of antibiotics, and the Harvard sling supported his abdominal wall. Siegel's wife and kid decided to postpone the bar mitzvah until Siegel stabilized. He couldn't go home, and it was decided to put him into a nursing home that offered a hospice floor. Siegel had been tottering on the precipice for weeks now. His body showed signs of severe muscle wasting. He was starving to death, as his intestines no longer would absorb much of the nutrients that were fed to him through his gastric tube. The GI docs had once again tried to give Siegel TPN. They had successfully placed a catheter into his subclavian vein located just under his clavicle and pumped in the slurry of protein, fats, vitamins, and minerals. The war to save him kept him on just this side of death. Because he couldn't get enough calories, his abdominal wall dehiscence would not heal, and the mess continued to be supported by Hercules's Harvard sling. The true evil was that Siegel's mind was still sharp enough to know his situation. Every day, Zach heard, he cried, demanding his son have his bar mitzvah, and he attend. Even Rabbi Leiber had been unable to comfort him, trying to explain that his son was automatically bar mitzvah whether he read from the Torah or not, and that the after-party was not a religious event.

Zach walked over to room ten and found Debbie, a senior nurse, taking down Siegel's dressings. It was a tribute to her professionalism that her face didn't display any disgust with bandaging soaked with a combination of pus, blood, and other necrotic material. The smell was devastating, but Debbie was pretty much immune to bad smells at this stage of her career.

"Mr. Siegel, what's going on today?" Zach asked. "The nursing facility says you were having a fever and are draining from your wound."

Siegel grunted in pain and exasperation. "I'm always draining, Dr. Maxwell, it always stinks, and I always have a low-grade fever, but the fucking incompetents at that torture-chamber nursing home sent me in because they get tired dealing with it. I tell them I will be kind enough to die on them so they don't have to clean up this mess, but I want my son's bar mitzvah." With that outburst, he lost all strength in his limbs, and the tears flowed from his eyes.

"I'm sorry, Mr. Siegel. Let me look, and maybe we can try to lessen the problem." Zach tried to sound convincing but failed. By this time, Siegel just obviously didn't care. His depression was the only emotion he was capable of. Even the pain that he felt seemed to be a null area in his life.

Zach took down the dressings that were saturated with a vile-smelling green-yellow cream and tossed them into a red hazardous-waste bag. The layer of tough, fibrous, tissue that was the only thing holding Siegel's abdomen together was starting to rot. The blue Prolene threads that had connected the long incision were tearing tissue that was no longer viable. Siegel only had a matter of weeks, if he was lucky. To send him back to the nursing home would probably just hasten his demise.

"We will try a drying agent in the wound, Mr. Siegel, and try to get some tissue growth. Maybe, if we are lucky … "

"There is no more luck, Zach. You and I both know this will never heal, but lucky for me, I'll die before the cancer really goes after my other organs. Leave it be. I don't want more treatment and, what's more, I'll die before I see my son's bar mitzvah. I'm tired, Zach. Can I go back to the nursing home or my room now?"

"I'll admit you, Mr. Siegel. Please don't give up."

"Rabbi Leiber, you need to re-set up the bar mitzvah." Zach had found the rabbi in the small chapel office eating lunch. Even though PAY officially had a kosher kitchen, Leiber, always the uber-religious man, brought his own.

"Dr. Maxwell, do you want some *gribenes?* My wife packed more than I can eat."

Zach looked at a greasy-brownish clump in an old Tupperware bowl, and thought it looked like rotted intestine. "Even if I knew what that was, I think I'd pass, but thanks anyway."

"You don't know what you're missing. It is from heaven. You know, you take …"

"Rabbi, please, the bar mitzvah."

"Of course, but you know the rest of the family doesn't want the service anymore. They especially don't want the party. That part I agree with, and as I told them and you, technically, the son already is bar mitzvah."

"Yes, yes, I know that, but this is Siegel's dying wish. Can't you just set up a service, and call the son to the Torah? Or do something so Siegel can die in peace?"

Leiber sighed. "Of course. I'll talk to the family. How much time do I have?"

Zach laughed without humor. "I'm not a fortuneteller, Rabbi. I'd say yesterday, so for a more exact time, I'd ask God."

Zach's beeper went off. "Dr. Maxwell, 3313 stat, 3313 stat." Zach went to a phone to call in. "Fuck, that's about Siegel. Better work fast, Rabbi, or tell God to slow down the inevitable."

Siegel had had a stroke. A tiny clot had managed to migrate up to his brain, blocking the blood supply. He was slurring his speech and couldn't move the right side of his body. The nurses had caught it immediately, and called Zach stat. He had examined Siegel, and called Ike and Hercules, along with Dr. Mitchell, the neurology resident. All of them accompanied Siegel to the CT scanner, confirming the neurology resident's diagnosis of a left-sided cerebral vascular accident, or CVA. The CT had shown no bleeding in the brain, and normally the patient would have received a drug to try to break up the clot, or a catheter would have tried to retrieve the clot, opening up the blood supply in the area. Because Siegel was such an unstable patient, and such a bleeding risk, nothing could be done. He was returned to his room and Zach went to a phone to notify his wife.

At this point in his career, Zach had already pronounced countless patients dead. It was part of the business. He knew the day he would pronounce Siegel was quickly coming. He needed to make sure Siegel's last wish was fulfilled. Siegel was his patient, a patient he had not been brave enough to fight for in the beginning, but over the months, a patient who had taught him never to bow to a diagnosis or therapy he knew instinctually was wrong.

"Rabbi Leiber, Monday in the SICU. We need to bar mitzvah Siegel's boy. We can do it before rounds, it will be quiet—like at six in the morning. The sun will be up, and we will have about forty-five minutes till everyone shows up for rounds."

"Zach, we need a Torah, prayer books, yarmulkes, and most of all ten Jewish men."

"Rabbi, this is PAY. There is a whole Internal Medicine residency of observant Jewish men. You put out the word to your compadres, and make sure they show up. Tell them it will be a mitzvah."

"But, what about … "

"Don't worry, I'll take care of the rest of it."

"Hey, Shoshie. How would you like to help out with a project against hospital policy, and what are you doing Monday morning at six?"

"Zach, I've told you a million times I'll have sex with you anytime you want it, but I refuse to perform in the operating room suite under those surgical lights. Mrs. Braverman told me they only change the pads every two years. I don't need your favorite organ to get an infection. I will do it, though, in Labor and Delivery. Might be good practice."

Zach chuckled, thinking he was a lucky guy. "You are hot stuff, but Labor and Delivery might be too much practice at this time."

"Might be fun, sweetie. In fact, just the thought is making me incredibly horny."

"Well, let's save it for later. I reserved the Pathology lab for seven. We'll only have a ninety-eight-year-old male stiff, and an eighty-nine-year-old female left to watch us. Can you help, and can you be here at 6 a.m.? I'm going to get Leiber to bar mitzvah Siegel's kid."

"Only if I can bring Abie and Uncle Isaac. Wait, where are you getting a Torah and an ark?"

"I haven't figured that out yet."

"I'll take care of it. Uncle Isaac is owed some favors from among the Ultra-Jews."

"Well, let me know if I can … "

"Help? Just show up in the Path lab. God, I'm horny. I must be ovulating, better wear two condoms."

Zach's week was a horror of work. Garber understood Zach's attachment to Siegel and tried to give him some covered time from his E.R. duties. Zach was in the unit, and placed the central lines necessary to run the drugs that would sustain Siegel's blood pressure. Siegel's kidney failure was the first calamity. Zach immediately called Nephrology, and Dr. Schwartzwald, the house dialysis expert, came up with a gigantic machine meant to filter the waste toxins out of Siegel's bloodstream. A second, special central catheter was placed in his right chest with both an arterial and a venous port, so dialysis could be performed. Unfortunately, Siegel went into cardiac arrest before the procedure happened.

"What the fuck?" Zach exclaimed as he ran into the SICU. "What happened?" Siegel's cardiac monitor was a jumble as the attendant gave chest compressions, and the nurse bagged oxygen into him. Zach reached for Siegel's throat to get a pulse and found the commotion from multiple people trying to help impossible to think through. "Everyone, please stop what you are doing," he yelled. All went quiet, except the monitor yelling the loss of pressure. Zach looked at the monitor and saw a sine wave where QRS waves should have been. "Okay, continue compressions, and who has the last set of labs?"

"The sodium and chloride were all right, but the creatinine is 7.8. The potassium was good too, at 3.4."

"When were those labs drawn?"

The nurse looked at the slip and found the draw time was an hour ago. "Just before Dr. Chenoiel made rounds."

Zach felt a cold sweat run down his spine. Chenoiel making rounds. Zach couldn't believe that anyone had put him on a clinical schedule in a place as important as this. The last Zach had heard they had put Chenoiel under an attending physician who was almost retired but still took off warts and lipomas on an outpatient basis. Bullshit had thought this was a place Chenoiel wouldn't cause any more problems. He was wrong. "Did Chenoiel see these results, and did he order anything for Mr. Siegel?" Zach asked with dread.

"Oh fuck," the nurse yelled. "He added potassium both as a hang and the main I.V. One of the floating nurses signed it off as being given."

Zach's mind went into overdrive now that he had a treatable condition. He just hoped it wasn't too late. "One amp $D_{50}W$ and ten units regular insulin, I.V. push, stat. If this works, get an amp of calcium gluconate ready."

One of the nurses opened drawers on the red crash cart, and found the prefilled syringes containing the medications Zach ordered. She then handed the syringes to another nurse to administer, mainlining the drugs through the central line port. There was a loud noise of mayo stands being tipped over, and Jake, looking disheveled and very out of breath, arrived at the bedside. "What the mudderfuck happened?"

Zach, looking grim, said, "We'll talk later."

Zach kept looking at the monitor and suddenly, as if they had never been there at all, the sine wave disappeared. "Stop CPR please, and check for pulses." The alarms on the monitor stopped, and the regular beep, beep, beep, of a regular heart rate started. Zach breathed a sigh of relief when one of the nurses said, "I have pulses. Someone hand me a BP cuff."

Zach turned away, after telling the nurses to administer the calcium in the I.V., and the Kayexelate down his G-tube. This disgusting medication would bind up the excess potassium that had caused the cardiac arrest.

"Zach, what happened? We haven't given him any potassium, his kidneys aren't working," Jake asserted.

Zach looked grim and started for the exit. "You didn't, but I'm going to kill the bastard who did." Zach took off, while Jake got a report as to what happened from one of the nurses. He quickly got to a phone and paged Ike and Hercules, stat.

⚕

Zach ran to the on-call rooms, looking for Chenoiel. His mind was one big white anger. His vision clouded because of the rage he had in him. He saw Chenoiel in the distance with one of the nurses from Pediatrics. It was obvious they were headed for the on-call room. "Chenoiel, I want to talk to you, you fucking asshole. Did you even look at Siegel's history before you wrote orders for him?"

The nurse separated from Chenoiel, stuttering a "see you later." Chenoiel was livid. "What is your problem, asshole, and what are you talking about? Besides, I don't really give a fuck, I'm going to have you up for review. You don't fuck around with someone senior, and you certainly don't have the right to open your mouth in a public corridor."

Zach's eyes were hard with anger and tears. "Your poor

excuse for a physical exam delayed his treatment, and now you almost killed him again. Your fucking potassium order put him in cardiac arrest, and look at you, you don't even give a crap."

For the first time a look of doubt clouded Chenoiel's face. "That's crap. Because of your ineptitude, I found his potassium was low and started replacing it. You are the irresponsible one here. I'm going to Bullshit and make sure he knows … "

"Knows what, boy?" Hercules had come down the hall, after running to the SICU. "You ordered the potassium. Your signature is there, and the idiot nurse wrote a note saying she asked you about the order, and you told her to administer it. So, I believe one of two things: one, you don't know enough about kidney function to realize that patients with a high creatinine should get their potassium with dialysis, or very, very carefully. If this is the case, you shouldn't be in a surgical training program because this is basic medical-school knowledge. My other theory is that you were in a hurry to get laid, having made plans with Ms. Pediatric Nurse, and booked the on-call room for a romantic two minutes with her. You were in such a hurry that you failed to check Mr. Siegel's notes, or previous lab work. If this is the case, you are guilty of criminal malpractice and neglect. This also disqualifies you from a surgical residency, and, if there is a God in heaven, disqualifies you from practicing medicine in any role."

Chenoiel looked like a trapped rat. "Bullshit will never kick me out of the residency. He is too worried about losing accreditation for the residency. Besides, if Bullshit even attempts to fire me, my father will have his hide, and the rest of you better start worrying about completing this residency."

Hercules's face was like a granite bust. His face showed no anger, sadness, or other emotion. "I want you to clear out your locker and be out of here in twenty minutes. At the twenty-first minute, security will come and get you." He started to turn around, but then remembered something. "Oh, I forgot." He ripped the PAY Hospital Doctor ID off Chenoiel's coat. "There, you are no longer a doctor here. That is the best I can do for now. Now leave."

"You can't do this. I'll have your job and my father will make sure you never practice in this country. It's back to Greece for you, Christospathos."

Hercules checked his watch. "Eighteen minutes." Chenoiel left to collect his property, and Hercules guided Zach to the coffee shop. It was still closed but there were lights on in the kitchen. Hercules yelled toward the back." José, you there? *Buenos días.*"

"Hola, Dr. Hercules. *Cómo estás? Que quieres?"*

"Juevos, pan, café, y papas fritas … doble. Por favor."

"Si, Doctor, con mucho gusto."

"Siegel is stable," Hercules told Zach as they sat at the table. "Jake has him on the Kayexelate and will keep an eye on his potassium. In the morning, the finale of this lousy play will end."

"Bullshit can't fire him. The board won't stand for it. Even if they attempted to, the Residency Review Committee will shut the place down," Zach commiserated.

"No, they won't lift a finger to save the bastard. The hospital and Residency Review Committee will cave the moment Siegel's family sues Chenoiel and the hospital board for not only hiring Chenoiel but letting him skip a year of training. The best part is they are suing that shithead who approved the jump in training, the head yammie bopper of medical education. The minutes from the board meeting show who pushed Chenoiel into the hospital." Hercules smiled.

"Siegel's family is suing? When did this happen?"

"As soon as I tell Siegel's wife the ex-Dr. Chenoiel tried to kill her husband, and especially when I tell her he made two attempts."

Zach was in shock. "Hercules, you can't tell on him because he made a mistake. I've made mistakes, as has Jake, and probably every resident here. You didn't report any of them."

"You are defending Chenoiel now, boy. Times have changed." Hercules eyed Zach with a wolfish grin.

"I'm not defending him. I'm just not sure. ..." Zach really didn't know what he wasn't sure of. Chenoiel was a horrible doctor. He had proven time and time again he just didn't give a shit about the patients, his fellow residents, or frankly anyone he worked with.

"I see you have worked it out in your head, boy. I would never pull this shit on a resident who made a mistake honestly. We all do. Medicine is not an exact science, and shit happens. No, I need to destroy Chenoiel because he can't be allowed to be a licensed physician, in this hospital, in this state, in this country, or anywhere in the world as far as I'm concerned. He makes mistakes because he doesn't care. His MD is a prize to him. It comes with a beautiful wife he abuses, mistresses who should know better, and eventually a fancy car, club membership, and mini-estate in the suburbs. To him the MD has nothing to do with patients and illness. He feels those two letters after his name earn him respect. He will never change, and therefore it is too dangerous to let him practice. He is no longer your problem, as you are no longer a surgeon. I am disappointed, but proud that we could start your education, and make sure you had the strength to further your career as you think you can serve. Emergency Medicine is a noble calling. In fact, and I will deny this if you ever quote me, it is more noble than surgery."

Zach was shocked. Christospathos was the consummate surgeon. To admit another specialty was greater than surgery was more than he expected. "Emergency Medicine is more ... "

Hercules laughed. "Of course it is. You are the surgeons of this generation. In the old days, we would be the ones who handled all the emergencies but we, in truth, we only know cutting. We don't do well with children, women, and hearts. You will know it all, or at least enough to stabilize a patient. The surgeons will all be in suburbia repairing hernias and ripping out diseased appendixes and gallbladders. Necessary work, but hardly anything one could write a sonnet about. Pray your decision won't kill you and pray that Shoshie will understand and support that streak inside you of heroism. Eventually, that personality defect will age you. Good luck, Zach, marry the girl, make many children, and be a hero to them. One day, Chenoiel will realize that he too could have been looked up to, but won't be."

Hercules squeezed Zach's shoulder, and walked out of the coffee shop toward the O.R.

Zach checked his watch and walked toward the SICU to make one more check on Siegel. He stopped first at the nurses' station and dialed an outside number. "Hey, beautiful, I am free tonight, and wonder if you'd like to come over? Take-out Chinese and Two Buck Chuck, direct from the fridge. Best I can offer." He listened and then smiled. "I love you, too. See you in an hour and a half."

Chapter 67

"**Mr. Alvarez, if you** keep shooting up with dirty needles, I can almost guarantee that you will continue getting these abscesses, and eventually get Hepatitis C or HIV." Zach finished clearing the malodorous yellow pus from the abscess site, and pushed the iodoform packing in. "You know the drill. Make sure you fill the prescriptions for the antibiotic, and make an appointment for the surgical clinic in three days." He told the medical attendant to finish dressing the abscess, went over to grab a cup of five-hour-old coffee, and sat at the nurse's station to complete the chart.

His beeper went off, and he saw the number was the SICU. A sour feeling hit his stomach. "Zach, if you want this bar mitzvah to happen, it better happen within the next couple of hours," Jake said.

"What do you mean? It was going to happen on Thursday, it's Monday. It can't happen today."

"Well, Zach, you had better talk to God. Siegel had another stroke and is now barely conscious. I don't think you can keep him alive till Thursday. Now, I am going back to Siegel to see if I can give you another couple of hours. Bye."

"Wait, Jake … " But the phone had already clicked off. He thought a second, and called Leiber.

"Zach, *ma schlomcha, Yid?*"

"Rabbi, you know I don't understand Yiddish, besides cursing words."

"Gut, so schmuck, you don't understand Hebrew either. One wonders how you became a doctor with such a limited intellect. You care to come down to the office? I have pickled *ptcha*," the rabbi said happily.

"I'd ask what that is, but it already sounds disgusting, and you don't have time to eat. I need everything ready in the ICU for the bar mitzvah in an hour. I'll call the family. You round up ten of the chosen people and get the Torah in there, stat."

"Impossible, my *goyishe kopf*. It can't be done in an hour and … "

"Listen, you self-righteous asshole. Siegel will be dead by sundown. He had one last wish and you are going to make God's punishment on him tolerable or so help me God, I'll tell everyone that God's representative in this fucking hospital couldn't move one scroll and gather ten of the fucking pious. God made the heavens and Earth in one day, and you can't bust your ass for one hour. I can't wait to see how you like that *ptcha* when that becomes known. Now, fucking move your skinny Jew ass!" He slammed down the phone and called in the family and Shoshie.

It was hard to tell whether Siegel was conscious when Zach got into the SICU. True to his word, Jake was by Siegel's bedside, adjusting I.V. medications. The stench from Siegel's rotting abdominal wall was overwhelming, but Sara, the boss SICU nurse, was already cleaning and using as much disinfectant as she dared. She looked up, and seeing Zach, gave him a wan smile. "He's still alive, Zach, but it was good of you to get the ceremony moved up. Your friend, Jake, is as good a doctor as you are, but … "

"Has Leiber shown up yet?"

"Not yet, but the unit secretary said he called, and told us he needed some space and he was on his way."

"His family and the bar mitzvah boy here?"

"Yeah, we told them to relax in the sitting room. I want to get him as cleaned up as possible, so they have as little horror to remember as possible."

Leiber came into the unit with two yammie-bopper residents, schlepping a small ark and tiny Torah. Leiber was very excited, "Rabbi Cohen-Henriquez loaned us this portable Torah and ark. He said he has had them since he was a chaplain in Vietnam. You owe him weekly blood pressure checks, by the way."

"The yammies are here?" Zach asked.

"On their way. Family?"

Shoshie walked in, followed by Abe and Isaac. "Oh Zach, are we on time?" She gave Zach a kiss on the cheek, which was caught by Sara who smiled her approval at Zach. Shoshie then went over to Jake and gave him a hug and kiss, and introduced herself to Sara, along with Abe and Isaac.

Hercules, Ike, Rupak, and the rest of his surgical team came in. "Are non-Jews welcome?" Rupak asked.

Leiber answered, "Indians are considered one of the lost tribes, and Hercules must be Jewish by now, working at PAY. Come, all gather around." Because it was traditional that Jewish men covered their heads during prayer, Mrs. Braverman had sent up a box of surgical bonnets that all donned.

The family was brought in with the bar mitzvah boy who immediately went to his father, and kissed Siegel's feverish cheek, followed by his wife who held his hand, her tears running down her face.

"Let us start," Leiber intoned. There was no place to sit, and very little space to set up a podium so Leiber used the nurses' station to prop up the prayer book. He sang loud and clear the preliminary prayers. They had wheeled Siegel's bed to face the nurses' station, and the nurses, doctors, and staff had filled all the space available to the back and sides of the bed. The rest of the patient beds took up the back of the SICU, where one of the Jamaican nurses watched the monitors. She said she considered this a mitzvah. No one asked her where she had learned that term. It was a given that PAY made everyone at least partially Jewish at one time or another. Siegel seemed to perk up and follow what was unfolding in the SICU.

"Dr. Maxwell, would you take the Torah out of the ark?" Leiber asked.

Zach nodded, and took out the Torah. Being a bar mitzvahed Jew himself, he knew what was expected, and marched through the crowd. He stopped by Siegel who, surprisingly, reached out to touch the Torah. It took a great amount of effort just to raise his hand a couple of inches off the bed. His hand then dropped, and Siegel closed his eyes, batting away tears.

Zach marched the Torah back to the nurses' station and sat with it in a chair. Leiber took off its cover, and gently placed the Torah on the largest desk area of the station.

In the Jewish tradition, the priest tribes were called first to read from the Torah, and Leiber's yammies provided those men. The third man was Siegel's son. Leiber called his name, and the son left his father's side to read the Torah.

The son's thin, reedy voice started to chant the ancient verses, carrying on traditions that Siegel had subscribed to, as had Siegel's father, grandfather, and great grandfathers. Zach was next to both Siegel's bed and Shoshie when he felt her squeeze his hand. He looked at her father, and saw the tears run down both their faces. She motioned him to look at Siegel. Zach saw the tears running down Siegel's face, and he was smiling, but at the same time, his color had turned dusky, in spite of the respirator providing him oxygen. A quick glance at Siegel's monitor indicated his heart rate had gone down to forty, and his systolic blood pressure was down to sixty. Zach moved quietly to shut down the monitor. He knew Siegel had arranged for a DNR. This was

Siegel's victory. He had lived to see his son reach manhood, now he could rest.

The last verse chanted, Siegel's son looked up, with a sigh of relief on his face. As the cheers of mazel tov were shouted, the newly proclaimed man looked at his father, blue, with eyes closing and realized his father was dead. He ran to his father crying, holding him tightly. "No, Daddy, no, don't leave, please, don't leave."

Siegel's wife turned white, the tears of happiness now turned into tears of mourning for the husband she no longer had. Siegel's heart beat its last beat, but the smile remained.

Chapter 68

"Zach, it's Mom." The phone call had woken him from the deep sleep of a resident who only could sleep every thirty-six hours.

"Mom, what's wrong? Is Dad okay?"

"Why would you think anything is wrong, Zach? Can't a mother call her son?"

Zach felt the bed shift, and a very beautiful and naked Shoshie stretched. He had been so tired that he had forgotten she was there. Suddenly he was very embarrassed. Zach's love life prior to Brooklyn was subject to a scrutiny and investigation from his mother who even the KGB could learn something from.

"Good morning, lover, want a go at this?" she asked, as she dropped the sheet, exhibiting all her glory. Zach almost dropped the phone to do his duty but the tinny voice from the receiver drove him back to reality and deflated the beginnings of what could have been a wonderful start to the day. He mouthed "mother," and put his finger up to his mouth to quiet her and was rewarded by a very confused expression on Shoshie's face.

"Mom, look, I have to leave for the hospital. What's up, or can this wait?"

Now his mother's voice had some confusion in it. "I just wanted to tell you, Mimi is getting married, and you are going to be our representative on Long Island."

It was Zach's turn to be confused. "Mimi? Which one is that?"

"Mimi is not a that, Mimi is a she, and the daughter of your Uncle Jack. It is next Sunday, and they want you to meet someone," she admonished cheerfully.

Zach broke into a cold sweat. "Meet someone" was a euphemism to get fixed up, like on a date, or worse. "Look, Mom, I'm pretty busy and I think I may be on call that day."

"No, darling, you aren't. I already checked with your schedule, and you are free. In fact, for the whole weekend," she gushed. "And be ready to be wowed!"

"Wowed, Mom, what does that mean? I don't want to be wowed."

"Zach, is that your mother? I want to say hello," Shoshie whispered.

Zach put his hand over the receiver, and whispered to her, "Not now. She's really busy and I've got to get into the hospital."

Shoshie just gave Zach a strange look, then jumped out of bed and went into the bathroom. Zach was in total mental collapse mode. The screechy, tinny, voice in his ear needed a response, and his girlfriend needed an explanation.

"Look, Mom, I need to run. I'll call you later about this, but remember, no wow."

"But Zach ... "

Zach hung up on her just in time to see Shoshie, disheveled but dressed, heading for the apartment door. "Shoshie, where are you running to? Look, we've got to talk."

"Talk, talk? I just wanted to say hello to your mother. I mean she must be curious about who her son is sleeping with."

"Uh, well ... about curious."

Shoshie froze. "She doesn't know about me? Are you kidding?"

Zach felt like running, vomiting, and taking a very loose bowel movement at the same time. He was guilty and trapped. He tried to open his mouth to speak, but the words kept getting caught on his tongue. Zach sighed, and said, "No, she doesn't."

Shoshie's face froze into an expression of mourning.

"I just didn't want the complications," Zach murmured.

"I'm a complication, a complication?" she screamed. "You fucking asshole." She opened the door and ran out into the hall.

Zach jumped out of bed and ran after her, but she had run down the stairwell. The tenants of the building had heard the commotion and come out into the hall to see what the noise was all about, only to find Zach naked.

Zach reflexively covered his crotch and with as much dignity as he could, walked back into his apartment.

He called her every chance he got through the day, but she wouldn't answer the phone. Finally, just as he was about to see the first vaginal itch of the evening, Uncle Isaac picked up the phone.

"You hurt her. Why did you do that? What happened, she won't talk. My brother's blood pressure is raging because he is afraid for her. He is very angry, and if he knew I answered this call, he'd be mad at me. Maybe you should stay avay far a bissel?"

"I don't want to stay away. I just handled things wrong, as usual. Please, Isaac, tell her to meet me. I need to talk to her. I want to be with her, and I understand how wrong I was. I just have to figure out how to fix it."

There was a pause over the phone. "I'll try to talk to her and then to him." With that he hung up.

She hadn't called by 11 p.m., and he was out of his mind with worry. He also knew he had to take care of the other problem, his mother.

She was a formidable woman, European-born, deeply in love with her family, and especially her sons. There was no sacrifice she wouldn't make, no enemy she wouldn't battle. Her sons were the most important people on Earth, and she was their guardian. This maternal instinct might have been acceptable when he was young, but it didn't stop as he started noticing girls, and wanted to go out with them. The intrusiveness had become a big problem. Naively, he had brought girls home on occasion. His mother was always polite, but there was this air of "show me if you measure up." Zach would always get the post-game show of his mother pointing out his date's faults. Zach stopped bringing his girlfriends home, and eventually convinced his mother he never dated anymore.

Shoshie had been in his life for months now. Why hadn't he told his mother? Why would he have? Their relationship so far rode the waves of the residency and his immaturity. The ups and downs had inevitably drawn them closer to each other, and to the shores of engagement. He was sure Shoshie was the one for him. But Zach knew exactly why he hadn't said anything to his mother. He didn't want to hear how Shoshie wasn't good enough for Prince Zach. He wasn't a prince; in fact, sometimes he didn't think he was much of a human. Now his mother was the last person he wanted to debate the pros and cons of the woman he loved.

He picked up the phone and practiced his conversation with his mother. "Hi, Mom, I can't represent the family at that wedding. I have a girlfriend and it's serious." He shook his head, and hung up the phone. He needed to fix this face-on. God help him.

Shoshie called him with a terse, "Coffee shop, Avenue U, at 8 p.m." and hung up.

He thought it was hopeful, but doubtful. He ran out of the E.R. and changed. The gypsy cab came and got him to the coffee shop at 5 of 8, and he found she was already there. He went to her table, and leaned over to kiss her.

"Please don't," she said coldly.

He hesitated, then sat down. "I want to ... "

"I don't really care. I have decided I read this situation all wrong. I had no right to expect much more than you gave. It was fun, the sex was fun, and your friends were fun."

"So, don't leave me. I need you and want to ... "

"Want to what, Zach? Zach, your family doesn't know about me. What do you think that makes me feel like?"

"Marginalized," Zach said. "I will fix this Shoshie, one way or another. You are too important to me, just give me some time."

"I always thought it was the Italians who were mamas' boys. I understand, but I am not going to be a secret. This needs to be resolved. I understand your love for your mother, and the rest of your family. God knows my mother and father can be intrusive, making life hell, but if you want a relationship, no third parties. You'll have to decide and decide soon. I want to be a real part of your life."

"And I want you with me, also."

"What do I do, Ike? I can't live through losing Shoshie. God knows she's put up with enough so far. But my mother is impossible. She'll never loosen up. She'll make Shoshie miserable, and then turn around and torture me."

Ike thought about the problem and said, "You know, Goldie and I never really had any problems with our respective in-laws. We were born here, raised here, and our parents were practically neighbors. I don't know if my advice will do you any good, but I think you have to come to the realization you are no longer a boy. You are a physician, you are managing a relationship, you pay bills, make sure you keep healthy, clean, fed. Understand, you are a responsible adult."

"So what? I mean who isn't. My mother won't understand any of that."

"Maybe yes, maybe no, but if you meet your mother with Shoshie on your arm, she'll realize you are serious about her and aren't a little boy anymore. In fact, don't you have a family wedding coming up?"

"Yes, but ... "

"Go to the wedding, then go see your mother. The family will see Shoshie, and then your mother will know you are serious. Yeah, she'll kill you anyway, but now it's her problem."

"Welcome Zach, we are so happy you could come."

The wedding was on Long Island, in one of the better wedding palaces. Jack was a second cousin from the branch of his mother's family who had come to the States from Europe before World War II. They were very successful, and owned commercial real estate in Manhattan, along with a bunch of steak houses. Occasionally, when he was in Manhattan, he went into the steak house for lunch on the family tab. In other words, family ate for free, as did any nun that walked into the place. Jack had, at one time, gotten such severe abdominal pains, he was rushed to St. Barnabas's instead of the more kosher Mount Sinai. He was in pain and scared out of his mind because of the black habits and the collars. The tortured depiction of a crucified Jesus on every available wall was like a look into hell. But the nuns were the nurses, and treated him with such kindness he vowed that any nun ever coming into a restaurant he owned would eat free.

"Jack, mazel tov on Mimi getting married, and thank you for inviting us. May I introduce you to Shoshie, my girlfriend?"

"I always knew you had good taste, but what I can't figure

out is how such a lovely lady would want someone as ugly as you are with her, huh?"

Zach laughed. "I ask myself the same thing every time we go out."

Jack looked at Shoshie. "So, what do you do? Where do you come from? Most importantly, why this schlub?"

Shoshie obviously had taken a liking to the large, round man with the kind smile on his face. "I am a dance teacher, looking for work. I come from Boston and most importantly, I like being with this schlub. He usually makes me happy, and I try to make him happy."

Jack's eyes bore into Shoshie. "I do believe you mean it. How come you haven't made an honest woman of her yet, schmendrick? I'd say she is a keeper and way too good for you."

Zach gave a melancholy smile, and said, "Because I don't deserve her yet, Jack."

"Hmmph, an honest and a very good answer. Now, if you'll excuse me, I must take care of a problem your mother caused. I'm glad you're partial to blonds and not redheads." Jack hurried off to the caterer.

Shoshie asked, "Do you prefer blonds to redheads, Zach?"

"Only if it is the gold on your head, Shoshie."

"Great answer."

They moved into the crowd of celebrants. He introduced Shoshie as his girlfriend, and she was charming. There were a lot of mazel tovs for Zach's good fortune finding such a lovely woman. He never met the girl he was supposed to be fixed up with, and that was just fine by him. The ceremony was fine, with the groom smashing the glass on the first shot, eliciting the shouts of "mazel tov." Dinner was then served, with the traditional kosher catering hall prime rib, chicken, or fish, and the bar was open. Zach found it funny that this was a first for Shoshie and him. Fancy food, open bar, dancing … their usual was the hole-in-the-wall Italian place, or take-out Chinese. Fancy was not served on a salary of $12,000 per year.

He had learned that Shoshie was not much of a drinker, usually limiting herself to a glass of wine or a beer, depending on what dump they were eating at. His apartment had a bottle of no-brand scotch and a half-bottle of white "Two Buck Chuck." Shoshie kept commenting on how great the Cosmos tasted. Wine was served with dinner, and Shoshie was on a dancing spree. Her face was flushed with happiness and the booze, and her outfit flared as she did twirls.

Finally, they sat down to dinner, with wine, and Shoshie continued to charm the residents of their table, intermittently dragging Zach back out to the dance floor. He was an incompetent dancer but did his best. Somewhere along the line, Jack patted him on the shoulder.

"Hey, can I cut in? Seems your girlfriend really knows how to shake a leg. You, on the other hand have two left feet."

"Jack, with Shoshie's permission, please take over."

"Well, young lady, care to dance?"

Shoshie, aglow and happy to give her feet relief from getting stepped on, responded, "If you think you can keep up."

"Keep up? You know how to Latin dance?"

She laughed. *"Vamos a ver."*

Jack yelled at the band leader, "Give me some Latin."

What happened next was extraordinary. Zach, of course, knew Shoshie could dance and he guessed Jack, who was rumored to be quite a Casanova in his day, could dance. They performed a Paso Doble which had everyone clear the dance floor for them. The cheering and toasting when they finished were deafening. Shoshie was glowing with perspiration and exhaustion. Jack was breathing like he had just run the New York Marathon. Shoshie flew into Zach's arms, her skin hot and wet. She murmured in his ear, "I love you, so much."

Zach just smiled, kissed her deeply on her lips and said, "I love you too, Shoshie." Tears flowed down her cheeks from happiness.

Jack came over, still short of breath, and said to Zach, "Well, Doctor, if you know what's good for you, you'll make sure this one doesn't get away, and you'll learn how to dance." He kissed Shoshie on the cheek and went off toward the bar.

Later that evening, Jack's wife Lila chatted with Shoshie and him. She was a nice, quiet, woman who had married Jack when he was just starting his business. He always said she was the rock he stood on when building his future. Without her, he'd have ended up as not much of anything. She gave Shoshie a look and quietly said, "Dear, would you do an old woman a favor and get me a double gin with a splash of tonic? Tell that bartender to use the gin under the bar, not the stuff for the guests." Shoshie gave Zach a look of worry, as he tried to signal all was good. "Sure, Lila, be back in a couple of minutes."

"Zach, your mother is already causing trouble. She needs to meet Shoshie as soon as possible, for all your sakes. Your father won't be a problem, but ... well, do what I advise. I love Shoshie. I think she will be good for you, but unless you take care of your mother ... "

"I understand, Lila. Why does Mom have to be like this?"

"Because she loves you and doesn't think there is anyone good enough for you. She doesn't do this consciously out of anger or hate. She doesn't act like this on a conscious level at all. She is just trying to protect you, even though we all form relationships without protection."

Shoshie came back bearing a large drink. "The bartender said this is what you wanted."

"Yes, on a very happy day, this is just what I wanted. I hope to see you soon, Shoshie. Now I'm going to find that husband of mine, and yell at him to save the calisthenics for us, later," she said with a wink and wandered away.

"Uh, not to be nosy, but what was that about?"

Zach gave her a sad smile. "She likes you and thinks you'd be good for me. She was just offering advice for the next step."

"The next step?"

"Yeah, the battle of the mudder, mudder."

"Zach, there is a short of breath in twelve. Can you take a look?"

"Sure." He was tired, this being 5 p.m. and him having been at it for ten hours. It started with the leftovers from last night, including two 'tutes who spoke Russian and had very malodorous vaginal discharges. One was straightforward, but the other had some sort of toy stuck up there that had embedded itself in her superficial mucosa. After carefully taking it out, he gently irrigated her vagina and tried to ignore her sighs of pleasure. He dumped the toy, a devil's head with horns sticking out, into Cidex, an industrial cleaner, and told the charge nurse that he was contributing a specimen for the museum. The museum was a small locked glass cabinet filled with the strange objects the residents had removed from vaginas and rectums. Most of the objects were pretty pedestrian—butt plugs, small bottles, vibrators. One was a true collector's item, a black rubber penis that measured eighteen inches in length and five inches round. The rest of the day had brought chest pains, real and imagined, lacerations, and a couple of appendixes. He was trying to write up his incomplete charts, but duty called.

A sad-looking, middle-aged man was on the gurney. His hair was carefully combed and his face shaven. He was wearing old clothes Zach was sure were from a second-hand shop or a shelter. His color was in the blue range, and it was obvious he had trouble catching his breath. Zach could hear the liquid sloshing in his lungs, and the high-pitched wheezing from the curtain. The man looked familiar, yet he couldn't place him. The patient, through his dyspnea, smiled the moment he saw Zach.

"Dr. Maxwell, thank God, you are here to save me again," he said, between gasps.

"I'm sorry, I saved you?" Zach looked at the name on the chart and was startled. The last time he saw Zinman the Third, he was being wheeled to the O.R. for the peritonsillar abscess Chenoiel had missed. "Mr. Zinman, so nice to see you." He realized his fault, and quickly said, "I mean, I'm sorry you are here. What's going on?"

"Can't catch my breath and I have a fever. I can't even eat, I keep puking, and I think I'm dehydrated. I haven't felt this way since the last time I saw you."

Zach suddenly knew why he didn't recognize him. This wasn't the Zinman of the sore throat, lack of cooperation, and the colorful language. "When did this problem start?"

"Well, after you correctly diagnosed me and I was on the ward, the Egyptian doctor started talking to me. Like you, he cared, and arranged for me to see a counselor. I sobered up, quit the drugs, and now live in a shelter for men trying to get more men like us healthy."

"That is tremendous, but the shortness of breath?"

"I am always a little short of breath. I quit smoking, but two packs a day for forty years is a lot of smoke to cure. This is the first time I ever got a fever and vomiting with it. Plus, I can barely talk. Can you help me?"

"That's what I'm here for. Let's take a listen." Zach listened to Zinman's lungs and heart, and then saw that his ankles were swollen. The vital signs noted that his respiratory rate was elevated, and his temperature was 102. Pretty much a setup for a pneumonia. Zach ordered a nebulizer with albuterol to open his lungs, an I.V. to hydrate him, and basic labs and blood cultures to see if he had bacteria in his bloodstream. He also ordered a stat chest x-ray to look for a pneumonia.

After reassuring Zinman he'd be back, he went to complete his charts, and wait for the x-ray to be done and to give time for the medication to work. Fifteen minutes later, the nurse yelled to him to recheck Zinman, as he seemed to be worse. Zach trotted back to Zinman, only to find his respiratory rate had gone up and his O_2 sat, the measure of oxygen in his bloodstream, had gone down. Zinman was barely talking and looked terrified.

He checked the x-ray and saw why Zinman was in so much trouble. Instead of nice, aerated lungs, the area was white with fluid, and Zinman's heart was immense. "Look, this is going to get better, but not immediately. I have to put a breathing tube in you and get some of the fluid off your lungs."

"But if I go to sleep I won't wake up." He huffed out the words one by one. Please, don't."

"Look, Mr. Zinman, if I don't do this you will die. Your heart can't handle this kind of strain."

Zinman closed his eyes and nodded his consent.

"Get him pre-oxygenated. I want a four-curved and an 8.0 tube now." Zach checked his laryngoscope. The light bulb was bright and screwed in tightly. Occasionally, the doc tubing a patient didn't check, and the light bulb was loose enough to separate from the blade of the scope and go down a patient's trachea.

"Sat is 90 percent, Zach. I think that's all we're going to get," the nurse said.

"Let's go then. I need eight of morphine, followed by succinylcholine. Stat kids!"

Zach watched as the meds were given. He counted to ten and told the respiratory therapist to stop bagging the patient. He entered an almost meditative state, where he was one with his blade, tube, and Zinman's cords. He didn't even notice an older woman coming into the room and observing him. Three seconds later, the tube was through the vocal cords, and a CO_2 detector showed a golden color, from light purple. Carbon dioxide was detected, meaning the tube had gone down the trachea, and not down the esophagus. Before he looked up from Zinman's face, the older woman walked out of the area.

"Great job, everybody. Let's start him on sixty of Lasix, then start him on a dose of cephalosporin and a macrolide. I'll call the ICU and anesthesia to give vent orders."

He leaned over toward Zinman's ear and said, "All over, and it went well, you'll stay asleep, and we will get the fluid off you and take care of the pneumonia." Zach never knew if a patient on a respirator heard or comprehended anything he said, but he thought it couldn't hurt to reassure them that progress was being made. He walked to the charting area to make his phone calls when he saw her.

"What are you doing here?" he asked, shocked.

"Why, a mother can't see her son at work?"

"I just wasn't expecting you." He gave her a kiss. "Welcome to my world, Mom. It ain't pretty, but it has a certain *je ne sais quoi.*"

"I can see that. You seem to be at least a prince, if not king of your domain," she gushed.

Zach took a breath. It was this attitude that caused so many problems. He was better than his friends, girlfriends, mentors. He didn't know where this came from, but it caused a lot of problems in his life. "Mom, why are you here?"

"I want to meet your girlfriend. Jack was very impressed, but then Jack gets impressed by anything over a C-cup. Does she have over a C-cup, darling?"

"Enough, Mother, that was uncalled for, and certainly way over the line." He took a deep breath. "Why aren't you happy for me? She is a nice girl, pretty, kind, and her parents have the same background as you. I'd love to introduce you, but if you're not going to be civil, there is no point."

"I'm always civil, and you are bordering on disrespectful. Is this what they taught you in medical school, to yell at your mother?"

"No, but Mom, this girl is the one. Please don't fuck this up for me."

"I would never do that, dear. How about I take the two of you out to dinner? I'm here for a couple of days and am staying with Jack."

"Uh, I don't know if that is a good idea, Mom."

"Why?"

"Because the last dinner I had with a girlfriend and you, ended up with the girlfriend locked in the ladies' room, crying, and muttering how you are the devil incarnate."

"You exaggerate. Besides, she was mentally unstable."

"Mom, she was a grade school teacher who counseled PTSD victims as a volunteer. How much more stable can you get?"

"Those grade schools can drive anyone insane. So, tonight at 8?"

"Let me check with Shoshie and I'll give you a call."

"We're checking with Shoshie now, are we?"

"Mom, don't push it."

She chuckled. "I didn't say a word, Zachary."

"Don't worry Zach, it's one little dinner. She can't scare me."

"It's not a matter of scare, it's a matter of torture. Look, she is a great mother and supportive of almost everything I ever did. She encouraged me when everyone, inside and outside of my extended family, said, forget it. She just won't accept any of the girlfriends I bring home."

"And how many girlfriends did you bring home, Dr. Maxwell?"

"Believe me, few became fewer as time went on, and then there were none."

"Well, she must feel bad about that, so maybe she has learned to be more accepting."

Zach just gave Shoshie a worried look. "We are going to meet her at Café Vesuvius at 7 p.m."

"Aw, the place you introduced me to Jake and Sandy. I seem to remember after that meal you took me home for dessert." She laughed.

"Let's hope we are both in condition to sleep after that."

Café Vesuvius was a small, family-run Italian restaurant in the middle of Greenpoint, in Brooklyn. Jake had recommended it as a place of semi-neutral ground small enough that intimacy was protocol yet big enough that flying cutlery probably wouldn't stick in anyone's body.

"Mom, this is Shoshie, Shoshie, this is Mom."

Shoshie looked fabulous in a bright dress that was conservative in cut yet showed curves. Her face was bright, young, and wholly beautiful. "Mrs. Maxwell, it is a pleasure to finally meet you. Zach has told me a lot about you."

Zach's heart started to rev up. "Crap, open challenge to Mom." She knew her history was exposed, and she couldn't stealth her way in.

"I'm sure he has, dear. I'm sure you understand I'm very protective in matters pertaining to my son."

Fuck me. Zach was now sweating. The first declaration of his mother's immovable position.

"He is a man, Mrs. Maxwell, and he doesn't need protection from me. I love him," Shoshie countered.

Round one ended when the waiter came to get drink orders.

"I'll have a martini, extremely dry, three olives," his mother ordered.

"I'll have the same, but skip the olives," Shoshie countered.

"Hey, maybe both of you want a glass of wine. I mean

neither of you are big drinkers, and those are big drinks," Zach implored.

"Dear, we're here to celebrate. Don't be a party pooper," his mother responded.

"Maybe you're right, Zach. I'll have a Chardonnay," Shoshie said.

The waiter was about to go when, "Don't listen to the party pooper. Have a proper drink … unless you have a problem with alcohol," his mother smiled.

"She doesn't have a problem with alcohol, Mom, she just doesn't drink a lot." Zach was frantic.

"No, you're right, Mrs. Maxwell." She turned to the waiter, now also sweating. "Give me that martini but make it a double … still no olives."

"Shoshie … " he begged.

"What?" she asked. Her eyes red and glowing.

"Fine." Zach gave up to the inevitable.

"So, what are your intentions toward my son, Shoshie?" his mother asked.

"Mom …"

"No, Zach, I'll answer that. I have no intentions, Mrs. Maxwell. Zach and I are together, and enjoying learning about each other. This isn't a conventional boyfriend-girlfriend relation-ship because of Zach's work. I understand it's demanding, so we work around it. But, it is going great so far, and I can't speak for Zach, but, well, I am where I want to be."

"Mom, you have to stop. Let's just enjoy …"

"I take it you're sleeping with him."

"Okay, that's enough. Mom, apologize now."

"For what, darling? This is the twentieth century. I assume she is normal and has been tested."

Zach stood up. "Mom, you have been inappropriate in the past, but this really was horrendous. You owe Shoshie an apology, but we are going home. The waiter will get you a taxi back to Jack's. Come on, Shoshie."

"No," Shoshie said quietly.

"Please, I told you this was a bad idea. Let's go."

"Yes, dear. Zach is upset. I'm not sure why, but don't worry. I'll find my way back to the hotel. Maybe you and I can talk at a later time ... or not, if your relationship doesn't last. Zach is famous for short relationships."

"Come on, Shoshie." He was trying to drag Shoshie out of the restaurant.

"Sit down, please, Zach," she requested. "Mrs. Maxwell, I don't know why after talking to me for less than five minutes you seem to have taken such a dislike to me. So, let me answer some of the questions I'm sure you think you have answered for yourself. First, he doesn't need protection from me. I'm not after his money, and I don't want to be an obstacle to his career. If he wants to break up, I'll be very upset, but this is not an arranged relationship that neither of us can get out of. We are getting to know each other, and the relationship will go forward as we are ready for it to go forward. Second, I love him, and I believe he loves me. It has taken a while to recognize this, but it is wonderful. I can't imagine a day without Zach in my life, and I hope he feels the same. Third, I trust him, and I know he trusts me. These points, in themselves, are a reason we should be together. And yes, we are sleeping together when we can, and anything further on that subject is none of your business."

There was a thick silence between them. His mother had stiffened at Shoshie's words, and looked like she was going to respond, but didn't. Shoshie looked like she was waiting for the firing squad, and seemed puzzled when there wasn't a blast from his mother.

Zach was about to tell his mother that everything Shoshie said was true and she'd have to respect both their wishes when the beeper mercifully went off. Zach looked down and saw it was the

E.R. He gave both of them a look and said, "I have to answer this, please no trauma."

"This is Maxwell, I'm off."

"Zach, this is Garber, can you come in, we are balls to the walls, and just need some help clearing. I'll make it up to you somehow. Please."

Zach looked over to the table, where Shoshie was looking miserable and his mother had on a stone face but was fidgeting with her napkin. Even from across the room, her knuckles looked white. "Give me a half-hour."

"Thanks, Zach. See you then."

Zach went back to the table. "I have to go into the E.R., Mom. I'll get the host to get you a cab. Shoshie and I have to go."

"What a shame, it has been such a lovely evening."

"Come on, Shoshie. I'll get you home, and then I've got to go."

"I'm going back to the apartment, we can take one cab," Shoshie responded.

"Mom, the host will tell you when your cab is here. I'll call you tomorrow."

His mother looked preoccupied. "Uh, okay, tomorrow. Go save a life."

Zach gave her a little kiss. "Tomorrow."

Shoshie was strangely silent on the way back to the apartment. She showed no anger and responded to his explanation of his mother's behavior with a neutral expression. He kissed her, and she responded with a half-smile and ran into the apartment building. Zach wanted to run after her, but he had promised he'd go be a doctor as fast as possible. Reluctantly, he turned away from the apartment and entered the hospital.

Chapter 69

"**My belly hurts.** Someone do something!"

"That sounds like your patient, Zach." Zach opened one bleary eye. He was on his third night shift in a row, after helping tame the onslaught of patients the night of his mother's arrival. He hadn't heard from her, and Shoshie, while friendly, was quiet. He was now exhausted, and at 3 a.m. the shift wasn't quite over enough to see the light at the end of the tunnel. It had been relatively quiet after a multiple stab wounds, so he had been able to doze off in his chair. The nurses had dimmed the lights at the dictation station, and aside from the screaming of the one patient, only the beeps of normal sinus rhythms could be heard.

"You are going to fucking love her. Make sure to get out the gloves that cover your arms if you do a pelvic." The nurse giggled as she headed to the break room.

Zach got up, shook out his arms to relieve the cramping, and went to the source of the screaming.

"I'm in fucking pain. The green man put something inside me! Get it out, get it out, you cunt," she screamed at the nurse.

"Now Ms.," he glanced at the chart, "Horney." Jesus, what a name. "There is no reason for that kind of language. The nurse is trying to help you."

"GET IT OUT, YOU FUCK," she screamed, as a sudden

gush of vaginal blood and fluid saturated the sheets, and then dripped onto the floor.

Zach froze. Ms. Horney was a 350-pound monster of a woman, with a belly that was a mountain of fat. She was now diaphoretic and pale. "Ms. Horney, are you pregnant?"

"You fuck, I'm not pregnant. My maidenhood is untouched by any man."

Zach got her to lie down and went through multiple layers of malodorous, filthy, clothes to finally get to skin. She was huge, and her abdomen was spasming "Man, she is term if she is a day. Get Neonatal down here stat, and get the incubator warmed up."

He grabbed the Doppler and, without much hunting, he found a fetal heart rate of 160. "FHT 160 and this baby wants out. Ms. Horney, you're pregnant and you're in labor. The good news is the baby will be out very soon."

"But, I've never let the devil's rod enter my holy place. Aghhh! It hurts."

"I need sterile gloves. The incubator and heat lamps on, and where is Neonatal?"

"I don't have a baby, it's an alien!"

Her vaginal area was hard to see under her overhanging abdomen and even harder to examine. Zach needed to get his fingers in her vagina to see how far dilated she was. The smell of unwashed body was making him gag and his eyes water. His only thought was this was going to hell in a handbasket.

"Get me a mask, but spritz a little benzoin in it."

The nurse, understanding Zach's problem, found a disposable mask with an eye shield and after spritzing the benzoin, put it on Zach's face. There, he could see and not gag as the sweet smell of the benzoin this close to his nose almost overcame the worst of the genital sweat.

"Godammmmmittttt, that fucking alien is trying to kill me," she screamed as another spasm hit.

"Almost there, the baby's head is showing."

"Aghhhhhhhhhhh!!!"

The baby slid out in a gush of mucus, blood, and unmention-able fluids. Zach tapped its blueish foot, and was rewarded with an indignant scream, turning the baby into a pink, feisty, howling, human being, and not an alien as advertised.

"Congratulations, Ms. Horney, you have a bright, healthy-looking, baby boy."

Ms. Horney let out a gasp and croaked, "I do?"

"Yes, you do. Do you have any idea what you want to name him?"

Ms. Horney looked around beaming and said, "Spock, his name is Spock."

Zach didn't miss a beat and announced, "Nurse, take note, Spock Horney was born at 3:18 a.m. with an initial APGAR of nine. Live long and prosper, Horney family."

Chapter **70**

He trudged to his apartment. Aside from Ms. Horney and baby Spock, the hours were spent with the desperate of Brooklyn. Heart attacks, stab wounds, babies with high fevers. About 4 a.m., the place was under control and Garber told Zach to go home and get some sleep.

Sleep, something he used to do as part of life, was now a treat, a reward, and something that was only enjoyed in short episodes between beepers going off. He opened the door and found Shoshie sitting with his mother. They both looked at him like he was some sort of zombie.

"Shoshie, Mom, what are you doing here?"

"We have been talking and waiting for you. We made you some dinner, thought you'd be hungry."

"I see no blood on the walls. You guys okay?"

His mother responded with a sad smile. "I'm going back to the hotel, could you call me a cab?"

Zach went to call a service.

"Don't worry, Zach, I'll find my way down, and yes, I still have my mace and whistle." She chuckled. She went to Shoshie and embraced her. "I'm trusting you, remember that."

She went out the door. Shoshie looked at Zach and said, "Go with her, and make sure she gets into the cab safely. I'll be waiting for you."

He ran to catch up and they waited for her cab. "What's going on, Mom?" he asked. "I have never seen you react this way with a girlfriend. You're not going to pull one of your famous kill-the-relationship moves, are you?"

"No, dear, your mother is not going to ruin anything. She is a nice girl, and if you don't fuck it up, I might be expecting a grandchild in a year or two. She loves you, Zach, and I think you might love her. That might be enough. Anyway, the cab is here, and I'm exhausted. I don't know how you survive these hours, but you are young. Give your mother a kiss and be well, I'm off."

He leaned in to give her a kiss and she hugged him. "Dr. Maxwell, I remember when you were my Zachie like it was just yesterday. Be healthy and happy." She gave him another peck and was in the cab and gone. Zach turned back toward the elevators.

Zach opened the door to the apartment and found the living and dining rooms empty. He went to the bedroom and quietly opened the door. A bundle was under the sheets. "Come to bed, Zach. It's been a long day, and longer night."

"You got that right," he said, going into the small bathroom. "Why did my mother come over here? Did she take another stab at trying to separate us?"

"She was lonely and wanted to talk, and so I did. You know, she's not as bad as I thought. She is just very protective."

"Protective? What is she protective of? I'm here learning medicine in a big hospital, just like she always dreamed. I have a girlfriend, not abnormal considering I lived like a monk during medical school. What does she want from me?"

"To be happy and successful. I understand it's what all the mothers want this year. In any case, I think she came to make peace, at least for the time being. Now, why don't you strip and spoon me, and we can sleep together, where the emphasis is sleep."

"Yes, ma'am. Your wish is my command."

"Oh, by the way, Garber left a message that he found coverage for you, to make up for the extra night. He says to stay home and relax. I invited your mother to lunch."

There was no response aside from a gentle touch on her hip, and some not so gentle snores.

Chapter 71

"**Oh my God,** you are going to kill me, woman."

As promised, there were no urgent phone calls yelling at him because he was late for a shift. So instead, he slept till nine with a beautiful woman beside him. Slowly waking biological urges were recognized by both and satisfied. He was happy and wished this could happen every morning. He turned on his side and kissed her, and then again, and then lower on her body.

"Hey, sex maniac. Haven't you had enough? It isn't I who will kill you, it's you who will cripple me."

"Shoshie," he said happily, "we're young, healthy, and have a day off. I'm just taking this opportunity to explore new territory. This territory in front of me," he said, nuzzling her breasts.

"Okay, thirty seconds more, and you have to hit a cold shower while I make some coffee. That's if I can walk."

"Come on, Shoshie, we don't have anything to do today."

"Yes, we do. I told you last night I invited your mother to lunch, so we have to be domestic."

"Domestic? What does that mean? And why did you invite her to lunch? If we have to meet her, let's meet at Dunkin' Donuts or some other fine establishment."

"Zach, please help me with this. I want her to accept me. If we build a life of any kind together, I don't want my new family to hate me. Plus, we can't afford a nice brunch if we go out, and she knows it, so she'll insist on paying. We're adults, we should treat her. Please, do this for me."

Zach smiled at her. "Okay Shoshie, brunch it is. I'll get showered and you get a list together."

She squealed with pleasure. "Oh, Zach, thank you."

He gave her ass a farewell squeeze and went to shower.

"Some more coffee, Mrs. Maxwell?

"Thank you, dear."

Zach was nervous. All the happiness and feelings that all was right in the world came crashing down when his door opened, and his mother walked through it. He kept interrupting the both of them, trying to steer the conversation to safe subjects. He had them at bay now but could tell they were both losing patience with him.

"Mom, of course Shoshie wants to raise kids and have a career. Shoshie, my mother didn't mean that women shouldn't have careers while taking care of the babies." He was beginning to lose patience with himself. Oh well, maybe two hours left in this epic visit, what could go wrong?

"Well, Zach's dad and I thought I should try to stay in our home until he had established himself in his career," his mother replied. "I mean think about all that effort, time, and money we put into your career, Zach. Maybe a woman with money herself, a sort of add-on pot o' gold, could allow a career for Shoshie while raising the children. More important than Shoshie's career goals, you did talk about a pre-nup of course? I mean, it cost you a fortune to get where you are now. Shoshie, he is going to need all that money to pay back the loans and past living expenses, and whatever else he makes in the future he needs to live. He even needs a few things just so the patients feel comfortable with him, a BMW,

Rolex, you know his 'badges of office,' so to speak. If things don't work out between you two, he can't just hand you a blank check."

The room went silent, and the temperature dipped into minus territory. Shoshie's face was frozen in rage. Zach saw she was trying her best to control herself, but unless he intervened quickly, his apartment was nuclear toast. "Mom, you don't believe that, and I'm pretty sure Dad could care less. Please explain that to Shoshie. Tell her it was a bad joke." He went to Shoshie to hold her, but she stiffened and gently shoved him away.

"That was no joke. That was a mother who, for some reason, doesn't approve of her son's girlfriend, and is trying to shut the relationship down. She doesn't understand that I love her son and want to build a lifetime relationship with him. I'm going, Zach, before I say something that will kill your relationship with your mother or me. Goodbye, Mrs. Maxwell."

She grabbed her wrap and stormed out of the apartment. Zach looked at his mother, and just shook his head. "You had to blow this one, too." He ran after Shoshie.

"Shoshie, don't go, please." He caught her just as she was getting into a cab.

"Zach, there isn't a future for me having your mother around. I get it, you love her. She's your mom, and she helped get you here and make you the man you are. How you weren't inoculated with her shit though … I don't know. I love you, but I won't torture you and myself with this albatross. Go back to her. Don't call me. When and if I can get my head straight, I'll call you." She slammed the taxi shut and the car sped off. Zach stood at the curb, watching the dust rise from the road in the cab's wake.

He walked into the apartment praying for silence and darkness. Instead his mother was standing there. Zach could see the wrinkles at her eyes, and the subtle aging of her skin. She looked like she had shrunk from twenty minutes ago. Zach caught his breath. In all his years living in his parents' house, he was witnessing something that had never happened before, his mother crying.

"I don't know what happened. I just opened my mouth and my brother's words came out. I'm so sorry, Zachie."

"What do you mean your brother's words? Dad wasn't rich, in fact he was making $97 dollars a week when you met him. He didn't even have a college degree at that point."

"And that was a big point when we got married, and it soured the relationship he had with my family from then on. Your father was never a businessman, but he was smart, and he provided for me and then us. He never wanted to take a dime from them, and the occasional times I took money, like to help pay your medical education, he was not only mad at me, but unreasonably mad at himself. My brothers wanted an easy life for me, and after all these years I had forgotten how happy we were building a life together."

"Mom, while I guess I understand, you've done so much damage. Shoshie is a good woman and we love each other, but this thing you have, well, you need to work that out for yourself. I won't re-expose Shoshie to you until you figure a way out of your sickness. I love you and owe you, but dealing with your prejudices is just too high a price. Go home, please. Between the hospital and Shoshie, I just won't have time to visit anytime soon."

He put on his jacket and grabbed his keys. "Just close the door on the way out."

"Zach, please don't go. Besides, it's freezing out there."

"I told you Mom, I have no time for anything except the most important, and that's Shoshie. Have a safe trip home. Give Dad a kiss for me."

He was out the door before she could get another word in.

Chapter 72

How many times had he been at this particular door, hat in hand, begging forgiveness? The door opened and Isaac was there. He didn't carry the shotgun, and his face looked sad. "She's not here."

"Isaac, please help me. Where is she? I came to apologize, again. I seem to just fuck this up, but I love her."

Isaac sighed. "You know, I had a similar problem. Meine parents were dead, but my oldest brudder, also now dead, vas religious. He found out that Luva vasn't Jewish. He made a lot of trouble, and he had very gut reason. Hitler vas killing all the Jews and Poles veren't better. Luva was a Pole.

"But you married her."

"Ya, but my brudder considered me dead and wouldn't speak to me … and then he vas dead, at the hand of a Pole. Luva converted when she got pregnant. Go home, Zach, and find someone else. Shoshie loves her father, and to Abie, your mudder insulted not only Shoshie, but him, his viebel, and the ghost of all he lost in the war."

"I need to talk to her. Please Isaac, where is she?"

"Gone, now go. That shotgun is around here somewhere." He slammed the door hard, leaving Zach cold and on a dark porch.

He turned to leave and got a half a block when he heard a whispering from some bushes. "Zach, kom in hai-ah." It was Luva. "Isaac vill kill me. Ach, here." She handed him a scrap of

352

paper and ran back to the house. Zach looked at it and hurried back to the bus stop.

<hr>

"Zach, you just can't take off now. I'm short-staffed and the neighborhood thinks this is a free smorgasbord of pelvics and work notes," Garber said.

They were standing in the middle of the E.R. with noise, action, and smells happening all around them. "I understand, I just need to take care of a personal problem."

"Hmmph, so you fucked up with Shoshie, huh? That's a shame. She seemed like a girl that's got it."

"How did you know?" Zach questioned. Was it that obvious? He hadn't been able to sleep, eat, or more or less do anything besides come to the E.R., and see a massive amount of patients who probably had bigger problems than he.

Garber laughed. "Do you think you are the first resident I've had that had girl or boy problems? In fact, do you think there has been a resident anywhere that hasn't gone through this kind of problem? Man, look around you. This shithole will kill a relationship that God himself on high put together."

Zach felt ashamed, and hung his head, mumbling an apology that it wasn't "this place." Garber was right. He had fucked up, and now he wanted to try to repair the problem, but she was too far away.

"Did I hear that mumble right? Your mother broke you up. What kind of man lets his mother run his sex life? Jesus Christ and Moses too, your mother? Shoshie is sexy as fuck. Christ, grow a set. I finally did with my fourth wife, shit!" Garber paused and stood in deep thought. "Tell you what, I think Rosen will do you a favor if I ask. He's a shut-in anyway. Let's see if he'll take your three-day over the weekend, and you take his in two weeks. Maybe you turn those peanuts into casaba melons by then."

Zach looked at Garber. "Thanks, I owe you big time."

"No problem. We all go through these life events. In any case, your work will improve once you get this taken care of."

"We need a doc stat in three," a nurse yelled out over the noise.

Garber gave Zach a pat on the back. "They are playing your song. Go win one for the Gipper."

"Huh? The Gipper?" Zach questioned.

"Just get out there, and save the patient's and your life."

Zach ran for it.

The situation resulted from a simple misunderstanding. A French tourist arrived at JFK International to visit friends in Brooklyn. Though his English was on the rudimentary level, it was good enough to be understood, so when he got into a cab and asked to be taken to 212 Beekman Street in Brooklyn, his driver, after giving him a strange look, did. Beekman Street was in the East New York section of Brooklyn, while Beekman Place was in DUMBO. DUMBO was an area of opulence and relative safety. In a further piece of bad luck, 212 Beekman Street was the home of Little Anthony's crack den and money-sorting house. The inhabitants of this establishment were hurriedly packing away crack-making equipment and money for a quick move. Through informants they were aware of a large raid planned by the NYPD, and they planned to be no-shows. Unfortunately, the French tourist was ignorant of the characteristics of this neighborhood and got out of the cab, to waltz up to the door and bang loudly. When no one answered, he banged again, shouting in French for his friends to let him in. In the last piece of bad karma, the employees of Little Anthony's, at least the ones with guns, didn't understand French. Through the thick door, the tourist's French sounded like the police had come. They quickly opened the door and blasted away with their guns.

The tourist was lucky in taking only three bullets to his chest and abdomen. When the police and ambulance showed up he was still alive, barely, and needed the fine fix-it shop known as PAY.

"Vital signs?" Zach immediately took command of the situation.

"Sixty over thirty, 140, thirty-six and a sat of 86 percent," the nurse responded. She was a veteran of hundreds of similar cases, and hadn't panicked over one of these for ten years.

"Okay, lines, fluids, now." He quickly did his first assessment, noting the patient was barely conscious, had no breath sounds on the left side of his chest, and his abdomen was distending before his eyes. He took another look at the throat, and decided there was no tracheal deviation, so for now, no tension pneumothorax. ABC popped into Zach's head. Airway, breathing, and circulation. With the patient semiconscious, who knew how long he'd have a gag reflex, preventing stomach contents being regurgitated into his lungs. The pneumothorax was preventing good oxygen exchange, causing hypoxia and of course that blood pressure was the result of bleeding. His thought process took less than a second, and his decision less than that. He glanced at the chart, noting name and age.

"Mr. Laurent, you have been shot in the chest and abdomen, and are going to need surgery. I know you have problems breathing. You have blood in your left chest that collapsed your lung. We're going to put you to sleep, and then get to work. Do you consent?"

Laurent whispered, "Am I going to die?"

Zach responded, "Not today, but we have to start fixing you now."

Laurent nodded, and Zach grabbed the laryngoscope. "Morphine and sux, please. Also, valium, titrate by twos. I need an eight ET." The patient dropped off to sleep as the meds hit his system. They were just the treatment for decreasing pain, and paralyzing his muscles, making the intubation easy. Zach placed the CO_2 device on the ET tube and announced, "Gold on the CO_2 monitor, now if someone would paint the left chest quickly with Betadine, and I need a chest tube tray, also the auto-transfuser, we can give him back his own blood from the chest."

Zach placed the chest tube, getting about 200 ccs of blood. The oxygen saturation came up, as did the blood pressure. He ripped off his gloves, and called Hercules, who told him he would send someone down to fetch the patient to the O.R.

"Pretty slick, boy. One would think you were a surgeon."

"Hey, Hercules, I thought you were going to send one of your adoring surgical slaves down here to collect this mixed-up Frenchman. You need to air out his abdomen and find the hole," Zach instructed.

"I did. Pal and Gervasio have the duty. I am taking a quiet day to catch up on life."

Zach was dumbstruck. Christospathos was the hardest-working doctor, resident, or attending at PAY. He never took a day off. He had never hinted at even taking an hour off.

"You feeling okay? I don't think you can survive without the hours under that big O.R. light."

"Yes, everything is okay. It was my wife's and my anniversary yesterday."

"And you were here. She pissed off?"

"Very."

"So, what are you doing here? Shouldn't you be on all fours getting smacked on the behind? You know, that thing you married guys get as a bonus of wedded bliss," Zach said with a laugh.

"Just picking up some stuff from the office, including her present and card, which I failed to remember to bring with me when I got home last night. If that doesn't work, I may be banging on your door for a bed."

"Zach's motel for the wayward husband is always open for a golden blade."

"You know, Zach, I like Shoshie and while it is not my business, having followed your antics for these last few months, I have a recommendation."

"Okay, I'm game, but just to fill you in, she isn't seeing or talking to me. My mother fucked up the meeting of the women in Zach's life."

"You mean you fucked it up. Never let your mother or your mother-in-law come between you and the woman you love. There is bad juju in that. You need a woman in your life that loves you and supports you through all the inconsiderate things you do, overtly and covertly. Take my word for it, there will be days you are so tired you will ignore her. You will yell at her and treat her like shit. None of it is excusable, which is why you need a woman who understands … then whips you."

"I don't think Shoshie is interested in being treated like shit. In fact, I believe she has put in a contract with her father, the guy with the shotgun, to have me shot."

"Details. Dump your mother's crap, get on your knees, beg forgiveness, and take your spanking like the pussies we all are. The father will fall in line right after. Take my word for it. My wife's father had a large sickle that he threatened to use to disconnect head from body."

"Thanks for the advice. Garber is letting me out of jail for the weekend and I will give it the old college try."

Zach had never been to Boston before. He wasn't into the Red Sox, Patriots, cheap beer, liberal Catholics who weren't liberal where skin color was involved, stupid-sounding dialects, and he hated Harvard and their stupid bowties. All in all, it was an adventure. He didn't think the beat-up car he had would make the 438-mile round trip, so he took the bus.

The bus was filled with college students and people going from Chinatown, Manhattan to Chinatown, Boston. Zach didn't care. He was in a bus, cut off from the hospital and his family, and planned to look out the window, or doze. Mostly he wanted to think in peace. His residency in Emergency Medicine would be finished in two years, and he no longer planned to face that alone.

"Chinatown in ten minutes," the driver yelled, and cheers from the passengers went up. Zach hadn't even realized he had spent the entire four hours in thought. He grabbed his small bag filled with a change of underwear, toiletries, and a fresh shirt. He looked out the window and thought he had never seen such a nondescript city. "Well, Beantown, here I come."

Shoshie lived in a section of Boston called West Roxbury. A blue-collar, Irish-looking section that was slowly gentrifying as home prices took off. He splurged on a cab, and was driven through the city, seeing old brick buildings and newer glass and steel structures. He saw the Charles River, and a sign pointing the way to Fenway Park and the Red Sox. Finally, the cab pulled up to a small white house with black trim. A postage-stamp front yard had yellowing grass, and a chain-link half-fence kept the house and yard enclosed.

He walked to the door and knocked gently. He suddenly felt he was in a déjà-vu situation. There was Abe holding a shotgun, this time aimed at his groin, his face almost purple with rage.

"You defile mein daughter, you *shtick drek*. You make a *nafke* out of her? I shvear dis time I'll kill you."

"Abe, please," he pleaded, "I need to speak to Shoshie."

"You vill speak to no one in this house. *Gey avek* and *legyn in drerd un bakn bagyl.*"

"Abe, please. You know I don't speak Yiddish. I need to make this right with Shoshie."

Abe was about to have a stroke, yelling, "You had your chance!"

A voice came from behind Abe, and Shoshie came down the stairs. Her posture slumped as if defeated, with her mascara running down her cheeks.

"Abie, stop it. While he deserves to be shot, it isn't worth you going to jail, and me having to clean up the mess. Zach, get out of here before I can't hold him back, and he actually shoots you."

"Please, Shoshie, I'm sorry."

"You are always sorry. You just don't know how good you could have had it, and now you'll never know. Please just leave."

"Ya, you momzer, *gey avek*," Abe yelled, as Shoshie turned to go back up the stairs.

Abe was about to slam the door closed when Zach yelled to Shoshie. "I love you and want to make this right. Please, I'll wait at the coffee shop on that main street, Centre Street? Please ... " But his words were bounced away by the slammed door.

It had turned cold and rainy. It fit Zach's mood perfectly. He ordered a cup of coffee and found a seat where he could watch the door. He pulled out a board prep book, mostly to distract himself from his current situation and waited ... and waited.

"Hey man, that's your fifth cup of coffee. You're not going sleep a wink tonight, besides you've been here for hours. You homeless?"

The waitress had come with the fresh cup of coffee to replace the old cup. Zach had never felt so alone. This was like being in a bad French movie. That's all he needed—some mournful jazz in the background, an ashtray full of butts, and a Gauloise hanging from his lip. He had really blown it this time. He sighed and started to collect his book and laptop. Time to go home and get on with his life.

The door to the coffee shop opened, and Shoshie walked in. Zach scanned her face, but no hint of forgiveness was evident as she strode over to his table. She stood before him, silent.

"Shoshie, I love you. I swear you will always be the priority in my life. I should have backed you up, but I was shocked. You are everything I want, and everything she told me she wanted for me. I just didn't understand her.…"

She hugged him hard and then kissed him. He returned the hug with a deep passion. He wanted to protect her the rest of his life from all the hurts out there. She broke the hug.

"I can't be second, Zach. I understand she is your mother, but I'm the woman you'll be with the rest of your life. It has to be you and me, and what we build."

He took her hand and said, "Would you be my wife?"

Chapter 73

"**Goddam, you're getting married?** Are you outta your mind?"

"I'm going to tell Goldie your advice on marriage. I predict you will spend the next twenty years sleeping on that very lumpy couch you own," Zach said to Ike.

"You are correct, so I'm going to tell Goldie, if you ever mention this conversation to her, that you are a liar and are just getting cold feet about entering into holy matrimony."

Zach laughed at him. "Ike, she's going to believe me, not you. You'll be fucked, or, should I say, never fuck again."

"And to think we used to be good friends. Can you give me a little more retraction, ex-friend?"

They were in the E.R., working on a patient who had a perirectal abscess. The O.R.s were full from the aftermath of the Feast of San Gennaro, a religious event that usually turned into multiple shootings and stabbings. Ike decided that, instead of waiting for a nice O.R. to contaminate with the gallon of pus the drainage of this ass would bring, he'd open it in the E.R. It didn't need saying Ike was no one's friend at this point.

"I think that does it for the time being," Zach said, stretching his back. "You going to bring him up?"

"Yeah, why don't you finish your note? I'll write his orders and he should be good to go." Ike paused at the sounds of a very loud patient cursing out someone. "Shit, I'll go see what's going on."

"No, you finish this guy. It's my department and my problem. I'll see you later, and remember my threat to you about Goldie."

"Yes, indeedy. I will."

Zach went out into the main E.R. area, and found a very large man, shouting almost incoherently. Zach calmly went to the man, making sure he kept looking him in the eyes, and always kept his body in a position where he could jump out of the way if the guy started swinging.

"Hi, I'm Dr. Maxwell," Zach said with a smile. "Can I help you? You're scaring all the kids in here. Tell me what the problem is and I'll try to fix it."

"You killed me, and then brought me back to life with someone else's body."

Well, that was a new one, he thought. Must have seen *Frankenstein* or read the comic book. "I don't think we do that at this hospital, but maybe if you can sit down, I can get the information and help find out who did this to you."

This seemed to make the man angrier. "You're full of shit. You killed me and re-animated me. Now you'll pay." With that, he pulled an object from a pocket in his jacket. In an instant, Zach knew he was about to die and dived for the ground, but the man's shot went wild. Zach looked up, and saw Ike fumbling around in the nurses' station. Zach sprang up and tried to tackle the man. The man was very strong and managed to stay on his feet.

Ike yelled to Zach, "Brace yourself."

"What?!" Ike dropped onto the man and pulled out a syringe loaded with a clear liquid. With one lunge, he buried the needle in the man's neck.

The man screamed, and then croaked, "I'm dying." He collapsed, dropping his gun, and quickly turning blue.

Zach was in shock. "What did you do to him? He looks like … "

Ike completed his thought. "Like someone paralyzed. I

pushed 120 mg of succinylcholine into him. It was the quickest way I could think of to put him out."

Zach's eyes went wide. Succinylcholine was basically curare. Ike had blow-gunned the guy, and he now had about three minutes till brain death. "We got to get this guy intubated double quick."

"You're telling me. With our court system, I'll get the chair for killing him, while if he had killed you, they would have let him out of jail in a year. Let's get him up on a stretcher."

"No time, get the tube cart, I'm going to bag him. We'll tube him on the floor."

Zach grabbed the BVM mask off the wall and started bagging the guy while the nurse came to help and got an oxygen tank. Ike showed up with the cart, and Zach took a breath to figure out what the best position was to tube this guy. Well, he thought, the paramedics intubated on floors, he could too. He lay down on the floor with his stomach to the ground and called for a laryngoscope. He fumbled, trying to get the hang of the blade at an eye level. Finally, he was able to manipulate the scope, held out his right hand for the tube, and passed it through the cords. He grabbed a syringe from the nurse, blew the balloon up, and then checked placement with end-tidal CO_2 device. All was good. In the meantime, Ike had gotten an I.V. in, and had given him Ativan to snow him, and pancuronium so the patient would stay paralyzed while the tube was in.

A crowd had now gathered, including a bunch of NYPD officers with guns drawn. They secured the pistol, which was still on the floor. Hercules and Bullshit had, during the action, run down to the E.R. when they were notified of the situation. "Mudder, mudder, what did you guys do to our E.R.?" Dr. Moskowitz said, shaking his head.

Zach, whose nerves were strung tight, said, "We were saving lives, like you taught us."

Moskowitz laughed. "I don't think I taught you to paralyze

a man in self-defense, but what the fuck, good thinking. At least I don't have a mass casualty event comprising residents, nurses, ancillary personnel, and patients."

Zach cleared his throat. "Uh, actually it was Ike who thought of it. I was busy trying not to die."

"Well, you both get credit, though I don't know what agency it gives you credit for. Let's just say you have credit in my heart." Moskowitz smiled.

"Thank you from the bottom of my heart, ex-chief. I take it I can get a free appendectomy for the asking."

"Sure, we have a new third-year med student who is ready for you. Wears glasses with lenses like the bottom of Coke bottles, also a pronounced hand tremor. He should have that worked up."

"Guess I'll pass, ex-chief."

"Okay, it's your belly pain," Moskowitz said, his face now serious. "Seriously, good work. You sure about this E.R. thing, Zach? We'll take you back, and I'll square it with Garber."

"Thanks, Dr. Moskowitz, but I think this is where I belong. Besides, there aren't many guys here who have surgical experience. Makes it easier for your guys."

"It's your life. Don't make it too easy for my guys. I don't want them too used to it. Chances are, they won't have a surgically thinking doctor when they get out in the real world."

Moskowitz walked away, leaving Zach to try to clean up the mess that had accumulated since the last case. He picked up the next chart and read, "Patient wants alien spores removed from rectum." Just another day in the E.R.

Chapter 74

It was 5 a.m. and he sensed a presence hovering over him. He cracked open one eye, trying to remember where he was. He was in the call room. There had been a lull in the human traffic of the E.R., and he lay down to catch a few winks. It seemed his head had just hit the pillow.

"Du glacht fleisch or pulkes?"

Zach tried to shield his eyes from the lights coming into the dark call room from the corridor. "What the fuck are you ... Abe? What are you doing here? How did you find me?"

"I tried your apartment, but no one answered the door, so I came to the hospital. I told the nice nurse I was looking for *mein zun*," Abe said, smiling sheepishly. "So, fleisch? I think it's better."

"Abe, I need to get some sleep while I can. There are a horde of patients descending on this hospital just to see me."

"Just to see the best doctor, *mein zun*," Abe scolded. A tear dripped down his face and then a big smile appeared. "You made mein Shoshie very happy."

"Well, you won't be happy when she finds out I died from lack of sleep."

"Ach, you are such a kidder. I'll leave you alone, but tell me *fleisch* or *pulkes* ... meat or chicken?

"Got me again, Abe." Zach scowled. "What is that question about?"

"The wedding party. People have to eat, you know."

Zach took the pillow and put it over his face. "The reception … oh fuck!"

Chapter 75

The next weeks were a whirlwind. Zach found himself either working his ass off in the E.R., or embarking on an errand with Shoshie for the wedding. Abe had sent Rya, Shoshie's mother, down to Brooklyn for the particulars. Zach fumed most of the time because he had just never pictured getting married in a synagogue with all the trimmings. He certainly didn't want to do it in a kosher catering hall wearing a penguin suit. He had finally had it one day, after a particularly savage night shift that ended with a six-year-old who had caught a bullet in the chest. Fortunately, aside from a chest tube, the kid would make it, but fuck, he thought, they're now involving children?

Zach walked into the apartment to find Shoshie making coffee. He was surprised she was there, having refused to let her move into the apartment. He decided it too dangerous an area for her to live. Zach had promised to go looking for another apartment somewhere safer, but who had the time, and he loved the convenience of rolling out of bed and into the hospital. He knew Shoshie wasn't understanding it, but for the time being she put up with it.

"Hey, this is a pleasant surprise. What's up?"

"Nothing, I just wanted to see my future husband. I'm trying out the breakfast routine in this scenario. You know, the one where my weary husband gets home from an exhausting night on call, and I have coffee and breakfast waiting, then put him to bed."

"Hmm, the putting to bed part sounds good, not that breakfast with you ever sounds bad."

"Great, sit down, I'll make you coffee and some eggs and lox."

Zach froze. "Shoshie, what are you buttering me up for? I'm not going to like it, am I?"

"Why would you say that?" she asked innocently, but as if a storm cloud had passed over her, her smile fell, and she looked agitated. "Look, I know Abe and Rya can be a little over the top, but can you try to cooperate with the wedding plans? It would mean a lot to me and mean a lot to them. They have been looking forward to this, probably since I was born."

"Shoshie, it's not that I don't want to get married, it's just this big Polish affair. I'm getting married to you; you, me, your parents, my parents, and a rabbi. Then let the honeymoon begin, and we all live happily ever after. Your parents are going to spend a fortune on this, and remember, they aren't wealthy. My parents are sticking by the parents-of-the-groom-pays-for-the-photographer thing. I have $326.34 in my checking account, and I guess you might have less. It just seems to be a big waste of money for an affair that lasts three or four hours. Besides, as much as I like your parents, they are bothering the shit out of me. I have doctoring stuff to do, and when I'm not doing that I want to be with you."

Shoshie was quiet, and obviously not happy. "Come on Zach, let's get you to bed. You need to sleep before you go into the hospital again."

"I'm off tonight. Last night was the third night, and I have two glorious days off. What do you want to do besides wedding crap?"

She smiled weakly. "I don't know. Why don't you get some sleep and we'll figure it out when you get up? Now go get some sleep."

✐··········

He woke up with the light coming through his bedroom window.

He reached over and didn't find Shoshie, which was unusual as when she was in the apartment, she usually napped with him so their schedules coordinated, or just quietly read in bed till he woke up. He was used to waking up to her smiling face, and she wasn't there.

He got out of bed and walked into the living room. Shoshie was sitting on the couch, writing in a large green notebook. She looked up and gave him a tentative smile. "We need to talk about the wedding."

"Shoshie," he protested, "we talked about it, and I don't want to fight."

"I don't want to fight either, but we didn't talk about it. You told me your side, and that was the end of the discussion. Zach, I love you, but we need to discuss and compromise in the relationship. I know you aren't used to having your orders questioned in the hospital, but this is our relationship. It has to be comfortable for us and that includes me."

"I didn't mean it that way, but I don't like the intrusion of your parents and the show they plan to put on, especially as we both know they can't afford it."

"They have been saving since I was born. This was their dream, and their dream became my dream. I think most little girls want the dress, the altar, the canopy." She laughed. "Maybe it's in our DNA."

Zach was silent, thinking about what Shoshie said. Was he an asshole, expecting what he wanted was what it was going to be? Damn, would he want a relationship with someone with that attitude?

He looked at her sheepishly. "Do I really have to look like the penguin, and what the fuck are pulkes?"

Chapter 76

Thirty-six months later

Dr. Maxwell, Family Medicine is on line four, and Surgery is on line five."

Zach corralled two phones from the nurses' station and punched the flashing "4" line from one, and flashing "5" line from the other. "Jake, Ike, I have you both on. Your favorite patient just came through my doors, and he needs the both of you."

"Fuck," came the spontaneous response from the phones. Jake sighed. "How much herring did Leiber eat this time? Can we try to diurese him and send him home, or is this an admit?"

Ike chimed in. "If this is just congestive failure, he's Jake's. You hear that, Jake?" he yelled through the phone.

Zach told both of them, "First, sorry, he needs admission, and second, there is a little for both of you. His kidney function sucks, so he may need to go on dialysis this time, and second, his foot is looking dusky, as in no blood reaching it. If he needs dialysis, I'm guessing this will be a permanent thing, and he is going to need a fistula. Like I said, a little for the both of you."

Ike now sighed. "Double fuck, is there still time to go through an E.R. residency? Surgery sucks."

"Yeah, Zach," Jake added. "I want E.R. also. All you guys have to do is determine if the patients need to be admitted, and if they're sick or not. We have to do all the real work."

Zach looked at the electric doors opening to the E.R. and smiled. "Yeah, it's all fun and games here, Mr. Doctor Associate Chief of Surgery and Mr. Doctor Residency Director of Family Medicine. Shoshie is just walking in and we are going to have a nice lunch with wine at our favorite French restaurant."

"Liar, she doesn't drink wine." Jake laughed.

Ike now sighed. "Jesus, have our lives become boring. We used to go to bars, go dancing … "

"We never did shit like that. Oh … except the bars. Look, just because Shoshie, Sandy, and Goldie decided to get knocked up at the same time doesn't mean we still can't have fun."

Jake sounded content. "Yeah, we can have fun, just a little more quiet fun. Besides, Sandy is still nauseous for anything except kimchee."

"And Goldie's ankles get real swollen when she stands too long."

"And Shoshie has gas … 24/seven. What's a husband to do besides invite his best friends over for takeout Korean barbecue, including kimchee. Booze for the boys, an ottoman for Goldie, and a couple of gallons of seltzer."

"Sounds good to me, Associate Chief of Emergency Medicine. Now you just go enjoy that French lunch, and we'll send an intern down to fetch our problem man of God," Jake said. They both hung up their phones, as did Zach. With a smile, he saw his beautiful and very pregnant wife head into the breakroom with their takeout salad Niçoise and some French bread.

The End

About the Author

DOCTOR IRV DANESH was born in Brooklyn, New York. Before he started kindergarten, he and his family had schlepped to five new homes because of his father's jobs. This was to be a recurrent theme throughout his life. Like the main character of his first novel *Doctor Taco*, Irv just didn't concentrate well in college. Women, and the lack of them, had a lot to do with that. After the rejections for admission to medical schools in the States arrived, Irv joined the diaspora of similar, slacker, pre-meds, and journeyed south of the border.

Two years of cultural and academic re-education enabled Irv to trek back to the promised land of Brooklyn. More specifically, Irv was nurtured at the world's largest community hospital, Brookdale University Hospital Medical Center. This mega-hospital provided him enough stab wounds, gunshot wounds, blunt trauma, and general patient stupidity to regale his friends with stories for years to come.

After two years of surgical training, he decided he didn't want to spend the rest of his life removing gallbladders or doing bariatric surgery. Being somewhat of an adrenalin junkie, he was in the right place at the right time to snag a residency at Thomas Jefferson University Hospital in the new field of Emergency Medicine. He has practiced in inner-city Emergency Departments for thirty-six years.

Dr. Irv's job statistically has a high rate of burnout. He fought through two of these periods, the first by moving to Boston and serving as Assistant Professor of Emergency Medicine at the Tufts School of Medicine.

He continued his career as Associate Director of Emergency Medicine at the Lawrence General Hospital in Lawrence, Massachusetts. It was here that he had his second period of burnout. He again was in the right place at the right time, helping birth USA Network's *Royal Pains*. Irv started as the show's Medical Consultant, advancing over three seasons to Co-Producer. His MacGyver-like vignettes, such as skull-drilling, fishhook-chest-wall-stabilizing, and other pseudo-medical procedures, would never be allowed in conventional, AMA-approved medicine. Then again, Dr. Irv marches to his own drummer.

Doctor Danesh can now be found at the freestanding E.R. in East Boston, working nights and dreaming of retirement.

Doctor Brooklyn is the fictional account of a typical doctor's training in the high-acuity, high-pressure specialties of Surgery and Emergency Medicine. It is also the story of finding love while still being responsible for too many patients at all hours of the day and night.

Dr. Irv lives in Marblehead, Massachusetts with his lovely and grammatically correct wife. He loves the change of seasons, except for the winter, which he curses every year.

His three artistic sons, and one medically inclined son, all left for other parts of Massachusetts and New York.

All in all, he would rather be in South Beach.

Doctor Brooklyn: *Love & Life at the End of a Knife*

Dr. Irv Danesh

www.doctorbrooklynbook.com

Publisher: SDP Publishing

Also available in ebook format

Also by Dr. Irv Danesh

The Loco Life of Doctor Taco

Available at all major bookstores

www.ingramcontent.com/pod-product-compliance
Lightning Source LLC
Chambersburg PA
CBHW071205250626
47159CB00001B/215